ALSO BY
SCARLETT ST. CLAIR

When Stars Come Out

HADES X PERSEPHONE
A Touch of Darkness
A Touch of Ruin
A Touch of Malice

HADES SAGA
A Game of Fate

ADRIAN X ISOLDE
King of Battle and Blood

GOOD TO THE LAST DROP

— R.A. Parker —

TIMEWALKER
PRESS

TIMEWALKER
PRESS

Timewalker Press
P.O. Box 1434
Salinas, California, 93902

Printed in the United States of America

Publisher's Cataloging-in-Publication Data
Andresen, Peter Garth

ISBN: 978-0-9854285-7-0 (paperback)

Book Cover Design by ebooklaunch.com

For Flotsam, who was at my side through every word.

Prologue

On September 15, 1995, in a remote bay off a verdant Caribbean island, Tomaso Garcia experienced a less than stellar moment as he died in the arms of a tempestuous woman. His reckless bravado had thrown him into her path only to have her tear out his heart (along with a few other organs).

She had been born as a wispy danseuse off the West African coast, only a week earlier. Unseasonably hot tropical waters (and a deceased French engineer, Gustave Coriolis), heavily influenced her budding personality. Her name was Marilyn, and like her namesake, she was voluptuous and exercised an element of control over every man she met.

By the time she found Tomaso, she had transformed into a cruel dominatrix capable of pushing normally placid sea waters deep into inland valleys with her one hundred and thirty mile per hour winds. Tomaso had his last conversation with Marilyn as he battled her savage winds and waters. His last words were not kind and heard only by him.

Tomaso, along with Che, his twin brother, were in the import-export business. They exported cocaine out of and American money into Columbia, South America. Their mother named Che for having been born with an inordinate amount of facial hair, making him look like her hero, Che Guevara. When he was a child, she would comb his wispy beard, place a little beret on his head and encourage him to carry a small .22 CAL pistol in a holster to school, unloaded of course. Columbian schools had their rules.

For the week prior to his death, Tomaso had unknowingly been running his 43-foot Bertram fishing boat, The Miss H. Whitlow, ahead of Marilyn. He would have successfully outrun her had he not dropped anchor outside of Fish Bay on the South side of the island of St. John in the US. Virgin Islands. It was there that he planned to drop off a large amount of cocaine and pick up an equally large volume of cash hidden by his hirsute younger brother.

The drop-off point was a challenging scramble up a rocky cliff on a deserted finger of land, which jutted into Fish Bay. Tomaso accessed the cliff with his Zodiac rubber boat. Che's earlier access was via a goat path that led along the backbone finger of land. The previous day Che had faithfully buried their most substantial sum of drug money ever collected beside a rock that resembled a hand, missing an index finger. Brown plastic suitcases held millions of dollars collected from their circle of drug dealers in South Florida. The brothers always made sure to never be in the same place at the same time on drug runs.

Che earned a Ph.D. in Ornithology while attending Night School at the University of Antioquia in Santa Fe de Antioquia, Columbia, years earlier. He and Tomaso worked days during that time, packing cocaine into plastic-wrapped 2.2-pound capsules for a local gentleman named Paolo Escobedo. They toiled for years in the hot jungles of Columbia for Escobedo until they decided to leave his employ and start their own business of stealing cocaine from Escobedo and distributing it to America. In their early careers as cocaine thieves and dealers, they had multiple run-ins with a curious leopard in the jungle near Escobedo's cocaine lab. It was from those experiences that they named their budding cartel "The Brothers Leopardo."

Che commissioned a jeweler in Cartagena to celebrate their success by making them matching leopard rings of thick gold, rubies, emeralds, and diamonds. The leopard face emblem became their signature stamp on every kilo of cocaine. Che rewarded the Jeweler with a generous 9mm intracranial "tip."

Their distribution network took advantage of Che's Ph.D. and teaching position at the University by employing an elaborate strategy to use Caribbean islands to perform their exchanges of money and cocaine. The Miss H. Whitlow carried nerdy Ornithology students on board for alleged oceangoing, multi-island field trips throughout the Caribbean. If they ever encountered Customs or DEA at sea, the brother in charge would unleash the nerds on the police until they bored the cops off the boat. The plan worked well for years until Tomaso met Marilyn. After he and The Miss H. Whitlow went missing, Che believed that his twin had double-crossed him and went on a manhunt to find and kill Tomaso. Che felt as hurt as he did murderously. The brothers Leopardo came to a sad end.

Acknowledgments

EDITING and EPITHET REDUCTION-Tom (Boy #2) Parker

POSITIVE VIBRATIONS- Emilia Carangelo

GENERAL LITERARY MENTORING- Peter G Andresen

PLOT & CHARACTER DEVELOPMENT-Jeff.Frank.Pat.Kim.Sally.
Roberta.Ray.Jim.Spike.Makena.Flotsam.Rosie.Cowboy.

CARIBBEAN BEACH BAR INSPIRATION: Foxy's (JVD), Ivan's
(JVD), The Beach Bar-Formerly Pusser's (STJ), Cow Wreck (ANE),
Joe's Bar (Water Island), Skinny Legs (STJ), Woody's (STJ)

-1-

CONCRETE JUNGLE

I attempted to make doctorly concerned facial expressions as I listened to what would be my last patient for the next two weeks. I held a pen taking notes, but my mind held a flyrod. I was absent for this patient. I gave an occasional nod, a gentle 'um hum,' and imagined the flyrod flexing as I cast to fish over a tropical reef.

As one of my medical school mentors said, being a good doctor is a lot like being a good sex worker. You don't need to care about the other person. Your job is to make them feel cared for. So, like a good doctor, instead of moaning, I said 'um hum' in my doctorly concerned tone. Instead of rotating my hips, I nodded my head. Well, come to think about it, the whole head nodding thing could fit both scenarios. I was being paid to service my patient's needs with my actions and not my emotions. I wanted this to be a quickie.

"OK, Patricia, finish physical therapy and see me when I return from vacation," I said and handed her a prescription for a muscle relaxant.

"Doctor, there's one last thing."

Ah yes, that one last thing, that fatal insignificant little detail that can extend an office visit into a marathon. *Alright, Ky, benign smile, and* "Yes, what's that?"

"Well, doctor, since my car accident, I've had a strange symptom."

"Tell me about it." *Hold the smile.*

"Whenever I sneeze, cough, laugh or even bend over, I pass, pass-oh God, this is so embarrassing." She turned her gaze.

"Out?" I asked.

"No."

"Huh? You pass blood, urine, wind, what?"

"I don't just pass wind, Doctor. It's bigger, worse." She started crying.

"Have you become incontinent?"

"No, it's in between." *What the hell is in between?* "Patricia, please help me here."

She extended her head and jaw toward me and made hard eye contact, "Fine."

"Wha...?"

Through her tears and in an irritated tone, "Doctor, if I cough-I fart, I bend-I fart, I can't even make love. My husband Lee won't even touch me, saying that if he puts his thing in me, he's afraid he'll puncture me, and I'll fly across the room like a kid letting go of a balloon." I handed her a tissue.

"So, since the accident, you pass a lot of gas?"

"Yes, when I cough or...."

"OK, OK, but why do you think the car accident caused you to become a serial farter?"

Oh, I could have worded that a little better. Beyond her, flecks of gold blazed in the highest valleys of the mountains, West of Fort Collins. The aspen trees were turning color, a sure sign of another early winter. My solace was knowing that within the hour, I'd be on my mountain bike with my dog, riding the trails that could ultimately end up in those fluttering, brilliant groves. Within 18 hours, I'd be on a jet for my first trip to a funky Caribbean Island to fish and perform a sunset wedding for friends. I badly needed time off.

"Well, it started after the wreck," she said.

"Did you injure your abdomen?"

"No, I was rear-ended, no tummy injury."

"Any trips to Mexico, drank any well or river water?" I was thinking of intestinal parasites.

"No."

My mind was in a frustrating loop, whiplash-farting, whiplash-farting. "Do you really think they're due to your car accident?"

"Yes. I don't know. Even Lee thinks it is. He says that the force of the accident must have blown out my O-ring." She said with a straight face. "Can that be surgically fixed?"

"I don't know. I think I slept through the O-ring lecture in medical school."

"Doctor," she started to cry again. "Even Eleanor, my chihuahua, won't sit in my lap. She goes to Lee now." I handed her another tissue. "This is so embarrassing. Once it goes, it really goes, and I can't help but push. It's uncontrollable, like when you're having a baby. The stupid doctor yells at you to stop pushing. Yeah right, like he's ever had half of an eight-pound baby hanging out of him. You can't just stop in the middle of it. You have to push." Sorry about the stupid doctor comment." She said, looking down.

"Alright, Patricia, while I think about this, let's get a weight on you."

"127 pounds."

A smile lit her face, "OH MY GOD, IT'S WORKING."

"What's working? The scale? Of course, it is. I have it calibrated every year."

"No, the trees, I mean my new diet. Wow, it's working."

I inspected her chart, "Let's see, holy cats, you've lost almost 30 pounds in three months. That's not healthy." I said like a stern doctor should while scolding a bad patient. I wasn't very adept at that sort of thing. I still needed practice at being commanding.

"How's my hair look, like seriously, your medical opinion?" *That one came out of left field.*

"Your hair, why?" I wanted to get back to the accident-related issues so I could finish and leave my office. I had the pre-vacation impatience that makes the last day of work seem like a week, and she pushed it into a month.

"Not shiny like an otter?" She asked.

"Otter, otter, like a sea otter?"

"Yeah, long, and silky and shiny like an otter or beaver. Ya know, flowing." She raised her chin, shaking her hair like a TV shampoo model.

"Patricia, I'm confused. Beaver hair is short and thick, not long and silky."

"How would you know, how many beavers have you examined?" She said in a petulant tone.

I wanted to say something about GYN clinics in medical school but held my tongue. "Beaver hair, otter hair, Patricia, you gotta help me here."

"I'm on the Aquatic Mammal diet to lose weight and make my hair shiny like an otter, or better yet a beeeever. I saw this, like new diet on the Dr. Larry show. Dr. Larry guarantees weight loss and hair just like an aquatic mammal. Does it, you know, like shine?"

"Who the hell is Dr. Larry?" I asked with immediate regret.

"You know, The Dr. Larry show. Liiiive from Chi-car-go," she said with an emphasis on the 'car.' "Weekdays at 3 O'clock. It's a medical health and beauty show. Ya know, When the Doctor's in, baby, you're on."

"Oh really, what kind of doctor is Doctor Larry?"

"He's a real doctor like you. He's so cute, well for an old guy, in his signature pink scrubs."

"A doctor in pink scrubs?"

"Yep, he's a real, well," she paused, "he IS an Osteopath, but he used to be an ER doctor and saved thousands of lives."

"Tell me about the diet," I asked with a pained resignation at my upcoming dietary education.

"It's so simple," her Beagle-innocent eyes widened, "just trout and Supershakes three times daily."

"Supershakes?"

"Yeah, you buy them from AquaticMammal.com."

"What's in it, do you even know?" I asked.

"They make it from powdered trees and some herbs. But you never answered me about my hair."

"Hold the hair question. Powdered trees?" I wasn't sure I'd heard her correctly.

Patricia's eyes narrowed. She extracted a white plastic tub from her purse with a label of a smiling beaver eating a trout with its paws. "Supershake mix." She coldly said as she handed it to me. I felt stupid and inspected the label. "Powdered birch, powdered aspen, powdered assorted North American Decidua, organic garlic powder, and biotin. Holy shit, you weren't kidding." I could have chosen a little better verbiage. "How long have you been on this, this diet?"

"About, let me see, June, July, Aug.... about three months."

"And your wreck was four months ago. I don't think your wind issue is from your accident. It's from eating this powdered tree stuff. It can't be healthy for you."

"Well B.S. to that. Dr. Larry promised a leaner, sexier me with long, flowing...."

I cut her off, "Yeah, I know, silky, flowing beaver hair." The unintended and exceptionally unprofessional vision that danced in my head took even me by surprise.

"Patricia, please understand, humans aren't designed to eat stuff that's been harvested with a chain saw. Does that make sense? It's the same reason that the indigestible fiber in beans causes us to, well, expel wind. The bacteria in your colon make methane as they break down fiber, or in this case, aspen trees. By eating your beaver food, you are causing a population explosion of gas-producing bacteria."

"Dr. Elliott, I'm sure your theory probably only applies to the Blanca version of Aquatic Mammal Supershake powder." She was challenging me.

"The Blanca version?" I asked, realizing that I needed to stop asking questions and let her fart herself into beautiful hair and cachexia.

"Yes. Supershakes come in two varietals, the basic Blanca version, ya know, from like harvested live trees. I guess they cut them down with a chainsaw. I never really thought about it. Anyway, it doesn't matter cuz I bought the Anejo", she countered with confidence, "it's a little more expensive. Dr. Larry says it's aged and worth every penny."

"You're talking in tequila terms and making no sense." My ear tips were getting hot.

"No, not Cuervo, silly doctor. The Anejo is, like, better. They take down abandoned beaver dams and grind them up to make the Anejo. I think Anejo means aged wood. It makes for a smoother flavor and easier digestibility, Dr. Larry promised."

My ears quit functioning as I hit my patience wall. I didn't possess the energy to talk Anejo, flowing beaver hair, or gas. I needed time away from all this. I needed to escape from this patient, from the practice of medicine, from Colorado's, frozen nine-month winters. I needed not to be here anymore. I chose to be succinct.

"Patricia," I said in my commanding doctor's voice. "It is my medical opinion that it was not your whiplash that has caused your wind issues. It's the beaver food or whatever you call it. Eat it at your own risk and Elanor's risk too. I need to go. Oh, and for completeness's sake, Cuervo is not a one hundred percent Blue Agave tequila. It is known as a mixto." I opened the door for her to leave, smiled sweetly, then shut it firmly behind her. "Safe," I said to myself out loud as I hurried to the back office. I flung her chart at my desk and picked up my keys.

"Hey buddy, where do you think you're going?" Rosie, my wife, and physician-partner asked.

"Huh, me?"

"Yes, dear."

"I have a heavy date. His name is Spike, and I promised him a bike ride before we leave."

"No leaving 'till you deal with those." She tapped her finger on a pile of small red and white paper slips. Each was a call from a patient, attorney, insurance adjustor, or pharmacy. I would have welcomed a rattlesnake on my desk with more enthusiasm. In self-pitying disgust, I said, "I don't know why, but whenever I'm about to leave town, the Universe sends out mysterious signals to the pains in the ass of my world. They sense that a great distance is about to grow between their little needy little mouths and my nipples. I feel like the friggin' Capitoline wolf."

"Well, my she-wolf, sit down and start feeding, or we'll never get out of here." Rosie had spoken, and I had no choice but to obey.

Toward the middle of the pile, I saw a note that clenched my throat in anger. I noticed Rosie studying me. It read 'Percy from Right Team Insurance, denying payment on all claims for Paula Tomlinson. Ordering an Independent Medical Exam with Dr. Gibson. Wants call back.'

"That chickenshit little dog-raper. I want to choke that little flit. God, please give me five minutes in an alley with that shit-head, only one of us would walk out, and it wouldn't be him." I said as my hopes for an early escape dwindled.

Percy Hayes was the lead adjuster for Right Team Auto Insurance and affectionately known as "Purple Hayes" by the attorneys and doctors who had to deal with him. He earned the moniker "Purple Hayes" for always wearing a purple jumpsuit to court when he testified on behalf of his employer and was a legend at Right Team for his celebratory "Hayesing" of doctors and insurance clients. It was a term he'd given himself for slapping a cowbell, strung from the ceiling of his office when he got coverage for a patient or payment to a doctor denied. He would stand in his doorway and rock his hips as he sang, "Another one bites the dust, HEY, HEY," and slap the bell. Then, the entire office of adjustors would arise in unison from their micro-cubicles, clapping their hands, and echo back his victory, "HEY, HEY."

I dialed the number and muddled through an analemma phone menu. Eventually, Percy answered, "Hello, this is Mister

Percy Hayes." I hated Hates for several reasons. One: was his job. He made a living, making my patients even more miserable than their original injuries by denying payment for their legitimate medical care. Two: was his criminal record of cruelty to animals. He and his mother had received convictions for taking free puppies from garage sales and selling them as training bait to pit bull fighting rings.

"Hayes, this is Elliott returning your call about your unfortunate insured, Paula Tomlinson. I understand you're denying her bills and sending her to the snake-pit for an IME with Gibson." I said, feeling no need for pleasantries.

Responding with a hint of perkiness, "Well, good afternoon to you, my Dr. Elliott. Do you know her claim number, sir?"

"No, I don't have her damn claim number. You're the one who called my office less than an hour ago. I would expect you to have it." I could feel that burning sensation in my ear tips again.

"Humm, let me see if I can pull her up on my computer without the claim number, it may take a sec." I imagined him inspecting his perfectly polished fingernails and wondered if he could see his nose hairs in the reflection.

"No, I'm afraid I'm going to need that claim... ooh wait, let me try one more thing." He seemed to love wasting my time.

"Uh-huh, oh yes," he paused, "claim denied, have a nice day."

"Wait, wait, what the f-f," I caught myself, remembering that insurance companies record all phone calls. If the phone call content were favorable for the caller, the recording would end up "lost" if ever requested by subpoena. If the caller made any stupid statements, the call would be played back to jurors if the case ever made it to court.

"Hang on, Hayes, just tell me why? She got splattered in a wreck that wasn't her fault and is facing a lot of pain and treatment."

"Oh, my Dr. Elliott, we caught her in a nasty lie in her telephonic sworn statement. She stated that she had no prior injuries of significance, but our investigation uncovered the true facts. At age 18, she was involved in a snowmobile accident in Utah and was under Chiropractic care for six months."

I couldn't hold my anger, "Are you shitting me? She is 54 years old, and you are going to deny her care for an accident from her teens?"

"Well, Dr. Elliott, that's not my call. It will be up to Dr. Gibson's Independent Medical Examination to determine if she had preexisting injuries, which, of course, would preclude our payment for this most recent accident."

"Hayes, why are you doing this to this poor old gal?"

"Dr. Elliott, we all need to play by the rules." He said in a grammar school teacher tone, pushing me to the edge of my temper.

"Who's rules you purple-clad, cubicle-dwelling little shit, certainly not the rules set by compassionate humans." I had just called someone a shit in the same sentence with using the word compassion. I had lost this battle with my own words. I needed to end this conversation, go home and be with my dog.

"Oh, my Dr. Elliott, have we had a bad day?" He was chumming the waters of my stupidity. I choose to avoid the bait.

"No, Hayes, it's all good." I said, hoping to salvage as much from the conversation's wreckage as I could, "I want what's best for my patient and to get paid for my work."

"Isn't that precious. Is there any other way in which I may service you today, my Dr. Elliott?"

Not taking the prudent high road, "No, Hayes, I'm feeling well serviced by you already today, thank you," and hung up. I put my forehead in my sweating palms, wishing that we were going to Hawaii rather than the Caribbean.

I noticed Rosie staring down at me, holding the top of her pen in her mouth. "Aaah, another happy ending from your friend Percy I see?" She said with a self-satisfied smile. Her double entendre hit me almost hard enough to jolt me from my self-pity and anger.

"Screw this. I can't do this anymore." I was referring to not only the day but my reluctant career as a physician and the perpetual fight with insurance companies. I was emotionally exhausted. "Let's go home and leave this stuff here. It'll be waiting for us when we get back from Saint Outhouse." I said, referring sarcastically to the Island of Saint John.

"Yeah, it'll be waiting for us."

Sweat ran in rivers off my chin and nose as Spike and I climbed our favorite mountain bike trail. The long, warm evenings of Summer had passed, and the Fall's abridged day had already pulled its sun back behind the Rockies. Indistinct shadows grayed the dirt under tall pine trees. Our intended endpoint was high above town, through aspens and scrub oak, to a dirt road beyond Horsetooth canyon. The road had originally been an old railway line, cut into the granite hillsides by unfortunate "Coolies" a century before. Its original use was to carry gold ore from mines high in the Rockies to a smelter, West of town. With the iron rails removed decades ago, it was now a rutted dirt road used by partiers, road sign shooters, and lovers without a private place to have sex at night. The ditches on either side of the road lay decorated with discarded whiskey bottles, underwear, and condoms. Local bears chewing on the latter two were often spotted at night.

We watched the Rocky's jagged shadow creep East, devouring the browning plains of Colorado until it met the flat horizon. Spike shared my water, and we headed home for me to pack before the pre-dawn alarm started my first day of vacation. The adrenaline of racing my dog downhill felt invigorating and healthy, utterly different from the stress adrenaline that squeezed my heart through most workdays. I needed sleep, I needed laughter, I needed not to be me.

I spent most of the night mentally ricocheting between my problem patients and trying to remember which essential things I had forgotten to pack--the stuff I wouldn't be able to buy on a remote Caribbean island. I felt guilty for leaving my difficult practice in the hands of my young medical resident, "BJ." I laughed out loud at myself for being so neurotic.

"Why are you laughing in bed?" Rosie asked, startling me.

"Sorry if I woke you. I'm just trying to keep my whole world straight in my brain."

She stroked my forehead with the backs of her fingers, "I thought that I was your whole world." I felt like a jerk.

"Will you make me a promise?" Her tone tightened.

"Sure," I hoped it wasn't some monumental task, "what is it?"

The intensity of her facial expression shone in the flicker of the bedside nightlight. This was not a good sign. 4 AM seriousness surely meant that I was in trouble or that the upcoming assignment was just plain awful. I braced.

"Ky, you've been on edge for a while, and I'm afraid you could kill someone if they pissed you off." Her eyes narrowed, "You've done CPR on a lot of men younger than you, right?"

"Yes, why?" This wasn't our fluffy, pre-vacation chatter.

"Babe, you've been acting, and I understand you're stressed... like a wild man." She was pleading, not requesting a promise.

"Ok."

"I know you don't want to go to Saint John, aside from skeletonfish fishing."

"Bonefish." I corrected her.

"Whatever. I know the Caribbean doesn't hold much appeal for you, but please quit making negative remarks like calling Saint John things like Saint Outhouse. For me, please try to relax and have some fun. I know it's not Kona, but Saint John can be beautiful in its own way. Jessica and I have had wonderful trips down there, and Chuck loves you. He's excited and wants to show you the life that he's built for himself. I wasn't supposed to tell you, but he didn't even own a Bonefish pole and bought one for his time with you."

I forced a smile as I looked into her dark eyes. "Rosie, I appreciate your approaching me like this." I knew that I had become irritable, and I might on rare occasions act like a shit, but that wasn't my true nature. I must have become a bigger shit than I realized for her to act so coyly around me. "That Chuck's spending money on a Bonefish rod when things are so financially tight for him after the hurricane is touching."

"He loves you. You're like his only sane brother." Chuck was the only one of her brothers who turned out to be a human being, and I harbored a great degree of filial love for him. "Baby, I'm sorry I've been cranky. Life isn't unfolding according to my game plan. I feel that I'm too young and worked way too hard to feel this disappointed with it all." I had the immediate realization of having not just opened a can of nightcrawlers but also thrown them into the bed with us -- time for a quick recovery.

I stroked the length of her nose softly, "Except for you. I love you. You are the best part of my world. The rest of the bullshit is bothersome and unimportant." I knew how lucky I was to have her. She swallowed and lowered her head. "Make me a promise."

"I will. What is it?" It was best to agree. I'd stepped into a steaming pile of my own words and had to extricate myself with a modicum of graciousness.

"Promise me you will try to have fun on this trip. Don't pre-judge the Islands, don't pack the asshole patients and insur-ance companies into your suitcase. Leave them for BJ. He's smart, and you've taught him well. Everybody will live for two weeks without you. I need you to relax, please. I'll make it worth your while, remember travel rule number one?" Her hand left my face and found a part of me that always responded to her touch.

"How could I forget?" I recited, "Every day while on vaca-tion, at least once." She smiled and opened the sheets to see what was staring back at her. "Yes, Dr. Elliott, at least once a day while on vacation, preferably twice, and today is the first day of vacation."

"Yes, Mrs. Elliott, I promise on both accounts." I threw the sheets back and experienced that which told me we were al-ready on vacation, and we hadn't yet boarded an airplane.

When and where wisdom makes its brief appearance in my life can be strange. It can't be predicted. As I wrote the alpha-bet with my tongue, I realized that *my entire life doesn't have to be perfect in order to produce perfect moments.* I promised myself that I would adopt that philosophical approach for this trip. I'd wasted too many years waiting for my life to be perfect before embracing the perfection of the small moments. For the next two weeks, I would make the effort to mine the perfect moments of what they had to offer.

-2-

RIDE NATTY RIDE

The doorbell rang as I applied my post-shower Rogaine. Through the peephole, I saw Dr. Jeb Chevali poised to make his grand entrance. He was supposed to have a new girl with him. This wasn't anything unusual as "the new chick" was a familiar theme. He'd met this new chick, Chiara, a few months ago. His description of their dating status was 'Chevali succinct,' "I'm banging a new bitch. She's pretty hot." For him, that was a supreme compliment. I was sure that she was going to be a stellar human.

I opened the door, and Spike greeted him. Spike liked Chevali. He was, as usual, smiling, tan, and in excellent physical condition. His only imperfection aside from brown Copenhagen specks on his lips and teeth was a cauliflower ear, an old college boxing war wound. Otherwise, Chevali, with his predictable Porsche 911 parked in my driveway, was perfect. Usually, I would have hated him were I not so familiar with his flaws, which made him human, and fun.

"Hey asshole, you gonna let us in?" That was Chevali-speak for 'good morning, my dear friend.'

"Us?" I saw nobody else.

"Oh, yeah." He stepped aside to reveal a pixie of a woman standing behind him. She smiled sweetly and stepped around him. "Hi, I'm Chiara." She spoke with an accent and politely extended a thin hand to shake mine. Before I could introduce myself, Chevali blurted, "This is Doctor Elliott."

The strength of her handshake wasn't unnecessarily firm, as if she were trying to prove something but more robust than expected from such a diminutive woman. She was well less than five feet tall and well-muscled. Her shoulder-length hair was in jet-black ringlets projecting a Mediterranean version of the young Shirley Temple. Her voice was unusually deep, and her eye contact unexpectedly drew me in.

"Please call me Ky. That doctor stuff doesn't fly around here."

"Tutto Bene." She said and raised to her toes and kissed my cheek while still holding my hand. I felt Rosie behind me and turned, "Rosie, this is Chiara, Jeb's uh," and before I could find the correct verbiage, Chiara popped in with "Chick for the trip."

Rosie responded by talking through a half-smile, "Hello, I'm Rosie, his," pointing to me, "politer half." Chiara bounced to her toes again and kissed Rosie's cheek, thereby letting me off the 'too familiar hook' for my kiss. I was relieved.

"Now that we have all had a group kiss, can I come in?" He angled his way through us and spoke to Spike. "Hey buddy, you going to miss your mom and dad? Don't worry. I'll make sure that they come home safe." Spike jumped up and gave him a nose in the mouth. Chevali smiled and wiped his mouth. "Spike," I laughed, "go wash your nose off."

"Would you like anything to drink, coffee or perhaps a glass of San Pellegrino?" Rosie asked Chiara.

"I'd love that, thank you. It's bottled a few kilometers from the village where I grew up." She answered as there was another knock at the door. I opened the door, "Jessica," I yelled and threw my left arm around her neck, pulled her into me, and reached down to smack her ass. It was round, firm, and gave a report that reflected miles of road work. She strived to act like a lady but loved my inappropriateness and always felt compelled to act offended. This time, it was a halfhearted slap on my cheek, followed by a kiss.

"You two at it already?" Rosie hurried out of the kitchen to hug Jessica. "Can you believe it's been almost two years since we were in Saint John? Rosie eased Jessica back to inspect her. "You look wonderful. Where's Baine?"

"He's out in his Bronco, putting the windshield reflector up and spraying stuff on his tires to protect them from the sun."

"You didn't bring dipshit. Well, there goes that threesome I've been fantasizing about." Chevali said. I cringed, feeling sorry for Chiara, and expected her to fling her glass of San Pellegrino on him. Instead, she stepped up to Jessica and tilted her head back to make eye contact.

"Hi, I'm Chiara, I am with Jeb, and I've been dating him for a couple of months. I don't think he couldn't handle the two of us at the same time. Too old." Jessica spoke to Chevali. "Oh, she's got your number. You're in trouble now." He smiled thinly.

Jessica looked down at Chiara, "Don't I know you?"

Chiara replied, "You seem familiar too. Do you have kids taking piano lessons from me?"

"No kids. Ah! the country club?" Jessica said, smiling confidently.

"No."

"Young Republicans?"

"No."

"Junior League?"

"Oh, hell no," Chiara answered.

"You play the piano, right?"

Chevali answered for Chiara while grabbing his crotch, "Yep, that's why I'm bringing her. She loves it when I tickle her ivories."

Chiara answered, "Si, I mean Yes, I play professionally, give lessons, and play the pipe organ at an enorme church East of town."

"That's where I know you from. You're the organ lady." Jessica frowned at her own words.

Chiara said, "Eh, I've been called worse."

Jessica put an arm around Chiara's shoulder, steering her away from Chevali. "Honey, we need to talk."

"What is it?"

"Chiara, you seem like such a sweet girl, playing our church organ and all. You're a part of our flock. But, what do you know about Jeb?"

"What are you asking?" Chiara asked.

"I've known him for years, and I know his little peccadillos if you will. Yes, he's a psychiatrist, but do you know what he is really like? I don't want you to get hurt, honey." Chiara lifted Jessica's arm off her shoulder and stepped closer until their faces were almost touching. "Porca miseria. Jessica, is it? I know Jeb, and I know he is a, how do you say? Hound dog. I like that about him, no fakeness. Just because I play the organ at your church doesn't make me one of your hypocritical flock. It's a job. And so you know, I've been hit on by a lot of men and women from your church, including your bisexual pastor and the church's most significant contributor.

Jessica stiffened, "Well, that's unlikely since my father is the most sizable contributor to the church." Chiara paused, putting her hands on her hips, staring blankly at Jessica, and said, "So, if you want to save my soul or judge me, unpack your bags now and stay home. Because when I'm on vacation, I drink, I swear, I make sex at all hours. Loudly, all of it. This is my vacation, and I won't be scrutinized by you or anybody else. And if I hear one word about my free time activities from anybody back at the church, you and I are going to have another, very antipatico conversation." Chiara stood her ground, expressionless.

Jessica stepped back. "Well, I wasn't trying to judge you, or...."

"Perfetto, then let's put this conversation behind us," Chiara said as Jessica's boyfriend Baine scurried through the doorway. "Hi." He made no eye contact and spoke to the room.

I felt sorry for him and moved to shake his clammy hand. He projected the charisma of a toad. The confidence in his handshake was half of what Chiara had, "Hey amigo, how have you been?" I asked and didn't care, but I wanted to be kind to Jessica by making Baine feel welcome.

"Good, I guess." His voice was flat. A thin mustache followed the contours of a half-smile as he looked around the room, "Hi Jeb, Hi Rosie, Hi..." When he saw Chiara, he stopped speaking.

I said, "Baine, this is Chiara, Jeb's vacation date." *Great, that made her sound cheap,* and before I could try to undo what I had said, she approached Baine. "Hi, I'm Chiara. Jeb is my boy toy for the trip to the islands." I immediately liked her. She possessed the kindness to wipe off some of my inconsiderate-host patina, which I had artfully smeared on myself. Baine took her hand, "Pleasure to meet you. Are you Jeb's ice skater from Norway?"

"Nice one Baine, that Sicilian accent is a dead giveaway, isn't it? Yeah, she's Sonja Fucking Henie." Chevali said from across the room.

"No, but I do know how to Ice skate," Chiara said, dropping his hand.

I was about to offer everybody coffee when two Harleys rumbled up my driveway. Their headlights crossed back and forth across my living room ceiling. Rosie looked at me, wide-eyed.

In my world, unexpected Harleys in my driveway at odd hours can be either a good thing or a bad thing. Without a word, Rosie slipped into the bedroom and reemerged with a folded towel in her hands, and handed it to me. The towel was heavy, .357 Magnum heavy. I had my finger on the trigger when the front door flew open.

"Where the hell is my Sissy at?" A gruff, cigarette-hardened voice boomed from my club brother Jason as he barged into the room without a knock. I stuffed the towel and its contents between two sofa cushions and stood tall to hug him firmly. I patted the back of his leather vest and felt the hard, inflexible patch sewn to its back.

"You come for breakfast?" I asked.

He spoke through his disarming grin, "I love ya brother, but I didn't get my ass up this early for free food. I need a kiss from my Sissy."

All eyes were on him, and nobody uttered a word. He smiled at the owl-eyed onlookers, "Haaaa, Sissy." He clomped his way to Rosie, picked her up in his arms until her feet left the ground, and kissed her face multiple times. "How ya doin' Sissy?" He asked with genuine affection in his voice.

"I'm well, Jason. I think you know most everybody here," Rosie said.

"Most everybody." He said as he put Rosie back down.

"Who's this little darlin'?" His smile widened as he spoke down to Chiara. She stood motionless for a moment, then straightened her spine and strode up to him. Jason was a foot and a half taller than she, thick with muscle and sleeved out on both arms with prison tattoos later colored-in with civilian happy colors.

"Hi, I'm Chiara."

Jason did something that I'd never seen him do before. He kissed her hand. "The pleasure is all mine, Chiara. I'm Jason." She blushed.

"Ky and I go back Lotsa years. How do you know him?" He asked.

"We only met today. I'm traveling with *thesea* guys and my date, Jeb." She turned her head as if to guide his eyes toward Chevali. Jason's eyes flashed from embracing her to him. He growled and turned his attention back to her. Chevali didn't move. I was glad.

"Bullhead, can we talk in private?" Jason referred to me by my road name. He slid his thick black boots backward, making small skidding sounds on my tile floor, and said to Chiara, "If you will excuse us, please."

"Why, of course." She replied in her confident, gravelly voice while Chevali, Baine, and Jessica stayed silent. Baine was deathly afraid of Jason. Jessica couldn't abide him or my other motorcycle club brothers.

Jason and I walked into the bathroom, "What has you up this early? Is there a problem we need to fix?" I asked.

"Nope, I wanted to wish you a safe trip, kiss my Sissy, and get your patch for safekeeping. You told me a civilian was gonna be stayin' in your house while you were gone. I just want your colors safe." He referred to my motorcycle club vest or 'patch.'

It was a simple leather vest with few sewn-on cloth names and artwork to the outside civilian world. To the motorcycle club member, it represented years of hard work, his identity, honor, and a chosen family for whom he would willingly sacrifice everything. The patch that signifies his motorcycle club membership must be earned, never given. Even though the member had the privilege and responsibility of wearing it, the club owned the patch. It held similar importance as the American flag to a combat veteran. Even more, nobody outside of a 'full patch' member had earned the right even to touch it. There were always rival clubs and Federal agents who would love to kidnap specific club's patches. The Feds and other clubs' members had committed heinous crimes to do so. For them, it would be the equivalent of counting coup on an entire club, not just one member, hence Jason's concern for my patch's safety.

Jason was the beating heart of our Motorcycle Club Chapter. Since his youth, he had been a 1%er and brought a massive level of respect and knowledge to our Chapter. He was as "Old School" as it got, boot leather tough, and as loving as he was dangerous. To the rare "Old School" bikers like him, being in a 1% club *was* about love. His explanation of that fact was what first attracted me to club life. People often see the puerile actions of lesser bikers, idiots on Harleys, and mistakenly extrapolate their actions to genuine bikers like Jason. His unfailing love for his club brothers and their families served as a beacon of actions greater than words, which we all strove to emulate. He was known throughout the biker and Fed worlds like very few living men and commanded deep respect from both.

Jason enjoyed bringing up new members, "prospects," through the arduous process of becoming a full patch club member, as he had me a decade ago. I was still his student. He was my sponsor and mentor. He tested me to see if I possessed the balls and brains to extricate myself alive by placing me in seemingly untenable situations. In doing so, he often put himself between death and me. All he ever asked of me was allegiance to my club. I loved him deeply and had proven it.

"Where's Roscoe?" I asked about our latest prospect.

"Outside guarding the bikes."

"From who, the coyotes?" We lived in a rural part of town.

I rolled my vest up with the patch inside and handed it to Jason, thanking him. Before leaving, he had forehead kisses for all the women. Jessica acted like it was painful. He had a handshake for a stunned Baine and an arctic glower that would frighten God himself for Chevali.

-3-

COMING IN FROM THE COLD

I slept through the flights from Denver to Miami. Our ascent from Miami International airport gave me the first glimpse of the Caribbean since I graduated from med school in New Orleans. I had not missed the Gulf and imagined Puerto Rico, our next stop, to be much more pleasant. We reached our cruising altitude over the middle of the Bahamas' meandering island chain. Dark, featureless islands floated, separated by swirled waves of sand beneath clear green waters and odd-shaped punctuation marks of deep blue trenches.

The captain's garbled voice shot from the volumetrically abused speaker above my head, jolting me awake. Our jet dipped low over the city of San Juan, and I could see straight into the windows of brightly colored apartments. I felt like an airborne voyeur. Below, cramped mildew-covered homes with rotting tin roofs followed a serpentine maze of streets. It looked like Miami Beach from the air, but with more black mold eating the buildings. To the East, high-rise hotels stood shoulder to shoulder, blocking the view of the beaches that they bordered.

Our approach took us over a crashed prop plane that lay dead off the end of our runway, not a reassuring sight. On the Mainland, somebody would have removed it within days of such an untimely demise. Its dull, mildewed fuselage, mostly reclaimed by jungle foliage, spoke of lying there for a long while. The green on white contours made it look like a partially grown airplane Chia Pet. *Welcome to the Third World. The Caribbean beckons you with open arms.*

Adjacent to the modern passenger terminal, ancient propeller planes, the stuff of aviation history, surrounded well-aged Quonset hut hangars. DC-3s squatted proudly on the apron with their noses in the air. Long silver wings supported massive propellered engines that had likely powered them from the Coca fields of Columbia to abandoned airports along America's gulf coast. It could have been a scene straight out of WWII.

The San Juan airport Terminal for Interisland Flights (Airline doublespeak for small, crappy planes) smoldered beneath the air-conditioned modern terminal. The Interisland Flight area was a hot, seething pit. The escalator down to it needed an overhead sign reading, "Lasciate ogne Speranza, Voi ch' intrate." With each second on the descending escalator, the temperature rose, as did the sounds of people yelling and children crying. The humid stench of travelers' body odor and onions deep frying in old grease attacked my nostrils. Wall-mounted TVs blared multiple channels, some in English, others in Spanish. Traveler's languages and dialects spun together in an Osterizer of unpleasant sound. The windows facing the tarmac reflected the frenzied indoor scene like huge smudged mirrors. Discarded food littered the rare unoccupied seats with enough calories to feed the children running underfoot.

I chose to stand, attempting to decipher what the airline personnel said in their Carne Guisada of Puerto Rican Spanish through blown overhead speakers. The air tasted as if each molecule had visited the lungs of every person who had entered this room in its decades of use. Fresh air and quiet had not occupied this place since its last day of construction. I slid my way among bodies slick with greasy sweat to find our flight information on a monitor. Gate number 4 would be the funnel through which we would eventually squeeze for our last flight of this all-day excursion. I was tired and wanted the flying part to be over. I hated flying, especially in small airplanes.

I forced shallow breaths, imagining millions of airborne mycobacteria inviting themselves to take up residence in my lungs. A sudden flash strobed through the windows. At the second flicker, I elbowed my way to a window that ran with rivulets of exhaled humidity racing down it. Water gushed over the rain gutters scattering the lightning flashes that bounced off wet the runway. Frantic screamers behind me overpowered the sound of thunder.

"Great," I said to my reflection in the steamy window, "now a weather delay." The word 'delay' hadn't cleared my mouth before a rattling speaker buzzed in a mystery language. All I could make out was the word 'four.' I searched through the throbbing clot of humanity, and Rosie's panicked eyes, fifty feet away, caught mine as harried passengers began dragging their yowling children and suitcases toward Gate 4.

I pushed gently at first. Imagining an oversold flight leaving me behind and pushed harder. If a man were to push too hard, there would be glares, words, and possibly a fist in the face. I'm usually not smart enough to back down. To avoid a night in a Puerto Rican jail, I followed a large, aggressive woman wearing a turban and a neon sweater moving toward Gate 4. I tried not to imagine the heat and smell inside that sweater. As she shoved, irritated people spun sharply, and upon seeing a woman, they moved aside. I felt like a quarterback following the Center on a quarterback sneak. At one point, I peered above her bowling mass and caught a glimpse of Rosie's blonde head floating away in a flash flood of dark heads. Turban lady led me straight to Rosie and Gate 4. I thanked her, and she replied with a look of disdain.

Our cramped, twin-engine plane blasted to life, and within seconds we were rattling down an unlit taxiway. Relentless rain beat the plane's thin skin as we rolled into a featureless night punctuated by staccato glimpses of the runway and a mountain to our right. After takeoff, the flight pounded us with bucking black air and lightning ripping between clouds at our wingtips to the vacant sea below. Spine compressing updrafts and jaw clenching, molar cracking down drafts entertained us until a thick Spanish accent machinegun splattered words from the ceiling. The pitch of the prop blades indicated a change in their angle of attack, and lengthening dips followed fewer upward slams until we bounced onto a runway. The plane rolled to a halt, peering into the windows of the Saint Thomas U.S. Virgin Islands airport. My scratched Timex watch indicated fifteen hours of travel time so far. Problem patients, upcoming trials, termites in my basement, as well as my animals and club brothers were all out of my reach. I felt a twinge of freedom tempered a hint of panic.

I removed my domineering watch as we walked through the airport. Despite the twenty nine dollars it would take to replace it, I wanted a vacation without owning a watch. I was about to divest myself of it in a trash can when I noticed a young black girl tormenting her toddler brother. Their parents were nowhere around them. I crouched, getting eye to eye, and smiled at him, "Hey little buddy, it looks like you don't have a watch," and strapped it to his tiny motionless wrist. "Do you know how to tell time yet?"

He stared at me as if I were from another planet and inhaled sharply. Tears ejaculated out of his widened eyes onto his face and shirt, and his arm shook as if a pit bull was eating it. He squealed with a look of abject horror and ran crying toward the Women's bathroom door. I told the little girl that it was OK that I meant no harm. She yelled something about a "white debil" and outran her little brother, who had a two-scream lead on her, slammed herself against the women's door, fell back on her butt, bounced up, and rammed it again.

"Nice job shithead, why don't you try candy instead? It seems to work better for you with little kids," Chevali said and walked toward the interior of the building. I watched for angry parents and thankfully saw none. A concerned crowd watched the hysterical children beating the women's room door with their terrified little bodies. Nobody noticed me yet. I felt stupid.

"Nice job, Santa," Rosie said, "I'll get the bags, you find a taxi, tell the driver we're going to Red Hook harbor, and try not to show your face."

"Gee, Red Hook sounds like something out of an old Disney movie," I said.

"Just go before the kids' parents beat your ass, Ok?"

Feeling like a pedophile was an unfamiliar and uncomfortable sensation, like a wet hair shirt, kind of snug at the neck. Outside of the terminal, a row of vans parked in the Taxi zone. A group of black men sat smoking on concrete planters in the faint yellow light of parking lot lamps. At the doorway to the terminal, a man wearing civilian clothing and nothing to designate him as anybody official was directing luggage dragging tourists to the group of disinterested appearing taxi drivers. He gestured to specific vans, speaking loudly and rapidly. I approached him in the jaundiced light of the building. "Hello, do I talk to you about a Taxi to..." the screaming kid incident had blown the name of our intended destination out of my brain. "Oh, yeah, Captain Hook harbor?" I was apparently not the first confused tourist with whom he had ever interacted. His bloodshot eyes gave me nothing as he replied, "You want Captain Morgan's or Red Hook?"

They both sounded right. "The place where boats go to Saint John?" Imposed pedophilia caused short-term memory issues. He yelled to the row of smoking Taxi drivers and gestured for me to move in their direction. One of them stood up in the gloom and politely asked me, "Red Hook?"

"Yes, sir."

"How many?"

"Six, including me. And enough luggage for twenty."

"There's a two 'dolla' charge per bag." At that point, I wasn't about to argue. I wanted to get away from the airport and to another island where I could blend in with ordinary tourists. I asked, "Do you mind if I sit inside your van while we wait? He wore a puzzled expression. "If you wan," and opened the sliding van door. "Leave open?"

"Yes, thank you." The van's laundromat-like humidity made my clothes cling to my skin. The only respite from the heat was a hint of warm breeze coming in off the ocean a few hundred yards away. I waited in the van, peering through face grease-smudged, tinted windows that made everything outside look like a muddy pond. I felt pervert-like, watching people, not wanting to be seen.

Baine appeared first, steering a mountain of luggage on a minuscule cart, followed by Chevali and Chiara, each traveling light with only medium-sized shoulder bags. Rosie and Jessica stepped into the dim light holding two drinks each, laughing and chattering. I searched for an angry black woman, police, and two hysterical children, and eased my head out of the van to call Baine.

The lanky driver glistened with sweat as he loaded our gear into the metal basket on the top of his van. I understood why he was charging an extra two bucks per bag. He would be earning it. The Taxi's air conditioning smelled like a frat house laundry hamper. I found myself breathing shallowly again, discouraging mycologic invaders from finding a lung in which to take up residence. Outside, the buildings and the night people of St. Thomas had similar appearances of consumption by tropical entropy. In downtown Charlotte Amalie, the main town, broad blue tarps displaying the letters "FEMA" covered many commercial buildings' roofs. I asked our jovial driver, Lewiston, about them.

"Oh, dey FEMA tarps from deh hurricane last year, almost to deh day." He turned around to face me as he drove. Chiara shrieked and frantically extending her right hand toward the windshield as if shooing his attention back to oncoming cars. He got the message and turned his face forward. She mouthed the words 'NO MORE QUESTIONS' to me. I mouthed back, 'I'M SORRY.' Lewiston's eyes reflected in his rear-view mirror as he watched us. He continued, "Da hurricane, she tore deh roof off mos' of deh buildins, and now insurance comp'nys be pretending like we done it ourselves. Dey is only giving fitty cent on a dolla to fix 'em, so FEMA has to give da tarps while everybody sues dey insurance comp'ny. Dem says it gonna be years, if ever. An deh U.S. gobment idn't helping none. Dey says it between people and dey insurance comp'ny."

"I guess the devil knows no borders," I said, watching the hapless denizens of the St. Thomas night gather under the pale glow of street lights, sitting on rocks and stubby walls danger- ously close to the road. I hoped for them that our flight's storm wouldn't move their way. Most of the buildings not covered by FEMA tarps were small cinder block homes with flat concrete roofs with rods of re-bar sticking haphazardly skyward. Their black silhouettes looked like the charred skeletons of trees re- maining after a forest fire.

We crested the twisting mountain road that separated the island from North to South. I could make out the contour of the hills and valleys by the patterns of lights of the homes scat- tered on them in the gloom. It was unlike any place I had ever been -- thousands of unfinished houses lining unpaved streets with people winding into and out of an ill-defined darkness.

In the bay below us, the lights of enormous cruise ships in port projected their perfect order. Row upon linear row created a visual contrast between 'the haves' and those who watch 'the haves' temporarily enjoy their island home. I felt like I should feel guilty but didn't. I was guilty of nothing here, except apparently for an emotionally injured kid with a new watch.

Red Hook harbor's unlit gravel parking lot was half-filled with junked cars. Shadow people scavenged the light of anemic street lamps on the road beside it. Muddy water-filled potholes, some of which seemed large enough to swallow a Volkswagen. Lewiston expertly navigated the water hazards before coming to a stop in the center of the gravel lot. We disgorged from the van into the same hot, still, night that had greeted us at the airport. Lewiston threw our bags onto wet gravel after climb- ing a duct-taped and wired ladder to the top of his van. Baine stayed with me while the others went to buy ferry tickets from a cluster of outhouse-sized kiosks scattered on a concrete pad by the ferry docks. The swastika-shaped uneven and chipped docks moored four unlit commercial-sized boats. There were no workers around the docks or the outhouses except for a few dazed appearing people sitting on a short, broken cinder block wall. In the quiet humidity, thousands of flying bugs tornadoed in the haze between them and me.

Each of the four double-decker boats was about seventy feet long, battered relics of a long-past era. Silver skins shone through dozens of scratches and worn patches on their hulls. Bald, squashed car tires lashed to their sides, protected already dented hulls from the ragged dock edges. The sad fleet rocked slowly to the cadence of an unseen sea beyond the black water of the harbor. Oddly angled, nonfunctional street light poles defined the boundaries of the docks. I assumed that angry hurricane whipped seas had slammed poorly moored sailboats into them. Sharp-edged pieces of boat fiberglass and ripped moldering seat cushions hung high in the trees beside the docks. Despite travel brochures describing St Thomas as "Paradise," this place spoke to me with a patois of a hardscrabble life.

A rattling and slamming sound moved toward us. An old black man, wearing shiny dark pants and a fully buttoned, well-worn collared shirt, appeared out of the dark. He pulled a homemade 3x5 foot metal skateboard with tiny metal wheels that repeatedly dropped into potholes, jolting his arm and body. It sounded like horses running over a steel bridge. "Carry dem bags to deh dock?" He asked.

"Sure," I figured he knew where to take our bags. He stood motionless, gesturing to us to load our bags onto the giant skateboard rather than lend a hand. Once loaded, he huffed and pulled the baggage-laden skateboard to the edge of the concrete area where the outhouses stood. He stopped, lifted a rail, and dumped our gear onto the concrete. The bags at the top of the heap slammed hard onto the unforgiving pad.

"Forty dolla." He held out his hand and spoke through edentulous wet gums. The pale skin of his palm and fingers shined in the featureless light.

"Forty dollars?" I shot back, "You pulled our bags for less than a minute. Do you really think you are worth," doing a quick calculation in my head, "twenty-four hundred dollars an hour?"

"Dat's the rate, fo dollah puh bag."

"Well, your math is as bad as your value. It would only come to thirty-two dollars."

"Yup, but deh be a bag loadin' fee uh eight mo dollah." His hand stayed motionless, palm up.

"You didn't load the bags. We did."

"Yeah, but I unloaded 'em."

"You turned your skateboard thing sideways and dumped them. I'm not sure that qualifies as a skillful unloading worthy of an eight-dollar fee."

I was about to give him an exceptionally generous five dollars when Baine squeaked and gestured with his nose behind Skateboard man. We were not alone. Our haggling over money had aroused the attention of some West Indians. Lizard-lidded eyes focused through me as their owners leaned on rusted car hoods.

"Surrounded by Indians, I see," I said to Baine, who stayed silent. I thought about my great grandfather, who rode through Indian country as a Pony Express rider in the 1860s. Unlike him, I was unarmed, a rare, naked feeling for me. I wasn't

going to pay forty dollars to haul my bags a few feet on a glori-
fied skateboard, yet I didn't want to land us in a fight in our
first hour on the island. Baine's wide eyes darted from me to
Skateboard man, to the watchers in the dark, and back to me.

"Huh, a West Indian version of a Mexican Standoff," I said
to Baine, who again didn't respond. (I used the term 'West
Indian' referring to the Caribbean Islands by the name given
them by Christopher Columbus.) He appeared to be unhappy at
that moment. "Man," I said to Skateboard man, "I'm not giving
you forty dollars for hauling our junk a few feet." Unfortunately,
I was getting mad and was about to resign myself to throwing a five-dollar bill at his sandal-clad feet and letting the shit
go down. A familiar voice from behind startled me. "Hey, you
live around here?" It was Chevali walking forcefully toward
us. The Skateboard man seemed bewildered at such a stupid
question.

Ok, here it goes, I thought. Chevali loved to fight, and I figured it was on now. I felt semi-bad for what I was going to do
to Skateboard man and his eight stoned Indians. One of them
reached for something under his untucked shirt. I would go for
him first. He was tall, skinny, and wearing a plastic shopping
bag on his head that read 'Publix' upside down. "I'm not gonna
get killed by some asshole wearing a shopping bag as a hat,"
I said as I pushed Baine behind me and faced the bag man
while Chevali chattily continued.

"Hey my friend," he said to Skateboard man, "I need to
score some weed. Can you possibly procure me some?" He
was toe to toe with Skateboard man, who smiled a gummy
grin. The other Indians stood still and exchanged glances. I figured that he was jockeying himself into a position to start the
party.

"How much you wan," Skateboard man asked. I expected Chevali to knock the old man out, but he took a step back. His actions puzzled me.

"I dunno, a couple of weeks' worth? I'm on vacation, and I want to stay stoned for most of my time here. I need stress relief, Ya know. My life is complicated. I've got a lot of personal and financial stressors. Do you have any idea how much I spend on lawn maintenance alone? I'd bet my gardener went to the same business school as you, my friend." He laughed and slapped Skateboard man on the shoulder.

The Indian circle relaxed and laughed too. Over their shoulders, I watched Rosie and the other gals handing our bags to a couple of sweat-stained guys throwing them through an open window on one of the boats. "Nubian Princess," in white lettering shone over her lime green paint job.

"Here's the deal, you score me the weed and my skinflint friend here," Chevali gestured to me, "will pay you half the money he owes you now. And when you get back, the other half. I'll pay for the bag of dope then too."

"I can do dat."

Chevali motioned for me to give him the money, and I handed him a limp twenty-dollar bill. I thought about how many years I had gone to school and going into unfathomable debt to earn the right to make a fraction per hour of what Skateboard man did. I was confused with his wanting weed. He hated the stuff.

"Good job, buddy," he said with a fake smile as he shook my hand. I felt something in his palm transfer to mine. It was a ferry ticket. While I was haggling with Skateboard man, Chevali had moved our bags next to the Nubian Princess as the girls secured our ferry tickets. He was saving me from myself.

Skateboard man and his friends left the parking lot while deckhands untied the Nubian Princess' bowline. We trotted for her in the dark until I handed my ticket to the deckhand, boarded, and searched for Rosie. All I could see were the backs of black heads, their owners facing forward at a peeling paneled wall. Every other surface in the room was bare metal aluminum. Frenetic, clanking music chopped from speakers mounted next to a wall-mounted air conditioner wheezing coolness into the open room. The staccato noises ricocheted harshly off metal walls, floor, ceiling, and metal seats. The outside 'walls' were glassless open windows separating the room from the tropical air outside the confines of the boat. I gave the deckhand a 'where are my people' look. He dispassionately waived a finger to a metal ladder behind him and rolled his eyes up toward the metal ceiling of the passenger area.

"Aaaah, upstairs?" I asked him.

The slightest nod signaled that my guess was correct. I climbed the steep metal stairs that opened to a hole that revealed unexpected stars above my head. The white, painted handrails felt sticky and cool. Untarnished bare yellow metal spots, polished by the hands of thousands of travelers, shown through on their painted tops. The ship was of World War II vintage. I suspected it was war surplus, then repurposed as a civilian ferry. When the massive diesel engines slammed to life, I couldn't help but wonder how many overhauls the engines had endured. The hard vibration of rough running engines caused the hair in my nose to itch the inside of my right nostril, making me want to sneeze.

The boat's upper deck was open to the night air and half-filled with primarily white passengers talking and laughing. To the front of the outdoor rows of seats was a glass-walled wheelhouse.

The captain's shadow moved to block and unblock green control panel lights. Gulls and other mystery birds clung to the guy wires above the wheelhouse. Once underway into the featureless darknight, the birds flapped their wings until achieving liftoff. Eventually catching the updraft off the bow, they glided effortlessly at the same rate as the boat. Occasionally one would angle off to the side and dive into the night only to reappear behind us and flap frantically to meet his squadron above the wheelhouse free ride zone.

Baine stood to take a picture of the birds in time to save two ladies behind him from being fecally assaulted by one of the birds. The twirling salvo hit his camera, and in the harsh lights of the top deck, a fantail of semiliquid bird crap sprayed off his lens. Two neat half-circles stuck to his neck and forehead. He lowered his camera and began cleaning his camera with his shirttail.

Jessica screeched, "No, not your shirt," and searched in her backpack. White bird excrement clung to his neck and forehead, brightly framing his face. Chevali and Chiara's snorting laughter quickly infected the other passengers. Baine apparently didn't feel the warm crap and stayed emotionless, blinking like a white-faced Capuchin. Jessica glowered at the laughter, grabbed his other shirttail, spit into it, and began wiping his face. Baine batted her hands away, "What the hell, you're spiting..." Jessica threw up her hands, sat forcefully down, and said, "Then you clean it, shitface." The onlooking passengers were rocking, holding their stomachs, and shaking their heads. Baine calmly turned toward the brisk wind coming around the Nubian Princess's bow.

I felt strangely at home on the pitching and rolling night sea. Substantial waves from odd angles occasionally slammed the side of the Nubian Princess, and as she shuddered, warm waves showered unsuspecting passengers. I was finally happy and did not want the boat ride to end. I wanted to stay on her, in the dark, swaying to the cadence of the Caribbean Sea. I held Rosie's hand as our bodies rhythmically bounced into each other. I was in love with the night and her in that perfect moment. I recognized it without trying.

All too soon, the engines wound down, and an unexpected pleasantry greeted me as we entered the tranquil bay adjoining the little town of Cruz Bay on Saint John. Distant sounds of talking and music rode a cool layer of air that wafted out onto the bay's water, bringing with it the island's smells. Alternating bouquets of garlic, fish, and steak cooking over wooden fires mixed with the gentle scents of island flowers releasing their night perfumes. I hadn't eaten any real food since leaving Ft. Collins more than sixteen hours earlier. I was hungry, fatigued, and filthy with sweat from stress and hauling luggage. I was grungy from the air of that little piece of traveler's hell in the basement of the San Juan airport, three rancid-aired airplanes, two taxis, and a boat. All I wanted was a hot redeeming shower and sleep. Hunger would have to wait until morning.

"We're here," I said softly as the other passengers gathered their belongings. Rosie awoke with the facial expression of confusion, which came from having dropped far over the edge of unconsciousness and aroused too soon. The boat's transmission ground into reverse. She spun an effortless 180-degree turn and backed into the dock with a squeaking thud.

The first passengers to disembark were the lower deckers. They formed an impenetrable line to a narrow aluminum gangplank, which sagged and bounced them down to the Cruz Bay dock. Children scurried, sandwiched between asses to the front and large round thighs to the back. Their parents made no eye contact with those topsiders who had made their way to the bottom of the stairs. There would be no blending of topsiders with them. They would go first while we waited. "That's rude," I said to Rosie. She put an index finger to her lips as if to tell me to shut up. I did. We retrieved our wet bags from a heap on the dock and waddled toward town.

"Look for Chuck," Rosie said, ducking her head side to side to see around the passengers as they fanned out to occupy the width of the dock. I wondered if I would recognize him. I hadn't seen him since he and his family visited us in my sophomore year of medical school. I always liked Chuck. Everybody liked Chuck. He was affable, funny, and a generally good guy. He had been an outstanding High School athlete and turned down multiple college scholarships to start his life on Saint John.

"There he is," Rosie said excitedly to Jessica. I visually sifted through the wall of people waiting at the street end of the dock but didn't see him. Rosie trotted to a middle-aged man with a round belly and greasy ballcap and hugged him. He had a drink in each hand, and the force of her affection caused him to spill some onto the concrete. His high-pitched laugh, uncharacteristic for a man of his large size, was a familiar one. It was Chuck. His smile confirmed the identification, but he had aged poorly in paradise. It showed in his sun-damaged skin and his weight, but not in the 'Chuck smile.' His eyes caught mine, and smile crinkles grew at their corners. We had a long history of genuine affection, obviously not tarnished by the years separating us. He handed the drinks to Rosie, saying, "Bushwhackers for you and Hoot," and walked a rolling gate toward me. I reached out my hand to shake his. He flung it behind him and pulled me into his fleshy, sweaty arms in a hug. He needed a shower as much as I did. I instinctively hugged him with the 'biker hug,' holding him firmly in my left arm and slapping his back, searching for a weapon with my right. I felt stupid.

"Damn, you've gotten ugly," I said.

"And you smell like a rotten old dog ass." He spoke through a smile.

I stopped the macho bullshit, "Seriously, it's good to see you." His smile widened as a small amount of fluid collected but didn't spill from his lower eyelids. In a lower voice, he said, "It's nice to see you, Hoot. I'm happy that you finally came down to see my island."

We piled our waterlogged luggage into the back of Chuck's filthy little Jeep. Stained rags and rusted tools littered sand-filled corners. A splintered wood 2x6 ran horizontally behind the front seats to prevent their collapsing backward. Shoulder harness seatbelts hung vertically from the roll bar. Their retraction and buckling devices appeared to have long rusted out of commission. Rosie got into the passenger seat and flung the useless belt across her chest, as did Chuck. Chevali wiggled the limp seatbelts and asked, "What the hell are those supposed to do?"

Chuck replied, "It's the law here that front-seat passengers wear a seatbelt. If the V.I. cops see you without one, they'll fine the shit out of you."

"But not the back seaters. That's idiotic." Chevali said.

Chuck turned a palm upward and swept it in front of him, taking his attention to the chaotic throng of people around them. "It's an Island 'ting, mon, get used to it, don't fight it, breathe slowly and be with it. Always remember, they don't call this Love City for nothing, remember LOVE CITY, this is where you are now."

The rest of us walked the fifteen minutes to our destination, a villa named Tamarindo, where Rosie and Jessica had stayed on previous trips. I didn't mind walking. It was pleasant to be moving without the encumbrance of baggage. My Bushwhacker, with multiple shots of rum, softened the uphill hike. Time blurred as conversations melded with the dark road. I sunk into a world of fatigue, sticky clothes, a warm night, and the smell of rotting garbage as we passed big green trash bins outside of a hotel. I imagined a cockroach version of a Roman orgy in it.

Villa Tamarindo greeted us with brightly lit windows. Chuck showed us around, helped with the bags, and suggested meeting him at Trunk Bay beach the following day. After he left, I quickly peeled my clothes off, thought seriously about burning them, and searched for the shower.

Our bathroom was spacious and bright with white, yellow, and green floor tile and walls. One entire wall was a hand-painted scene of tiny yellow birds on vines sitting in a white lattice with a blue ocean and green islands in the background. It smelled pleasantly of orange blossoms and Clorox. A mobile of hand-painted wooden fish pirouetted in the air above the toilet. The custom shower required a step-down into a tiled basin about six feet in diameter. There was no shower curtain. It was open to the bathroom on one side and to the night on the other, via two walls of jalousie windows.

I helped Rosie down into the shower with me. A turn of the faucet handle had tepid water spraying wonderfully over us. We swayed together in the soft, cleansing spray. I used a bar of soap to liberate the smelly grime from my body. The stench coming off me was truly impressive. The soap dislodged torrents of vile, foul-smelling filth. I smelled of death. *I smell of death?* It worsened to become death and rotten flesh. I wondered if it was Rosie who stank and felt embarrassed for her. In the years we had been together, she had never smelled so putrid. I wondered if she had hidden some horribly infected body part from me. It couldn't be me. *I couldn't smell this badly of death and decay. No living human could, not even Rosie.* I had gone weeks without showering while Elk hunting and never stank that bad. I sniffed a frowning Rosie.

"Are you OK?" I asked.

"Better than you, you stink like...."

We said "death" in unison as a shrill "FUUUUUCK ME" came from Chevali's room next door. I couldn't imagine that they were already having sex. I cradled a handful of shower water, raised it to my nose, and sniffed. "Holy shit, thank God it's the shower water and not you. It smells like holy hell, like something is rotten in the water. Rinse the soap off, quick."

She snapped back, "I thought it was you." She ducked under the malodorous spray and whimpered. Foul rivulets swept dull soap bubbles down her body, only to replace them with the stench of disease.

I answered a knock at our bedroom door. It was Chevali, dripping wet and naked with his right hand cupping his groin. Shampoo swirls made his hair resemble a poorly decorated cake. "What the fuck is going on with the water?" He asked as if I had some specialized plumbing knowledge.

"I don't know, but whatever it is, it's long dead and not of this mortal world."

"What do we do?" He looked ridiculous.

"Hell, if I know."

Jessica, dripping and clad only in a towel, padded up behind him and inspected his naked ass. Pleasure showed on her otherwise disgusted face. "Hi," she said coyly. She had quietly been after him for years. The human embodiment of 'opposites attract.' He was less than enthused by her, considering her a snob, and often took measures to embarrass or repel her. Jessica said, "The water stinks." He removed his hand off his groin and turned to face her. "No, shit." Her eyes dropped to his crotch. She swooned lightly, giggled and trotted wordlessly back to her room.

He grinned and talked to his pecker, "You do it to 'em every time, my friend." I didn't see what he was so proud of as I glanced at him, wiggling and soapy. Rosie, at my side, was red-faced and reeking. "Oh, sorry Rosie," he said and regrabbed himself, "what do we do?"

"Let me see if there is a phone number upstairs in the main house that I can call." Why I became the director of plumbing perplexed me, but I wanted to fix the situation as much as the rest of them. I opened my suitcase, spit on my fingers, and wiped them on my towel to avoid contaminating my stuff with the cloying yuck that had taken up residence on my body. Carefully, with only the tips of my thumb and forefinger pulled clothing out of my bag until I reached my new, unworn flip flops. One still had a ROSS DRESS FOR LESS sticker. I walked upstairs, kicking a couple of giant roaches out of my way. I feared that once they got my scent, they would be chasing me in hordes.

The great room was just that, but I was in no mood to admire anything. I searched for the obligatory 'Welcome to the Villa' renter's information and found the property management's name and number. "Valerie with Mango Property Management" was greeting me from a photo on which someone had drawn a mustache and goatee. I found an ancient yellow rotary dial phone and dialed the number of the person who could deliver us from this odiferous debacle.

There was no dial tone. I pulled on the thin phone line only to find rat turds and frayed tiny white, green, and red wires locked in a static spray. My heart sank when I saw the time on the oven clock, 10:47. We were sunk. I relayed the happy news to each couple by speaking through the slatted doors of their rooms and returned to our bedroom. Rosie lay naked, face down, rhythmically breathing in sleep. I laid next to her and, for a few minutes, replayed the day in my head as I watched a dust encrusted, fake rattan ceiling fan as it spun cooling air onto us. I rolled over onto my stomach and buried my nose into the bedspread. It smelled sweet of sunshine and clean breezes. Sleep came quickly.

-4-

WAITING IN VAIN

I awoke with traveler's panic, that semi-conscious confusion in strange surroundings, unfamiliar sounds, and being
naked on a bed rather than in it? The panic worsened as the
smell of rotting morbidity struck my consciousness. *Oh, sweet
Jesus, what the hell died.* Leaning over, I sniffed my quiet, un-
moving wife. *It's her, she's dead.* A guttural sound from a bad
place deep within me shot from my throat. She flinched, lifted
her head, and scowled. Her unhappy expression brought it all
racing back -Villa Tamarindo's rotten shower water, Jessica's
giggling at Chevali's little pecker, a screaming child wearing my
Timex. "Oh, I must be on vacation," hadn't entered my brain.

"Good morning, my sweet, uh, my sour." Her unchanging
frown signaled that I was alone in the enjoyment of my humor.

"What now, Einstein?" were her first words of greeting.

I asked in irritated confusion. "I've been on this island for a
grand total of seven hours, and I'm supposed to be the one to
solve the shower dilemma?"

"You're the doctor. You solve everybody's problems."
Sarcasm was competing with the smell of rotting carcass to
surround her.

I was thirsty. I hadn't eaten much in twenty-four hours,
yet my thirst outpaced my hunger. My head had the annoying

thump of dehydration. My mouth was dry, making it difficult to enunciate words with more than one syllable. Upstairs, the refrigerator contained only leftover food, and the faucet only yielded fetid water. Left-behind bottles of liquor held no interest. It was hot, and I was sweating away my last drops of circulating fluid. I pinched the skin on the back of my hand, and it stood semi-erect like a pale rooster comb to the count of five without a hint of skin retraction. It was bad. If I were in an E.R., they'd be hooking me up to an IV. I hadn't washed my face or brushed my teeth.

Outside in the shade of a wide veranda, my sweating friends sat, swatting at invading flies. Beyond them was a blue sky kissing a blue-green ocean filled with happy green island humps floating off to the horizon. I didn't care. My misery grew with each sweat droplet. Sailboats glided effortlessly on calm Caribbean seas, pulled along by unseen gentle tropical breezes. Sweet little yellow birds flew in circles above our heads. I didn't care.

"Let's go into town, eat breakfast, and find the property manager," I said, assuming a leadership role I had no desire to occupy. The miserable-appearing group gave weak nods, and we lumbered toward town. I noticed little of our vacation surroundings and aimed for the shade of successive trees as we walked. Nobody was talking. I figured they were all as dehydrated as I. Rosie was pale, Jessica had bedhead, Chevali kept sniffing himself. Chiara bounced along with her head-turning side to side, taking in the scenery to which the rest of us were immune. Baine had a zombie stare as he held Jessica's hand that lay on his shoulder while they walked. The concrete roadway reflected the sun's rays deep into my broiling brain. I was hell hot. My tank top and running shorts were too much clothing.

We stopped at the first little restaurant and plopped into hard plastic chairs. My thighs required exaggerated lifting movements to unstick them from the plastic every time I changed position. A dour waitress filled our water glasses that we drained in seconds. After a couple of pouty refills, she gave up and plopped her water pitcher on our table with a thud. I had a strange feeling of not being welcome.

I leaned back to relax after eating as my brain began to function in a mode other than misery. It quickly became evident that we were an island unto ourselves. The other patrons had scooted their tables away from us. *Can they smell us?* The nasty scowls from otherwise happy vacationers told me that my hypothesis was correct. I didn't care. I already had my friends. I only wanted to resolve the water situation and take a hot, clean shower. I motioned to the reluctant waitress, making the universal hand signal of writing on my palm. She hurriedly delivered the bill in a coconut half-shell with a rock holding it in place. She scratched her printed name off the bill, keeping her identity safe from us.

"Excuse me, ma'am?" I asked politely. "Would you be so kind as to direct us to Mango Property Management?" The waitress flicked her hand and snarled the directions, "There, upstairs behind that yellow building. You aren't going to be here long, are you?" She stood, tapping her foot, glaring past me at the ocean, waiting for payment.

I slowly thumbed through my wallet and said, "Yes, in fact, we're searching for a place to buy to move our tribe here." I positioned myself upwind from her.

"Tribe?" She leaned back as I edged closer to her.

"Yes, we are a tribe of Yahweh devotees." I had no idea who the Yahweh's were, but I had seen their signs back in

New Orleans when I was in medical school. "We're starting a commune here on Saint John, a place where free love can flourish." I said as I grabbed both Rosie's and Baine's hands, kissing each of them, "Unfettered by society's harsh judgment and stifling rules." The waitress appeared as if she were about to vomit at my feet and shuffled away.

"Did you really have to do that?" Rosie asked me without a smile. Baine's head cocked like a dog hearing a mouse in a woodpile as his eyes darted between Jessica and me. He said nothing.

At the base of the steep wooden steps leading up to Mango property management, the group appointed me to report our water and rat-phone issues. I lightly knocked on the door and let myself in. It was meat locker cold. Squished behind a card table desk covered with papers, brochures, and files, sat an exceptionally large woman. Her yellow dress was many, many meals ago, too small. Her ample, stretch-marked tits struggled to explode out of it onto the table.

I'd read about a St John custom. It dictated that when first addressing locals, one should begin the conversation with the appropriate salutation, 'Good morning,' 'Good afternoon,' or 'Good Evening.' They thought mainlanders were rude in starting conversations without the proper greeting.

"Good morning, my name is Ky Elliott. We are renting Villa Tamarindo. Are you, by chance, Valerie?" I was proud of myself for remembering this custom and was expecting a similar, respectful response. I waited, no response. She kept writing, ignoring me. Huh, maybe it was hard to hear me above the raging air conditioner a foot behind her head. So, louder and slower, "Hello, my name is..." She cut me off and without lifting her head, snapped back, "I heard you the first time. Let me finish what I'm doing." So much for pleasantries. She plodded along until finally slapping her pencil down. "What is it you want? I'm very busy." She must not have gotten laid that morning.

I told her about the demon water spewing from the showers. She answered, blankly talking to my chin, "It's a catchment system. Frangipani flowers can drop onto the roof and give the water an odd, harmless smell. We had it tested, and it won't hurt you. Good day." She put her head back down, exposing grey roots, and grabbed her pencil again. I wasn't accepting that answer. "Ma'am, I need to speak to Valerie, please."

"You just did."

Maintaining my composure and not wanting to make a new enemy every hour while in the Virgin Islands, I said, "Valerie, the problem is not one of a few flowers on the roof, there is something big, bad and exceptionally dead...MUERTE," (for some unknown reason, I threw Spanish into the conversation as a point of emphasis), "and rotting in the water system. I know catchment systems inside and out, and I'm familiar with frangipani flowers' pleasant yet 'off odor' in said catchment systems. And what I'm smelling is death, not tropical flowers."

I had never been in a building with a catchment system, nor did I have the foggiest idea of how frangipani flowers looked or smelled.

"The people who just left before you didn't complain."

I spoke to her bad dye job, "I don't give a rat's ass about the anosmic morons who just left. I'm telling you that there is something dead in the water that we showered in last night. We smell beyond disgusting, and as a physician, I can tell you it's a health hazard. If any of us ends up sick from this dangerous contamination, you and your management company will be held legally responsible." *Ha, got the bitch with that one.*

In a dismissive tone, Valerie said, "Flowers in the rain gutters, but to keep you happy, Doctor, I'll send Pedro out this week to check it. You are fine, now have a wonderful vacation."

I had to shift gears. "If you will excuse me, Ma'am, I'll return in a moment." She flicked her hand as if brushing crumbs off her card table in my direction. "Love city my ass," I said as I held her office door open and called down to our group sitting in the morning's swelter. "Hey everybody, Valerie wants to speak with all of us at the same time."

We took up half of the office and Valerie the other half. Baine closed the door behind him as I shut off the air conditioner. Valerie whipped around with tits swooping clockwise to face me. I feared her inertia would twist her through an entire '360.' "Get your fucking hands off of that air..." She suddenly wore a pained expression as our funk greeted her.

"Uh, huh," I said, "Take a deep breath of the happy ass frangipani flower essence. So now that we have your attention..." She looked panicked. There was no escape route from the crazy, stinking mainlanders. She was too obese to move with all of us in her office. The death stench rose with every degree of temperature. It was wonderfully cloying. "Is this the innocent smell of a few flowers in the rain gutters?" I asked.

Horror grew in her widening eyes, as did the unmistakable smell of rotting flesh. "Out, out, get the fuck out of my office, you Motherscunts," Valerie yelled.

"Ma'am," I asked calmly, "what are you going to do about the water situation?"

"Fine, I get it, something dead. I'll send Pedro out in the next day to check it out." She held her nose and fanned herself.

Keeping my hand poised on the air conditioner switch, "Next day won't do. We are paying hundreds of dollars per

hour between us to be here on vacation. I want it fixed today."
I want to speak to your boss NOW."

Valerie growled, "I am the boss. This is my business, ass-hole." Her eyes were on fire. Sweat ran down her face and cascaded down onto her mountainous chest. Tit-funneled sweat stained the fabric under them, forming a wet frown along the dome-like top contour of her belly.

"Understand me. We are going to the beach and will be back at the Villa around four. I expect this health hazard to be resolved and the water sweet by then." I paused and added, "Health hazard fixed now." Valerie's response was a sage grouse-like vibrating growl.

As we descended the stairs, Chevali smiled up at me, "Good job Ky, in less than twenty-four hours, you have done more to singlehandedly unravel a century's worth of race relations in the Caribbean than any man alive."

"Thanks, asshole, it's not about race. It's about what's right. I wouldn't give a shit if she were green."

Jessica added, "She was."

We walked in the unforgiving sun to the Taxi parking area by the ferry harbor. The Virgin Island version of a Taxi was a pickup with two rows of metal seats welded length-wise along the sides of the bed with no seatbelts. The roof was a slice of pink and white striped canvas stretched over thin metal tubing. It vaguely reminded me of the vehicle driven by Ricardo Montalban in an old TV show, "Fantasy Island."

The driver stopped at scenic overlooks and spoke to the passengers through an electric megaphone mounted behind his cab, giving a brief history of the bays below. I wasn't in the mood for fluffy tourist entertainment. I wanted to immerse my hot, stinking body into some fresh seawater.

We hopped out onto the sunbaked asphalt parking lot of Trunk Bay at noon. The waves were an impressive six inches high. The ocean water was so clear that the Park Service boat anchored fifty feet from shore seemed to float in green-tinted air, casting a perfect hard-edged shadow in the sand below it. We sprinted across the burning sand, and as I entered the water, I instinctively sucked air into my lungs, bracing for a temperature shock that didn't come. The water invited me into her. I waded out to testicle level, the unwritten cutoff depth for wading in cold water, and without hesitation continued to armpit depth. "Warmer than Hawaii water," I said, to Chiara who was next to me, treading water.

"You're right. This isa perfetto." She replied through polished white teeth and then tucked and rolled forward, doing a couple of watery summersaults. With each revolution, her tanned ass cheeks, unhidden in a thong, reflected the sun. I glanced up to see Rosie watching me admire the little revolving globes of hard flesh. She had an unthreatened 'caught ya' look in her eyes. All I could do was smile and exaggerate my already guilty facial expression.

Baine and Jessica waded out to us. "Water's warm," he said flatly.

Chevali replied, "Yup."

Baine waded to him, "Do you take baths?"

"Only if I have a chick in the tub with me." He reached out and swatted Chiara's ass when it rolled to the surface. The tone of the smack spoke of an enviable muscle to fat ratio.

"I like baths," Baine said.

"Huh?" Chevali answered.

"I'll take a bath rather than a shower at least once a week."

"Is that so?" Chevali was looking at him with that one-eyed

discernment you give crazy people, wondering if they are about to explode.

"Yep, sometimes I use oregano bath salts too."

"Oregano bath salts, what the hell for?" Chevali asked.

"They are organic and help detoxify your skin," Blaine answered, rubbing water onto his arm.

"Why, is your skin toxic?"

"I, uh, don't know."

"Then why use detoxifying bath shit?"

"I read about it in Prevention Magazine, it's supposed to...." His voice trailed off into the universe of annoying beings.

"Gee, that's really cool." Chevali's eyes plead with Jessica to reel Baine in. She was oblivious to them, staring at Chiara, spinning in the water. Rosie also seemed captivated by the black head hair alternating with her shining ass cheeks. Chiara's right cheek had an impressive burn scar, well-healed and about three inches long.

"This is..." Chiara said before sinking and leaving undulating fingers of hair where her head had been.

She bounced off the bottom and said, "Malto amazing," providing a glimpse of a grin.

She sank again and bounced up. "I never want..." Sank and bounced up. "To leave this...."

Sank and bounced up "Place ever," and started to tread water while the rest of us stood. Rosie leaned into me, "Damn, a spinner and a Yoyo."

"Poor Dr. Jeb," I said, and I ducked underwater to grab a handful of wet sand to scrub my torso. "Ya know, I just had an unsettling thought," I said to nobody in particular. "Sharks are attracted to the smell of decaying flesh, and we're creating a

chum slick of death from whatever is rotting in the cistern."
Searching eyeballs met my statement.

Chevali waded back to knee-deep water, trailing plumes of
sand in little eddies underwater. Each of us followed, attempting
to act calm and not panic, except for Baine, who stayed chest-
deep. He wore the facial expression of a man, trying not to appear as though he were peeing underwater well past the time
for a long healthy pee. I wondered if he had a prostate problem.

Jessica called to him. "Hey Baine, aren't you worried
about..." She stopped herself, eyeing the people in the water
near us, "Did you hear what Ky said?"

"Yep."

"Baine, honey," Jessica said through gritted teeth, "don't
you want to come back here with the rest of us?"

"Are we leaving already?" He said.

"No, Honey, please come back to the shallow water. We all
smell a bit like..." She whispered, "death."

"I'm fine. It's almost like my bath at home. Except there, I
can turn up the hot knob. If it gets too hot, I can turn the cold
up knob to regulate the temperature."

"Baine, get your ..." She paused when a nearby woman
frowned at her, "over here." She patted the surface of the water beside her. He stayed motionless.

"Hey Forrest, y'all come on over. We got us a box of choco-
lates right here." Chevali put his hand on top of his head, imitating a shark fin.

Jessica snipped, "That doesn't help, being a shit to him."

"Oh really?" He pointed to Baine swimming toward us.

Chevali said while splashing water into his armpits, "It's a
gift, ya know, communication with simpler animals, cats, gold-
fish, Baine."

Ignoring him, she said to Baine, "Nice of you to join us."

"Thank you, it's nice to be here," he replied with ignorant sincerity.

The warm water made me cooler than I had been since landing in Puerto Rico. I scrubbed the clinging oil of death and tropical grime off me with sand and seawater and sat back in neck-deep pleasure. The scent of saltwater wafted on a breeze, which lowered the temperature of my head, emotionally and physically. I was again pleased to be with my senses. No stench or clamoring people in airports. Gone were my sweat-heavy clothes cultivating bacteria in their fabric. A gentle sea surge rocked me, slowly filling my shorts with sand. I felt lovingly embraced by the environment and looked ashore.

Hundreds of sunburned and quiet people lay strewn on towels reading or wading along the waveless shore. The quarter-mile-long beach was bordered on either side by tall, black rock slopes and steep green hills which angled toward the shoreline. A soft, onshore breeze carried the sounds of humanity away from me. I reached down, scooped handfuls of coarse sand, and tossed them underwater, creating drifting sand clouds. Small, white fish swam through the clouds in hopes of catching a meal. The water was rocking me, slowly yet powerfully scooting me. In defiance, I fruitlessly dug my toes in the sand. No sounds entered my brain. I heard only my breathing and watched new friends swimming around me, having lunch in my stirred-up sand. The broken trees that climbed the hill behind the beach were perfect in their imperfection, and in that second, so was I. My wife and friends, quiet and chin deep, swayed in the surge. Most had closed eyes. Rosie's hand found mine in the sand, and I gave it a small squeeze, bringing a slight smile to her otherwise slack face. Was I somehow feeling a sense of home?

We slogged, waterlogged, and still stinking toward the Taxi area a few hundred feet uphill from the concession area and showers that we had missed on our way to the beach. *SHOWERS?*

"Shit baby shit, showers," I said, hearing the unmistakable sounds of people showering inside a long brown, mostly open-air building. It was time to change plans.

"We can't assume Valerie would fix the water problem on a Saturday, agreed?" I said to the paused group. "I, for one, was not impressed with her commitment to customer satisfaction. Since we gotta go out in public for dinner, lets we buy soap and shampoo at the little concession store and shower here."

Chevali and I secured little bars of travel soap and bottles of shampoo. He and I took adjoining shower stalls on the Men's side so we could share the shampoo bottle. I spoke over the sounds of the other showering beachgoers to ask him for it. The shower stalls were a foot above head height and opened to the ceiling, allowing breezes to blow through. Water splashing and laughing conversations echoed off the pitched ceiling to create a hint of voyeuristic acoustics.

"Incoming." He tossed the shampoo bottle over the wall to land at my feet. "You won't need much with your hairline." The shower water was hot and pleasantly stung. I scrubbed away death, sweat, airport grime, and unloaded sand that had hitchhiked in my shorts.

"Hey, Rosie?" I spoke up toward the roof on the lady's side of the showers.

She replied, "Great shower, huh?"

"Yep, but one small problem."

"What's that?"

"Once you are clean, what are you going to wear that doesn't smell like a sewer pipe? All of our clothes are shower-yuck stinky." I heard a few chuckles from other showering tourists.

"Oh hell, what are we going to do?" She asked.

"I don't know. The only piece of cloth within ten feet of me that doesn't smell like the devil's ass is my towel," I said.

"Me too." A voice from a direction other than Rosie's.

Chevali grunted from his shower stall. I filled my mouth with water, planning on spitting it on him and yelling at him to quit jerking off in the public shower. I pulled myself up to peer over the wall between us to get a shot at him.

He stood, facing away from me. His left hand was on his hip, his right hand was in front of him, rhythmically moving back and forth. His white, round ass was churning. *Oh God, oh hell, I really did catch him jerking off.* I did not want to see this. As I started to let myself drop back, I noticed an extra pair of muscular brown legs in front of his. Chiara was in his stall, bent over, and he was doing her doggie style standing up in the shower. So, I spat water on them and asked, "Anybody got hair conditioner?"

She yelped and shot forward, disengaging. She was magnificent naked. Every inch of her wet, glistening body was tan except for her small pink nipples and teeth as she smiled shyly. He flung around and glared up at me. To my disgust, I was facing his little pecker again for the second time in as many days. I hoped that this was not setting the tone for the rest of the vacation. His following action took me by surprise. Without saying a word, he slowly pulled her hips back in line with his, pushed on her shoulder to bend her over, and re-entered her. As he did this, her eyes never left mine. Her head bowed down, and she rolled her eyes up, puppy dog style, to hold my gaze. Once he restarted his rhythmic motions, her eyes stayed locked on mine and fluttered shut while she smiled. He ground into her, grinning at me, and gave her an echoing swat on the ass. I couldn't take anymore and retreated down back to my stall to wash off my new sweat.

I spoke in Rosie's direction, "Hey Rosie. I'm gonna say screw it...."

Before I could finish my sentence, both Chiara and Chevali added, "Me too."

Ignoring them, I continued, "And just wear my towel back to town."

She replied, "But what are we going to do with our rotten clothes?"

"Let me think..."

I couldn't shake the mental movie of Chiara happily screwing Jeb in front of me. She smiled up at me. *Shit, this is awful.* I hated feeling guilty for my thoughts. I wrapped my towel around my waist and went outside to meet the non-copulating members of our group in the shade of swaying coconut trees. Standing in moist sand, clad only in towels, each person held their retched clothes out at odd angles. We waited, watching mongeese scatter from bush to bush in the periphery until the shower lovers joined us.

"Hey, there's Chuck." Rosie pointed to the parking lot. He slowly lugged two SCUBA tanks uphill. His shirt was wet, and sweat stains rimmed the circumference of his hat. She called and cautiously ran to him, taking short choppy steps holding her towel to her chest with one hand and over her butt with the other. She gesticulated, rubbing her armpits as if in a shower.

He nodded. She pinched her nose and bent over, pretending to vomit. He turned to face us, pinching his nose, rocking back and forth, laughing at us. Chevali and I had the same reaction. After checking to make sure the coast was clear, we lifted our towels as we faced him. He stopped laughing, let go of his nose, and extended his hand in our direction with his thick thumb and forefinger about an inch apart.

"Bastard," I said.

Rosie returned, "I told him about the water situation. He said that Valerie was a useless cow and doubted that she would do anything. And if the cistern isn't completely sealed, that all kinds of animals can get into it. He's going to come up and look at it for us in an hour."

"Man, if that shit isn't fixed, I'm going to be one mad son of a..." Rosie stopped me with her narrowed eyes. "Vacation, Ky, vacation."

"Yes, mom," I paused, "and now we gotta do something with these rotten clothes."

"Like what?" Jessica asked.

"Screw it. I'm going to bury them," I said.

Baine and I scooped out a hole under a big rock as feral cats eyed us. "I hope they don't steal them," I said to Baine, "it would be a loss for all involved parties."

"Ya know cats have an amazing sense of smell. In fact, the customs agents in Spain have started using cats rather than dogs to sniff luggage for bombs and dope."

"Seriously?" I asked.

"Yes, I refereed the divorce of a cat breeder who breeds a Manx, Siamese mix for that specific purpose," he continued, "when I was a boy, I had a cat. His name was Baine too."

"Wait, you named your cat after yourself?" I asked.

"No, my Dad did it. He thought it was funny. He would put cat food on my plate and my hamburger helper in the cat's bowl some nights just to watch my face."

"He had a good sense of humor?" I asked, trying to inject levity but thinking he had an asshole for a father.

"No, not really, unless it came to me." His voice was flat.

I scraped sand over the clothing hole and switched subjects, "Just like the pirates, burying our treasure on a Caribbean Island."

The return to Tamarindo ignited my anticipated frustration. Nothing had changed. We had the same stinking water. "I can't believe the blatant disregard for her guest's health and enjoyment. This place is beyond fantastic." I said to Rosie as I swept my hand beyond the main house and huge veranda. "Look at this view," pointing to the little harbor beneath us that opened to a calm ocean and a dozen uninhabited green islands. Sailboats at anchor rocked slowly as a ferry cruised into port. "All of this, and to let it be ruined because that incompetent bitch is too stupid or lazy to do her job. We are paying..." Rosie shot me her 'shut up' facial expression. "Vacation, Ky, vacation, Chuck will fix it. He's been living down here for more than a decade. He'll know what to do. Go inside and drink some rum."

"Screw rum. I want tequila?" I was losing touch with my happy place.

Chiara said, climbing the stairs and smiling through her question. "Let's see if the last people left us any rum. I'm a thirsty girl."

"Hey, who said rum?" Chuck arrived with a shopping bag in his arms, "Not only did I bring rum, but dinner too," he said, walking into the main house with the confidence of someone who knew the place. He reached into the bag, imitating a pirate unsheathing his sword, and held a bottle of brown liquid in my direction. "Hoot, this is the good shit. I got it just for you because I know you're a liquor snob." His smile was wide.

"Isn't good rum an oxymoron"? I asked.

"OOOh nooo, Hoot, this is the best rum in the Caribbean." He massaged the label, "this was the rum given to British Royal Navy sailors every day onboard ship until the 1970s. It's sippin' rum like that yuppie Patron shit you used to drink."

"Still do," I replied with a hint of unexpected shame, hoping that nothing I did was yuppie-like. It was the right time to be humble since he seemed sincere. "I've read wonderful things about this stuff. I don't think you can get it on the mainland." I lied, I had never read anything about it, but I wanted him to feel like I appreciated his efforts.

In the kitchen cupboards, I found mismatched, dusty shot glasses. Many contained withered bugs having found their final resting place. They got a quick rinse from a gallon jug of store-bought water and dried with a kitchen towel of dubious cleanliness. Chiara stood at my side, bouncing up and down. "Me too, Me too?" She asked shyly. Her hair was in ringlets from the humidity and uncoiled and re-coiled as she bounced.

Chuck said, "Hell yes, we gotta' kill this bottle tonight. It won't be any good in the morning."

I reluctantly accepted a shot glass of Pussers rum, forced a smile, and took small investigatory sips. Chiara downed hers in one swallow, apparently with a mouthful of air as she immediately belched.

Chuck flinched, "Damn, you thirsty?"

"Yep, and I love Pussers. I had it in Tortola years ago," she said.

He poured her another, "Siiiiip it this time." She did and adorned each sip with a painfully familiar moan. I tried to turn off my inner movie screen of her in the shower, gazing up at me with wet, swinging hair. I refocused on my rum, expecting the overly sweet, bland rum we drank as teenagers and hadn't bothered to drink since.

My last rum experience was of slamming flaming Bacardi 151 shots in my father's kitchen, catching my face on fire, and burning all my eyelashes off. I learned that eyelashes functioned like miniature eyelid shock absorbers and spent the next week blinking like a spider monkey because of the strange sensation of my eyelids crashing into each other.

This rum was a different species and invited another, longer pull. It offered strong and subtle flavors. The volatile alcohol rolled into light tropical flowers and fruits that ignited the length of my tongue. Swallowing changed the characteristics at the back of my throat to oak and melted sugar. I liked this stuff and surrendered old memories to the joys of a new friend. My eyelashes were safe tonight.

The well-used kitchen of Tamarindo, like the rest of the house, had seen younger days. The kitchen counter Formica was a blue floral pattern, and I suspected it had been popular in the seventies. It had worn to a dull white beside the stove and at the corners. The evening's sounds of conversation, laughter, and clanking pans and dishes all melded with the warm buzz of Pusser's rum. Chuck and I grilled the steaks outside in the warm and humid night while squadrons of mosquito's dive-bombed any piece of skin not drenched in "OFF."

"Thanks for bringing dinner, Chuck."

"It's cool, Hoot. I'm super glad you decided to come down."

"Me too. It's been an adventure so far with the whole rotten water thing."

"Let's find the cistern. I did some repair work on this place. I think I know where the access holes are. First, let's find the outside port for the water trucks."

"Water trucks? As in bringing water to the house? There's no city water?"

"Nope, only in town. When there isn't enough rain to keep the cisterns full, tanker ships come with potable water from Puerto Rico. Then, water trucks deliver it to the homes."

"Water trucks? Wow, what a weird deal," I said.

"It's life on a rock Hoot. Let's locate the watering port. It should be toward the front of the house."

We followed the winding concrete path that connected the pool area to the fence at the driveway. With a flashlight, he spotted an eight-inch diameter metal pipe jutting out a few inches from the rock facade that wrapped the house's base. "Oh, that's bad," he said.

"This is where they dump water into the cistern? What the hell, it's wide open to the world." My dumfoundation grew.

"Yeah, it should have a cover. He searched the ground with his light, "There it is." Chuck picked up a haphazardly shaped piece of window screen, shaped into a cap of sorts, laying in the dirt. "Damn water-truck drivers are too lazy to do this." He said, replacing it over the open pipe.

"Are you serious? That hole leads to the water we drink? A cat could climb in there and shit in the water."

"Worse than shitting, he could go for a last swim. Let's go to the living room and open the cistern."

Chuck moved a large woven floormat in the great room to reveal a 3-foot square of terrazzo that had no grout around it.

"Here it is," and dug his thick, tan fingers into the crack and hoisted it onto its side. We all circled to investigate the cistern. The source of the contaminated water lay in three feet of water, surrounded by inch-long eggs that had escaped her rotting abdomen.

"Fuck me running. A goddamn iguana, how did that bastard get in there?" Chevali was the first to comment, followed by a female, "Oh Gross."

"Mamma Mia." Chiara.

"I showered with that on me?" Jessica.

"I brushed my teeth with that?" Baine.

"Shit," Chevali responded, "I wondered if you had a new mouthwash, Baine. Your breath's been sweeter than usual. Jessica, I'd still slip him the tongue if I were you." She huffed and walked stiff-legged back to the kitchen.

"What the hell do we do now?" I asked, happy now that I was no longer in charge of the water disaster.

"We gotta get her outta there first. I'm just not sure how," Chuck said.

"Hey, a wait." Chiara left and came back with the swimming pool skimmer, "You thinka thees could awork?" Her Italian accent thickened with her rum intake.

"Only one way to find out," Chuck grasped the shaft of the skimmer and ran it down to the demised iguana's depth. Each slow, gentle swath pulled up an easily dismembered body part but also kicked up clouds of rotten iguana sediment. If he captured a leg, a loop of gut would swirl off. He painstakingly deposited the iguana slime into a wastebasket. The eggs proved to be the hardest to retrieve, either rolling away from the leading edge of the skimmer or disintegrating into a cloud of future reptile mush. The process took nearly an hour, making the house reek of morbidity and bacterial reclamation, driving all but Chuck and me from the house.

Immediately after his reptile removal efforts, he said that he remembered, a little too late, that the house had two separate cisterns. We found the other cistern cover under a wicker chair on the far side of the room and opened it up to find a full, fresh, clean-smelling vat of 10,000 gallons of water. With the simple turn of a valve knob located under the house, we had clean water. I poured a gallon of Clorox bleach into the second cistern, just to be sure. We ran faucets and showers until the stench of hell gave way to that of light bleach.

The bottle of Pusser's ran dry before our mood to party did. I stepped outside to escape the noise of drunk conversations and walked beyond the veranda to be alone under the dark sky, throbbing with uncountable stars. I leaned against the rusted, wrought iron handrail that encircled the deck and looked back into the house. My friends were talking, laughing, and wildly gesticulating in the story. I felt lucky. I thought back to the physically and emotionally walking wounded who filled my practice, my dogs sleeping without me, and an upcoming trial in which I would be an expert witness going up against the unscrupled, puppy murdering insurance adjustor Percy Hayes. My heart was thumping in my neck when a soft voice came from the dark, "Hey, you OK?" It was Rosie.

"Yep, doing great."

"Why'd you leave? Chuck was worried that you might be getting sick or something?

"No puking. I simply needed to see the stars and remind myself of where I am.... in life and on the map. Sometimes it's easy to forget where you are in the world, ya know?"

"Yep, where are you right now?" Rosie asked.

"Trying hard not to be a stressed-out prick with my head in Colorado and trying to be contented on a tiny island thousands of miles from reality." I pulled her to me and kissed her face.

"Thank you for coming out." She smelled like "OFF," a happy scent for me. We watched the stars quietly until she asked, "Seems like everybody likes Chuck, huh?"

"Who doesn't?" I said, noticing the darker outline of an island on a featureless sea beyond the bay. Absent stars on the horizon defined its low silhouette. "What Island is that?" I asked.

"Lovango."

"Lovango?" There were two lights on it. "That's where I want to live. Fuck the world, give me Lovango, you, me, and the animals."

"And what would you do for a living?" Rosie asked.

"I don't know, anything but a damn doctor."

"Ky, you are on vacation. Please be here with me, only me. Leave the assholes in Colorado." She kissed me passionately and began rubbing my belly.

"Remember vacation rule number one?" She asked. I could see her teeth reflecting a moonlight smile in the dark.

"Yep."

"And you know you are a day behind on your duties," she said.

"Hey, that's not fair, the whole iguana water thing."

"Buddy, rules are rules. You have run up a sex debt and owe me two tonight. I intend upon collecting my due."

We returned to the others inside, where I began washing the dishes by hand. Each time Rosie delivered a plate or dish, she would slide her hand into my loose shorts to encourage a degree of tumescence. Her affections necessitated my leaning into the counter to maintain my dignity. I was throbbing like the stars of the night sky above our heads, promising an interesting exit to our downstairs bedroom.

When Chuck announced his departure, I forced myself to imagine showering in rotten iguana water, causing me to lose all visible signs of Rosie's repeated assaults.

"Amigo, thank you so much for dinner and the iguana hunt," I said.

"Happy to do it, Hoot. Why don't you guys meet me in the morning? I have a foursome for a shore dive in Frances Bay.

"What time?" I asked.

"I'll pick you guys up at 7:30."

"I'm into it, man," I said.

I spent the next two hours attending to Rosie's desires. I wanted to give her everything she could want from a night together under a rusted ceiling fan circulating warm tropical air on our sweating bodies. When we rested, the sounds of Cruz Bay town had died down, replaced by singing voyeuristic Coqui frogs whistling and cheering from outside our louvered windows.

-5-

THANK YOU LORD

I started my morning standing under Tamarindo's veranda overlooking Cruz Bay, eating New Zealand yogurt, and watching boats glide in and out of the harbor. Unlike me, the whole world was not on vacation. Most of the ferryboats were running between Cruz Bay and the island of St. Thomas to the West. Some made a sharp right outside the harbor and headed East to the British Virgin Islands. Sailboats motored out to the open sea, unfurled their sails, and headed in every direction.

Chevali appeared shirtless and wearing orange micro-shorts that would have invited his molestation in most big-city parks. He stopped at the top of a short flight of stairs leading to the main house, turned, and began urinating down onto a potted cactus at the base of the steps.

"Hey Jeb, how'd you sleep?" I asked.

He grabbed his jaw and moved it around while he peed with his other hand. "My jaw is sore from eating pussy all night. I feel an anaconda that just ate a gazelle."

Jessica, clad in a red bikini, stealthfully climbed the stairs with the prowl of a trout about to snatch a fly from the surface of a stream as she visually consumed him from behind. She quietly stepped up, shoulder to shoulder with him, "You're mixing your metaphors, mister sore jaw."

"Wha, what?" Chevali flinched and quickly stuffed himself back into his shorts.

"You mixed your metaphors. Anaconda live in South America, and gazelles are from Africa." She said dryly, still standing next to him. She put her nose to his mouth and sniffed. "Smells OK, maybe her mommy had time to teach this one some personal hygiene before she quit High School."

Jessica was usually professional, cultured, and calm. She could confidently discuss the intricacies of medical devices with surgeons and possessed the charm to keep them entertained when she took them golfing, tennis, or shooting trap. The tropical heat had unleashed the 'Vacation Jessica.' Her typically straightened and expertly coiffed hair hung in an unruly but attractive mass of twirls. Instead of staying hidden behind layers of bra, high buttoned loose shirts, and coats, her breasts were pleasantly swinging in her loose bikini top like kids in a hammock. Chevali stepped back, "Jesus, Jessica." She halted her pursuit when Baine arrived at the stairs and asked, "Hey, what are you guys talking about?"

"Mouthwash," Chevali said.

Baine started in, "Ya know, I read that mouthwash is one of two leading causes of oral cancer."

"Yeah, What's the second?" asked Chevali, feigning interest.

"Oral sex," Baine said. Jessica coughed, looking trapped.

"WHAT?" Chevali asked.

"Yep, just ask Ky. He'll tell you," Baine said, handing off a conversation of which I wanted no part. I said nothing, so he continued, "HPV virus can live in your private parts and is spread by regular sex and oral sex. It causes cervical as well as head and neck cancers."

"This is frightening. I'm getting a breakfast beer," Chevali said.

Jessica followed him, taking unusually small steps.

Baine continued, "Yep, I quit using mouthwash and having oral sex because of that article."

"Poor Jess," I said.

"No problem, my breath is fine," Baine rambled on. "I brush my teeth every day with fluoride toothpaste. Sometimes, for vanity sake, I'll buy the whitening toothpaste, cuz I don't want to look like a damn woodchuck", he droned on. "Teeth, unlike bone, don't get continually replaced by the body. Did you know that your skeleton is replaced with new cells every five years? But not your adult teeth. They must last your entire life. That's why I brush with a soft brush and not too vigorously." I didn't know if he thought he was funny or entertaining. He missed at being either.

"No, Baine, I said, "I was talking about the no oral sex thing, poor Jessica, as in she doesn't get any oral sex." He continued, "I'm fine with missionary style any day, no need for putting my mouth down there, ya know, the old nose-to-nose tango is good enough for us." He wouldn't stop, "Do you know where the term missionary style came from?"

"Yes, in fact, I do," I replied, wanting him to stop. He didn't.

"It comes from the South Pacific Islanders, who did it doggy style until the European Missionaries taught them about Jesus and how to have sex like white people, ya know, face to face." He was educating me on the world's history of sex.

"Yes, I know missionary style very well. I remember it from High School." I interjected through his blindingly boring mind-vomit, "Hey Baine, let's go inside and grab some coffee." I said and motioned for the sliding glass doors.

"Sure. I like coffee. Do you know that Coffee didn't actually start in Columbia but was introduced…"? His words became an auditory blur. I turned my attention to a Tamarind tree at the edge of the deck and a bird with a strange amelodic song that didn't follow any pattern. Its song crescendoed up and down, slightly warbling. I finally caught sight of it. Brownish, rather drab, the size of a blackbird but with a sharper, longer beak. As it sang each note, he would dip or thrust his little body up, then down. The up thrusts came with crescendos and the dips with decrescendos.

"Jeb, what do you want to do with the day?" I asked from across the kitchen. "Any desire to join the rest of the kids and hit the beach?"

He replied without glancing at Chiara, "I need to go for a run, make some phone calls and watch the news." He headed for a large TV in the corner of the living room.

"HOLD IT." I raised my voice and held out my right hand, facing him. "I have a very simple request, please, please don't turn that damn TV on while I'm in the room. I don't want to hear one second of news while I'm down here, please?"

"Good Christ, Ky, it's only the news," he said.

"I know, I'm sorry, but when I'm paying for time away from reality, the last thing I need is a dose of it in the form of the miserable news. I know the economy is shit, I know someone is getting murdered, I know crazy-ass dictators want to start a war with America. I don't want to hear it. I simply want to be a happy ostrich." I visually searched the room. Everybody was silent, staring at me. I felt like an ass for my outburst.

Jessica was the first to speak, "You know, Jeb, Ky is right. I have to listen to that depressing junk every day because of my position in the Young Republicans. I hate it."

Chiara said, "I don't need it."

Rosie silently nodded *yes.*

Chevali blinked. "Can I at least watch ESPN?"

"All damn day, baby," I said in a loud voice.

Chiara turned to Rosie, "Can I go with you guys. I don't want to watch TV."

"Fine, fuck it, let's all go." Chevali acquiesced.

Chuck's Jeep skidded into the small parking area in front of Tamarindo. "Hoot, haul your ass out here."

I threw our beach bag into the rusting floor of his blue Jeep CJ-5. Its dull paint hadn't seen a coat of wax, perhaps ever. Rosie got into the front seat, and the rest of us crammed ourselves into the small open-air passenger compartment. Chiara sat on Chevali's lap. Baine sat on Jessica's. There was no roof, except for a piece of splintered and mildewed plywood over the driver's compartment, held in place by rusted baling wire. The large front seats belonged in a Soyuz space capsule, and dirty brown foam squeezed out from breaks in their brittle plastic-coated fabric. Nonfunctional shoulder belts swung uselessly, like a castrated Doberman's scrotum.

Chuck pumped the brakes going downhill, causing the brake pedal to smack the metal firewall in front of it. Fortunately, the hill leading to town was short. The Jeep's suspension was nonexistent, and potholes transmitted thuds to the junction between my neck and skull, an investment in a headache yet to come.

He turned left into a covered parking area under the Wharfside Village, a three-story minimall of shops, restaurants, and bars. "Everybody out. You guys can Taxi it to Francis Bay. Hoot, you're gonna help me fill the SCUBA tanks." Rosie and Jessica walked directly into the closest store while Chevali, Baine, and Chiara waited outside. Better them than me. With Rosie and Jessica, any shop was an automatic stop.

We pulled up to Frances Bay, facing a rental Suzuki Samurai that was in the same condition as his CJ-5. On the driver's window was a yellow sticker with a red arrow that pointed left from the vantage point of the driver, "THINK LEFT." The morning's divers waived through the windshield of the little Suzuki. They smiled sweetly, and it was then that I saw an angular array of yellow, misaligned teeth. They looked like splayed teeth of logging handsaws.

"Shit, they're going to shred my regulators," Chuck said.

– 6 –

GONNA GET YOU

I fell asleep watching SCUBA air bubbles travel West as Chuck and his divers retreated into the depths from my seated position in chin-deep water. I was the only human in Frances Bay when I slumped over in the water and awoke with a confused startle. Inland, our group walked toward the beach from their Taxi. Chevali picked up something from under a tree. Rosie, Chiara, and Jessica were conversing and laughing. Baine was a few paces behind them, hopping and pulling something out of his foot. Jessica and Rosie, and Blaine positioned themselves on beach towels and appeared to be comparing bracelets.

Chevali walked out to me, "What a fucking waste of time," he said as he sat in the water with me and bit into an unwashed fruit.

"Looks like you kids had a happy stop at the jewelry store?" I asked.

His jaw tightened as he motioned to Baine, who was pointing to his wrist. "Yep. I think they tried on every piece of shit jewelry in the joint before buying."

"Him too? Are you serious?" I asked.

"Dead," he answered, peeling the red and yellow fruit with his teeth.

Chiara waded out to join us, sitting on the sandy bottom

beneath glassy calm water. Beyond them, the water darkened with increasing depth. Bright emerald green gradually gave way to a dark blue that floated a half dozen islands to the North and West. Chevali bit off and spat a piece of peel in the water toward Chiara. It drifted toward her chin, and she splashed it back at him, "Cazzo." Expressionless, he spat another mouthful toward her and motioning with his fruited chin toward Baine, "Does that asshole ever shut up? I had to listen to him empty the contents of his bird brain on anybody who would stand still for the last hour."

I said, "I find his depth of knowledge fascinating. How about you, Chiara?"

"Absolutely, and he doesn't spit mango peels at me, like this pisello." She splashed water at Chevali.

He dug into the fruit with his front teeth, and yellow juice ran down his chest into the water. "This is fucking wonderful. Ya want a bite?" He smiled at me through teeth crammed with yellow pulp.

"Jeb, and no offense to you, Chiara, but I wouldn't put my mouth on anything yours had ever been on."

Completely unperturbed, he held it out to Chiara. She said, "I agree with Ky."

"You didn't say that last night," and began slowly licking the mango with the tip of his tongue and imitated her moaning.

"You really do enjoy being a maiale, and she stammered, "a-a-a pig."

He had no verbal reply but smiled a yellow, stringy smile of mango stuff. He lurched forward, clutching her in his arms, and kissed her limp mouth, wiping mango on her face and darting his tongue into her screaming mouth. She wiggled free, stood in the knee-deep water, jumped up and flung one leg around the back of his head, then sprang up and shot her other thigh at his throat, squeezed, and fell into the water. On the way down, she reached up as if to high-five me. His head disappeared underwater. Her face popped out of the water. She smiled at me, "Six years," she sank and reemerged "of Kung Fu" before her head sank again. He stood up, extricated her from his neck and threw her into the water, grabbed the half-eaten, floating mango, and began gnawing again. She coughed out a mouthful of water and rejoined him at his side quietly, facing the shore.

I rotated a few degrees on my knees in the coarse sand to face the Island of St. Thomas. Beyond it was a workday in Ft. Collins. Although I liked the exact spot I was in, I still couldn't stop my imagination from traveling to Hawaii. It would still be dark there. I re-centered myself in Frances Bay, thousands of miles from my nearest patient. I didn't have to see patients or testify in court today. I could generously help myself to this supreme moment, breathe a happy breath, and let my attention float to a pair of pelicans on my left. My ass cheeks relaxed into my luffing loose shorts.

A familiar metallic, rhythmic chime coming from the beach made my heart pound in my neck. "Hey Ky, do you want me to answer the phone?" Rosie's voice carried over the water, and I said "Yes" without my conscious mind having the opportunity to register the implications. She brought my work cellphone, invading my peace on a deserted Caribbean beach. *Shit the bed*.

"Um, oh, oh, shit...Ky." Rosie held the phone away from her as if it smelled bad. Her words and actions yanked me at light speed away from the pelicans, warm water, and Chevali's pulp-filled teeth. They jerked me back to a reality that I had invested thousands of dollars trying to escape. Maybe my secretary needed the location of the fish food for the office tank. I slogged out of the water and put the phone to my ear, "Hello."

"Ky? BJ, here, I need your help." It was my resident BJ, and I wanted to hear his voice about as much as I wanted a hemorrhoid. I dropped into doctor mode, letting all emotion drain through my feet and into the sand.

"What is it?" I asked.

"Hey, Tomika Sheridan took an overdose last night. Her attorney called the office."

"Is she alive?"

"Yes, so far, she's in the ICU on the vent."

"Shit."

In a true lady-like fashion, Jessica mouthed some words to Rosie, stood up, smiled, kissed my cheek, and walked down to the water, leaving us alone.

"The cops called and wanted a list of all the meds you had her on."

"Shit again, did you give it to them?"

"Should I have?"

"Sure, it's OK."

"Then yes, I did."

"Does anybody know why she did it?" I asked.

"Well, her attorney said it was because her insurance company stopped paying for her shrink and Prozac about six weeks ago...a Gibson IME cut her off."

"Shit, tell her attorney I'll pay for both if she lives. She's got a couple of kids, damn it. So, with all this going on, are you alright?"

"Uh, I don't know. I...a... never had to deal with a suicide attempt before. Are you pissed at me for calling you?"

I was. "No, man. It won't be your last, trust me."

"What do I do?" I wanted to say, 'get the hell out of the practice of medicine while you can,' but didn't.

Rosie was pale, her eyes locked onto mine.

"Just call if she dies. There's nothing else we can do." I said to BJ.

"Sure, Ky, will do."

I was worried BJ wasn't going to be able to handle the pressure and thought about aborting my vacation and flying home. Besides, although the Caribbean was pretty in its own jaded way, it still wasn't Hawaii.

"Hey, is Alley there? Can I talk with her?" Alley was my secretary, and although she didn't know medicine, she had an innate sense of when something was wrong. She also had an uncanny ability to spot borderline personality patients from a hundred yards away. I trusted her judgment.

"Here she is...."

"Ky?" Alley asked.

"Hey baby, aside from Tomika, is everything Ok?"

"Smooth as silk, don't worry, BJ and I have it handled."

"You sure?" I asked.

"Yep." She sounded confident.

"Well, if BJ gets wobbly, please call me," I said.

"Yes, I'll call if we have any wobbles. Now go drink rum, get laid, and sunburned."

"Shit, can you print that on a bunch of my prescriptions? That's the best thing I could prescribe for about half of my Patients."

"Done, and please give Jeb a healthy kiss on the lips for me," Alley said.

"Oh, not you, Alley? He hasn't soiled you too? Do we have to burn you when we get back home?"

"Not yet, but he's in my sights. I'm gonna shag him one of these days, in between his teeny boppers."

"God, help us all. Thank you for keeping a lid on stuff, adios." I sat in the sand next to Rosie and watched the rest of our group laugh in the waveless water of Francis Bay. Rosie asked, "Bad?"

"Yeah, I guess," I explained the situation while she picked grains of sand off her legs.

"If Tomika dies, I gotta go home. There will be calls to make, and the cops will be up my ass. My vacation just got a big black eye. I might as well friggin fly home early." She stopped my self-pity party with, "Who's going to perform the wedding ceremony for Boddington and Ramona if you leave?"

"Oh hell. I guess I forgot that the whole world doesn't revolve around my sorry life."

"Ky, look around you. Your sorry little life at this moment is on a tropical island thousands of miles from all of them. Even little Percy can't mess with you here. Please be here with me now. I need lunch. Let's go into town and eat, take a nap, and shower so we can meet Boddington and Ramona when they arrive. They're coming on the five-o clock ferry from Red Hook. It's noonish, and I could even eat your cooking."

I waded out to gather the others. They basked like a troupe of Japanese Snow Monkeys napping in the water, except for Baine. He was staring at a bee that had crash-landed in the water and was struggling to fly. He gave it a quick flick with his hand, only to have it land in a spray next to Chevali, arousing him. With water dripping from his nose and eyelids, he peered down at the struggling bee, then at me.

"Who the hell was calling you?" Chevali asked.

"Oh, it was only Alley."

"Everything good? He scooped the water under the bee, carefully elevated his hand, and flung it up in the air, giving it a launch, freeing it from an inevitable watery grave.

"Yeah, she needed to know where I put the fish food. Let's go find some lunch."

I forcefully released the idea of leaving the island early and laid naked on our bed at Tamarindo. The fan breeze felt pleasant on my heated skin. The last conscious sensation I remember was enjoying the smell of sunshine in the crisp, white bedspread. I fluttered down into a place of innocent perfection between sleep and wake, between dream and reality, barely awake enough to have semi-directed thoughts. If they drifted to unpleasant, I left them and arose toward ordinary consciousness. I visited that place where ideas evolve as watercolors painting themselves. Unlike being in a complete dream state where I had no choice but to fight the dragon, I could hit the reset button and return to an unpainted canvas in this current state. I floated in a mental Shimadhi tank under a ceiling fan where I wasn't anything but comfortable. I had no place to go, with no duties or responsibilities to attend. The walls that protected me from reality eventually thinned, and I found myself lying with Rosie rhythmically breathing. It was time to meet Boddington and Ramona at the ferry dock.

- 7 -

MISTER CHATTERBOX

Watching the dented 'Native Son' ferry lumber into Cruz Bay gave me that 'friends are coming' thrill of excitement. Rosie and I were alone, waiting for them at the dock. Boddington and Ramona had never been to the Caribbean, and I borrowed Chuck's lead by having Bushwhackers in hand for them. The ferry rotated a slow 180-degree spin as a hitchhiking seagull above the wheelhouse fled inland to St. John. I waived, wondering if it was the one that had splattered Baine. The captain backed carefully into the concrete dock, and the old tires tied to her stern squeaked painfully from the compression of the ferry's inertia.

The topdeckers descended the outside stairway and stopped, letting the bottomdeckers exit in mass before them. The unsmiling bottomdeckers bounced down the gangplank onto the dock. The topdeckers pointed excitedly and prattled as they waited their turn to exit. In the middle of the bottom deckers, a familiar blond head appeared and moved to a different cadence. Most of the people around him lumbered with large, externally rotated thighs and knees, preventing their splayed feet from pointing forward as they walked. Boddington was a head taller than most of them, muscular, and moved with a predator's purpose in his gait. Evidently he hadn't received the memmo about who rode where in the ferry. Ramona followed behind him, fiddling with her sunglasses. Boddington recognized Rosie, and a broad smile grew under his handlebar mustache.

He and I met while in pre-med while taking a summer course in organic chemistry in Utah. Our assigned roommates were typical pre-med geeks. Mine barely spoke English, and his was a Seventh Day Adventist who made the mistake of trying to correct Boddington's swearing within the first few minutes in their dorm room.

In the dining hall on the second night, I noticed that we were both painfully obvious outliers by wearing Wranglers, tee shirts that declared our identity to the world, and boots. Everybody else dressed as though they were at a math competition, wearing the clothes of pale and puffy indoor people. I sat amongst a group of nerds who talked excitedly about taking the Medical College Admissions Test soon. A couple of them bragged that they had already pre-read the textbook we were going to be living out of for the next eight weeks. My mind was on the well-muscled thighs of a gal who sat in running shorts eating by herself, another different kind of outlier.

A booming voice from behind jolted me from my plate of fried catfish, asking, "You takin' the organic chem class?"

"Yep," I said and took another bite of my muddy fish. "You?" I asked.

"Yep..., uh, I got another question."

I looked up at him and nodded.

"You ever feel like you landed on the wrong fuckin' planet? He looked slowly over the room of jabbering pre-med nerds.

"You mean like this intellectual shit show." The poster child for unwashed hair, probable future neurosurgeon across the table, kept his head down and shoveled soup rapidly into his dipped head.

"Yup." He said, followed by thirty seconds of silence. "Hey, I got a question for you."

I swallowed, "What's that?"

"You want a roommate, ya know, someone who ain't gonna keep you up all night reading Science Digest by flashlight?"

"You're in luck. I left my magazine collection at home, so in a word, hell yes." The nerd next to me recoiled. Boddington smiled and held out a hand for me to shake. I stood up, took his hand, and introduced myself. "I'm Ky." His handshake was that of a confident man. "I'm Brian, Brian Boddington. Was that you who rolled up on that noisy son of a bitch yesterday afternoon by the dorm?"

"Ya mean that?" I pointed to a parking lot full of sensibly compact pre-med cars. Two exceptions stood out, my Harley Road Glide and a big brown pickup.

"Damn, that sucker is loud," he said.

I aimed my fork at the four-wheel-drive Ford pickup with a trailer hitch, "I don't imagine that's yours?"

"Yeah, that's 'Ol Buck, we've been down the road for a few years. How'd ya know?"

"Wild guess on my part, I said."

That was it, done. I told my assigned roommate Koichi that he'd be rooming with Boddington's assigned roommate. They had no choice, nor did they protest. That first night we stayed up all night drinking Jack Daniels, swapping girl stories, and pissing off every nerd on our dorm floor.

Boddington strutted along the dock and spoke over the heads of the bottomdeckers in his usual loud tone that would have passed as angry yelling for most people.

"Damn you Ky, look at you in them Jesus boots." This was Boddington-speak referring to my flip-flops. Unsmiling West Indians turned and glared at him. Ramona got the vibe, and he didn't. She hid behind her sunglasses while he seemed oblivious and spoke as he walked toward us. I kept my cool and didn't engage as one guy caught my eye and muttered, "Motherscunt." A too familiar West Indian term of endearment. I handed the Bushwhackers to Rosie, just in case.

"What 'ta hell ya got in your paws there, Rosie?"

She hugged them and handed them each a Bushwhacker, explaining what went into making them. They were not typical Boddington drinks, but he graciously accepted it and kissed Rosie on the cheek. In a low, un-Boddington-like voice, "Thanks for all of this, Rosie poo, I love you guys." Returning to his triple-decibel voice, he said, "Son of a buck, I don't remember the last time I had rum for dinner." He raised his eyebrows at Ramona, "Shit, musta been at least a week."

Whipped cream clung to his thick mustache and sprayed as he talked. "I'm thinkin' about a half dozen of these bad boys, and I'll be ready for an after-dinner drink." He downed his Bushwhacker in three gulps, and Ramona, who was usually not much of a drinker, finished shortly after him. I sensed we were in for a classic Boddington night. A thin, older black gentleman approached us, dragging a hauntingly familiar 3X5 foot metal skateboard, "May I assist you with your belongings?"

"Why sure little fella, I gotta find the sons a bitches first". Boddington turned to me. "Ky, where'd they put our shit?"

The skateboard man indicated that their bags were the

only ones still on the dock beside their boat, "May I retrieve them for you, sir, and take them to your vehicle?"

Before I could warn him, Boddington said, "Sure buddy, just put the nicer bags on top of the old beat-up ones cuz if you squish her shit," he shook his elbow toward Ramona, "buddy, I'm gonna pay hell all damn vacation." The man who was old enough to be Boddington's grandfather said, "Will do sir, the missus' bags on top of the gentleman's," and rattled off toward the far end of the dock.

"Boddington," I said, "I didn't have a chance to warn you, these guys rip everybody off, he's gonna charge the crap out of you for moving your bags a hundred yards."

Ramona's mouth turned down. Boddington's mouth didn't, "Huh, we'll see about that. Now, where the hell do we find us some more of them Bushwarmers, I got a microbuzz a goin', and I don't want it fadin' on me."

"This way," I said and walked toward the shore. "I gotta help rent a vehicle for the crew. Take your bags over there, to the Pussers bar. Rosie will show you the way, and I'll meet up with you up in a half-hour or so. Jessica and Baine are waiting for me at a car rental place just down the road."

"Baine, ya mean that dumbshit judge she's been boning for the last few years?"

Ramona hit him in the arm, "Be nice. He's not that bad. Maybe she loves him."

"Well, that'd be like falling in love with a dog turd. It don't hurt the dog turd much, but it sure puts a mess on you." She laughed, "Stop it. Jessica is such a kind person. You wouldn't want to hurt her feelings over her dating a drip. Oops, did I say that? Whoa, time for another Beaverwarmer drink." Ramona was already starting to slur.

The rattling and overloaded skateboard appeared with its old man. "Sirs?" He said, addressing us in a quiet voice. "May I assist you in loading your vehicle? I'd be most happy to do so."

"We ain't got us a car yet. We're headed to that bar yonder for a cool one before they're all drunk up. I can take them bags from here." Boddington said.

"Nonsense, sir, I'll be glad to transport them for you at no extra charge. I'm a touch parched myself." Skateboard man replied, smiling.

"Well then, let's vamoose and commence to some real drinkin." Rosie held me back as they walked. "Oooh Ky, Boddington's gonna flip if this guy tries to rip him off."

"I warned him," I said. "He'll be fine."

"Ugh."

A cereal box-sized, hand-painted pink sign, richly decorated with generations of bird droppings and mold, identified the rental lot, **Long Ben's car rental.** It hung crooked on the side of a pink tool shed. A dozen Suzuki Samurai parked at odd angles in a mud lot that had the appearance of a car graveyard rather than a rental lot. Each had rusted and dented bodies. Yellow and red stickers obscured part of the driver's side windshields, "THINK LEFT." Mildew chewed at their tiny fabric rooves.

I knocked and opened the office/shed door. Cold air and noise slammed me from a hissing air conditioner reverberating in the plywood room. Before I could cross the threshold, an unfriendly voice commanded, "Shut deh damn door before you let out all de cold air."

An instinctive reaction fell out of my mouth, "Well, fuck you too," and I hadn't even seen the speaker's face.

"What? The voice grumbled, "I can't hear you over de air conditioner." Despite my waning belief in Love City's love, I let it pass.

The "office" was a windowless pre-fabricated toolshed. A hole cut in the side held a window-mount air conditioner on full blast. Papers weighted down with chunks coral on his desk fluttered like frustrated birds incapable of liftoff. Long Ben sat under a bare lightbulb in a squeaking rolling chair with upholstery that looked like a badger had shredded it. His thick, black arms rested on polished, grey metal. Without rotating his massive head up, he said, "I'll be wit you next," and continued talking to Baine and Jessica.

"If you don' buy de island insurance, an' you get in a wreck da police will hold you in jail until deh car repair bills are paid. There is a twenty-dollar 'sand deposit' for when you bring it back full of sand. I keep it. There's a no smoking deposit, when you bring it back, an there is a cigarette butt or ashes in da car. I keep it. If it smells like smoke, I keep it. You be drivin' on de left side of deh road. Do not take it off paved roads or driveways." Baine waited for Long Ben to draw a breath before continuing his welcome to paradise tirade. "Mr. Long Ben, I am an attorney, in fact, a judge. I would call into question the constitutionality of holding a person in jail until any bills are settled, lest there be an accident." He turned to Jessica and nodded.

Long Ben arose from his chair and leaned across his cluttered desk, resting on thick knuckles. "Mistah, mainland attorney, my brother-in-law is deh Chief of police on dis island, and neither of us gives one shit about your mainland constituinity.

You wreck my car, you go to jail, an I don give one crap if he feed you."

Long Ben sat back down and continued his instructions, "Total fee for deh rental be nine hundred and seventy dollah, dat include insurance and other fees. If deh car is returned clean an undamaged, I send your refund for your deposit wit-in six to eight weeks. There be a one dolla charge for de stamp, too." He ran a finger through the maze of lines on the humid-ity-wilted contract. "Initial here, sign here, initial here, three phone numbers of relatives or friends who I be calling before you leave. There be a two thousand dollar hold on the credit card until deh car is returned in good condition. Sign here, both of you. I need copies of driver's licenses an one of you passport, so you don't give me no six for nine."

Baine said, "We weren't told to bring our passports when we made the reservations."

Long Ben started to wad up the papers.

"Wait," I said," I have mine."

Long Ben looked questioningly at me, "You wit dem?"

"Yes," I couldn't help myself, "I be wit dem."

"Den gimme your damn passport an sign an initial every place dey do."

I had an issue with his unnecessary abruptness. "Was that a request because it sounded like a command, and you ain't commanding me." Jessica put her hand to her mouth. Baine seemed to shrink a foot as Long Ben stood and stepped to me. "Oh, you tink you scrappy dude?"

"More than you want to find out," I said.

We were chest to chest, and he stank of stale sweat and old beer. His belly was cold on my chest. He was a foot taller than me and outweighed me by what I figured was a hundred pounds of blubber. My first plan of attack was to give him a 'Mike Tyson'.... push him back a few inches with my forearms and deliver an uppercut with everything I had. I waited for him to twitch. The stalemate held for a few seconds until his belly jiggled against my chest as he laughed.

"You a funny Bukra," and smiled down at me. I smiled back and said, "You smell like you drank your lunch," and gave him my passport to put in the world's oldest working copier. It coughed out a Paul Harris rendition of my passport, and it was time to inspect the vehicle.

Baine meticulously documented every scratch, dent, ding, and tear. At the same time, Long Ben crossed his sweating arms over his protruding belly and stared into space. We rented the only non-Samurai on the lot, a mini pickup mimicking the larger taxis in town, complete with rows of seats running lengthwise in the bed of the truck. It had a homemade metal skeleton roof to support a pink and white canvas top. Twist ties affixed the moldy canvas to the thin metal tubes of the roof skeleton.

Long Ben handed me the keys, "And der a two hundred fifty dolla charge for lost keys, each of dem. An be sure to drive on the left. You are not on deh mainland."

I spoke to Long Ben as I handed the keys to Jessica, "The only time I drive on the left side of the road is when I'm drunk. Give me an hour, and then I'll take over."

I asked Long Ben, "Hey, did you get enough to drink for lunch?"

"What you say?"

"You need a drink after the tough negotiations? What kind of beer you drink?"

"Caribe."

"Ya think they have any at the Pussers bar?" I asked.

"Uh, yeah?"

"Walk over, and I'll buy you one." He nodded in a confused acquiescence. Jessica drove the seventy feet and parked the truck next to a SCUBA tank-filling shack. The parking lot had a low ceiling, and noises from the bar echoed through it: rock music, women's laughter, and that which drowned out all the rest, Boddington's voice.

He stood at the end of the bar, surrounded by transfixed strangers in a semicircle around him. The skateboard man sat slumped on his skateboard on the bar floor as he struggled to keep his eyes open. Ramona, three seats away from him, smoked a cigarette, and talked through her swaying hair to a much younger guy. Empty Bushwhacker cups lay squished flat in front of her. I'd known her for twenty years and had never known her to smoke. The young man edged closer and whispered into her ear. She tossed her head back, laughing, almost throwing herself off her chair.

"So, I grabbed that silly sombitch by his damn lapels." Boddington hollered and grabbed the air-opponent in front of him with both hands, yanking the imaginary adversary toward his face. He turned his head and asked the group, "Can you believe it, friggin' lapels? I pulled him off his damn feet and kissed him square on the mouth." He paused, and the entranced crowd stayed silent until Chiara asked. "You kissed him on the mouth?"

Boddington yelled with a grin, "Damn right, kissed that bastard right on his mouth." He managed to get even louder, "With my forehead, HA! I headbutted that prick right in the lips." He mocked a head butt and throwing the adversary to the ground.

"Knocked his bitch ass clean out. That's how I got this here cut right over my eyebrow." He patted his forehead. "Blew his teeth clean through his lower lip an' drove 'em into my damn skull." The group joined him in laughter as he slapped the men on their backs and winked at the women. He motioned to the bartender to give everybody in his group another round of drinks. The bartender had the appearance of a sixteen-year-old surfer, with sun-bleached hair and the smooth facial skin of a young, trouble-free life.

Boddington slipped over to his wife, gently kissed her on the top of her head, pulled the young man to him with one hand, spoke a few words directly into his ear, and refocused his attention on Ramona. The young man threw some cash on the bar, picked up his cigarettes, and left without making eye contact with anybody. Boddington caringly put his arm around her, speaking quietly. She pushed his arm off her and puffed her dark hair from in front of her face, and slurred, "Screw that, he was a cutie... a toy." Boddington ordered her a bottle of water.

I asked the bartender for a Caribe for Long Ben and a shot of Patron for me.

He asked me, "What's a Patron?" *Being thousands of miles from reality can have its downsides.*

"Any Pusser's?" I asked. He appeared concerned, "It's a lot more expensive than our regular stuff. Yeah, we got a bottle that usually only 'Ski' drinks.

"Well, how much is it?"

"Four dollars a shot," he said apologetically.

"Make it a double. I've got some catching up to do here."

Rosie nudged me. "Boddington told me they haven't eaten since breakfast, seventeen hours ago. Look at poor Ramona. She's a mess, smoking and flirting with some kid." Ramona was now face down with her hand on a water bottle that wavered then tipped, sending a small river into her face. The bartender brought me my Pussers shot and Long Ben's beer in one hand and a can of OFF in the other. "You'll need it. The mosquitoes are crazy this time of year."

"Thanks, amigo." I searched for Long Ben. He was absent. Not wanting his beer to get hot, I gave it to Jeb, who was petting a cat that the others tried to shoo away. Long Ben never showed up.

While I sprayed myself with OFF, I said to Jeb, "Thank God Boddington chased little mister hottie off. I was afraid Ramona was going to rape him under the bar. And to top it all off, Boddington apparently paid the skateboard guy with alcohol."

"He's in as bad of shape as Ramona," Chevali said. The small black man now laid, curled up on his skateboard, resting his head on some crunched-up plastic glasses, his hands clasped between his knees. His eyes fluttered as he noiselessly talked and laughed to himself while people gently stepped around him.

"It's time to feed everybody," I said.

The roar of intense drunkenness died down as our group ate bar burgers and greasy fries. For the first time in hours, the voices of the other bar patrons, being only moderately drunk, overpowered Boddington's. Ramona was having difficulty finding her mouth with her burger. She missed, and it skidded across her cheek, leaving a trail of mustard, mayonnaise, and ketchup. Boddington laugh-talked, "Sombitch Ramona, you look like a clown on acid."

Without wiping her mouth and oblivious to his remark, she struggled to see him from under heavy eyelids, "I need to go home. Where the hell is home, anyway?"

Rosie and Chiara punctuated their conversations with laughter and hugs. I was pleased to see her being kind to Chiara. I'd feared that she would be an outcast, the unwitting victim of Chevali's assembly line of perpetually younger women. In her mid-thirties, she was twice the age of the one he brought on last year's trip to Kauai.

At the far end of the bar, Jessica talked with her hands to a couple of women. She made broad sweeps and then held her hands to her chest, imitated driving a car, and taking pictures. The prettier of the two leaned over, and Baine's eyes followed her cleavage as she searched her purse by her ankles. Her breasts were easily visible below the generous neck of her loose dress. Jessica's eyes followed Baine's eyes down as she bent. Her foot slammed his as it rested on his barstool footrest. She didn't miss a beat in her gesticulations. Baine yelped and turned his head toward the emerging lights of St. Thomas.

"Hey Rosie," I broke into her conversation with Chiara, "we should probably get this crew up to the house before Ramona boots at the bar."

"You think she is that bad?"

"Check out her new makeup job," I said. Boddington was holding her from falling off her barstool as he nonchalantly talked. Ramona's hair stuck, plastered to the condiments on her face.

I got the bartender's attention and asked for the bill. It was more than a day's income for me, and I thought about how fortunate I was. I watched Baine staring blankly toward the ocean. Although I had zero fondness for St. Thomas, it, like Colorado was an ocean away. Everything that wasn't on the tiny island of St. John was a million miles and two weeks away. It wasn't Hawaii, but St John was already developing a personality of her own. Like every person, place, dog, or motorcycle, it had good and bad aspects without caring about my opinion. If I were going to discover that sense of peace that I had promised Rosie, St. John and I would have to accept each other unquestioningly.

At that moment, with my wife and flawed friends, I found a touch of that peace. My skin, warm from the day's sun and the night's wet air, felt perfect. The sounds of friends and strangers played pleasantly in my ears as happy meaningless bar conversation. Thirty feet away, a female Rottweiler played alone with a coconut at water's edge, as Marley sang from speakers over my head, and "GRAAAAAH." Ramona rocked her head back and resoundingly belched.

"Nothing good can come of these eructations. Hurry up, yank her ass outa here, and I'll catch up with you all at Tamarindo," I said to Rosie.

I stayed behind to pay the surfer dude-bartender and walked out onto the sand in front of the bar. The too-thin female Rottie ran up to me, and playfully dropped her coconut at my feet. I called up to the surfer dude, "Hey, amigo, who does she belong to?" I asked.

"Some assholes left her here and sailed off a few months ago."

"Who feeds and cares for her?"

"Nobody that I know of." Surfer dude answered.

"Order me the biggest burger ya got, rare, and a bottle of water."

I fed her bit by bit in the dark while we walked along the beach toward Tamarindo. She led me to a dugout she had burrowed in the sand under the concrete road. I gave her water by pouring it in my hand for her to lap up. "Hey, sweetie, come home with me tonight. I'll give you more food when we get there."

Coquis slowly nudged the sounds of Ramona's belching from my brain as I fell asleep naked under my ceiling fan for the second time that day. One of my hands held Rosie's while the other lay on soft, rising, and falling fur next to my bed as both Rosie and the dog softly purr-snored. Tomorrow morning would come soon. I was going fishing for Bonefish with Chuck.

– 8 –

Don't Rock the Boat

One year earlier.... Most boat captains would have watched the weather forecast. Tomaso, fueled into a false sense of invincibility by snorting pure flake cocaine, traveled blithely Northward from his home port of Barranquilla, Columbia. His intended anchorage was Fish Bay off the Island of St. John, US Virgin Islands.

The evening sky grew increasingly dark, and gale-force winds picked up quickly. Typically, it was a smooth motor in his Zodiac from the Miss H. Whitlow to the rocky cliff below the drop-off point. Dittlif Point's phallic thrust into the Caribbean Sea made it an easy target. But tonight, lightning spattered around the Miss H Whitlow. The waves that raged from every direction would have made lesser men seasick, he thought. He falsely remembered facing more significant seas in previous drug-cash exchanges. He was wrong.

Tomaso kissed Serena, his DEA alibi/nubile Ornithology student, and struggled to place a large suitcase of cocaine into his tossing Zodiac. He told her that it was a load of game cameras to record a rare nesting pair of bridled quail doves at night in stormy weather. "It's only a passing storm. Make us some tea, and I will be back in an hour." His 'passing storm' was a fast-moving and unforgiving wall of wind, rain, and thirty-foot waves named Marilyn.

He lashed the suitcase to his waist with a nylon cord, which he then tied to the Zodiac. He fired up the outboard and headed toward the shore. Marilyn's Rain shot sideways with such force as to nearly blind him from seeing island house-lights that were his usual travel beacons. Once at the rocky cliff base, he could not see well enough to free himself from the Zodiac. Thinking that he cut the section of rope which con-nected the suitcase of cocaine to the raft, he cut the wrong rope. It was he who was free of the suitcase as a wave crashed into the boat and hurled the suitcase into the pitching, black water. Unbeknownst to Tomaso, the suitcase was floating un-der the surface, still attached to the Zodiac. Thinking that the raging black sea had claimed his cocaine, he screamed at the storm, "*Chinga tu Madre, ese chingado Oceano no vale una verga.*" Marilyn's wordless answer was another fast-moving wave. His brother was going to be furious at the loss of the suitcase of cocaine. Tomaso's only option was to retrieve the money Che had left the day before and return to the Miss H. Whitlow.

The money buried at the base of amputated finger rock was in large suitcases identical to the one submerged and still tied to his Zodiac. Seawater and rain pelted him as he struggled to carry them down the slick cliff. Once in the bouncing raft, he tied the money-filled suitcases to his waist and the raft. Che would never believe him if he lost both the cocaine and the money. The wind whipped sea spray obscured the Miss H. Whitlow lights as he motored at full throttle in what he thought was her direction. Waves, as tall as a three-story building, grew as his cocaine-induced bravery waned. Fifty yards to his right, the Miss H. Whitlow was taking on water, and her twin diesel engines were flooding as he passed her, unseen. Within minutes she would splinter on the very same rocks from which Tomaso had just come. The winds were strong enough to rip the pearl buttons open on his Larry Mahan cowboy shirt as he motored full speed toward the mangrove swamp of Reef Bay in total darkness. Heaving waves flung him from the crest of one wave to the next, his airtime enhanced by the hurricane-force winds. The suitcase of cocaine acted like a sea anchor, keeping the Zodiac from flipping.

Tomaso's last seconds of consciousness were spent staring twenty feet down into a wave trough revealing the tops of mangroves. He was confused as lightning shone the remains of an old sugar mill off to his left. He would come to rest far inland from the natural shoreline. His body, the Zodiac, and the bulky suitcases containing cocaine and 2.26 million dollars in American $100s, all lumped together and wound around a temporarily submerged tree.

-9-

High Tide or Low Tide

At sunrise, I introduced our new roommate to a skeptical Rosie. "Her name is Sandy...I named her after her home on the beach." I smiled at my slack-faced wife while my head mildly pulsed.

My first-morning urine was coffee turbid. *I might be a little dehydrated*. I trudged upstairs to the main house to retrieve cold bottled water from the refrigerator. Despite Chuck's assertion that the water from the tap should be safe, I'd expended too much time, money, and effort to spend my vacation yelling at porcelain. I heard his Jeep and hurried outside to avoid having him wake the others. The brown bird that lived in the Tamarind tree right off the deck was already singing that which passed for a song in his bird world.

"Hey Chuck, how are you this morning?

"Good. You ready?" He motioned to my feet. "Hoot, it's a long, hard hike down to Reef Bay. You're gonna die in flip-flops."

"I'm fine, man," I said.

"You're going to need more traction than those."

"Well, my shoe collection didn't make it down here, so I'll make do with what I've got."

"And what shoes are you going to fish in?" Chuck asked.

I raised my left foot and wiggled my left flip flop.

He sighed forcefully, and I was starting to feel stupid. I'd researched everything in print about Bonefishing, except for footgear.

"You got money with you?" He asked. I patted my wallet and smiled.

"The dive shop will be open soon. We gotta get you some better shoes." He pointed to his feet in black, open-toed sandals with nylon webbing that securely crossed over his foot and heel.

The Manta Ray's Cafe was a shoe closet-sized restaurant in Wharfside Village. Large, glass front refrigerators in the dining area leaked condensation in puddles and rattled, making conversation difficult. Rust chewed at their hinges and corners. The arched concrete doorway and windows were open to the shoreline only a few yards away. The water between St. Thomas and us was dark, not yet touched by the morning sun, hidden behind St. John's mountain backbone. The front door and shutters were thick. Multilayered wood hung on heavy gauge iron hinges jutting from deep inside the foot-thick walls. I imagined hurricane-driven wind and waves uselessly battering them last year. I paid for our coffees and pastries. My coffee tasted like it was brewed the previous week, and the deflated pastries looked as if someone had been brooding on them. Their earlier, fluffier lives had long since passed.

Chuck introduced me to the restaurant owner, Murray, who appeared to know him well as they talked about the ongoing recovery efforts from last year's hurricane. Marilyn had destroyed his bakery, and his insurance company was stalling on paying him, so he opened the tiny Manta Ray's Cafe with borrowed money from his grandmother. Murray was thin and wore finger-smudged round glasses. His hairline followed the contours of a satellite map of Florida, while his bulging eyes made me want to palpate his thyroid gland.

I asked for cream, and he handed me an open jar of powdered creamer from under the counter. I wondered if it had been open all night to cockroaches pushing their legendary limits of immortality in the face of the jar of poison. The morning's turbid swill presented a challenge, and as with a few other things, I needed it more than wanted it. In my Styrofoam cup of steaming blackness, I watched my distorted reflection swimming on the little waves that ricocheted around the inside of the cup. "Dorothy, we ain't in Kona anymore," I said to the coffee. The idea of improving its flavor with creamer seemed like a long shot. I handed it back toward Murray, and Chuck snatched it at the near pass-off point and poured a chunky white pile into his coffee. He stirred it with a dirty finger, which he then sucked with a satisfied flourish.

Chuck's fingernails couldn't have been blacker if he'd changed his transmission that morning. The only thing greasier than his fingernails was his ballcap that read "Key Dog Dive Shop." I tapped the logo on his cap, "Where's that dive shop?" He squinted at me with a look of concern and gestured to the wall separating us from the shop next door. Murray smiled at Chuck and said, "Ah, family." I felt stupid and wanted to point to my coffee, saying, 'Ah, bear bile,' but took the high road and forced a smile.

The dive shop owners treated Chuck like family. Their small, shy black lab 'Makena' hung with me while I inspected shoes in the corner of the shop that smelled happily of neoprene.

"Well, Hoot, ya find anything that will work?"

"Maybe. What do you think of these?" They were the exact shoes he was wearing. "No, you can't buy those. We would look like momma dressed us alike." He was right.

"How about these?" He picked up a leather sandal, similar in design to his. The sole sticker proclaimed they were waterproof leather and "MADE IN BRAZIL." I questioned whether there was such a thing as waterproof leather and concluded that they were attractive enough to wear to work back in Colorado. I wore them immediately, like when I was a kid at J.C. Penny's, getting new shoes for grade school.

Aside from failing brakes, riding in Chuck's Jeep brought an involuntary smile to my mouth. The few West Indians who were up at that hour waived and called, "Chuck, OK." Their words' inflection posed as a statement, not a question. He would grin and wave back with "OK." He was contentedly a part of the island and her people.

Turbulent wind and the Jeep's motor noise kept conversation to a minimum while we wound up Centerline Road. Beyond the little town of Cruz Bay, there wasn't much in the way of human habitation. Grass nibbling goats and pigs laying in the mud along the road replaced the tourists on the streets retreating behind us. Wet tropical forest scents grew more pungent as the trees grew thicker and taller. Many of their limbs lay broken and twisted by Marilyn. The jungle seemed impassible. After a half-hour and a couple of turns off the Centerline Road, we pulled into a muddy parking spot. The smell of burning crankcase oil swept up to me as we slowed. "Is the burning oil gonna be a problem?" I asked.

A nonchalant Chuck reached under his seat for a plastic bottle of off-brand 10-40 motor oil and smiled, "We can check it when we get back. Let's go, Hoot, those Bonefish are waiting for you, and it's a long hike down." He gestured to a leaf-covered trail that disappeared into the darkness of a jungle canopy. "When was the last time you came here fishing?" I asked, expecting an answer like 'two weeks.'

"Uh, never."

"Are you serious? You've never been down there before?"

"Well, by boat. I hate to hike when I don't have to." Chuck's eyes diverted in apparent embarrassment.

"That explains the belly, son." I rubbed the front of his stretched tee shirt as we stepped out of the Jeep toward the trail. Chuck stopped, put his foot on a small boulder, and began assembling his fly rod.

"I thought you said it was going to be a couple mile hike?" I asked, curious as to why he would assemble his fly rod at that point.

"It is. You'll want to do this too." He said as he rotated sections of fly rod together.

"Why?" I asked.

"Spiders... it has a bad reputation."

I don't fear spiders, per se, but have a healthy respect. If I catch a bug in my home, I'll release it outside. Spiders get squashed, splattered, sworn at, and if hanging in too high of a place, sucked up with the vacuum's extension hose. I hate spiders. I don't fear them. I do check my underwear each morning before I put them on, as the thought of a brown recluse or black widow biting my private parts is a bit disquieting... just not fear evoking.

"Don't screw with me, man." I wondered if Rosie had told

him about my underwear ritual, which also extends to shoes, pants, and bedsheets. But I think everybody does that.

"I'll walk in front." He said in a neutral tone. He was messing with me, but to play along as a good guest, I quickly pushed all the pieces of my new fly rod together. I felt irritated with myself because I hadn't familiarized myself with appropriate Bonefishing footwear or the indigenous arachnids. Chuck walked with his fishing rod tip angled up in front of him like a defensive saber. We stepped cautiously under the high jungle canopy that filtered the emerging morning's light over a muddy trail of snaking tree roots.

I stayed a few paces behind him with my fishing rod at the same height and angle as his until he stopped and said, "Here ya go, Hoot." Something the size of my hand hung, suspended at face height in the middle of the trail. Sadly, he hadn't been screwing with me. I wanted my shotgun. With a swipe of his fly rod, he removed the black and yellow hunter and the web that spanned the width of the trail. The spider quickly disappeared under some leaf litter. The bastard grinned at me with the glee of a sadist to an arachnophobe. I put my mind on the unsuspecting Bonefish in a bay beyond the spider highway and wished that I had my tall hiking boots.

The trail steepened and dove into a dimly lit world alive with the scents of a throbbing tropical fecundity as I reluctantly assumed the point position. Birds squabbled and talked about us in the canopy a hundred feet above our heads. We didn't speak much since the slippery trail required concentrated effort to keep from sliding, tripping, toe-stubbing, or root surfing. It was an elbow fracture waiting to happen. Yet, about every ten feet, my attention arose from the trail to the space ahead of me. I wanted to avoid my face becoming a spider's breakfast.

I never imagined that my new fly pole would lose its virginity to a pound of spiders before ever seeing a fish.

After a water break, Chuck again took the lead. I followed as an inner demon took control. I had missed out on years of screwing with Chuck and slowly arched my fly pole forward toward his right ear. I carefully made the slightest contact and yelled, "OH MY GOD." He squealed, ducked, and lurched forward, slapping at his ear, "Shit, shit, shit," until he felt my pole tip with his hand. "You Muddascunt, that's not funny."

I proudly smiled. "Ya know, since my arrival on this Island, I'm continually greeted with that term. I'm assuming it's a West Indian term of endearment?"

"No, it means you're an asshole." I figured he was feigning his irritation with me.

At random intervals, corroded little metal plaques on posts stood in front of exotic trees. Some were partly legible with an artist's rendition of the tree etched into the metal along with the name (both conventional and scientific), country of origin, and potential use. The farther we went, the more still, humid, and quiet the jungle became. Above us in distant tree limbs, sunlight squeezed itself into slits of light, holding steady at steep angles through the thick air. None of them reached the ground, swallowed up by a more considerable darkness.

A stirring sound to the right in the dark undergrowth caused us to stop. We made eye contact. He nodded. I cautiously took a couple of steps forward, and a snorting black mass shot toward us and abruptly slid to a halt, spun, and flung mud on us as it bolted away. The wild boar crashed through the thick jungle uphill and away from us. The heavy hooved squealer sounded like a boulder mowing down the forest. It stirred another huge boar to again crash toward us, closing the distance rapidly. It was about to be piggy pinball, and I didn't want to be the flipper. I started yelling while jumping up and down and waving my arms. Having grown up hunting in California, wild boar had chased me scrambling into the safety of oak tree limbs more than once. I continued flapping as I instinctively searched for a tree to climb, and as I started to move toward the closest one, Chuck yelled, "No, Hoot, stop." I quit flapping and turned to face my porcine aggressor but could no longer see or hear it.

Chuck appeared to be having a standing seizure, heaving and held his abdomen in cramped laughter. When he was able to regain a modicum of composure, he swung his fly rod toward the tree which I had been moving toward as my pig escape route.

"Holy hell. Thanks, amigo." I said after seeing the tree trunk.

"Yep, I know, that's why I yelled."

The tree was grey, smooth-barked, and easily five feet in diameter and with thousands of sharp, inch-long thorns protruded from its bark. The plaque at its base read, "MONKEY NO CLIMB TREE" ... Kapok...Ceiba penetrandra...stuffing for mattresses." *Stuffing for mattresses? Maybe for masochists.* "Thanks, Chuck, it would have shredded the shit out of me," I said, pointing to the sign, "And hey look, it's called a Chuck no climb tree."

"Eat me, and by the way, great job on the pig. It passed out laughing at you, Doc. I think it may need CPR."

"Crazed Pig Resuscitation?" I asked, waiting in vain for laughter.

His gaze passed to my right, and he walked past me. "Wow, I'd heard about this."

He waved his fishing rod to a little ravine off the trail and a stone house foundation remnant. Only the first couple of feet survived. It was about six by ten feet, without any remaining signs of a roof. Rusting pieces of tin plates and cups lay scattered on a mud floor. "You know the story? "I asked.

"Slave quarters." He motioned to the stones that made the dry-stacked mossy walls. "A hundred and fifty years ago, the Dutch brought their own prisoners here, and once they all died, they imported African slaves to clear the jungle and grow sugarcane."

Inspecting the steep, densely forested terrain, and said, "I can't imagine how that could have ever been accomplished without bulldozers."

"That's why most of them died early, worked to death, until the revolt."

"The revolt?" I asked.

"Uh-huh, in seventeen seventy-something, it was one of the biggest slave revolts in the Caribbean. The slaves kicked the shit out of all the European planters and their families, took over the island, and held off soldiers from Europe for about six months."

"Six months, that's it?"

"Yeah," he said, "then the Danes came back, killed a bunch of them, and it was back to status quo with plantations, slaves, and all that misery for another hundred years."

"What about us, the Americans?"

"The U.S. didn't come here to start our version of screwing up the island until World War One. We bought it to put in a military base."

"The U.S. didn't own slaves here?" I asked.

"Naw, by the time the U.S. bought the Island, slavery had thankfully been gone for half a century."

"Huh, now I guess we just enslave the islanders with American TV and consumerism, like the rest of the world," I said as I walked on.

The trail steered us out of the steaming jungle and into an odiferous mud flat flanked by pineapple plants, which unfortunately had no pineapples. It smelled strongly of wet earth and vegetative decay, a strangely clean stench. The stifling canopy had succumbed to a bright sky and welcome, cooling breezes. I was dripping with sweat, squashed mosquitoes, and pig-flung black stuff. Rounding the final corner, a surprising cluster of dilapidated brick and rock buildings stood in odd shapes with fallen, rusted tin roofs on our left. "Wow, what's all this?" I asked.

"It's the Reef Bay sugar mill. I'll show it to you later. I gotta get to the water to cool off." He sounded irritated with playing tour guide.

Reef Bay's deserted yellow sand beach opened to a rambling, open ocean that stretched to a sharp horizon. To my right, a black, rocky hillside angled steeply into the calm water of the bay. Above the rocks, the thick verdant jungle guarded her secrets. Between the rock wall and us, a fifty-foot-long, twisted metal boat dock laid sideways at an angle across the sand. One end of the pier hung, perched triple head height precariously against the hillside.

I pointed to it. Before the question could leave my lips, Chuck blurted, "Hurricane Marilyn, last year, Park Service still hasn't fixed it yet." He struggled to unpeel his clinging shirt to reveal what previously had been a sculpted abdomen in his youth. Now, a white, hairy bulge extended from barely below his nipples to hover above his belt. Chuck had gotten fat, and judging by his mood, I figured it best to hold my verbal barbs for later. I flung my shirt and new, muddy Brazilian Reef walkers onto the rocks and walked into the soothing water. "I'm so damned hot, I'd expect to see steam coming off my ass," I said. He was already chin deep in the water, staring out to sea. No reply.

After the cool down, I attached my fly reel to and threaded fly line through the guides of my rod. I tied thick blue fly line to a tapered leader, leader to tippet, and tippet to a brass-bead-eyed, fluffy pink fly. Each step required a unique knot. I looked up to see Chuck's mouth arched downward at the ends, "How do ya set this shit up, Hoot? I didn't have time to read about that."

He held a naked reel in one hand and a box of fly line in the other. I'd forgotten that he wasn't a fly fisherman and didn't want to make him feel bad, "Wow, nice setup. Let's put this dude together and go get 'em." He handed me the equipment, looking like a kid handing his mom a broken toy.

A half-hour later, we started our assault of Reef Bay reef, the alleged home of St. John's Bonefish population. My reading on the subject had instilled in me a world of confidence until I stepped into the water. I stared at the featureless saltwater flat bordered by blue water, a half football field to the West. We waded, crunching on sea snails, sank in muck to our ankles, and dodged holes, coral heads, and sea urchins. The shallow water was hot, not warm. While pleasing to my legs, I couldn't imagine it having much oxygen-carrying capacity to support the sea life surrounding my feet. I relaxed and enjoyed this new environment beyond my expectations.

To the West, the scalloped shoreline of St. John revealed successive little peninsulas jutting seaward. There were no signs of humanity in any direction except for a sailboat far out to sea. The only sounds were of my breathing, slow sloshing in the knee-deep water, and the swooshing of my fly rod when I took practice casts at imaginary Bonefish. Chuck was in silent running mode watching for fish. We were brother predators on the hunt, yet where I had expected to find excitement, I found peace.

We zigzagged our way up and down the reef for over an hour when I noticed that the sun-bleached hunks of coral exposed above water level appeared to be sinking. The tide was coming in. Cooler water swirled on invisible currents to cool my legs as I waded at the edge of the reef. Just beyond the length of my fly rod, the bottom dropped sharply, turning the water dark blue.

On the shoreline beyond Chuck was a familiar shape that was non sequitur with my surroundings. I stopped and instinctively crouched and submerged to my waist in the 85-degree water. He stopped and cocked his head in apparent confusion at my body position. I wondered if the heat and rum hangover were making me hallucinate and gestured toward the shoreline with my nose.

He also crouched. Without a hand touching his cap, it rotated upward on his head. His eye corners crinkled behind his sunglasses. "Cay deer," he whispered, "I've been down here for years and never seen one. I thought it was a bullshit myth."

"She's tiny," I said, watching the fragile doe amble along the shoreline. She had white spots on her rump and was nibbling obliviously on bushes. Her front hooves were on the sand, and her back feet in the saltwater while her white tail wiggled rapidly. She appeared to be as happy and peaceful as I was feeling.

"Aside from car bumpers, I'd guess she has no predators on the island?" I whispered. Chuck nodded.

I felt privileged. The island was sharing something with me that she rarely did with the thousands of people who visit her monthly. "This is cool stuff," I said.

"Yep. I've got a friend who's a biologist for the National Park Service. She told me that they don't exist South of the Florida Cays."

"Don't ya love it when nature proves man wrong," I said as a shadow moved sinuously through the water to my left. "Shark?" I asked loud enough to make the doe disappear into the brush with a short hop. The sleek fish was three feet long and dark. A yellow triangle broke the surface backlit by the morning sun, making it glow against the dark water behind it. The fin curled toward us and climbed upstream toward our scent under the water. "Did you bathe this morning? That bastard wasn't in the neighborhood until you dipped your ass in the water," I said.

"It's only a baby. As soon as it sees us, it'll move to deeper water." He stayed still. My comfort level with sharks existed at a different level from his. I expected a hasty exit by either the shark or me before it was within my discomfort zone for dangerous animals. I stood, and true to Chuck's prediction, the fish skittered off into the sun dancing water, making its exact whereabouts unknowable. "Good job, Hoot, you showed the poor little thing who's boss."

"Screw that. I knew it wasn't going to eat me whole, but maybe take a hunk a chunk of calf muscle or worse." I said, grabbing my crotch, half in jest, "which could pose a small problem for the longevity of my much-needed vacation."

"It's a small Lemon shark. They use these flats and mangrove roots as a nursery."

"Oh, that's reassuring, fishing in Godzilla's daycare center,"

I replied as two more moving objects appeared, closing the distance between us and the shoreline. Two more sharks. They swam to the left of a group of grey missiles at a depth of a few feet. "Bonefish amigo," I whispered.

I recognized their shape and color from the hours of videos I had rented from the local fly shop. They stopped to drop their noses onto the sand while their tails, silver and wet in the sunlight, broke the surface. The tails rocked slowly a few inches above the surface, indicating that the fish were feeding off the bottom. I recovered a photograph in my mind of Bonefish "tailing" in one of the videos. "There they are," I said, "cast about fifteen feet ahead of them, let your fly settle to the bottom, and when they get to where it lays, retrieve the fly by making short strips." I was quoting from book learning and zero experience.

Chuck's head swiveled toward the Bonefish, then to the shapes to our left. "You gotta do something about them while I cast." He said, fumbling with his line. The sharks were only a few feet away. Using my fly rod like a rapier, I thrust the tip underwater toward the pair, and they scattered. "What the hell, man?" I said as he took a strong back cast before presenting his fly to the Bonefish herd. *Why are the damn sharks homing in on us?*

Whhhhzzz, his reel chattered as he completed the forward portion of his cast. His rod and fly line hung frozen in their position behind him. His fly caught the one piece of remaining reef sticking above the surface. He seemed surprisingly calm, "You get 'em, Hoot, I'm screwed."

I stripped a few yards of fly line off my reel to make loose blue rolls of line on the water around my knees, took a loop-building cast, and then shot my fly to a position ahead of the herd. I got lucky. I was amazed at the ease with which my heavy

#8 weight rod could fling a giant fly. I was accustomed to the smaller rod that I used for trout fishing. The Bonefish meandered toward my fly, and I began stripping six-inch sections of line toward my groin. My heart pounded in my neck as it only does when a prey animal is about to succumb to my hunting skills or I'm about to get laid. The sensation brought with it an easy smile.

Strip, *wait a second*.

Strip, *wait a second*

Strip, *HOLY SHIT.*

The line ripped through my stripping hand and shot forward, uncoiling the floating coils at my knees. The fly line held taut to engage my reel, and the rod vibrated and jerked with unexpected violence. I wondered if a shark had taken my fly. The reel whirred loudly until I applied a braking action against the spinning spool with my left hand. Spontaneous laughter erupted from a sadly foreign place within me. I wasn't prepared for the happiness that flooded my brain. My throbbing neck and convulsing diaphragm propelled me into a rarely inaccessible quality of spontaneous laughter. Chuck, too was infected, talking through his laughter. I couldn't make out what he was saying, but I immensely enjoyed sharing the experience with someone I loved.

The reel suddenly stopped, and the rod nearly lurched from my hand. The fish was still on the line and headed for the two menacing sharks that would normally devour it, but its splattering rage scattered them. The blue fly line on my reel was bird-nested and stopped fast by its disorganized mass. I cautiously pulled on the fly line ahead of the disabled reel, retrieving a few inches of line at a time as the rod vigorously shook from one direction to another. The fish fought harder for its life than any of the largest trout I'd ever caught. When I sensed a weakening in the fight and pulled a little harder on the line, it nearly sliced my finger flesh. Hemmingway's "Old Man and the Sea" came to mind with his description of the friction from fishing line cutting and burning the old man's hands. While my fish was a bit smaller, my fish's fight instilled a similar sense of responsibility within me. I needed to land my fish quickly to avoid this athletic animal falling to the same fate as the old man's. We had sharks in the neighborhood, and the commotion was going to bring more in for an easy meal if possible.

I eventually steered the fish to Chuck's knees. He grasped the line and pulled the spent fish into his wetted hands. Using a pair of suturing hemostats that I inherited from my father, I carefully dislodged the hook from the fish's mouth. I kissed it on the nose and silently thanked whatever God blesses stupid fishermen. It shot out of my hand with a screw-you splash to disappear amongst the coral and sand. I'd caught a Bonefish with my very first cast. I knew luck, not skill, had been on my side.

I held up my useless reel to Chuck, "Thanks for your help. I'm gonna be a while, so why don't you keep hunting while I see if I can unfoul this mess."

"No, I'll give you a hand." His grin was a little too wide while his eyes searched the water behind me.

I'm not sure whether I jumped or screamed first before it registered in my consciousness. We were knee-deep, alone in water filled with overly curious sharks. The hit to the back of my right calf caused a slight reaction on my part. I was above Chuck's six-foot head, looking down on the bill of his greasy cap while I exhaled a shriek that could seemingly reach Puerto Rico. It was uncharacteristically high-pitched for me. In the past, when injured by hooves, mountain bike wrecks, or fists hitting me, my verbal reaction was a deep grunt at worst. That morning's noise was in all shame, the scream of a little girl getting hit on the ass with a wet soccer ball on a playground. It was the scream of a goat being stabbed. It wasn't my scream. I had no such scream until that moment. Perhaps the primal unconscious thought of being food helped that scream find my vocal cords and, to my chagrin, Chuck's ears.

I landed with a splash, barehanded. The spasms of jumping and screaming caused me to eject my fly rod to the water behind my flailing body. In an irony that twisted my skittering mind, I found solace in Chuck's fits of laughter. The bastard couldn't talk, and could barely inhale through belly quaking, shrieking roars. He cried and pounded his thigh through frothing water. I lifted my leg out of the water, expecting to see a bloody crescent taken out of my calf muscle...yet I was intact. It had only given me a tasting bump with its nose. Before he could pump oxygen into his purple, shaking head, the fish came in again for another taste and had two friends. The third wasn't so small. He composed himself enough to join me in moving like a pair of unmounted jousters fending off barbarians with our fly rods. I turned my rod backward and hit one of them with the butt of my rod. He held his rod by the butt and slashed the water in front of the advancing shark trio until one of them bit and snapped it. Side by side and continually parrying the sharks, we retreated to the last piece of coral sticking out of the water and regrouped. "What the hell was that about?" I asked.

"Jeez, Hoot, I've never seen anything like that unless there was food in the water. Those little shits want to eat us." He paused and inspected his new fly rod. An umbra of disappointment shadowed his face. "Shit, I hope the warranty covers shark bite." His sadness made me hold back from chastising him.

"I'm sure it will. When I closed my trout rod in my truck door, Orvis took it back, and for thirty bucks, I got a perfectly new one within a week." We stood on the exposed coral chunk, watching the sharks swim in expanding circles around us until finally disappearing.

Over his shoulder, I saw our school of Bonefish tailing about twenty yards away. "Hey amigo, I gotta find a private place onshore. Why don't you take my rod and get one of those?" I handed him my fly rod. He sloshed parallel to the shore as I headed in. I attempted to wade as quietly as possible and aimed for the spot where the little deer had disappeared into thick bushes. The sharks reappeared about halfway to shore, first circling, then darting in singly, then in pairs. I quickened my step, and by the time they were swimming within inches of my feet, I jumped safely onto the sand. I began to wonder how my leather Brazilian reef walkers were tanned. I lifted one to my nose, and its smell was vaguely reminiscent of the shower-head death water at Tamarindo.

After watering a tree, I witnessed another pleasurable experience. Chuck was thigh-deep in water and about to release a Bonefish when his gaze caught mine. He held the fish in the air, gave a happy yelp, and gently placed it in the water. I slid into a trance of sublime emotion when my eyes held his for that second. I had known this man since he was a kid. My emotions of sharing this supreme fishing moment with Chuck were a confusing mixture of filial and an unfamiliar version of paternal love. I had experienced these same emotions when my hunting dogs made me proud. Shared experiences define the texture of the bonds between men, as well as with their dogs.

I remembered back to being a kid, catching my first trout with my father in a small stream in the Big Sur region of California, and the look of love and pride on his face. I thought about the bond I had with Jason, shaped by hours of riding Harleys with the boys in the club. My mind went to an instance when he and I were back-to-back, surrounded by a dozen bikers of a rival club, and what it took to extricate ourselves alive. Shared near-death experiences of violence and adrenaline etch themselves into your brain. Shared fishing experiences embed themselves into your heart. In that moment of swirling emotion and memories, I enjoyed another unpretentious perfect moment. I stood still and observed him fishing for a while before cautiously wading back out.

"I was wondering if the mosquitoes had carried you away. It must have been a hell of a shit." Chuck's words brought me back from inside my head to a saltwater flat in the Caribbean.

"How many did you catch?" I asked. "One, but he fought like a tiger shark. Damn, this is fun. I can't believe I've lived down here all these years and never did this. Thanks, Hoot." He had that smiling, spent expression of a man having just gotten laid. "What the hell are you thanking me for? It's the Bonefish that are magical." I spoke over the sounds of the rising tide, which was already up to my waist. "Why don't we get out of the water before the sharks return."

"After you left, they didn't come back. I wondered if you still had the smell of dead Iguana on you?"

"I've showered a lot since we cleaned up that mess. I'd hope like hell that isn't the case."

"Oh well, at least we didn't end up as breakfast," he said.

"Speaking of breakfast, that dried-up cowpie I ate is getting lonely. Why don't we go into town and eat?

"I could go for a Goat Roti right about now," he said. *What in the hell is a Goat Roti?*

On our climb up from the beach toward the jungle, we passed the ruins of the old sugar mill. "What's the name of this place again?" I asked about the dilapidated buildings. "Reef Bay Ruin," he said. Reef Bay held a perplexing energy of hope for me amongst the ruins. Maybe it was the Bonefish?

-10-

Fussing and Fighting

After a dinner of rum and some kind of fish, our group noisily meandered onto a street filled with West Indians and tourists. A shifting blur of black and white faces voiced politely "excuse me's" as people on the crowded street bumped into one another. No two people, except for our ambling group, seemed to be moving in the same direction. The poorly lit street pulsed with the smells of food cooking, alcohol on people's breath, and pungent tropical plants releasing their scents to hang heavily in the air of the wet, still night. Occasionally, stray dogs approached the tourists but gave a wide berth to the West Indians. Baine ignored them, Boddington spoke kindly to them, Chevali petted them.

A thin female mutt scurried past us, head down and cowering with a quick, worried stride. Chevali and I slid out of the stream of foot traffic, crouched near a rock wall, and faced her from a few feet. "Hey, sweetie," I called while Chevali made a soft clucking sound with his tongue.

She stopped but held her ground and scrutinized us. Chevali opened the box of dinner leftovers and tossed her a piece of fish. Her eyes never left us. She took a couple cautious steps toward the dinner remnant and cautiously sniffed it. A group of staggering men approached. One, wearing a colorful knit bag on his head, yelled "Ge hyo Muddascunt" and kicked her in her rib cage. She screamed and was fortunately able to dodge the next, more prodigious kick. His foot slammed into the wall behind her, and he fell, grabbing his bleeding toes, and rolled onto his back, screaming, "Skettle." I thought I could see bone sticking out of his great toe. Chevali moved with fists clenched toward the man, "You kicked my dog, asshole." I held the back of his shirt.

"Fuck you and de dog." The downed man replied. Chevali swatted my hand, but I held firm saying, "If you would please be so kind as to allow me..." I lifted an eyebrow and motioned to the bleeding man with my head. He relaxed, smiled, and stopped pulling away from me. He bowed and held out a sweeping hand, palm up as if guiding me toward the swearing man.

"Hey buddy, I know first aid. Let me see your foot."

"Fuck dat bitch," he said, motioning toward Chevali.

"I know, I know, he's a silly man with a big heart when it comes to stray helpless dogs."

"Fuck deh dogs... You hep meh foot?" His emotionless friends stood with their backs to him, seemingly bored with his injuries. The moving mass of tourists split around them to put us in a human shadow. He held his foot up for me to inspect the bleeding, angled toes. The great toe indeed had an open fracture.

"This is sure to become a horrendous bone infection in this environment. That's gotta hurt. Let me help you." I held my hand to help him up. As soon as he clasped my hand, I stepped on his broken foot as I pulled him up. I felt things crunch under my thin flip-flop. His reddened eyes locked onto my gaze. His mouth opened wide enough to accept a billiard ball. The only sound he made was a wheezing "HAAAAAAR" as the air left his lungs. His legs crumpled, and he fell to the street. His choking gasps caught the attention of his friends. They turned to face us with bloodshot eyes that told of many a smoked spliff that day.

The supine man swore and muttered in a language other than English, pointing to his foot and me. One of them moved toward me when Chevali stepped between us. "Anybody for Sushi?" and slammed the box of leftovers into the advancing guy's face while stepping behind his right leg, tripping him, and driving him down onto the road. Food chunks clung and wiggled in his beard as he lay, mumbling on his back. His already distant gaze focused on something far beyond the dark sky above him.

The third of the trio stood wide-eyed and motionless, watching Chevali, who feigned a short punch, and he scattered through a gathering crowd. Chevali walked to the dog kicker, who was up, hopping on one foot, trying to make a getaway. "Oh no motherfucker, let me deliver a message from the island dogs to you," and swung a roundhouse kick at the guy's stable leg. For the third time that night, the dog kicker hit the ground, crying. Chevali said as he stood over the whimpering man, "I know I'm only a tourist, but if I see you hurting another dog, I promise you that this evening will have seemed like a vacation for you." The dog kicker muttered and glared at him, "If meh catch you, teach dem live heh."

"Sheraton hotel asshole, I'm at the pool every afternoon. I'll be the one with an umbrella drink in my hand and my unbroken toes in the water."

From the downstream side of the human current came an irritated voice. "Ky, damn it, where'd you go? We've been looking all over for you. You friggin disappeared again. I swear you have ADD. I'm going to attach a leash to your ass." Rosie had found us. She scowled at the two guys on the ground, then at Chevali's sheepish grin. "Oh no, no, no, what did you do?" She spoke through pursed lips, her head tilted left, a sure sign of displeasure.

"Oh honey, we were simply helping these poor gentlemen. Something happened, I don't know what. We wanted to see if either of them needed any medical help." I Smiled and cocked my head to match hers. "See, everything appears to be perfectly fine," and held two thumbs up. "Let's go find the others."

Woody's was a minuscule restaurant a few feet back from the island's main street. Outside, plastic tables and chairs filled the sidewalk between the restaurant and the street. Inside, to the right of the entry, a short bar adjoined a dining area the size of a pickup bed. In the back, a poorly ventilated kitchen pumped out heat and the smell of hot grease. Rowdy drinkers drowned out the wall speakers' thumping reggae. Boddington's voice dominated the cacophony.

"Damnit, Ramona, hold still while I set the table for this young buck here." She was lying on the bar giggling with her shirt pulled up, showing the bottom of her untanned breasts and her yoga pants down to the top of her wavy escutcheon. Boddington poured tequila into her jiggling navel from a bottle of Culo Diablo tequila that cascaded down her flank and pooled on the dark wooden bar. Rosie, at her head, was taking pictures and talking to her. Boddington threw a small handful of salt and almost hit his target. He turned to a thin young man with a butch haircut and thick, black-rimmed glasses who was part of a group of U.S. Navy sailors on shore leave.

"Son," Boddington commanded, "ya aim your tongue for the hole, not the hair." Boddington ran his hand from her groin up to her navel. "Now go get her for God and country." The sailor bent forward as if to obey orders. "Whoah, boy," Boddington pulled the man's tee shirt that was wet with sweat. The sailor froze and focused his unblinking eyes on Boddington, who stuffed a lime wedge into the man's open mouth. "Gotta have your salad before the main course, now suck 'er hard and spit out the rind, boy."

The sailor appeared to have his bravery provoked by Boddington's encouragement, cocked his head back, and spat the rind behind the bar, almost hitting an overly tattooed female bartender. A smile came to his face, and he plunged face first onto Ramona's abdomen, startling her. She squealed and started wiggling and then moaning as the sailor tongued her belly. He sucked and tongue flicked her navel. She arched her back, closed her eyes, grabbed his head, and pushed it toward her crotch. He tried to pull his head away, but she clung tight and began humping his face. Behind crooked glasses, his eyes rolled wildly while her writhing pants muffled his screams, "No, No, stop... help."

He pushed himself away from her with both hands, grimaced at Boddington, and hunkered like a guilty dog awaiting punishment. The laughing crowd of onlookers grew quiet and adopted his facial expression. The music seemed to get louder as the drunks quieted. Ramona, lost in her own world, was obliviously grinding her pelvis. Boddington's face changed expression from a smiling-happy to serious. Chevali stepped between Boddington and the sailor.

"Ramona baby, you're hot as hell, my turn." He swiped a whipped cream can off the bar, drew a sputtering, fluffy white "X" on her gyrating belly, bent down, kissed her belly, and blew whipped cream onto Boddington, the bar, and the sailor. Ramona kept humping her hand to the beat of the reggae music. Chevali, with whipped cream covering his face, shouted "My turn," and scooped Ramona's knees from below, lifted her butt off the bar, gave it two hard spanks, and jammed his left arm under her neck. He picked her up and handed her off to Boddington, saving the sailor.

"Take this woman home and give her what every man in this bar wants to." He raised his fist in the air and yelled. The crowd shouted back, and laughter resumed. Boddington smiled at Chevali with a limp Ramona in his arms and said, "Thank you. You saved me from myself, I owe you," kissed the top of Chevali's head and carried Ramona through the parting crowd.

Chevali tore his shirt off, jumped on the bar, laid flat, grabbed the bottle of Culo Diablo tequila, and spoke to a small group of swaying women, "Who's next?" I quickly seized the shocked appearing sailor who was trying to escape. We struggled back to the bar through the bouncing women about to devour Chevali. I stuffed the whipped cream nozzle in his mouth, pushed the tip down until his cheeks expanded, chipmunk-like, and whipped cream shot from the sides of his mouth, and plunged his head into Chevali's abdomen. The unfortunate sailor bucked and tried to push away. With his eyes closed and head back, Chevali smiled and moved his head side to side for a few seconds until he discovered his prize.

"What the fuck?" Chevali yelled. I let go of the sailor who had whipped cream covering his face and under his glasses.

He stood straight, then ducked as if there were incoming rounds and ran for the door.

"You bastard, that's not funny. I'm not queer." Chevali was red-faced. Chiara and Rosie were hugging each other, rocking, and laughing. Baine and Jessica standing at his feet, gasped as if they had witnessed a mugging.

"Well then, try this on for size, big boy," I said as I poured Culo Diablo tequila over his chest, nudged Rosie to his far nipple, and picked up Chiara with one arm and hefted her to the nearest nipple. They latched on like puppies at feeding time. Next, something happened that sent my head spinning for the second time that day. Rosie and Chiara unlatched from his nipples, came face to face, and shared a searching French kiss. Drunken onlookers screamed and encouraged them. Chiara winked at me, put her hand up in the air, high-fived Rosie, and arched up to kiss Chevali. Chiara pushed him off the bar, climbed upon it, and flung her shirt into a leering, cheering crowd, and laid face up in her running bra. He yanked her shorts down to show the top of her clean-shaven pubic mound and bit it making her squeal.

I overheard Jessica speak into Chevali's ear, "I'd sure like to have a private body shot with you sometime." He acted as if he had stepped into something cold, bad, and wet. He turned his attention back to Chiara, whose abdomen was the subject of another Sailor's attention.

At Chiara's feet, Baine took a long hit from his light beer and regarded her toes as if counting them in his mind. The tattooed bartender pushed the sailor away, clutched Baine's shirt, and pulled him up to Chiara's belly. He searched with pleading eyes to Jessica. The bartender squeezed a lime wedge on Chiara's navel and encouraged Baine to join the game. He attempted to pour some of his light beer on Chiara when the bartender pulled it out of his hand and yelled, "tequila asshole, not light beer for fucksake." Baine spoke back, flatly, "But, I don't like tequila."

The tattooed bartender replied in a dominant tone that made him assume the countenance of a schoolboy enduring a nun's ruler. "I don't give a shit if you like it or not," she said, thrusting the Culo Diablo bottle toward him. "It's not about liking tequila, so man up and drink." She poured tequila onto Chiara's belly and pushed Baine's face down. He complied, and when he brought his head back up, the bartender put a hand on the back of his head and the bottle to his mouth, "Now it's time to learn to drink like a man. Drink it, little man, drink." Baine wearing the same boyish compliant facial expression, drank multiple gulps as she steered the bottom of the bottle skyward. When she pulled it from his mouth, tears were rolling from his eyes while he coughed and gagged.

Rosie asked the bartender for the bottle and walked to Chiara's head. She squeezed a lime wedge into Chiara's open mouth, ran a salted finger over Chiara's lips, and took a swig off the bottle. She leaned forward until her mouth hovered a couple of inches from Chiara's, dribbling tequila from her mouth into Chiara's. They kissed again. Chevali laughingly yelled to me, "We may be out of luck for the rest of the trip."

Baine's eyelids hung halfway into his iris', and his face more lax than usual. He teetered again over Chiara's feet and lasciviously ran his fingers between her toes as if slowly masturbating her. He squeezed lime over her toes, loosened the tequila bottle from the bartender's hand, and drizzled a stream over Chiara's foot. His weaving head sunk toward it.

"What the hell are you doing?" Jessica reappeared, screaming at Baine, snatched the bottle with one hand, and slapped the back of his head with the other. "NO," as if scolding a puppy who had peed on the floor. "Home, NOW," and pulled him from the bar into the crowded street.

When I was able to talk through my laughter, I said to Rosie, "Baby, I need to take you home right now," giving her a look of intentional sexual hunger.

"Take me now or lose me forever." She said, tossing a movie line through a tequila and Chiara-wetted grin.

I pulled a wad of money from my pocket, and the first two bills revealed big head Benjamin Franklins. I caught the bartender's eye, handed them to her, and yelled, "Does this cover enough of this mess for all of us?" She smiled and nodded her head, yes. I felt stupid. I just paid two hundred bucks for a few hits from a bottle of Culo Diablo tequila. "Please keep the rest as a tip for putting up with these weirdos." She smiled and motioned to Rosie, "If you two ever want to party, I work here and at the Ancient Navigator most nights. We could do some real damage." She smiled and blew a kiss to Rosie. This island was indeed opening herself up to embrace us. Rosie smiled at me with a pondering expression on her face, which surprised me. She then focused her gaze intensely into my eyes, "Tonight, I share you with no one."

"I never thought it was an option," I said. "It never was... before tonight." She said coyly, bent over, and roughly bit my right nipple through my favorite tee shirt.

Halfway to Tamarindo, we stopped at the quiet beach where Sandy, the Rottweiler, had her hovel. Mast lights from sailboats rhythmically swayed and reflected in broken pieces on the water around a small boat that floated a few yards from shore. "Mi Bumpsey" was about twenty feet in length, too small for anybody to live aboard, and her deck was open to the night sky. She rocked slowly in the splintered moon shadows of palms.

"You game?" I asked.

"What if someone sees us?"

There were few street lights, no people, no cars. "Who? It's dark, and what nice tourists aren't asleep, are drunk in town." She took my hand and led me into warm water, and we pulled ourselves onto the boat. I grabbed a couple of seat cushions from the bench seats that ringed her inner deck and laid them out as a makeshift bed. She faced me and raised her arms above her head, allowing me to effortlessly remove her sundress with one hand. Interrupted moonlight danced across her long body as a breeze moved the palm leaf shadows above us, causing her pale breasts to glow intermittently. She laid back on the cushions and held her hands up toward me. My tongue met her salty belly, and she writhed with every slow tongue stroke. She pulled me up toward her face, and I removed my favorite "Bite Me" tee shirt from Hawaii and flung it into the darkness below the boat's steering wheel. The shirt's image of a snarling gecko was our private voyeur. Her abdominal muscles rhythmically contracted, pulling her pelvis to meet mine a few times when a car approached from the direction of town. I held a low position, imagining the potentially comic sight of my white ass appearing in and out of sight over the boat's gunwales, and waited for the lights to disappear.

A half-hour later, the excitement of having sex in the warm night air on a pirated boat caused me to shudder in pleasure as she arched her back and stifled a yell. I sank into her embrace, and Mi Bumpsey rocked us into unconsciousness. In my sleep, I rolled off her and the safety of the cushions and onto the hard fiberglass bottom of the boat. I awoke suddenly with a hot, stinging right ear. In semiconsciousness, I reached for my ear, thinking it was under attack by a centipede. My hand stopped short, with something encircling my wrist. In response, I threw my head back, which made the centipede sink its fangs deeper into my ear. Peaceful post-orgasmic grogginess gave way to a rush of anxiety mixed with searing pain as the centipede's venom poured into my throbbing ear. I sat upright and reached around my head to clumsily swat the attacker and found the blunt end of a fishing lure still attached to the line that ensnared my wrist. When I moved my wrist, it dragged a fishing rod toward us. I felt relieved but not lucky.

The night's dark sky had turned to a hint of pink, and the moon that had illuminated our earlier lovemaking had abandoned us. I struggled to free my hand and accidentally drove the fishhook through the entire thickness of my earlobe. I felt more panic as I envisioned an irate boat owner finding us naked, with my ear attached to his fishing rod. With the light of dawn coming rapidly in the tropics, I wanted off the boat. I released a little line from the reel to avoid ripping the lure through my earlobe, pulled my shorts on with my left hand, and told Rosie, "Let's hustle our asses the hell out of here before we get busted."

Inspecting my impaled auricular quandary, Rosie said, "I told you that you would become hooked on these exhibitionistic fantasies of yours."

"I'd say screw you, but that's what got us into this mess into the first place. I love you." I reached forward and kissed the mouth that Chiara and I shared only a few hours ago.

I slid into the cool morning water and held the rod high in the air while we waded to shore, where Sandy, the rottweiler joined us. We walk-trotted back to Tamarindo in hopes of avoiding arrest for theft of a fishing rod, trespassing, and having sex in public. Each stride caused the thick line to tug painfully at my ear. Once home, I headed for the kitchen to find a knife to free myself from the fishing rod. I was about to cut the line when Rosie called me from behind. I turned to face her with the rod still close to my ear, and a flash of light blinded me. "Gotcha, fisherman Ky." She took a flash photo of me. *Damn it.* I cut the line with another searing yank.

"Great, Ansel, now that you have taken another Pulitzer winner, can you help me find some pliers so I can extract this damn hook out of my ear, please?"

"Look at me for a minute. I think I like you with an earring. It gives you that swashbuckling, Errol Flynn sorta vibe. I want you to keep it. It goes with the Caribbean pirate theme down here."

"Be that as it may, the longer it's in, the greater the chances of a raging infection that could rot off the side of my head."

"Oh, I didn't think about that." She grimaced.

We rummaged through the house and found nothing resembling pliers. "To hell with it, I'll just coat it with Neosporin, and tomorrow we can go into town and find something to cut this bastard out of me. Let's try to get an hour's sleep before the others awaken."

-11-

No More Trouble

I awoke to the song of the brown bird in the Tamarind tree by the deck above our room. The sun was up, and my ear was throbbing. The dried blood on my neck felt tight when I turned my head.

"I need to get this filthy hook out of my ear so I can think. If Chuck sees it, he'll tease the shit out of me for the rest of the trip. I can't give him this much ammunition, and speaking of Chuck...."

"Yes," Rosie answered.

"We've been here for days, and he hasn't mentioned a girlfriend. Does he have one?"

"He's pretty quiet about his love life," Rosie answered.

"Hell, he's probably servicing half the tourist chicks on the island. I'll bet he gets more ass than a bus station toilet seat."

"Ky, you're gross. He's probably dating a sweet girl who's been busily working since we've been here. I'm sure he'll bring her to Ramona's wedding."

"Yeah, you're right. God knows anything would be an improvement over that beast he was dating when he lived in Reno. Shit, remember her? I swear she was more masculine than half the guys in the motorcycle club."

"She did have a thick neck," Rosie said.

"Thick neck, hell. She had a thick everything except intellect. I bet they shared his face razor in the mornings."

"You are such a pig." She said as Boddington's voice upstairs broke the quiet of the morning. "Geezel Pete, I'm getting married today. Where's my woman at? I need me a breakfast burrito and a hummer to get rid of this thumping hangover. Ramona honey, where you at?"

"Well, so much for sleep," I said, "let's get up and remove this thing out of my ear before it rusts."

The kitchen was welcoming with the scent of brewing coffee. "Whoa, buddy, what in the hell is that in your ear." Boddington saw my dangling lure.

"What are you talking about?" I feigned ignorance to my detriment.

"This wanger-danger right here, shit, it can't be real." He reached for my ear, and before I could duck, he gave it a sharp tug.

"Ooooh shit." I sank to my knees.

"Jeez Ky, this sombitch is for real. How the hell did you manage to festoon your ear with that? I never envisioned y'all as one of them Goths. Did them fish turn the tables on you yesterday? My uncle Elmer shot hisself in the kneecap once while squirrel huntin. Had a limp for the rest of his life. Us kids used to tease the hell outa him about the squirrels outsmarting him. It looks like you set the bar even lower for yourself, son. Seriously now, what happened?" He asked while I swatted his hand away.

Boddington, Ramona, and the others had me surrounded by the time I finished the story. Their back slaps sent me into a strange mixture of emotions. I felt pride for being adventurous, worry that someone may have recognized us, and embarrassed for having a fishing lure in my ear.

"One good thing about it." Boddington slapped my thigh.

"What's that?"

"At least you didn't get it stuck in your little pecker, Yeee. That would have been fuckin' great, a Caribbean genital piercing."

I spoke to the laughing group, "can we abandon Boddington's homoerotic pecker piercing fantasy and go to town for breakfast. Boddington, you can order some of those shriveled-up little sausages and daydream about Jeb in a Speedo."

"And after breakfast, we have to find a pair of wire cutters," Rosie added to my aching misery.

"Oh great," I said, "a group shopping experience. This shouldn't be humiliating."

The walk from Tamarindo took us through a quiet neighborhood of primarily rental villas. A firm breeze wafted uphill, populated with the scents of clean ocean and flowers. It cooled my face and arms from the direct morning sun. The narrow concrete road curved past a couple of green trash bins set nearly into the roadway above the Gallows Point hotel. The formerly entrancing breeze transformed into an overpowering stench.

"This curve in the road always smells like a ruptured colon-sigmoid, to be exact." Boddington was doing his best to encourage our appetites.

"What the fuck is that smell?" Chevali asked.

"Whoa," Boddington added, "that smells like a hot night of Osculum Infame."

Jessica quietly asked Baine, "What is an Osculum whatever, do you know?"

Chevali answered loudly, "Jessica, it's the smell that comes off a hot tub full of divorce judges involved in an underwater circle jerk."

Chiara swatted his's arm, "Be nice." She leaned back and mouthed the words "I'm sorry" to Jessica, who smiled and nodded. Baine seemed oblivious, engrossed in watching Chiara's red-painted toenails. He looked like a bass inspecting a popper on the water's surface. Jessica followed his eyes to the object of his attention and elbowed him in the ribs. He nonchalantly changed his gaze to the horizon.

Surprised that Boddington would be familiar with the Osculum term, I asked him, "how the hell do you know what an Osculum infame is?"

"Used to date this kinky bitch, she was into that witchcraft shit, I ain't got no idea what the hell it means, but she and her other clutchmates would giggle and talk about the funky smell. Kinda weird, I know, but they thought it was funny." Ramona glared at him. I wondered if it was jealousy or if he was revealing too much.

"Hey, where does everybody want to eat?" I asked.

Rosie said, "Chuck likes the Manta Ray's Cafe. He knows the owner."

"We'll give it a try," Jessica spoke for Baine, who kept his lips closed and his eyes pointing far down the road.

"I ain't never ate no manta ray. I wonder if I can get mine deep-fried with gravy." Boddington added.

"I had a pastry there yesterday. I can only hope his cooking is better than his baking," I said, hoping to stir debate for alternate restaurants.

Beyond the sigmoid stench curve, a wooden phone pole resembled a rusted porcupine impaled with hundreds of oxidized staples. They penetrated waterlogged, curled business cards and flyers advertising day trips on sailboats to the British Virgin Islands. One caught my eye, "Bounder." The flier, protected by a plastic sleeve, immediately gave me a modicum of confidence in the owner's intelligence. It pictured a small red sloop, a dog, and her owner, "Captain Tim."

"Hey, guys, look at this." I stopped and patted the flyer. "Doesn't Chuck like the British Virgin Islands?"

Rosie replied, "We've been there a couple of times. There's a fun little beach bar and a sweet old guy, Foxy, who sings all day for tourists."

I reached into the plastic sleeve and tore off a copy of Captain Tim's phone number. Beyond the pole and behind a short chain-link fence, a group of trees stood between us and the calm water of the bay, fifty feet away. Under the trees rested a small plot of above-ground graves made of concrete. I had only seen such things in photos of graveyards in New Orleans and Jim Morrison's grave in Paris. Some had professional appearing headstones. Many had homemade headstones with the deceased's names, birth, and death dates smushed into wet cement, giving them the quality of a child's finger painting. The white concrete rectangles had mildew growing on their sides, proportional to their age. One was open on the end, patiently awaiting the owner's demise. Rusting coffee cans filled with dirt, presumably once holding live flowers, trickled brown rust trails down the sides of a couple of them. Some had faded plastic flowers. My favorite had a brown beer bottle and shot glass sitting on top, an apparent tribute to an old drinking buddy.

A hundred yards later, we walked past the scene of the previous night's boat adventure. The owner was on board, rearranging the seat cushions. Hanging over the gunwale were my underwear and favorite tee shirt accidentally left on board in our haste to leave. The Hawaiian gecko seemed out of place, upside down and snarling in our direction. I faced forward so that he didn't see his fishing lure hanging from my ear. The direct sun on it made it throb.

"Hey, y'all doin' laundry or somethin'?" Boddington grinned at me after shouting to the boat owner, who looked up with an expression of anger. He yelled back something unintelligible and returned his attention to his boat. Boddington grinned at the man who waived him off like an irritating fly.

"Boddington, you're the reason that locals become irritated with tourists," I said, shaking my head, which made the lure bounce and hurt.

"No, buddy, I think you are." He retorted, hitting my shoulder hard enough to make my fish hook sting even more.

Once in town, we huddled around little white tables in the Manta Ray's cafe. Thankfully, the conversation shifted away from my ear and focused on the wedding to take place that evening at sunset. Chuck arrived as we collated the money for our breakfasts. My unselfish group of friends were arguing over who could pay more than they needed to.

"How are you, little brother, arms sore from wrestling Bonefish?" Rosie asked while hugging him.

I interjected, "More likely sore from wrestling his boyfriend's bone."

His face flushed red for a fleeting second, and I worried that I had offended him. Still, his yellow-toothed smile quickly returned, "No, Hoot, what's sore is my belly from laughing at you screaming like a little girl when the baby shark bumped you." He launched into his embellished version of the previous day's shark encounters. In the middle of his story, Rosie asked me, "Why didn't you tell me you had a run-in with a shark?"

"No need to worry over spilled urine."

"That's disgusting." She said as Chuck hit a crescendo of hoots and howls while protecting his crotch as if from shark attack. Not only our group but the other restaurant patrons and even Murray all laughed at me. I felt stupid. A round, florid woman with a New York accent jabbed her spoon at my ear and laughingly asked, "Is that from fishing yesterday too?"

Her husband stopped laughing, scowled, and said, "If you don't mind, I am a Dermatologist. That really needs to come out. How long has it been there? Are you up to date on your tetanus?" I make every attempt never to let anybody know I'm a physician out of my office setting. I held my medical tongue and said, "Thank you, sir. It will be coming out the very minute our stand-up comedian ends his melodramatic fish story, and we can buy a pair of wire cutters."

Murray spoke up, "Hey Doc, no need to waste your money. I have a pair in my toolbox in the kitchen." He disappeared behind a split bedsheet hanging by a horizontal string above the doorway. Not wanting to be the center of attention, I said, "No, I'll be fine. We can go buy a pair." Boddington said, throwing me under the embarrassment bus, "Bullshit, we gotta get that outa there before you die from ptomaine or whatever happens to infected human ears."

The Dermatologist spoke, "The big guy is right. Although ptomaine is unlikely, we need to remove it. Find those wire cutters, please." Irritated and becoming more embarrassed, I said, "No, please, I can do it myself, enjoy your breakfasts, I'll be fine."

"Here he comes. Wow, they're a little rusted." Boddington held my arm and reached over the counter to Murray. "Let me do it. I saw a short video about foreign body removal in Chiropractic College" and started for my head with the open-jawed brown tool. I ducked, "Damn it, can we please not..." The Dermatologist politely reached for the wire cutters in Boddington's hand, "If you will permit me, sir, this IS my forte."

Boddington replied, "If you insist, Doc, but I get to be the scrub nurse," and slapped the cutters into his pale hand.

"We need something to sterilize the field before I cut the hook," he said to Murray.

"You want Clorox or alcohol?" Murray asked.

"Alcohol will do."

Murray returned and handed a half-full bottle of rum to Boddington. He took a swig and spat it into my ear. "She's sterile now, Doc."

The Dermatologist sighed, "Chiropractor?"

"Yup, wasn't that cleaning job good enough for ya?" and spat a second mouthful into my burning ear. Rum streamed down my neck and shirt. The Dermatologist looked like he wanted to run but took a breath and focused on my ear. He held my ear lobe, and with a quick snip, the sharp end of the hook skittered across the tile floor. He gave the blunt end a yank to remove it. My ear vibrated with pain.

"There we go, but you need to start on an antibiotic today. I can call it into Bob, the pharmacist at the Chelsea pharmacy here on island. Last year our Schnauzer, Tommy Boy, contracted contact dermatitis while we were down here, and I called him in a steroid cream. Worked like a charm. What's your name and date of birth?"

I had no fight left in me when Boddington rang in with, "No damn antibiotics. All he needs is this...", and showered me with a third ear-full of rum "and a proper neck adjustment to

C-one and two.... the nerve supply to the auricular branch of the Vagus nerve and maybe a short shot to C-three for the 'ol lesser occipital nerve. I got it from here, Doc. By the way, ya got some first-class hands. I'd a been shaking like a dog shitting a peach seed if I had to do that to a human." Boddington turned and spoke to me, "we can do the adjustment with you sittin' in yer chair."

"No, really, Boddington, I'm fine." I smiled at the Dermatologist and thanked him. He nodded and said, "I've always wanted to see a Chiropractic adjustment, been curious for years."

I tried to stand up, but Boddington leaned hard on my shoulder. He had an MD audience and was going to do his best to educate the Dermatologist. "Stay still, son. It'll be over in a second, just like sex for poor Rosie." He placed a hand under the back of my skull, extended my head back, and WHAM, it sounded like someone stepping on a bag of potato chips inside my head. Before I could react, he turned my head to the other side, and again WHAM. I saw floating stars, and my ears roared. I wanted to vomit but held it in.

"Shit on a bunch of penicillin, you're cured now boy, but we may want a scooch of Neosporin on the holes for good measure." Boddington proudly wiped his hands together. The dermatologist stood motionless with his mouth wordlessly moving, staring at me.

"Betcha' heard the correction all the way over there, didn't ya?" Boddington said proudly to the Dermatologist. "We seated the Atlas squarely within the confines of the Axis with that one." Boddington blinked at me, "How's that feel, buddy?"

I hadn't noticed that my lips were numb until I tried to speak, "I phu umk hay," I sounded like I'd been to the Dentist.

Someone else was at the steering wheel for my mouth, and I was worried that he might have torn a vertebral artery. I didn't want to have a brain bleed on an island with no Emergency Room. I resigned myself to the fact that by the time they got me to a Neurosurgeon, I'd be a permanent GORK. I had faced death in much uglier places than this and sat listening, waiting for unconsciousness to descend. The Dermatologist said to his wife, "My word if I did that to a patient, I'd be arrested for assault."

Boddington visibly puffed up, "You call my work assault?"

The Dermatologist said, "It is rather violent, aren't you afraid of injuring people?"

"Assault? Let me ask you who carves people up with scalpels and then poisons them with drugs that are so poorly researched that they're continually recalled for killing patients. I help people heal themselves with positive intentions directed through educated hands." Boddington's volume was rising.

"I'll have you know," it was the Dermatologist's turn for righteous indignation, "that I graduated from Perelman School of Medicine near the top of my class." Baine stepped between the two and interjected, "Now gentlemen, please, please..." The Dermatologist turned on Baine, "What business is this of yours?"

"I happen to be a professional in conflict resolution, an officer of the court, a Family Law Magistrate." Jessica pulled at his hand, "Honey, maybe not now, this isn't...."

"THIS, Jessica, this is exactly what I do. I facilitate common-sense resolutions amongst opposing parties." Baine assumed a regal countenance for Baine. Chevali spoke from the back of the room, "He's a fucking divorce judge. He wouldn't know common sense if it bit him in his fat ass. So, back off

Baine and let these professionals settle it between them." The Dermatologist's face turned redder as Baine stood proudly between him and Boddington. "You're a divorce judge?" The doctor asked.

"That's a crude but semi-adequate term for my professional endeavors," Baine replied.

"Get away from me before I give you a black eye. You parasites don't resolve anything. You punish men for being successful. You're a legal bottom feeder. If it weren't for another of your lowly ilk, my new wife Ginger and I would OWN down here rather than just renting for a few weeks a year."

Chevali interjected, "Yeah, a legal carp." Then he giggled to himself and slapped Chiara on the ass. "Got him."

With my orbicularis dysfunction resolving, I uttered, 'snop.' Then, with a second more fortuitous effort, "All you assholes, stop." The room quieted, "Jeb, knock it off. Boddington, thank you, I feel great. Baine, don't ever put yourself between two pissed-off men unless you are wearing your silly robe and in your damn courtroom. Nobody gives a shit what you do for a living."

I spoke to the Dermatologist, "Thank you, my ear thanks you." I turned to Rosie," Please pay Murray for the Doctor and his wife's breakfast. Guys, we are all here on vacation. Remember what Rodney King said."

Boddington frowned, wordless.

"Can't we all just..." I said, open-handedly paddling the air between us as if trying to pull a thought out of his head.

"...Get..." I kept paddling toward me.

Chiara jumped up and down with her hair bouncing, "Along."

Boddington still looked puzzled. *OK, maybe I'll stick to quotes from country songs the next time I want his thoughtful input.* I was relieved that my mouth was working again and spoke to the Dermatologist. "Hey Doc, that spinal manipulation stuff really does have some merits. Thanks again for fixing my ear."

"You're most welcome. He smiled, and we shook hands. Then, in a move of class, he turned to Boddington, "It's evident that you too have skilled hands, Doctor."

Boddington smiled, "Well, what the hell, as do you kind sir."

-12-

My Cup

The guys left with Chuck to help him lug SCUBA equipment. I walked with the women until I found a cybercafé to check my email. My secretary Alley and I had agreed that all non-emergent communication would be by email, as cell phone service in St. John cost three dollars per minute.

The cybercafé was a small, poorly ventilated former store. Above the open sliding doors, a handmade sign read 'LOVE CITY CYBERCAFE' with an artistically challenged version of a pelican wearing reading glasses in front of a computer. The roof was FEMA tarp-covered. Against one wall, shoulder to shoulder tourists busily hammered off-white keyboards. Peter Tosh sang on elevated speakers to compete with their clacking. Green computer light images bounced and flashed on an older man's giant glasses as he typed and talked to himself. Behind a tall counter, a white guy in his mid-twenties, eyes closed, sported an explosion of unlikely blond dreadlocks and a Rasta tie-dye shirt. His head wobbled, bouncing an African continent-shaped medallion, and his ratty dreads off his unmuscled, flat chest.

"Excuse me," I asked. His head stopped in mid-bob. His left red-eye opened and inspected me. It was becoming evident that cheap weed was the breakfast and dinner of the local champions. "Uh, hey?" he answered.

"Hi, I'd like to rent some computer time when available. Need to check my email."

"They're like full," he said as his right eye opened.

"I can see that. Any guess as to how long it will be?"

"I dunno, like when someone is done."

"Why thank you, that makes it perfectly clear. Do you care to venture a wild guess? I haven't been to one of these cyber places before."

He grunted and raised his featureless shoulders, "You like want some coffee or homemade vegetarian pastries while you wait? They like rock." Behind him, on a card table, a half-full 'Mr. Coffee' coffee maker sat beside a jar of Coffee-mate and a white cereal bowl with brown sugar cubes and a plastic spoon. A loose weaved green bowl held a pile of smashed pastries individually wrapped tightly in plastic. I wondered if Murray was his baker.

"All vegetarian? I guess that means no real cream for the coffee?" I asked with zero intention of consuming anything but felt like screwing with him.

"Like, no man. Dairy cows are abused and forced into milk-slavery by heartless industrial farmers."

"Huh, I guess no eggs in the pastries either, a function of hapless poultry servitude, I'm assuming?"

He didn't verbally respond but sucked through his teeth as a woman said from behind me, "OK, all done, how much will that be?" *Thank God.*

He handed me a slip of scrap paper with a password and brief instructions on how to log on. The process was laborious, and the instructions minimally helpful. I wound my way around to AOL and got the familiar "You've got mail." I scrolled through emails from Alley and my resident, BJ. Each email jerked me back closer to my Stateside reality. My vacation-induced optimism deflated in spurts with every problem patient I addressed. My second to the last email was from Percy Hayes, the puppy murdering insurance adjustor. He had successfully denied another of my patient's cases in a court trial. I had seen how convincingly he could lie to a jury and worried about the patient's future. My throat tightened to what would have been a standard workday grip. Those unpleasant feelings made me aware that I had unwittingly achieved a degree of emotional vacation mode since being in St. John.

The last email was from Alley, a collection of thousands of dollars' worth of office-related bills, and a question, "How do I pay these?" I couldn't take anymore and wrote to her that I'd have Rosie call her tomorrow. I was percolating in my feelings of anger and hopelessness. I could have easily been sitting at my office desk in Colorado, watching the snow falling in my parking lot. Any vacation sunshine that had warmed me had immediately turned into an apocrine tarnish on my skin. I felt like saying "Screw it" and climbing on an airplane back to Colorado.

I studied my green reflection on the computer monitor. *How in the hell can a man have worked so hard to accomplish so much with no help from anybody and still feel this empty inside?* I thought about the varied definitions of the word 'success' and questioned my life's work. What made me happy? Was I working at a job, living in a place, and in a life defined by me or others?

The computer screen gave me no answers. Its small white cursor continually blinked and mocked me from a corner of the screen. I loved Rosie, my animals, and time in the Colorado mountains when warm, but I hated being a doctor in the modern world. I was not an overly responsible man by nature, and I had placed myself squarely in the middle of one of the most thankless hyper-responsible professions possible. I felt stupid.

"Hey man, like are you done, or is the computer froze up?" A hollow voice brought me back from my Dante-like self-pity inferno.

I didn't turn toward him, "Yeah, I'm frozen, and I'm done. What's the bill?"

He tallied my charges while I stared into my eyes in the dull jade computer screen, waiting for a revelation.

"Twelve fifty, plus tax, man." The white Rasta said from behind the counter. "I thought you said you didn't pay taxes." I was acting like an asshole, opened my wallet, and pulled out a twenty. "Here ya go," and put it on the counter, "keep the change for my reride tomorrow."

"Sure man, like what's a reride?" He said as he brushed it into a metal box below counter level.

"Attractive belt ya got on," I said, "what's it made from?"

"Like cow, I guess. Why?"

I glared into his red, alveolate eyes, "I hope it didn't give up its skin to make a belt to hold your pants up over your vegetarian ass," and walked out into the morning's swelter. The emails had successfully wiped clean any veneer of happiness.

As I walked toward 'home,' there was no breeze between the buildings, and the sun deliciously warmed my skin but burned my punctured ear lobe. I reached up and found another trail of crusted blood on my ear lobe and upper neck. *Wonderful.* I left it and started my walk back to Tamarindo. My facial expression must have shown my emotions when a humming West Indian woman carrying an armload of packages stopped in front of me. She was a bit older than I, wore an African print wrap-around dress that showed her ample hips and breasts in their lumpy outlines. Her hair twisted into a tornado and frozen in mid-spin with a pencil. "Why such a handsome man look so grumpy?"

"I'm sorry, what?"

"You seem like dem cat ate your canary." She smiled and shifted the precarious load in her arms.

"Uh, my canary is fine, really, thank you, ma'am. I appreciate your kind concern," and gave her a genuine smile.

"*Don'* call me ma'am. I not old enough." She giggled. "Listen to me now, and I *don'* care what it is, deh water make it bettah. Go swimmin in deh ocean. She will talk to you. God bless you. Now, go tell her what your worry be, an dat I, Mazie say Hello", and walked away humming to herself. Stunned by her forthright kindness, if not clairvoyance, I spoke to the back of her retreating tornado, "Thank you maa...", and caught myself," Mazie." I heard her chuckle.

The little town of Cruz Bay chattered with activity in the daylight. Cars and trucks not designed for the narrow, winding streets were in a constant friendly battle for the right of way. Locals, be they black or white, were always stopping, pulling over, or backing up to let each other pass. The only exception to the kindness rule was tourists panic driving on the left side of the road and the water truck drivers. The latter showed nothing but contempt for any vehicle, taking their swath through the middle of every road.

I stopped at Pusser's store in Wharfside Village. The tightly packed shop's shelves overflowed with brightly colored mariner's clothing and unfamiliar sailing paraphernalia. Being hot and fatigued, I didn't stay to investigate. I wanted only to buy rum and go home to sleep. The rum sat in neat rows next to a rack of white, colorfully decorated tin mugs with the Pussers logo, nautical flags, and drink recipes for Pusser's Painkillers at the cash register. I picked one up, and inside, on the bottom facing up, was a drawing of a lynched man holding a bottle. Above him were the words "PUSSERS RUM," below him read "GOOD TO THE LAST DROP." **This is mine**. I paid for the rum and my new one-of-a-kind tin cup. I put it in my fanny pack and headed for my bed a few minutes' walk away.

The walk took me along the partly shaded concrete road that was a few feet from the lapping waters of the bay. Mi Bumpsey was gone, and my underwear and gecko shirt had washed up on the beach. I picked them up and threw my underwear over the low-hanging telephone line to wave at the world and continued my walk with my shirt wadded in my hand. I was happy to have my shirt back. I walked uphill past sigmoid curve to an unmarked road that plunged steeply to my right and disappeared into the foliage. It was the only road that could lead to a hilly spit of land with a couple of partially finished houses a quarter-mile away. Between them and me was a shallow, green-blue bay. I felt like exploring despite my fatigue. The pot-holed concrete road was wide enough for one car and so steep that I worried about my reef walkers sliding. I took smaller than usual steps to not fall with my load of Pusser's, my new tin cup, and heaviest of all, the emotional baggage of the morning's emails.

The road leveled out to split the bay. On the left, a brackish pond, and on the right was the desolate, clear bay. Rocks lined the shore and protected the road from waves. I was sweaty, hot, and alone. The water welcomed me as I waded to thigh

depth on the fist-sized rocks with my new reef walkers protecting my sensitive feet and slowly laid back into the water. It
rushed into my ears, muffling all sounds except for my rhythmic splashes. I backstroked for a minute, dropped my feet, and
trod water. My arms moved in the water like giant, slow-motion
hummingbird wings while my legs made broad, slow strides to
propel me afloat. My mind crossed the sea in front of me to a
few tiny uninhabited islands breaking the horizon. I imagined
being alone on an island of only a few acres, insulated by nature's anonymity from a world that leached my humanity.

For a brief second, I thought about sharks but realized
that I would be more than happy to die here in this secluded,
warm little bay alone and unseen. I'd seen a lot of bad deaths
in my training and career. There were very few good deaths. I
grinned at the irony of finding a profoundly peaceful moment
in Caribbean water, leading to my pondering a good death. I
guess the times, places, and situations that make us the hap-
piest would also make the best times to die, the Universe's gift
of 'dying in the saddle' scenario. I felt tears well up and join the
water that caressed my chin. I was OK with death at that moment, but I wasn't inviting it. I just wanted peace to replace the
discomfort that defined my life and asked the water to give me
an answer, and that Mazie said 'Hi.'

She spoke to me with the rhythm of the waves and on the
seamless feathers of White-tailed Kite birds drifting overhead
on unseen air currents. The bright, clear Caribbean reflected a
faint iridescent green off the bottom of their ivory wings back
down to me. The tears kept flowing, but not out of sadness.
They were only tears. I didn't understand them, but I let them
flow unexamined in that moment of intimate lonesomeness. I
knew I could cry here, and nobody but the water would know. I

wanted to be there so badly that just being there wasn't good enough. It was OK.

Back at Tamarindo, with the intensely unfamiliar sensation of having cried still heavy in my eyes, I removed my clothes and lay naked on the white bedspread that smelled of sunshine. I felt foolish for having gone on another typical Ky Elliott epiphany hunt. I let go of my self-incriminations while the ceiling fan cooled me into unconsciousness and drifted away on the wings of Kite birds to faraway islands. I was OK.

-13-

MISTER BROWN

A warm hand ran over my chest while I slept deeply on my back. I hadn't moved. "The sun's not out, so it won't work." A soft voice pulled me nearly to consciousness.

"Huh?" I replied with my eyes still closed.

"The sundial can't work without direct sunlight." The soft voice was irritating the hell out of me. I opened my eyes to see Rosie hovering over me, smiling. Her blonde hair swept to one side over her neck so I could see her face.

"Did you say something about a sundial?" I was confused.

"Yes."

I was growing irritated with her questions and answers and said, "Oh hello, happy to see you, but what the hell are you talking about a sundial for?"

She bent forward and kissed me, then softly took hold of my erection that I had been unaware of sporting. "The sundial can't work in here without any direct sunlight. We need to put you outside by the pool if you want to see what time it is."

A gravelly female voice from the other side of the room said, "I'd a bet, oh, three-thirty, what about you guys?"

Chevali spoke confidently, "Na, that little thing couldn't cast a shadow past one o'clock."

Blood pounded into my head from my shrinking pecker as I ran for the bathroom. I quickly wrapped myself in a white bath towel until something in the toilet caught my eye. It looked as if a bull had shit in the toilet. Half of the mountainous mass was above the water's surface. I sprinted back into the bedroom. "Who the hell did THAT?" I asked while pointing to the poor toilet. The laughter quieted as they all shrugged quizzically at each other.

Rosie said, "The girls and I came down here to find some sunblock." Their heads turned simultaneously toward Chevali. Rosie continued, "He was right outside the door when we got here. Damnit Jeb, what did you do?" She walked into the bathroom and shot out, shrieking. "What the hell, Jeb, why?"

"Simply leaving your husband a personalized calling card." Chevali replied shamelessly. Jessica turned pale, verbalized monosyllabic grunts, and left. Chevali called to her, "You really should see it. If it were a bass, it'd be a real lunker." Then speaking to Chiara, "Can you fetch my movie camera, it's right inside our bedroom door. This deserves photographic documentation, and it's a real beauty."

"Oh, *Che Cazzo*," Chiara said, karate chopped the air between her and Chevali and followed Jessica.

"Nice job, asshole, now go flush that monster," I said.

"Gotcha good this time," he responded as he followed Chiara, "Hey, did you find my movie camera yet?"

I asked Rosie, "Why the hell did you bring them in here?"

"How was I to know you'd be asleep and trying to reach the fan with your pecker?"

"I don't know, shit, I was having a great nap, now all of this," and pointed to the bathroom, "and that."

"What are we gonna do with it," she asked.

"Hell if I know, it's not going down without a bucket or two of water. Or I guess we could adopt it and name it after Jeb."

"I'll go find a bucket. This is war, Ky. We need to get even. You think long and hard."

"I was, before you got here."

Footsteps were falling on the deck above our bedroom. "Sounds like the gangs all here. Let me go up and see what Boddington's plan is," Rosie said.

"I'm hitting the shower, but wait, we have to deal with the Chevali baby first," I whined with disgust to Rosie. "Rock, paper, scissors?" she said, holding her hands up in front of her chest.

"No. Thank you for offering, but I'll deal with it. Go tell everybody that I found tonight's sunset time. We have to be ankle-deep and performing the wedding by 7:20," I said.

"I will. *Bonne chance, mon ami,* thank you for being so brave in the face of such danger. You are my hero." She batted her lashes and kissed my cheeks. "Yell, when it's all clear."

After dealing with Chevali's creation, I was able to take a shower. Rosie joined me in mid-shampoo, "Hey baby," I asked, "what's the game plan?"

"Not good, we gotta' leave in 40 minutes, everybody's scrambling. Poor Ramona is in a panic, and I can hear Jeb doing Chiara in the shower, so scoot over before we run out of hot water."

Forty-five minutes later, I climbed into the pickup. Chuck was waiting in his Jeep under the shade of a tree in the driveway with a black guy in the passenger seat. The sun was changing from white to a bright yellow when we arrived at the unmarked trail that led to the secluded wedding bay. Everybody except for Boddington jumped out of the vehicles to walk to the bay. We followed Chuck to a parking spot off the road, and the three of us began walking.

"Hey, Chuck, who's the guy with you?" I asked.

"My roommate, Jimmy, rents a room from me. He's a waiter at Lime Inn. It's where we're going for dinner tonight." Chuck stopped Boddington and me and grinned. "Ha, what a sight, hold it right there," and raised his camera.

I wore Tommy Bahama silk short pants, a short sleeve, a light green Clergy shirt, and my new, mud-stained reef walkers. Boddington wore a top hat with a turkey feather in the band and a brown tuxedo jacket over a ruffled white shirt. Elk whistler tooth cufflinks adorned his sleeve cuffs. His Tuxedo lapels showed some wear at their edges. Knobby Knees peeked out from under his short-hemmed Tuxedo pants and above black Buckaroo cowboy boots (with a Bowie knife tucked inside the right one.) He carried himself with his usual posture of confidence.

"Love the Tux, Boddington," Chuck said.

"Yessir, she was my Dad's for most of his weddings."

"Most of his weddings? How many have there been?" Chuck asked.

"Seven or eight, I lost count. After momma died, he kinda went nuts and started marrying any bitch who would say yes. As far as the Tux goes, he said I could have it, says he's done with women."

"What about Ramona's family? Why aren't they here?" Chuck asked.

"Parents killed in a car wreck a few years back. She's got a younger sister, got all strung out on heroin after the wreck. Nobody knows if she's alive or dead." We stumbled and sweated down a twisting path into the welcome shade of trees. I could hear small waves on the shore and talk and laughter behind the trees.

Boddington nervously asked me on the way down, "Am I doin the right thing, ya know, marrying Ramona?

"Nope. Getting married is always a mistake."

"What? Shit, man I wasn't expecting that."

"Buddy, she is batshit crazy...so are you. The only question is whether you are willing to live with her version of and degree of craziness for the rest of your life?"

"Well, I figure she is willin' to put up with mine."

"Alright then, welcome to the Folly a Deux club. If being with her makes you happier than being without her, and if you are willing to grow with her through time, perhaps to the point of her outgrowing the need to be with you, then you are doing the right thing."

"Sure, I guess."

"Well, if you aren't sure, think about it now. You don't want to end up in a courtroom with Baine looking down at you."

"This is gonna be it man, my one and only marriage. I ain't gonna be like my dad and do this every few years with some bar bitch. This apple is falling far into another county."

"I understand, amigo. Speaking of him, why didn't he come down for the wedding?"

"He said he was too busy with the ranch, couldn't get away. Besides, he's afraid of flying."

"Wow, not even for his only son's wedding?"

"Naw, he's a busy man," he said while holding his head up with too much confidence. I let it go.

"I guess we're your family now," I said, gently patting him on the back.

"Damn straight."

The trail ended at a deserted cove, perhaps fifty yards in length, and hemmed in on three sides by jungle. The sun was about two fists above the horizon and would be hitting the sea to the left of St. Thomas in a few minutes. I took charge. "Alright, everybody, shoes off and in the water."

Ramona wore a short veil covering the back of her shoulders and a knee-high white dress with a minimum of lace and white nylons. She held a bouquet of vibrant tropical flowers. In her earlobes hung dime-sized black pearl stud earrings that Boddington had presented to her before we left. As we approached the water, I held Boddington back, "Hey, don't forget to remove the boots, don't want 'em ruined by the saltwater."

"Bullshit," he said and walked into the water. "I always said I'd get married and buried in my boots. It's how I'm doin' it. Let's put this show on the road", and found his place, mid-calf deep in the water next to Ramona. Everybody else stood as couples except for Rosie, who stood on the opposite side of Ramona from Boddington. Chuck stood next to Jimmy, who started to weep when I began speaking. Chuck handed him his handkerchief. Baine and Jessica stood further apart than any of the other couples. I positioned myself so as not to have the sun in anybody's eyes.

I began, "We are gathered here this evening, knee-deep in Nature's softness, in the presence of God, friends and a few voyeuristic fish, to join Boddington and Ramona in holy wedded matrimony...." Chevali had his movie camera rolling before we got into the water. Once I started speaking, he kissed the side of Chiara's head and left her while shooting a grinning selfie, then paned back to the rest of us.

-14-

I Can See Clearly

The Lime Inn was a large, open-air restaurant with no inn attached. Its green, slanted roof opened to the West, the ocean view obscured by rusted roofs and FEMA tarped buildings. Laughter, conversations, and plates clanking all mingled and bounced off the hard-tin ceiling. The owner, a one-armed gentleman, mopped his face with a towel slung over a shoulder as he greeted us. "Chuck, a pleasure to see you. Is this your family?"

"Some of them, yes. The smart-looking ones are their friends," he said as he slapped my head.

"Hi, I'm Chuck's brother-in-law, Ky. I was hired by his father to inject some brains into the family gene pool."

"Pleasure to meet you, sir. It seems as though you have taken on a prodigious project," he said while smiling at Chuck.

"Well, a thimble into the ocean still raises the sea level a bit," I said.

Jimmy took our drink orders and distributed two orange and white cans of OFF. Before he could recite the menu specials, Boddington interrupted, "Hold on, my friend, if it's alright with everybody, I'm gonna order for the lot of us." He raised his eyebrows to everybody around the table.

Jimmy said, "OK, Dr. Boddington, what will it be?" As he spoke, we took turns drenching our feet and ankles with the OFF. It smelled like summer vacation.

"First, I don't want to even think about food until we're done with our third round of drinks. Then I want the man of each couple to have an enormous damn steak, rare, and the women each get one of them biggest ugliest lobsters your boys got in the back. I'm talking about them spiny bastards, the size of my forearm," he paused and gazed around the table, "y'all can share. Then for dessert, I want a couple bottles of your oldest Porto, I'm talking the good shit, and if ya ain't got any, y'all got time to send a boy to the liquor store. I'd prefer a Graham's thirty-year-Old Tawney as a minimum."

Jimmy raised his eyebrows, "I'll see what I can find in the back of our cellar," and turned as if to move off.

"Whoah little fella, I ain't done yet." Jimmy turned back to face Boddington, who was leaning back on two legs of his chair. "For dessert, each of us to gets a big 'ol slice of your famous Lime Inn key lime pie and a hunk of your carrot cake."

"Very well," Jimmy said as his pen hurriedly scratched his order pad.

"Now, let this party commence." Boddington picked up his water glass, threw his head back to drink, and his top hat fell off, tumbling to the floor. "I'm gonna need me stampede string for this here sombrero," he scanned the room, then down to Ramona's legs. "Honey, I'm askin ya for a fashion sacrifice tonight."

"What's that?" She asked cautiously.

"You got any squirrel covers under them stockings?" He waived his water glass toward her lap, spilling cold condensation on her legs, making her jump.

"Yes, why?"

"Can I have 'em?"

"My underwear, here?"

"No, them white stockings. They gotta be hot as hell."

"They are. I'm dying in them." She ducked a bit, cautiously scanning the restaurant. "What do you want them for?"

"I need me a stampede string, don't want my sombrero getting' lost to head gesticulations. It's got sentimental value as of an hour ago."

"Please don't ruin them. They are Victoria's Secret and cost me a fortune."

"I'll guard them with my life."

Ramona wiggled her nylons off under the table while a conservative appearing couple at the adjacent table watched disapprovingly. Finally, she handed them to Boddington, "You sure about this? We are in a fancy restaurant."

"No problem, honey, I got 'er under perfect control." He extricated the large knife from his boot, and the woman at the other table gasped and started rattling her husband. He took a side glance at Boddington and tucked his chin to his chest, pretending not to look.

"You aren't gonna cut them, please, you promised," Ramona asked quietly.

"Nope, ain't cutting 'em. Just makin' my chapeau ready to accommodate 'em", and plunged his knife into his top hat right above where each ear would be. He positioned the nylon's crotch at the back of the hat, rolled it tightly, and ran a leg through each new slit. The nylon legs dangled, Beagle-like in front of his ears until he pulled them under his chin and tied a large white bow.

"Now this sombitch ain't goin' nowhere. Where's them

drinks at? I want a test run with a shot of Jack. See if she holds," he said while patting his hat. Ramona leaned in to speak to a beaming Boddington, and their eyes met. Her eyes closed for a brief second. She smiled at him, remained word-less, and picked up her water, taking a slow pull.

I moved my attention from my friends to regard the sur-rounding strangers. Sound faded into an indistinguishable fuzz of voices, music, and laughter. I watched the wait staff and owner move with honey bee efficiency bouncing from table to table, serving food, and watering the oblivious eat-ers and drinkers. The customers all turned into mouths. Most open and moving with food shoveled into some variation of a smile, then wiped with stained paper napkins. They drank from condensation wetted glasses, and if the ice had suffi-ciently melted, their teeth appeared oversized and distorted, magnified through the bottom of their glasses. Some floated tiny bits of lobster or pie or bread into the water that they then drank with the next gulp. Their upper lips were all sweating. A few had bouncing cigarettes hanging out, contaminating the air around them.

"Earth to Ky, earth to Ky." Rosie's voice pulled me back from the world of mouths. "Where'd you go?" Conversations, soft Afro-pop music, and the smells of the garlic and fish and bread came back to my consciousness. "Hey baby, just taking it all in. You know all these guys are here because of you." I responded, gesturing to our friends.

"What do you mean?" Rosie asked.

"How did they all hear about this place? You and Jessica came down here and returned home with pictures and stories. Your descriptions of these islands painted pictures in their heads, leading to it becoming their dream to fulfill. Your words whetted their appetites for an adventure to come down here. Kinda cool, huh?"

"Yeah, what about you? It wasn't your dream to come here. Are you OK with it? Do you kinda like it at all? I know it's not Hawaii." She had a special pleading in her soft eyes that were showing her age. The formerly firm skin that surrounded her blue eyes now winkled at the edges. Sun damage freckles occupied what had been flawless fields of collagen-rich Teutonic beauty in her youth. I held her eyes with mine, knowing too that I was not twenty-one. There are moments where your partner's flaws are selfishly disappointing. At other times like this, those inevitable changes that could have otherwise been a negative become something to love deeply. Her physical flaws had developed as our lives grew together in happiness, arguments, physical pain, and pleasure. Neither of my dysfunctional parents ever told me that it would be possible to love my wife's imperfections. I held her warm and sweaty hand and gave it a slight pulse. At that point, we could have been sitting in the New Delhi dump, and I would have said the same thing to her, "I love this place because you are here with me."

She leaned in and kissed me harder and longer than I would typically be comfortable with in public. I expected someone to interrupt us with a chastising remark, none came. I slowly pulled my lips from her mouth, noticed Chuck smiling at us, and he dropped his gaze as if in guilt. A strange ending to a profound moment. I expected him to have a girlfriend and wondered why he was alone. He'd gained a lot of weight but still projected his perpetually self-reliant and cheerful personality. He seemed to be, as had always been the case, loved by everybody in his sphere. His attention shifted to the far side of the room, following something. I could only see loud, happy tourists and waiters. I asked Rosie, "Does Chuck seem lonely to you?"

"I've wondered the same thing."

"I am a little worried about him. Do you think it bothers him to be in a group of couples, being the only single person?" Rosie asked.

"Rosie, you and I are the only married couple here. The others are single and screwing."

"That's unnecessarily cynical, and besides, Boddington and Ramona are married."

"Fine, for one grand hour. As far as Jeb and Chiara go, she's the vacation piece, and I'm not sure she doesn't have the same feelings or lack thereof for him," I said.

"She and I had a pleasant talk today. She really is a good girl, a toughie. I like her a lot."

"It's obvious you like her. That tongue swap last night had me a little worried that you might start batting for the other team.

"Oh Ky, that was innocent girl fun. It meant nothing. Girls can do that kind of thing, and it's totally fine."

"Innocent? If I kissed Jeb like that, you'd cut my nuts off. Hell, come to think of it, I'd cut my own nuts off."

"You sound a little worried about yourself, Dr. Elliott."

"Not funny. Like I was saying, take Baine and Jessica for instance. They are an oil and water cocktail if there ever was one. For starters, she has a personality."

"Oh, stop, at least he treats her well."

"I'm serious, Rosie. He is so damn boring. To her credit, she can stop being a Junior leaguer for a while and let loose down here. Her hair is messy and look at her tits. Have you ever seen Jessica without a bra on in Colorado? She even has nipples, look. But Baine, he's just a boring dipshit."

Baine wore a purple Izod golf shirt buttoned tight to his neck, and his collar turned up. Jessica held his hand between a glass of water and a plate of half-eaten bread, leaning in the opposite direction from him and laughingly engaging Chuck. Baine, his face reddened by the sun and slack from drinking light beer, was giving a slurred monologue to a disinterested appearing Chiara.

I leaned forward and turned my attention to him. "Doc Martins? Baine said, "Arch support is for wimps. Give me a pair of paisley Fluevogs on a tan foot, and I'm in heaven. Did you catch Madonna wearing those four inchers in Truth or Dare? The way they made her project her stride, whew, that was sexy. Can you imagine the lucky person who gets to do her pedis? Who do you like to wear when you go out, ya know, on those little black dress nights? I could see you in a simple but elegant pair of Steve Madden's loafer pumps. Normally I think any woman who wears spandex should have to obtain a license, but Steve-M really brought spandex to such a brave new world of dress shoes. I prefer a higher heel. But these days, those damn lesbian sensible shoes have influenced the market, and the low spark of high heel boys may be on the way out. I hope not. Goddamn rug munchers." He dropped his head as if in mourning.

"Why *woulda* you care so much about women's shoes?" Chiara asked.

"The perfect shoe," Blaine continued, "on a paradisiacal foot is a full-grain safe, guarding unimagined treasures. When divorcing couples come into my courtroom, I know each of "their stories by their shoes. Who has class, who is a dirtbag, white-collar, blue-collar, who can afford the most alimony, and who probably deserves it. Shoes say more than spread-sheets to me. Who cheated on whom? I have a little game with myself."

He droned on, talking to the side of Chiara's head. "I check his and her shoes under the respondent and plaintiff tables. I look at their attorney's shoes too and know who charges more per hour, just by their shoe choice. Anyway, I bet with myself on whether it was the man or the woman who was the cheater by their shoes, really. The cheating women usually have pumps with a little too much wear on the edges. Believe it or not, it's not the red pumpers who are the cheaters. The red pumpers are feeling insecure because their husband is boinking the secretary. To regain some level of attractiveness after fart-ing out a half dozen kids, they wear those new, too shiny red pumps. The men in penny loafers are always the rapscallions. They're trying too hard to dress conservatively, and God forbid if they have committed the crime of putting a penny in the little front pocket. I sock it to them. If they want to flaunt their stu-pidity, I let them wear it, so to speak."

He laughed to himself, drained his light beer, and held it up to a waitress who wasn't even serving our table, "Garson, Garson, un otro por fevor." She sneered down at him with a look of having scraped something off the bottom of her shoe and said, "I'll tell your waiter you want another."

"Merci buckets," he said and turned back to Chiara who was tugging on Chevali's shirt for help. Baine continued talk-ing to the back of her head, "Where was I, oh yes, loafers. The only exception to the loafer rule is the Gucci tasseled. They speak of an understated devotion to class...."

"Did you hear that bullshit?" I asked Rosie.

"What a weirdo, I had no idea. Poor Jessica," she said.

"No kidding. What the hell does she see in him?"

"Fashion consultant?" Rosie said.

"I guess I better remove the penny from the front of my loafers but come to think of it, they are Gucci tasseled. I'm safe."

"Ky, the day you trade in your Lucchese boots for tasseled loafers is the day we end up in front of Baine in court."

"Not food for thought," I said. "Speaking of food..."

The majority of the waitstaff followed Jimmy, loaded with plates of steaming food. Behind them, a waitress strained under a huge tray of drinks, rattling with ice and Baine's light beer.

Boddington stood and addressed the table. His top hat was secure with Ramona's white pantyhose in a bow beneath his chin. Hand hemmed tuxedo shorts exposed his pale legs inside his tall boot tops, "Y'all, this is just too damn good for words," his eyes got misty, "just too good. Please join us in our first meal as a married couple, we love y'all." He sat and mopped his eyes with the table cloth. "Now, eat." He cast his gaze downward as Ramona hugged him, rocking him side to side. I knew that the only thing that could ever make that man teary was love.

The conversations ran to comments about the food and the day's sunset ceremony. Couples shared fork loads of beef and lobster and drinks between them. After clearing the dinner plates, Jimmy appeared with a bottle of Port and poured a small taste for Boddington, "Cockburn's Aged Tawney 1955 Vintage Port." A tip of his well-secured top hat signaled that it was drinkable. I faked a smile when Jimmy poured me a glass. I had never been much of a Port drinker. My first obligatory sip of the thick, red-brown stuff opened a new world of subtle sweet flavors that developed in my mouth. The floral flavors jolted me to pause and pay attention to my sense of taste, as I had rarely done before. It was like drinking the best dessert I had ever eaten. "Rosie, holy hell, can you believe this stuff?"

"Wow, I think I'm in love." She inhaled through closed teeth and took another sip.

"I don't EVER want to be a snob about anything, OK maybe Harleys, but after this, I think I could become a Portoholic."

Boddington and Baine extolled the Port's virtues in a language the left me happily alone with my glass. "About anything grown in the Douro Valley in the mid to late fifties would get my vote," Baine said.

"If they had any on this little island, I'd like to find me a crisp Touriga Franca, but I'm thinkin' our choices might be a little limited by geography," Boddington said, swirling his glass and holding it up to a distant street light alive with swarming insects.

"I've gotten into LBVs in the last few years. None hold up to an Aged Vintage like Grahams, but I find them fun with winter desserts." Baine was ignoring his light beer for the first time in the evening. "This vintage is begging for a fluffy pastry. What did you order for dessert?" Baine asked.

"Well, I couldn't make my mind up about goin' sweet or tart, so I said screw it, I only get married once and ordered one of each. Everybody gets Key lime pie and Carrot cake." Boddington swung his head away from Baine to address Ramona. His roll-job of concealing Ramona's panty portion of his impromptu stampede string unfurled like a flag and draped over the back of his neck. He was oblivious and kept talking. Every time he swung his head, the panty portion of her stockings fluttered out, making him appear as though he were a French Foreign legionnaire.

"That was the best chow I've eaten years," Boddington said as he opened his shirt and rubbed his belly. I stopped Jimmy and asked him to calculate himself a generous tip and bring the check to me. He smiled and said, "That has already been taken care of by the gentleman sitting next to Chuck." Chevali smilingly nodded to me, elevated his delicate port glass with his middle finger extended toward me, and sipped.

The Boddingtons left, and Chuck led us to a dingy bar across the street called Fred's place. The hand-painted sign out front was an obvious target for drunk spitters who left a residue that provided for a healthy colonization by bacteria and fungi. The bar's bare concrete floor was below street level and guarded against flooding by a high curb that required traversing to descend the concrete steps down into the bar. It was typical St John construction with an uninsulated roof of dark brown 2x4 cross beams arranged in a disorganized lattice to support rusting tin corrugated steel sheets. It couldn't have held the weight of a man. Staples held black cloth insulated wires to the wood lattice over the two-car garage-sized dance floor lit by bare bulbs. Military-green walls echoing the harsh bare bulb light gave the back room an uninviting glow.

The actual bar was dark stained and chipped plywood, six feet in length, and stood diagonally in a corner. Behind the bar, a stubby shelf clung to the wall by corroded brass brackets at head height, supporting a half dozen cheap off-brand booze bottles. A Heineken logoed ice chest beside the bar contained beers floating in an ice slurry, which the bartender scooped into plastic glasses with his bare hands for mixed drinks. Painfully loud music conjured up visions of pissed-off men beating metal trash cans with spoons and singing in a staccato nasal whine ricocheted off unadorned walls. A middle-aged West Indian couple danced to a mysterious beat hidden within the music with their drinks swaying in front of them. The man's bald head bowed down, and his eyes closed as he shuffled back and forth in worn flip flops. She faced him smiling, chin in the air, swaying her Volkswagen fender hips side to side. The simplicity of the scene was somehow tender.

"They changed dance nights to Tuesday and Friday. We'll come back then. They bring in bands from all over the Caribbean. This place can really rock." Chuck yelled to us. I had a hard time imagining this place being anything but a mosquito feeding ground, even if they could import live music. I turned to Chevali, "Any desire to hang here?"

"Fuck no. I'm done drinking and could go for a swim. I'm sweating my nuts off."

"We're outa here, and Thank you, amigo," I said to Chuck.

"I'm going to stay here and wait for Jimmy to get off work, gotta give him a ride home," he said, pulling a Heineken from the ice chest. "You want to go diving in the morning, Hoot?"

"Hell yes, I didn't come all the way here to sit on a beach. What time?"

"I'll pick you up at 7:30. Anybody who wants to go needs to have their shit ready by then."

"Done, I'll ask around and herd the cats," I said, and I held out my hand to him. His hand was wet and cold from his beer, "Hey man, I appreciate you taking the time to play travel guide for this group of weirdos. I know you have a life and a business to run."

He smiled, showing his yellowed teeth, and said, "When we... I come to Colorado. I'm going to expect the same outa your ass."

"Consider it a fete accompli." He looked confused, and I said, "Done deal, amigo." He nodded his frayed baseball cap bill at me.

An ocean-scented breeze attempted in vain to cool us on the walk back to Tamarindo. A humid puff can only do so much cooling if it's 80 degrees. The concrete road glowed faintly as the shifting light from a shy Waxing Gibbous teased the night's darkness by peeking from behind boofy, drifting clouds. Their corpulent violet profiles poked holes in the background spray of stars. Waving palm shadows swept the miles of braided black tar used to fill decades of concrete road cracks. Sherman tank cockroaches challenged me for the right of way, but I had no desire to inflict any more cockroach guts on my new Reef Walkers. The satisfying crunch would not be worth the infectious aftermath. I stopped at Sandy the Rottweiler's cave and called to her. A low rumbling growl transformed into a whine as she erupted from the darkness to run between my legs. At my urging, she followed us home.

Except for Baine, we peeled off our sweaty clothes at Tamarindo's poolside and waded into the refreshing pool. Baine said he was going upstairs to watch CNN. Music drifted uphill, wavering loud, then soft on the warm air currents that swirled between town and us. Coqui frogs sang with it, never keeping tempo. The chlorine-scented pool water reflected the moon's light on wandering wavelets. I could easily make out multiple pairs of white breasts through the water, ramblingly distorted with the water's chop. Strangely, they were more beautiful than sexual.

"*Whata* the hell was that?" Chiara asked, scooting closer to Chevali. Jessica was to his right and snuggled as close to him as Chiara. He spoke to me by leaning around Jessica. "Ky, did you see that at the far end of the pool, toward town? Watch the water's surface... wait."

I ducked deeper until covering my mouth with pool water. Wavelets bounced up to lick my nose, and I instinctively pushed Rosie behind me and held motionless to observe the invader. On the town-side of the pool, a skittering black form dropped to the water's surface in an erratic flight pattern and then disappeared into the blackness. Two more fluttered down, skimmed the pool surface, and split into different directions. One jittered over my head, revealing the distinctive form of bat wings. *Bats in St. John?*

"Bats drinking from the pool," I said, almost not believing myself.

"There aren't any goddamn bats down here. How the hell would they get here?" Chevali expressed my thinking.

"I have no idea unless they hitchhiked in your wallet," I said.

"Or in your ass, no wait, that would be gerbils."

"No matter how they got here, there are more, look," I said.

I rotated my head back and inhaled the night sky deeply into my lungs and brain, wishing that moment never to end. Rosie slid from behind me and ran her hand across my low abdomen as she sidled up next to me. "They won't bite us, right?" I put my right arm around her shoulders. "Why the hell would they bite us? They eat bugs." I said as I ran my fingers into Chevali's hair, "Oh shit, shit, it's on you, duck." Rosie screamed and smashed her face into the water as he honked and jumped sideways. I may have broken the peace of the evening.

"Nice job, ass wipe." Chevali snapped.

Jessica said, "With that, I'm going to bed if I can pull Baine away from the TV." Rosie and Chiara followed her out of the pool. A little later, I heard Jessica pleading with Baine to come to bed. He said something about NATO airstrikes in Bosnia and having to watch the videos. Jessica's wet feet slapped off in short hard steps.

"I'm not ready for bed. You feel like a cigar? I brought a few Cohibas back from my last medical mission to Cuba." Chevali asked.

"Great, I'll fetch some rum," and got out of the pool to discover that the girls had taken all our clothes. "Hey amigo, we haven't any clothes. You may want to find one of your speedos, so the bats don't think that your pecker is a little grub and try to eat it?"

"Nope, I'm happy to let the night air dry my naked ass." He said with open arms as if inviting the night to embrace him.

"Sounds good to me," I replied, thinking that sitting naked with another man wasn't usually my style, but with him, I was fine. He was vociferous about his chosen sexual proclivity. In the past, we'd shared tents, hot springs, and hotel rooms. I wasn't worried as we sat in the featureless, cloud-filtered moonlight on nylon webbed loungers, drinking rum and smoking Cohibas. Above us, purple-edged clouds reflected the lights of Cruz Bay off their puffy underbellies, casting soft-edged shadows of the deck furniture. I could barely make out his face unless he was pulling on his cigar, illuminating him.

Thinking about the day's wedding, I asked, "You ever going to get married?"

"Been there, done that, never-a-fucking-gain." He answered, shaking his head, and making his cigar tip glow what appeared like a smile in the dark.

"I never knew you'd been married."

"Yeah, great woman, Shirley. I think I may have actually loved her."

"You don't know? When was this?" I asked.

"We got married the summer before med school."

"What about now, any chance of things progressing with Chiara?"

"Hell no, she's just the vacation slam piece. I made sure she knew that before we even bought plane tickets. No illusions, and she's fine with it."

"Lucky you. But seriously, you're never gonna marrying again?"

"Nooo, marriage is what stupid men do to try to ensure that the woman they're with won't screw anybody else. Men don't like other men porking their women, right? Besides, all marriage does is ensure the financial future of greedy divorce attorneys and judges like dumbshit in there." He pointed with his cigar at Baine.

"Ya think it's that bleak?" I asked, thinking about Rosie.

"I've screwed more married women than single, and for eighty percent of them, their husbands were cheating too. It's what humans do, I know. I'm a shrink. I don't give a shit about how educated they are or what kind of car they drive. Humans are all just furry little animals who will eventually succumb to the drive of their id."

"Maybe so, but don't want your best friend hanging with you forever?" I felt naive the second I asked the question.

"That's why I have Mavis." Mavis was his black lab.

"The forever monogamous marriage is unmaintainable post-Victorian bullshit. Think about it, when the church came up with the 'until death do us part' bullshit, the average Roman

man lived to be in his late twenties, and the average woman lived into her teens. There was a fifty percent mortality rate every time she farted out a kid. So, men weren't stuck with the same woman for decades, only a few years at worst." He sat up and threw a leg around each side of the lounge, and faced me.

"Look at it this way, when you get married, all you do is put everything that you have ever worked for and will ever earn in terms of alimony risk in the hands of assholes like Baine. Shit, did you see him the other day doing her fucking toenails by the pool? For God's sake, doing her nails in front of other men? I guarantee you that he hasn't had regular sex in months. They've been together for a couple of years, right?"

"Yeah, I think so," I answered.

"I get more sex in a week than he gets in a year, and he has to endure all of her whining and demanding. At around six months, I'd bet she started laying down the rules. After that, he had to ask for sex rather than simply screwing her like he used to. He's afraid of making her mad and never getting any, so now he asks. Once she has him asking for it, he's sunk because she no longer respects him. Their sex becomes measured and boring. She occasionally doles out unenthusiastic sex just to keep him around. But while they are making unpassionate "love," he held his fingers up, making air quotation marks at making love, "they each remember the past grunting, screaming, farting, swearing and headboard banging fucking. Right? Back then, her ass wouldn't hit the mattress for half an hour straight. Now, if he sweats on her, she wipes it off with an eeeewww, making him feel even more like shit. She used to scream in orgasm, but now she holds her breath to hide it, not showing her pleasure so he won't ask for it too often."

He was depressing me. *It's a good thing he didn't go into marriage counseling.*

"She'll probably cheat on him since she's lost all respect for him. She's tamed him with the same pussy that they're both bored with now."

"Jeez, you aren't in the least bit cynical. All bullshit aside, ya gotta believe in love, right? You said you loved your wife years ago. What happened to her, the marriage?"

"Oh, I loved her, but she caught me porking the housekeeper in the bathroom one day when she came home early from tennis. Kind of a bad scene. She beat the shit out of both of us with a wet mop."

I couldn't help but laugh at the visual image, "You said you loved her, so why were you doing the housekeeper?" He took a long hit from his cigar, "What's love got to do with it? Sure, I loved her, but every time that bitch bent over to clean the dog hair off the floor, I just had to try it, ya know. It's like all those islands out there." He gestured with his cigar to the darkness, and glowing embers fell in an arc around him. "No matter how amazing this Island is, don't you wonder what each of those is like? I loved Shirley, but the housekeeper's ass called to me like Bali Hai in that old play."

"Eh, you think you're capable of falling in love again?"

"Sure. I fall in love every few months. I love Chiara right now. When we go home, I doubt I'll ever call her again. All women, even Chiara, want to tame their men with sex. It's what they do. He flicked his cigar toward the West again, "Every woman I've ever screwed, humped like minks until they thought I was tamed. That's when the physical affection dried up, and they started expecting me to clean their poodle's puke off the carpet at 3 AM while they slept, rather than screwing. Never again."

"You've put a lot of thought into this, haven't you?"

"Yes, specifically, so I don't end up with my dick in one hand and a toenail paintbrush in the other like him," he said, pointing to Baine, who was asleep on the couch. I sat back in my lounge chair and thought about what Chevali had said. I was embarrassed by thinking he was at least minimally correct. He was cynical and jaded but seemed happy.

"What's the deal with Jess and you? She's been after your ass for years, and you always give her the straight arm. She's in fantastic shape, pretty, and I'll bet she could go a round or two. Hell, I'd take a shot at her if I wasn't married."

"She is the epitome of unattractive to me." He talked through cigar smoke exhalation. "Not that she isn't physically attractive, she is, but I couldn't stand having to listen to her. All she talks about is politics, religion, expensive cars, and golf. The sex wouldn't be worth it. Poke her a couple of times, and you'd be having to attend Junior League Charity Balls and political fundraisers, let alone having to put up with her feeling guilty and religious on Sundays. Sunday is my favorite fucking day, and she would be trying to drag us off to church. No way. Take Baine. I'd bet his nuts haven't bounced off her pretty little chin in over a year."

"That visual made my cigar not feel good in my mouth," I said.

"At least it doesn't have a scrotum."

"But she is attractive. That would account for something, right?" I asked.

"Dude, having a pretty woman who won't screw is like having a Porsche that you can't drive, sitting in your garage. Ya gotta make payments, wash and wax it, pay insurance, all to just stare at it and wish you were inside of it. Screw that. Trade it in for a Chevy that you can play with, have fun in, even if it has a little wider trunk."

I rubbed my cigar out on the concrete deck. "Alright, it's been a long day. Are you guys going diving in the morning with us?"

"Do ya think it'll be an easy dive? It's been a couple of years."

"I'm hoping so, the train leaves at 7:30 sharp. Have all your diving shit ready on the front porch. But for now, what do we do with him?" I pointed to Baine, asleep on the couch. TV flickers made him seem to be moving.

"Let me handle this," he said and walked to the porchlight. Using the night as camouflage, he captured a gecko that was stalking a moth.

"No, man," I whispered. He flapped his hand at me, reached in the door, and threw the gecko on Baine's face. I expected him to jump and scream. But instead, he twitched as the gecko climbed down his chin onto his neck while Baine talked to himself.

A crooked smile came to Chevali's face, "Why can't they have snakes on this island?"

I went downstairs to find Rosie asleep with her glasses low on her nose and a book on her chest. Sandy slept on the floor next to her. I laid down and watched the fan circle around over our heads. The rhythmic clanking of cable halyards on aluminum sailboat masts in the bay and coquis singing, petted me to sleep.

-15-

ONE DROP

One of the reasons I ostensibly go on vacation is to tempo-rarily lead a lifestyle that does not include jumping out of bed and scrambling to start the day. The morning's boat traffic in the harbor was the only human sound wafting through the bedroom louvered windows. I rolled on my side to see Rosie looking at me with one eye open, no expression on her face.

"Ready for a diving adventure?" I asked.

"I don't know...you?"

"Hell yeah. My only question is about Chuck."

"What do you mean?" She was talking with her face still half-buried in the white pillowcase, so only half of her mouth was moving. It made her uphill cheek puff out with each syllable.

"Have you spoken to him about starting us with a gentle dive? You know how he likes to do everything, balls-out, hair on fire. Jeb was concerned too," I said.

She continued to puff-talk. "When he took Jessica and me diving before, it was usually easy shore dives. Did he mention to you where he was thinking of going today?"

"Yeah, the Flintstone house? Have you done that dive be-fore with him?" I asked.

The pillowcase was working its way into the corner of her mouth, and she spat it out. "Uh, I don't remember."

"Oh well, a cartoon dive sounds easy, right?" I was confident in Chuck's appreciation of our dearth of diving time in Colorado.

The Boddingtons, not being divers, stayed behind while the rest of us jammed our bodies and gear into the little pink and white topped pickup. Rosie drove, and Chuck gave directions while we traversed the island to the Coral Bay side. From the steep, narrow road that wound out of town, I looked down at St Thomas and smaller islands floating on cerulean seas beyond her. Sailboats with triangular white sails preceded small wakes, while chunkier powerboats left long white "V" shaped expanding wakes that braided the waters between the islands. FEMA tarps covered many of the town's roofs. The roadside foliage was a vibrant light green at the tips of the bushes and trees, but the undergrowth was a brown and broken web. Hiking would be impossible without a chainsaw.

Adiabatically cooled air at the island's crest cooled me. Seductively captivating islands meandered in dark blue waters to the Southeast. I thought about Chevali's comparing islands to yet unconquered women, and I mentally ravaged each before moving on to the next. I could have easily been an islomaniac he-slut.

A couple of smaller bays indented Coral bay's jagged "U" shape, probable hideout bays for pirates only a couple of hundred years ago. Steep hillsides held the colorfully painted concrete block houses clinging to them. Any significant seismic activity could send them tumbling like the remains of splintered wooden homes amongst the slopes. Chuck would later point out how the wind from Marilyn blew the wooden houses off their foundations and rolled them along the hillsides.

Some survived the trip intact to end up lying on their sides. Others left a trail of wood siding, house chunks, and furniture smudged into the foliage for hundreds of feet. Concrete one lane roads wound serpentine coils uphill from the main road at the water's edge to their empty concrete pads. The bay held a dozen sailboats, moored and facing Southeast like fiberglass soldiers at attention. Less lucky boats littered the shorelines, remnants of Marilyn's tempestuous savagery.

Chuck's rental powerboat in Cruz bay was new and clean. It felt safe. She had wooden SCUBA tank holders inside her port wall and a blue canvas top to shade the captain. Before casting off, I attached everybody's SCUBA regulators to the aluminum tanks and honked each one with a short punch of the regulator's purge valve.

"Hey, there are only six tanks. Did we forget one?" I asked Chuck.

"Nope, six is right."

"Who's not diving?"

He peered at me through half-closed eyes and motioned with them to Baine, who was trying to squish his flabby frame into a wetsuit. "Hey Baine, you might want to hold on putting that on. It's a long hot ride to the dive site," he said.

"What's he going to do?" I asked Chuck.

"Jessica said he's claustrophobic and afraid of diving. He wants to snorkel above us while we dive. I told him that we're going to be a way's out to sea where it could get rough," he said.

"This ought to make for some fun watching, I said."

"I hope I don't have to rescue his claustrophobic ass."

Chuck carefully idled through the bay, weaving around different types of boats. Older, poorly maintained boats displayed wooden gunwales sadly faded and splintered by a relentless tropical sun. Their windows, dulled with dried salt spray. The rare, properly maintained vessels shone with well-polished chrome and wood, coiled ropes laid at strategic points for sail hoisting. Their sails were neatly rolled and tied with clean white ropes that securely bound them to booms. Small windmills attached to the boats spun noisily, generating electricity for the evening's blender. Tan, wrinkled boat owners waved while holding their breakfast Caribes and Bloody Marys.

Once we were clear of the watery parking lot, Chuck called for everybody to hang on and gunned the throttle. The boat's engines rumbled confidently until the hull planed to a flat angle of attack. Sometimes she slapped an oncoming wave, and the force caused our heads to bob in unison as if we were at a rock concert. Waves noisily slamming the hull stopped all conversation. I sat to the aft and held my hand over the edge. The hissing water against the hull peppered my hand, throwing it backward. My mind echoed back to Colorado and the mountains of paperwork piling up daily, and an anticipated unpleasant cross-examination by a hostile Insurance lawyer my first week back from vacation. I was dreading it and wanted to slide over the side of the speeding boat and disappear. The visual images caused hot acid to etch my stomach walls, intentionally left empty for the morning's boat ride.

Coral Bay's Earl Grey tinted water made the thought of swimming in it uninviting. Beyond the bay's mouth, the ocean turned a deep blue that could be meters to miles deep, calming and simultaneously foreboding. SCUBA diving in water where I can't see the seafloor from the boat made me feel like a fish lure.

Chuck backed off the throttle and pulled me back to the boat, but I returned with a putrid stress to pollute the morning's purity. We slowed in calm waters within the shelter of a crescent-shaped bay behind a football stadium-sized island. Chuck commanded Chevali to cast the anchor off the bow and reversed the boat to a firm stop, ensuring a stable anchor bite into the sandy bottom. He threw a length of rope with an attached empty Clorox bottle as a float from the stern as a diver's "oh shit" rope in case caught in a stiff current when resurfacing after the dive. I felt comforted by his attention to detail.

The bay was a calm, translucent green. The boat's shadow wiggled in the sand twenty feet below us. I liked it. No toothy submarines would be breeching to send me flying like a South African seal. A mild Westerly wind rippled the surface, blowing rotating wavelets around the flat bay.

"What's the name of this Island?" I asked Chuck.

"It goes by two names, Flanagan and Witch Island. Legend has it that witches used it in the past for weird rituals, but when the U.S. took possession of it back in the 1970s, they changed the name to Flanagan. Locals still won't go near it. They say that lights move around it at night."

"Does anybody live on it?"

"No, it's a bird Nature Preserve. The Park Service guys are supposed to arrest anybody who sets foot on it, but the Rangers I know, hate to go near it. Just walking on it can bring you a nasty curse by the old witches."

"Huh, I feel sorry for the birds." Baine limply added.

"Why?" I asked.

"Because they're all going to get cursed," Baine said, wedging into his wet suit.

Chuck leaned into me and asked, "There is something the matter with him. Is he, like, socially retarded?"

"I don't know, Jessica likes him, and she's cool. Maybe it's the prestige of dating a judge?"

"I'm really glad he's not diving with us. I wouldn't want to be responsible for him underwater."

"Well, the good news is with a divorce judge tainting the water around us, the sharks will stay away."

"Or try to breed with him. In either event, he'll be a distraction for them." Chuck smiled.

"Anyway, thank you for taking us on such an easy first dive. The calm water seems so inviting," I said.

He cocked his head, looking confused at first, but then assumed a commanding presence and spoke. "The dive today is a little complicated. We're going to a dive spot called the Flintstone house. It's a group of gigantic rocks stacked up to resemble the old cartoon Flintstone house. Nobody knows how they got there, but it's worth the effort, trust me."

Chiara's eyes searched the waters of the bay. "Where is it? Can you see it from the boat?" She held her hand to her forehead, shading her eyes.

Chuck scowled at Rosie, "Didn't you tell them?"

Rosie grimaced, "Oops."

"Oops?" I repeated her word back to her.

"Since you all have been so well informed, let me clarify a few details about today's dive." Chuck paused and spoke at Rosie. "It's a tiny bit technical." This obvious understatement was not a good sign. *Shit*.

Chiara leaned over the gunwale and searched the waters around the boat. "It's not down there?"

"See those rocks off to the right of the island." Chuck pointed to a cluster of rocks a few car lengths to the South side of the island. They were steep, jagged, and stuck up about fifteen feet in the air. *Unclimbable.* "See the small waves breaking between them and the island. That's where we will snorkel to. If it's high tide, we can descend and squeeze through an underwater passage between the rocks and the island. From there, we go a few hundred feet toward Norman Island on the other side. At about sixty feet depth is the Flintstone house. It's really cool." Idle chatter stopped as expressions of concern spread to everyone's faces.

"Chuck, Chiara isn't very experienced. Are you sure this is the right dive for us?"

"Sure, I did it with Rosie and Jessica. No problem, huh Rosie?"

Rosie looked diffident and questioned Chuck, "As long as we have enough high tide to spare, we should be fine, right?"

I felt irritated with Rosie not telling me about the dive. "Enough high tide, oh please do tell?" I asked.

Chuck took over. "Fine, I kinda misjudged the tide and wave action last time. If we miss high tide or the waves are too big to swim through the passage, we can go around the point there." He pointed to the far side of the steep, offshore rocks. "It drops off sharply out there....and for completeness' sake, there have been a few tiger sharks spotted from time to time, which seem to, maybe sorta live there. High tide is just now hitting. It'll be fine."

Chevali and Chiara stood in the slowly rocking boat, mouthing words to each other. Baine stood with one arm in his wet suit, wobbling like an amputee seal. Adrenaline sent my mind back to my desire never to see Colorado, my office, my patients, or a courtroom ever again, and I said, smiling at everybody. "Like my great uncle, Crazy Horse said, today is a good day to die."

I spoke quietly to Rosie, "and for you, my sweetness, a vigorous ass paddling tonight for not telling me about the dive."

"I've got the ass if you've got the hand," she said and jumped into the water, "Throw my gear in so I can put it on."

We snorkeled above a rippled sandy bottom and a few scattered rocks and fish. Snorkeling on the surface with a SCUBA tank is hard work, but the water was the perfect temperature to keep me comfortable. Slowly, the bottom climbed closer, and the water grew choppier until Chuck stood, rotated his mask to the top of his head, and spat his snorkel out. His fins generated a cloud of sand that tumbled my way. We were headed into a strong current. Chiara couldn't touch the bottom and clung like a baby chimp to Chevali.

"You're gonna follow me in single file. The water is too rough to snorkel, so we'll use our SCUBA air for swimming through the channel. Be careful of sea urchins stabbing you, and on the other side is a healthy garden of fire coral, so try not to get washed into it." He stared beyond the churning water of the rocky channel rolling toward us from the pitching sea. I figured he was timing the incoming swell sets as the rhythmless waves bounced me backward in the water.

"Go NOW." Chuck pulled his mask down, stuffed his regulator into his mouth, and disappeared underwater. Rosie and the others followed him. Chiara was between them and me in last place.

I followed her at a depth of about six feet. The waves over

our heads churned air into the water, transforming the top four feet into turbulent white water. Chiara's buoyancy wasn't correct, and she repeatedly floated upward into the frantic upper froth, which pushed her flailing body back toward me with every surge. I saw her grabbing the sharp rocks, and I feared they were going to cut her ungloved hands. I had to do something, so I pushed her fins forward, attempting to give her a forward boost. She instinctively recoiled and stopped kicking, causing her to slam into me with one leg on either side of my head, knocking the regulator out of my mouth and filling my face with her squirming crotch. The thin alternating white, yellow, and green stripes of her minuscule bikini bottoms slid down my face mask and onto my open mouth. Despite being in a near-drowning incident, I saw the irony of answered prayers in that fleeting second. I regathered my regulator and breathed deeply.

I grabbed what I could of her wiggling body. With her ass cheeks in my right hand, low abdomen in my left, I simultaneously pushed her off my smile and rotated my body under hers with me facing up. We were mask to mask. I held her tightly in my arms and kicked furiously. My shoulders bounced off the rocks, and I envisioned them being shredded. Fortunately, my shoulder straps took most of the punishment. After dozens of fin strokes, we emerged from the channel, and I released her body but held her hand to prevent her from floating upward.

We found the others at a depth of about fifteen feet. At first, Rosie seemed focused on my holding Chiara's hand. I had no idea if she had seen us emerge from the rocky canyon in our tense face-to-face embrace. I intentionally let her go, allowing her to float upward, then pulled her back down like a balloon. A look of relief spread to Rosie's face. I was curious about her concern, considering that she had her tongue down Chiara's throat a few nights before at Woody's bar.

Chuck immediately read the situation, and like any well-equipped divemaster with a bunch of rookies, had extra weights in the pockets of his dive vest. He calmly took Chiara's hand, pulled her down, and let her float back up a couple of times while putting a couple of lead weights into her BCD vest pocket. Once she stopped bobbing upward, he rotated away from her, waived us onward, and swam away.

Large rock slabs covered in coral horns, tubs, and fans of red, orange, green littered the undulating seafloor. The fish acted disinterested but still swam just out of reach and kept one eye on me. Rainbow-colored parrot fish alternately chewed at the coral with oversized beak-like mouths and shit sand clouds. The sound of pounding waves gave way to the clicking of thousands of unseen shrimps and my exhalation bubbles. I made the concerted effort to slow my breathing, not wanting to run low on air. My air gauge showed that I had already used a third of my air. Rosie's pressure gauge indicated that she had a nearly full tank. She was taller than me, but I outweighed her by thirty pounds. It irritated me that we could do the same exercise underwater, and she used so little air.

I moved effortlessly underwater, comfortably insulated from everything that was above the sea surface. Forty-five feet of water sequestered me from Colorado, more than the thousands of air miles between it and me. The slow swaying sea fans in a light surge, the rhythm of my fins, and my controlled breathing profoundly soothed me. My perfectly adjusted buoyancy allowed me to swim inches from the bottom and let my knuckles lightly drag in the rough sand from limp arms.

We followed Chuck around a rock the size of a school bus and came upon four fox-faced spotted eagle rays slowly flapping their brown wings parallel to us. Their impossibly long tails also rode barely above the surface of the sand. We followed them up an embankment to a jumble of garage door-sized rock slices arranged against all odds to form a house of rock slabs. The house had four sides, each sticking up about six feet high from the sand, covered by a slab roof. The house was the size of an average bedroom. It had a sand floor and excellent views of rocks, sand, and resident fish from the doorway. I imagined a massive hurricane formed it by throwing twenty-ton rocks around like a kid making an underwater fort in a bathtub. I felt uneasy inside it and worried about an earthquake dislodging the roof stone and squashing me in the sand. I inspected the roof rock and noticed something swimming above us. My mind raced to tiger sharks, and I wanted to close and lock the nonexistent door.

It was Baine, bouncing on waves at the surface, arms and legs paddling frantically in opposite directions. The crystalline water visibility made him appear to float more like a gangly kite in the air than a swimmer peering down at us. Relentless waves battered him with a surface current, fortunately nudging him toward Which Island and not out to sea. I was happy to be underwater.

I checked my air gauge and motioned to Chevali. The excitement of the stone house had taken a toll on my controlled breathing. Chevali pulled his gauge up to his mask and swam to Chuck, pointing to it. He batted the top of Chevali's head and tapped his SCUBA tank with a bronze clasp to draw everybody's attention and signal the end to the dive.

I searched for Blaine on the surface again, but he was gone.

The swim back through the rocky channel required no kicking as the changing tide quickly propelled me past the narrow rock walls and spat me into the glassy calm little bay. Instinctively having to be responsible for everybody around me, I counted the divers. All accounted for, except for Baine. I could easily make out the underwater hull of our boat, lazily tugging on the anchor line in the middle of the bay. I surfaced to join the floating group and spoke to Jessica, "Have you seen Baine?"

"No, I lost sight of him right as we turned back."

I asked the other bobbing heads, "Has anybody seen Baine?"

Their heads all rotated, "*NO.*"

"Shit, Hoot, we gotta find him," Chuck said.

I switched from vacation mode into work mode and said, "You guys swim back to the boat and watch for him. Wait there until we return. If you see him, use the air horn, one single long blast if he is OK, three shorts if there is a problem. Does anybody know how to use the radio to call the Coast Guard for help if we need it?

The girls all shook their heads. "*NO.*"

"Jeb, you?"

"I made Eagle Scout. I can figure it out, but...."

Chuck stopped him, "I want you to snorkel the rocks there and the edges of the bay. If there's a problem, call a Mayday on channel 16."

Chevali repeated, "sixteen, sixteen, sixteen."

Chiara interjected, "Easy to remember, the age of the last chick you brought on vacation."

I couldn't help myself, "Hey, reverse the numbers, and you get her IQ too."

Chuck's eyes narrowed on me. "How much air you got left?"

"Let me see." I picked Rosie's gauge console out of the water next to her and read off, "I have eighteen hundred left. Damn Rosie, you are amazing. I wish you spent our money as conservatively as you consume oxygen."

She replied while treading water and unbuckling her equipment, "Well, if you knew how to touch me right, I might breathe a little harder once in a while." She talked through a smirking smile and tilted her head.

"Damn it, can you PLEASE stop this bullshit and go find my fucking boyfriend," Jessica shouted and smacked the water with her hand. I had never known Jessica to lose her composure. She would rarely loosen up, be less proper, and even minimally crude at times, but only on tropical vacations. This was a whole new level of self-expression for her. *Does she really love that nerd?* It would be up to Chuck and me to either find him alive or recover his shark-bitten body. I wasn't looking forward to either.

My mask felt cool on my face as I swam on the surface toward the growing waves that were roiling through the rocky gash which we had easily traversed thirty minutes before. The water level was dropping, and the waves within it were growing. I had to yell to him over the sound of crashing waves, "Do you think we can make it through?"

"I don't want to waste time going around the outside. Follow me and kick like hell." He put his regulator in his mouth and sank.

There was no clear water at the entrance to the little canyon, only continuous waves blending a cappuccino of water and sand. A pulsatile roar replaced the peaceful clicking sounds of shrimp. I could barely make out Chuck's yellow fins pumping ahead of me and I grasped the sharp rocky walls to keep from tumbling in reverse. The wave action blew him backward, and for the second time that morning, and in the exact location, I had my regulator knocked out of my mouth by a diver's butt.

Seafoam and sand filled my open mouth and obscured my vision. Drowning would follow within minutes if I inhaled. If I lost my regulator at the end of an exhalation, I wouldn't have enough air to clear it of water and sand to save myself. My survival hinged upon my finding my regulator in the underwater sandstorm while clinging to rocks and kicking my fins to the point of almost ripping them off my feet. Despite all this occurring simultaneously, my most significant concern was having Chuck's ass in my face, as Chiara's had been earlier that morning. The memory of the texture of her bikini filled my mind's mouth. *Why does my brain go to such places? I'm about to drown. Why in the hell would my memory replay Chiara's bikini bottom stuffing my mouth while having Chuck's fat ass plowing into my face? What's the matter with me?*

My unconscious took control of my right hand to find my regulator while my left hand grasped the sharp rock wall, propelling me forward a few inches at a time. With my regulator back in my mouth, I gagged a lung full of water and sand out through it and stifled the instinct to inhale rapidly. I swallowed sand a few times, sucked in a short calm breath, and forcefully exhaled more sand and water. I inhaled more of the bad stuff, causing me to cough and inhale uncontrollably. I forcibly kicked, scratched, and coughed my way to the exit of the canyon's vortex. I felt nauseated and tried to swallow. My sand-etched esophagus felt as if I had deep-throated a porcupine. I tucked this little pleasantry away and searched underwater for Chuck until I heard him clanging the brass clasp on his tank.

He must be safe and near. Releasing my abalone grasp from the rock, I saw him calmly floating ten feet below me, arms crossed, staring up at me.

I rotated my palms up to multiple directions, physically asking *which direction do we go?* Barring Baine having been drug off by a tiger shark, his body would have washed back toward the island. Between coughing spasms and razorblade swallows, I did my best to convey this to him. He got it, and we headed toward the rough water side of Witch Island. I motioned to him that one of us should be at the surface to check the rocky shallows while the other should search at depth.

He maintained the deeper portion of the hunt while I ascended to the surface as my nausea worsened. I was glad to be going to the surface. My SCUBA training taught me to vomit through your regulator in the event of vomiting underwater. I distinctly remembered having zero desire ever to perform this maneuver. The closer I rose to the surface, the closer I got to vomiting. This was not good. At the surface, incapacitating ocean waves immediately assaulted me and riddled me with wrenching nausea. I filled my B.C. with air and bounced on the surface of each wave, making my nausea even more profound until I exploded. I shot what seemed like a gallon of sandy seawater in a three-foot arc. I puked enough sand to make a beach. I wondered if any of the Parrotfish beneath me were jealous as expanding clouds of sand-vomit encircled my legs and plummeted toward Chuck. I instantly felt better, placed my snorkel in my mouth, and swam parallel to the shore.

The underwater drop-off on the South side of Witch Island was steep and rocky, and I kept Chuck in view as we covered our search areas. *It's strange to search for something that you don't want to find.* I breast stroked a couple of yards from the jagged shore rocks as waves broke against them with enough force to rain back out on me.

Swimming on the surface of rough water with a SCUBA tank on your back is miserable work, especially if you are face down. It's much easier to float on your back and kick, but with a search underway, this wasn't an option. I was weak from fasting, a vigorous dive, volcanic vomiting, and now battling surface waves. Being dangerously dehydrated, I didn't want to become the second victim of the day. I couldn't leave Chuck alone in the water, so I decided to abandon my equipment on-shore and snorkel above him.

I hauled my bulky, SCUBA gear-laden body up and onto the hot sand in a small section of sheltered water. Exhausted, I lay in the sand, panting and coughing, with my face in a human footprint. *Baines?* I fought my heat weakened mind, question-ing what new unpleasant physical sensations I could experi-ence that day. No matter how hard I tried not to, I came up with both *pain* and *cold*. While the latter was unlikely, I had a sinking feeling that the former was inevitable. Severe dehydra-tion soon caused a throbbing migraine that was growing by the minute. I'd found pain and felt happier with the thought of find-ing Baine's body than Baine. I examined the footprint. It led to others leading toward the summit of the short island.

"Hoot.... what the hell.... are you alright...? I saw you puk-ing on yourself." Chuck called from the rough water only a few yards away. I responded while barely lifting my pounding head, "I'm fine, just wanted to work on my tan for a minute. You see anything?"

"No, not shit." He yelled back from the crest of a wave. The waves had grown to the point where he disappeared in the troughs, and we could only shout to each other when wave peaks thrust him skyward. I doubted the footprints could be Baine's. Even he wasn't stupid enough to climb over a haunted nature preserve that was sure to have him arrested or possessed by some pissed-off, disembodied spirit. I yelled to Chuck. "Footprints in the sand, leading up there." I lifted my trembling arm.

"You are not serious?" He disappeared behind a wave, then reappeared, "Please, Hoot, don't screw with me, I..." disappeared and reappeared spitting water. "I'm beat to shit and can't joke...."

I waited for him to reappear, "No Shit, really." I said quickly, and he swam toward me. I knew I should stand and help extricate him from the water but conserved my energy, rationalizing that he was younger and hadn't vomited out all his body's fluid and potassium. I closed my eyes, laid my aching head back in the sand, sweated, and waited. I could hear and feel every heartbeat in my head. I desperately wanted to wash the sand out of my shredded esophagus that was on fire from sanding itself with every parched swallow. *Oh yay, now I get to add burning to the unpleasant sensation list.*

"Hoot, you look like shit. Do you want me to get the boat?" Chuck frowned as he spoke down to me.

"I'm fine, only a little seawater hangover. Hey, you wouldn't happen to have a canteen on you, would you?" I asked in jest.

"I wish. Where are the footprints?"

I didn't raise my head but pointed uphill.

"Damnit if that asshole... I told everybody to stay the hell off this island." He was sputtering.

"Only one way to find out," I said and peeled off my stifling hot neoprene.

"I'm a bad human, amigo. At this point, I'd rather find his lifeless body so that I don't have to knock him the hell out," I said.

"You'll have to reach him before me."

We followed the footprints to the top of the scorched island. Every step in the unshaded sun made my head thump harder. The blistering midday sand, combined with occasional unattached cactus needles, tortured my feet. My feet were competing with my head for my least happy body part. My desiccated throat stuck to itself with every attempted swallow. My swollen esophagus didn't have the normal peristaltic movement to propel the rare drops of saliva toward my waiting stomach. My dry-sanded throat felt like two hunks of meat bouncing and clinging to one another.

At the hillcrest, an acrid stench stuffed my head into an olfactory dungeon. "What the hell is that smell? I asked. "Something must have died up here."

Chuck grimaced and blinked as if trying to clear his nose by fluttering his eyelids. "Watch your step. The cactus thorns may be the least of your foot worries."

"No kidding. Wow, that's awful." I added *stench* to my list of unpleasant sensations.

I watched our boat float motionlessly in the emerald water of the island's semicircular bay. The girls' voices bounced off the flat water up to my ears. Chevali was face down in the water snorkeling, combing the shoreline. St. John appeared close enough to hit with a rock, and I wondered where the nearest store was that had water and aspirin. The ends of the bay were rocky, but in the center was a curved white sandy beach with a few large rocks. My eyes followed a well-defined set of footprints in the moist sand to a lifeless body, curled up behind the shade of a boulder hidden from Chevali as he snorkeled to within four body lengths of it.

"That'd better be him." I threw a rock downhill at him, and it came up short.

Our descent through rocks, stubby bushes, and short cacti made my tender feet scream at me to stop abusing them. Fortunately, anger partially numbed them. I imagined multiple Baine recovery scenarios, some alive, some not, some starting with him alive and ending otherwise.

We found Blaine snoring in the fetal position, hands neatly folded under his head, resting on a pillow of his fins and wet suit. He had an innocent, child-like smile on his dreamy face as flies crawled around his mouth and nose. I was about to grab a foot and yank him back to an abrupt consciousness when he passed wind, loud and long. I lost my desire to be on the same island with him and backed away. We didn't wake him but wordlessly waded out into the bay and swam toward the boat. The refreshing water brought my migraine down to a Richter 7.

The girls appeared panicked as we swam up to the boat without our SCUBA gear. "We found him," I said while we treaded water off the port bow. Jessica's face reddened, and she sobbed onto Chiara's shoulder, "Oh God, oh no, oh God, please Jesus, no." "He's alive. Jessica, he's fine. Would you like to say hello to him?" I spoke up to her from the water.

"Of course, where, WHERE?" She shook her hands, palms up.

"Jess, he is totally safe and happy, I promise. I'd like YOU to be the one to tell him how delighted you are that he is safe and well-rested. Jump in and follow Chuck. She passed me swimming in the opposite direction as Chevali swam up to us and climbed aboard.

I need to drink water, or I'm going to die. I pulled two bottles of Queen Amina Water from the boat's icebox and threw one to a water-treading Chuck. I emptied mine in seconds by squeezing the thin plastic bottle, ejecting cold water into my parched throat. The cold made my head pound harder for a few seconds. After drinking his, Chuck filled it with seawater and threw it back to me, "Hey guys, watch out for Park Service boats. It's a nasty fine if we get caught on shore." He said and swam with Jessica toward shore as I told my story of the canyon swim, vomiting sandy seawater, the hot hike, and finding The Sleeping Buddha of a Baine. I sat under the shade of the blue canopy over the helm and pulled cactus out of my feet.

"What a fucking moron, that was stupid even for him," Chevali said.

"Yep," I said as Chuck and Jessica swim up to the island. I watched as Chuck put his fingers to his lips, indicating to her to stay silent, then lead her to the rock behind which Baine slept. Jessica's fists doubled. She started stamping her feet like a mad skunk and leaped behind the boulder.

Chuck later related that she jumped on him like Hulk Hogan doing an elbow slam into Baine's unsuspecting ribs. From the boat, we could hear them both screaming, her in anger and him in pain. I watched Chuck holding his belly in laughter until Baine appeared first, followed by Jessica beating him with wide swings of his fins. Each contact made a "whop" sound until he was safely in the water. If a man could have ever tucked his tail between his legs, it would have been Baine. He swam hard and fast for the safety of the boat. Jessica's raging insults never stopped as she power stroked the poor water with her angry arms.

I considered knocking Baine back into the water with a straight right to his forehead as he climbed onto the boat but withheld my anger. We still had to recover our gear from Witch Island before the spooks or the cops invaded our happiness. I asked Chuck once he was back on the boat. "How should we do this, over the hill again or motor back to the far side, and swim the stuff to the boat?" My brain, in its dehydrated and starved state, wasn't working well.

"Ooooh hell no," Jessica said. She jabbed her index finger toward the water and then Witch Island while glowering at Baine, who was alone in the sun at the far corner of the boat. "You get their SCUBA gear. Do it now." Her voice had a quality that spoke of a less than sexual finish to Baine's vacation. He turned to retreat into the water and revealed red, raised fin-induced welts rising angrily across his back and shoulders.

Chevali spoke up, "Hey, Baine, you may want to consider a little hand cream on those tonight to ease the sting." Baine held his jump long enough to turn and make eye contact with Chevali, but before he could respond, Jessica held her arm out, pointing toward the island. "No, now, go."

Red-faced and wild-eyed, she growled to Chevali. I expected Jessica to scold him for teasing Baine again, but she extended her hand toward Baine as if sicking a dog on a rabbit. "Fair game from now on, don't hold back," and she started crying with her hands over her face. Chevali said nothing but tenderly held her in his arms and rubbed her back while holding her head down to his shoulder. He then rolled his eyes upward with his tongue hanging from the corner of his mouth and imitated humping her leg. She didn't notice him. A pig among pigs, my friend Dr. Jeb Chevali, I loved him for that.

Once Baine had swum all the gear back to the boat, Chuck started the engines and jammed a UB40 cassette in the player. Chatter restarted about the swim through the channel, the spotted eagle rays, and the Flintstone house. Speculations on the structure's origin ran from massive hurricanes to witches and even UFOs. I sat in my spot at the back of the boat and watched the spray shoot up from the hull, forming transient rainbows in the fast-moving air at my shoulder. Baine sat opposite me with his hands between his knees while his head bobbed with the waves and not UB40. His blank stare at the boat floor momentarily made me pity him. We all occasionally do stupid things, and I was certainly no exception. I raised my voice over the roar of the Yamaha engines to him. "Were you able to see the Flintstone house from the surface?"

He spoke up, "Yeah, but only for a minute before the sharks showed up."

I thought I'd misunderstood him, "Did you say sharks?"

He nodded, "yes."

"You mean the eagle rays. I think there were four of them, right?" I said as I flapped my arms like a swimming ray. I figured he didn't know the difference. "No, I saw them too. They almost led you guys to the stone house. But two big sharks came from the other direction, didn't you see them?" Above the sensations of wind, sea spray, and the bouncing boat combined, I felt my heart pound in my throat and my head.

"No. How many?"

He held up two fingers.

"How big?"

"Longer than the walls of the stone house, by a few feet."

"How Close?" I was not liking his answers and tried not to believe him, thinking he was trying to justify his stupid actions.

"They were swimming in circles on the other side of the stone house while you guys swam in and out of it. They saw me on the surface and started to circle up in the water toward me. I couldn't warn you and had no place to go but the island. Let me show you on my camera."

"Show me on your camera. How?"

"It's a new type of camera called a digital. It doesn't use film, just some kind of computer thing. See."

He handed me the camera after extricating it from a waterproof plastic housing. It was palm-sized with a snub-nosed protruding lens. He tapped some buttons, "Simply touch this arrow here and scroll through the pictures."

I held the little silver thing in my hand, "Canon Power Shot 600, never heard of such a thing." The business card-sized TV screen showed a picture of us divers from above. I touched the little arrow. My heart thumped, and I swallowed hard at my swollen tongue. There were two striped sharks, each significantly longer than the Flintstone house, swimming a few yards off the far side of the rock house from us, the oblivious divers. "Holy hell Baine, why didn't you say something?"

"I didn't have much of a chance. Jessica was a little mad at me." I patted his shoulder, feeling bad about wanting to kill him only an hour earlier. "Let me help you out of this. Don't show these to anybody until I bring it up, OK?" He wore the expression of a stray cat, uncertain if he could trust me not to kick him. "Yeah sure."

-16-

Exodus

The floating splinter factory docks at Coral Bay undulated as a maze of sundried, twisted wood planks bounced with boat wakes and foot traffic. Hidden hinges joined each independent section to its neighbor, letting each find a separate cadence. Some were more buoyant than others, riding at differing heights above the water. Most canted a few degrees, and boats in various states of disrepair wrestled for space at their edges. Seemingly abandoned Zodiacs harbored pools of oily water dancing with floating debris and moldered life jackets. I figured the oil was a good thing, preventing them from serving as a flotilla of mosquito breeding ponds. A couple of sailboat masts jutted from the surrounding water at odd angles, marking unrecovered sinkings from last year's hurricane. Inflatable grey dinghies were the most numerous vessels at the docks, sometimes moored nose to tail to accommodate their numbers.

Chuck led us to a disorganized scattering of buildings near the water's edge. 'Skinny Arms' was an open-air bar with uneven and poorly maintained wood floors, built from the same 2X6 boards as the docks. Overhead rafters sagged under a patchwork roof of rusted metal and fiberglass corrugated panels -- the latter with black mold growing in their adjoining seams. The bay side of the roof was only a stained tarp, haphazardly lashed to broken rafters, undulating in a soft onshore breeze. The bar was homemade with warped and peeling house siding. Its top was dark-stained plywood, scarred with dozens of cigarette burns melted into the yellowed, thick lacquer. Behind the bar, a jumble of bottles stood at inebriated attention on crooked shelving. Brown rums poised shoulder to shoulder with bright red Campari, whiskeys next to cheap tequila. Grey Geese flew toward Jim Beam. The mirror behind them had a long break at the top-right corner. The missing shard exposed a lighter shade of wood previously shielded from the elements before Marilyn broke it. Duct tape covered the newly exposed mirror edge. Unfortunately, a large TV hung by thin rusting chains from the sagging ceiling and mercilessly blared CNN.

We pulled two green Heineken logoed tables together before I crumpled into my plastic chair. I sat with my back to the TV and under the wash of a dubiously mounted, hula hooping ceiling fan to hopefully drown out the news anchor's voice. It was futile. The waitress repeatedly filled our water glasses and asked for drink orders. Although it was past noon, nobody but Chuck ordered alcohol, asking for a ginger beer.

"How the hell can you drink beer now?" I stuck my tongue out like a dehydrated cow.

"It's not real beer. It's like a strong ginger ale. Take a taste."

I asked the waitress. "We've had an adventurous day at sea, is there any chance of parking a couple of these here for us, please?" I thumped our empty sweating water pitcher with my finger, expecting her to have a bad attitude. In contrast to my same request a couple of mornings ago in Cruz Bay, she was sympathetic. My sweating and medusa-haired friends sat motionless around our table. The sun had etched a photonic fury upon them, making sunglass and bikini lines glow. My forehead felt tight and swollen from the morning's irradiation. When I blinked, my eyelids stung from sunburn and dried salt.

The conversation at the table was scant. Baine sat quietly next to Jessica as she talked past him to Chiara. His eyes were on the TV's talking heads, discussing the shooting of a Rapper named something like Snowpack Forsure. A bunch of old white guys debated the ailing condition of the Rap World. I did my best to squeeze them from my head and caught Baine's attention. In a loud voice, I asked, "Hey Baine, you were gonna show me your camera. It's one of those new digital things, right?"

He scowled at me like I was stupid, "I did on the boat."

This guy could screw up a free dinner, "No, I mean how to use it, show me all the pictures and stuff, remember?" I shot him a bug-eyed look.

"Sure." He held it up toward me, "All you have to do is press this. When it dings, go to this button to select..." Obviously, he hadn't recalled my offer to help drag him out of the dog house. *OK, time to go into moron mode and drop down to his level.*

"BAINE, bring it over to me. I can't see it from there. I want to see if you got any cool pictures of our dive."

Still clueless, he sighed, walked over to me, and knelt, seemingly irritated at my dragging him away from the TV and bullet-riddled Rappers.

"Thank you, Baine. Let me see if there are any interesting pictures on your camera from today." My loud words were pedantic and overly enunciated to throw one more clue that I was trying to help him. He ran through the instructions for the little camera as if talking to a child. I was working hard for this one.

Holding the camera away from my face and trying to engage anybody at the table, "HOLY SHIT, SHARKS." *That should get 'em.* The conversations continued as if I had been talking to myself. Why is it, if you are trying to have a private discussion that everybody around you stops talking and points an ear at you? Now that I wanted to distract someone, anyone, I couldn't do it. But I had a ringer.

I held the camera up and turning my face toward Chevali. "Wow, what a great set of tits on that one," I spoke to the unconscious mind of a sex addict. His eyebrows raised, and he cut his conversation with Rosie, "Whatcha got, Ky?" He asked. I had precisely set the hook.

"There are pictures on Baine's camera from today." I handed it to him. "Look at the little screen, tell everybody what you see, Jeb," I spoke in the same exaggerated tone as when talking to Baine.

"I don't see any tits." He strained to examine the back of the camera. His comments caught Chiara's attention, and she leaned in attentively and said, "Nope, no tits." He tried to hand the camera back to me. Even Chiara had joined the mental deficient club. I was losing my patience.

"I didn't say tits. I said sharks, SHARKS in the picture on Baine's camera while we were swimming, pictures of big man-eating SHARKS right next to us. He took pictures of us diving with BIG ASS MAN-EATING SHARKS, look at the big, looong sharks swimming only a few yards away from our oblivious asses, getting ready to eat us, and instead, they chased Baine out of the water onto Witch Island as we mindlessly swam with two big ass tiger sharks the size of school busses."

Conversation stopped, and all eyes met mine. I pointed to the tiny screen as Chevali squinted again. "See those two big damn fish, not twenty feet from you." I pressed the button to reveal another picture of the two marauders swimming up, aiming for the lens, taken right before Baine got to the safety of the island.

Epithets and gasps accompanied the camera as it passed from person to person. Jessica stared at it, then at Baine, then back at the camera. He blinked back at her, seemingly unable to muster the words to extricate himself from her ire. I interjected, "Baine, you said that they chased you out of the water to the safety of the island. You had no choice, right?" I wanted Jessica to understand that his actions were excusable.

She was purse-lipped, and her head shook slightly. "Why did you stay on the island where we couldn't see you and not come back to the boat?" She asked in what seemed to be defensive anger. "I had diarrhea and didn't want to poop in the water by the boat." He countered. "I had to stay on the island for a few, uh, episodes. I guess I fell asleep in the shade."

Behind Baine, a green and white Park Service boat pulled into a slip behind Skinny Arms. Two West Indian rangers dressed in uniforms that appeared entirely too hot for the tropics, wobble-walked atop the pitching docks. They talked and gesticulated to boat owners, indicating someone about the same height as the shorter of the two rangers and pointing toward the East. One of the owners waived them toward the bar, and the rangers turned. I didn't have time to explain myself and stuffed my hat and sunglasses onto Baine, "Trust me, NOW," I said. Patting the tabletop repeatedly with my open palm, I caught everybody's attention and emphatically said, "Don't ask questions, just do as I say...."

"Yeah, eat me, captain fish breath," Chevali said and took a hit of water.

"Listen, please, please, please trust me NOW. We were only snorkeling around the half-sunken sailboat on the other side of the bay. We were NOT, NOT, NOT, on a boat by Witch Island." Chuck followed my eyes as I sprayed my words.

"Oh shit, Park Service." He sat at attention as they spoke to the female bartender.

She turned the TV volume down, allowing their voices to bounce off the tin ceiling to my ears. The taller of the two said, "And we got pictures of him from our boat, squatting and doing his business directly in the birds' nest. He soiled the only two known eggs left in existence. Now we need to assemble a team to clean the eggs and nest and hope the parents don't abandon them. He is middle age, about his height," pointing to the shorter ranger who was peeking down the top of a bikini-clad woman at the bar. "In a wet suit, really nondescript, brown hair, thin mustache, and a tattoo of a red high heel shoe on his right butt cheek."

The bartender said she had only seen about fifty people that morning who fit the description but that the ass inspections didn't start until the afternoon. Clearly, she did not like having police of any kind in her bar. "Ma'am, there are only two remaining mating pairs of these birds known to exist, and this guy is wanted for some serious crimes. Please, if you get any tips, give us a call." He handed her a business card. "We're going to town to have the pictures developed. Can we return and put a couple posters up of him?"

The bartender answered while mixing a cocktail. "Sure, no problem, we'll hang up a wanted poster of some weirdo taking a shit in a bird's nest before we start taking dinner orders. Sounds perfect."

"Thank you for your cooperation, and if you don't mind, we'll check around the restaurant." The shorter of the two spotted Chuck and walked directly to our table. "OK, Chuckie?"

"OK, Clarence, OK," he said, smiling. "Who dees people wit you?" Unlike his counterpart, who spoke perfect English, Clarence conversed in the local patois.

"Clarence, I mean officer O'Grady, this is my sister and her husband visiting from Colorado and some of their friends." Rosie and I both stood to shake his hand. She smiled a disarming smile. "A pleasure, sir."

"Hi officer, I'm Ky." His palm was sweaty, rough, and warm.

Chuck interjected, "He's a doctor," as if that somehow made our group less likely to violate the sanctity of an endangered bird's nest.

"Oh, what kind doctor, medical or college doctor?"

"College doctor?" I asked.

"Yeah, deh all over deh place this time of year for the annual bird count. Come from all over deh world to see our Virgin Island birds, especially deh Flanagan's Boobie. It's deh one time a year we allow guided tours of Flanagan's Island so deh can count deh Flanagan's eggs and watch deh parents dive for squid off the island."

"Human Doctor. I'm not smart enough to be an Ornithologist." I thought a little humility might lighten the mood. I was wrong. Officer O'Grady eyed each of us carefully. "Where you been dis morning?"

I took the lead, "We were snorkeling on that sunken sailboat over there." I pointed over his shoulder to the other side of the bay. He didn't move.

"Chuckie, you see a guy, my tallness, brown hair, and you guys see any boats dat come in from Witch Island?" Officer O'Grady seemed to have a hard time finishing a thought or line of questioning. His eyes scanned the restaurant and boat dock while he spoke. Chuck shook his head, "No mon, but not really lookin', why?" Chuck adopted the local vernacular.

"Dis white guy, we got photos from our boat, he on the top deh Witch Island doing his business in a bird nest, a Flanagan's Booby nest. Heem cover deh nest an eggs wit heem doodoo. What a mess, now we gotta clean dem up, so deh don abandons deh nest. We got pictures, gonna pos 'em up and catch deh sick muddah." Baine obscured his face with his menu, shaking so hard he could have used it for a fan.

Chuck asked, "Why didn't you go ashore and arrest him?"

"We were goin' to but got a call about a shark attack in Trunk Bay, and we had to go."

"A shark attack in Trunk Bay?" He asked in a louder voice.

"Yeah, Chuckie, a bad one. Dem baby lemon shark, two feet long, bit a German tourist's breast. Deh buggah wouldn't let go, and deh had to send her by Ambulance boat to deh Hospital on St. Thomas to try to remove it."

"You serious? Did they get it off?"

"Don know yet, haven't heard. But before leaving, we got some telephotos of da guy dumping in da nest. By deh time we get back, we jus found footprints an his doodoo on deh Boobie eggs."

"What a bastard. Be sure to give me a few of the posters to put up. When do you think you'll have them made?" Chuck asked.

"Last time we had posters made was when dat Dominican was catching turtles and selling deh meat to rich people last year. Took two days over on Saint Thomas."

"Well, throw a couple in my Jeep. I'll put them up. You know where to find it."

"Yes, I do." He turned to the table next to ours to ask questions.

Once Clarence was out of earshot, Jessica asked Baine, "In an endangered bird's nest, really Baine, a bird's nest?" Baine's eyes followed the officers moving from table to table. "I didn't know it was a nest. It was just a pile of sticks to me." Chevali leaned toward Baine, "And you thought the eggs were what, left by the fucking Easter Bunny, really dude? You could be responsible for wiping an entire species from the face of the planet with your squirting bowels."

"I didn't check that close. It was kinda an emergency." Baine looked in vain to Jessica for reassurance. As the officers circulated around the room, a waiter wearing an apron with a skull and crossbones on the chest made his way toward our table. He was thin and appeared unhealthy, with the sallow-green complexion of a heavy drinker and smoker. His abdomen was swollen, pushing the material of the apron ahead of his swaying body. He obviously had ascites from advanced liver disease and was in desperate need of a peritoneocentesis to drain the excess fluid from his swollen abdomen. His arms and legs were skinny, and skin hung from his bones without the fullness of muscle between them.

"Skinny," Chuck said with genuine warmth and introduced us. I shook his bony, finely trembling, cool hand. Skinny was soft-spoken and communicated through yellowed, angled incisors. He was pleasant and obviously sick, but his lithe movement belied his physical condition.

"You all out diving this morning? It seems like it's getting rougher by the minute." Beyond him out to sea, white caps were peaking on rolling waves that formed a watery train to the West. Chuck answered, "Nothing difficult, just playing in the water." I appreciated his vagueness.

"It's a pleasure to meet all of you, and I hope you come back to revisit us before leaving the Island." Skinny's kind nature was palpable in his mannerisms. He had an air of a tired and tortured soul, and I assumed that he worked to keep from wallowing in his fleeting mortality.

"Seems like a sweet guy," I said to Chuck, who smiled through a mouth full of food, "but we gotta hang around here until the Park Service guys leave. Can't let them see us hauling SCUBA gear around."

"No problem Hoot," he said with egg jiggling from his goatee. "By the time we eat and the women are done shopping, they will be long gone."

"Shopping?" Rosie heard her magic word and smiled broadly at Jessica.

"Yeah, each of these little buildings here," Chuck gestured with his Ginger Beer. "Is a little shop."

The ride home in the back of the pickup cooled me until I tapped on the roof of the cab above Chuck's head as we entered the center of Cruz Bay town. "Can you pull over by Woodie's so I can get out? I spoke to him through the open driver's window. I gotta go to the cybercafe and check in on the office." My throat constricted around my exiting words.

The Cybercafe was as uninviting as it had been the day before. The White Rasta, champion of all living things that don't have valuable leather skin, sat red-eyed and engrossed with his computer screen. I assumed he was watching animal porn.

Regretting our unkind words from the previous day, "Good afternoon, I'd like to rent some computer time, please." He didn't look up but reached into a coconut shell filled with little sheets of torn paper and handed one to the air between us. "This is the instructions, but before you start, leave a twenty-dollar deposit in case you decide to skip out."

I dug into my wallet, "Thank you so much for bringing a pleasant slice of the mainland to the Caribbean," tossed a twenty toward him, and found a computer screen that mirrored my disheveled caricature. The computer time flew by in a matter of years. I dealt with problem attorneys, insurance whore doctors, bills, and demanding patients, mad at me for not being there for them every day of the year. Once finished, I told the White Rasta to keep the twenty's change for tomorrow's assault on my peace.

I awoke in the early evening, naked under my ceiling fan, sweating on the bedside of my skin, luxuriously tepid on the fan side. I remembered a dream about Roman soldiers pillaging and raping their way through the English countryside, undoubtedly influenced by my day of dehydrating heat, tiger sharks, an incontinent idiot, and upsetting emails.

I quickly showered and joined our group on the deck in the fading light of a short tropical dusk. The gentle warmth of the setting sun and buttery smooth air lovingly massaged my warm skin. The billowing clouds to the North blazed pink, transforming into Japanese hanging lanterns for the evening sky.

"Christ, Ky," a smiling Boddington greeted me. "I'm glad it wasn't you, buddy. I thought I might have to come and save your scrawny ass," he said, thrusting a brown drink into my hand. Fresh ice cracked sharply in the warm rum. "Drink up, son, I'm thinkin we're going in for round number two any minute, and I may need your help saving some poor soul."

"Huh?" I asked.

Ramona was blushing and beamed a mischievous grin. Jessica looked uncomfortable, bending over the handrail as if trying to catch a glimpse of something trying to escape. Baine was in the house, watching TV. I took a sip of my rum, and while the flavors were pleasing to my palate, the alcohol burned my sanded esophagus. I took another swallow, hoping it would numb it. It didn't, but I continued drinking.

"What in the hell are you talking about, Boddington?"

"SHHHH, quiet, boy, you might scare the animals away." He turned to Rosie and Ramona, "He's like this even when we're hunting. Ya got you a totally silent wilderness, animals listening for the slightest hint of a human, and this bastard's gabbing on and on about his dog, his Harley, and them damn criminals he rides with, his blow-up dolls, anything. He just keeps his gums a flappin' while I'm trying to hunt up an Elk for dinner."

Then it started, apparently again. The sound of an open hand smacking an ass, growling, grunting, and swearing voices. *The sound of a bed squeaking?*

"Ouch, you little bitch, Daddy's gonna teach you a lesson." A voice from below the deck.

Ramona held her hand over her mouth while she and Rosie sheepishly ran in place in silent laughter. They were the second couple at that moment to be convulsing in their enjoyment.

"I've been a baaaad girl. And damn it, Daddy, I'm gonna make YOU pay for it." Followed by another smacking sound and a Chevali grunt.

"You little slut." More bed squeaking.

"Son of a bitch, I can't take it anymore. I'm too old to put up with this racket and too young not to want to join them," Boddington said as he strode to the handrail where Jessica stood. Her eyes darted side to side, and she was tight-lipped. He softly rubbed her shoulder, leaned over the rail, and yelled down to Chevali's bedroom. "For Christ's sake, Jeb, either fuck her or kill her, but whichever you decide to do, make it fast, 'cause you're costin' me dinner time, and I'm hungry enough to eat a bag full of horse flies. Now give it to her good, and let's vamoose. I gotta eat."

Silence, followed by giggling and a muffled, "Oh shit." Bed squeaking rapidly. Faster. More squeaking and a couple of crescendoing howls and a final ass smack. Silence. The sound of a shower.

Boddington hugged an obviously distraught Jessica, "It's OK, sweetie, the bloodshed is over. I think the guys in the white hats won." She put her head on his chest and wiped a tear from the end of her nose.

The pink lantern clouds previously strung in the evening's powder-blue sky faded to light stains against a violet backdrop of a night sky. Faint stars, coming alive for the night, defined the extinguished cloud's silhouettes. My new bottle of Pusser's Rum died a quick death.

We (I think it was only me...not totally clear on that memory, still) resorted to drinking from a leftover bottle of Culo Diablo tequila. I was missing my Patron and made the unfortunate choice to use cheap tequila to assassinate my memories of the afternoon's email unpleasantries. I became comfortably numb and numbing more by the minute as Boddington kept pouring. Chevali climbed the stairs to join us, grinning and wearing tented Ronald Regan eyebrows. Chiara was composed and serene. Rosie whispered to me, indicating that Chiara preferred to stand as the rest of us sat to make dinner plans. Jessica was dropping rum down her throat at a rapid pace, headed for a rare drunk.

Alcohol fuzzed conversation and laughter garnished the meandering walk to town. I didn't engage much but watched and listened. My skin still held the day's warmth, and sweat trickled down my torso to collect at my belt line. I was happy that I'd rehydrated enough to sweat. However, it appeared as though the rum and the night's unrelenting humidity aimed to rob me of my improving hydration status. The chemical irritation of OFF caused a mild burn where the sun had eaten my skin's defenses.

I spoke to Rosie. Her blurred eyes were a sure sign of my trip deep into the wilds of my private rum/tequila island. "Hey, you ever notice how when you're drunk, you can communicate with other drunks on a different plane, in that ethereal drunk-to-drunk transmission of thoughts that supersedes words? It's almost a telepathic thing."

"You mean like now?" She smiled an answer-question.

"Uh-huh. And you can spot sober people as easily as they can spot a drunk?" We both looked at Baine. He was holding Jessica's arm, protecting her from falling over the cracks in the road. His feet moved squarely, one in front of the other as if following an imaginary painted line on the dark road. Jessica's feet wandered like an alpaca caught someplace between a trot and a canter.

Rosie's eyebrows raised, elevating her wrinkled forehead as if gravity was wrestling her for control of its growing weight, "It appears as though Jessica, and you have been drinking."

She spoke to that internal place that only drunks can hear, and they were the funniest words in months for both of us. We began to quiver and held onto one another for stability until we crumbled onto the concrete street, crying with laughter. I didn't care if the cockroaches picked us up and carried us away. I was laughing too hard to stand. In their alcohol-induced haze, the others stood, calmly talking as we scrubbed the street with our legs and hands. I don't remember washing them before eating.

Dinner, wherever it was, was a blur. I do remember the sight of food, falling backward off my chair, and scowls from someone, "blow me," rolling eloquently from my lips, and Rosie telling me to be cool. I remember hitting that turning point where the unslurring little voice in my head spoke, "Ky," she said. "It's time to stop drinking rum and start drinking water. Listen to me, or you will make an ass out of yourself in public." I thanked her, not knowing why the voice of reason in my head was a female, and ordered another rum and Coke. And I raged on. I did remember urinating in the bushes outside the restaurant's restroom while a line of men and women watched while waiting for their turn. That was clearly not my finest hour.

We followed Chuck to the quiet little bar, 'Fred's Place.' It was full of people and alive with loud live music and bouncing bare bulbs hanging from rafters a few feet above my head. As it turns out, the bulbs were stationary. It was I who was jumping, dancing to, of all things, reggae. Not merely reggae, but the best reggae ever played in the entire world history of reggae. I'm usually not a dancer, but this was musical virtuosity of the highest order, and my feet couldn't stay still. Haplessly possessed by dancing spirits, I danced on. Reggae before this had an annoying monotonous beat that prompted a quick turn of the radio knob. My beautiful friends, family, and loving strangers from all over the world and I converged at that moment to move together with God's greatest gift of music. We were in sync with the perfection of 'One Love.' Our night of swaying synchronicity with every other living being on the planet would last forever.

"Uh, Oh." I heard me say to Rosie as we gyrated with the most benevolent group of people to ever gather in the name of rhythm. "Uh, honey...I hate to..." I intended to say, 'interrupt the passionate reverie,' but what came out was a loud verp, and the only word I could gurgle was, "VOMIT." *Shit, the little voice was right*. The race was on. She held my arm and guided me. I clasped my mouth with the international signal for: "GET THE FUCK OUT OF MY WAY OR YOU ARE GOING TO GET PUKED ON." We shot for the opening in the chain link fence that served as a wall between Fred's Place and the crowded street.

Just as we reached the top of the concrete steps, and to the abject horror of polite tourists on a pleasant, post-dinner stroll, it happened. I skidded to my hands and knees in the street and roaringly humiliated myself with the violent heaves of a human Vesuvius. The convulsive forces of ejection caused rivers of tears to cascade down my already sweating face. I was dangerously hemorrhaging without bleeding, and the only thing leaving me faster than my body fluids was my pride. I may have urinated on myself but was too busy gurgling and foaming to care. Tourist's and local's scowls of hatred and disgust enhanced the embarrassment that filled the vacancy left by my exiting decorum and...dinner. Chuck and Chevali stood over me, taunting and jeering as if they didn't know me. The cruel bastards were paying me back for my prior sins of publicly

humiliating them. As the eruptive phase of the evening temporarily eased, and despite my straddling a lumpy river between
my hands and knees, all I wanted to do was lay down and go
to sleep in the street.

-17-

Get Up Stand Up

Vacation mornings are like unopened Christmas gifts wrapped in their wonderment. They hold the promise of unyet fulfilled dreams. Like vacation afternoons and evenings, they are my favorite. I love vacation mornings.

The bright morning sun punished my dangerously inflated head with hateful photons of molten lead. I laid without moving all night, frozen in a Pompei victim contortion. My right shoulder felt dislocated. Lactic acid and spasm gripped my abdominal wall muscles. I was in the fetal position, and as I straightened my legs, the skin on my knee caps stung. Pain seemed to be the sensation of the day. I did not want to own my mouth. Rosie was snoring but sounded far away?

This mattress sucks.

My head was so heavy that I was afraid it might break off and decapitate me if I lifted it. I pondered as to how that might not be a good thing. I needed water badly. Opening my eyes produced a blurred, black, and white cat, staring at me, lapping up something by my head?

I am in bed, Right? Why is there a cat in my bed? My confusion was holding hands with total body pain in my first waking seconds. Then the smell hit me.

Oh, shit, here we go again?... What again?

I jerked my head up to relieve myself of a hot torrent jetting from my esophagus. My hair stuck, glued to the concrete floor, and my movement pulled a chunk of it out by the roots.

Concrete floor? BOOM, I almost hit the cat with that one. Where did that come from? Holy hell of hells. My head-Migraine. Bad throbbing migraine. Mouth beyond awful, but at least it isn't dry anymore. Floor? Cat? I think I just vomited magma. Again?

"ROSIE," I cried out.

The snoring stopped.

"ROSIE, why am I on the floor with a cat? Why?"

Oh God, every cell in my body ached. "ROSIE, every cell in my body aches, why?"

"Because you are a dumb ass," was her loving retort. Fluttering memories started returning, like the old-time flip-card cartoons. This was not a happy moment. Oh no, embarrassment joined pain and confusion in kicking my ass, and my eyes had only been open a few seconds.

"ROSIE, why am I on the floor?"

"I wasn't about to let you in my bed last night. You might want to check around you to see your handy work. There was no way I was going to let you share THAT with ME in bed."

I raised my head, and my remaining hair flapped down, wet onto my forehead. I might have had a bad night. "Did I spend a lot of money on dinner last night?" I was hoping that this morning's cat food had been a cheap dinner.

"Yes, dear, in fact, you bought dinner for everybody at our table and the table next to ours. I think about ten people in total. Remember falling backward off your chair and knocking the nice lady's dinner into her lap and calling her husband a shithead?"

"No, was he a shithead?" I asked.

"No, he was a very nice plumber from Des Moines."

"Was it an expensive restaurant, ya know, good food?"

"Oh, I don't know, why don't you see if you recognize the remnants of Fillet mignon and Chilean sea bass and key lime pie and a chocolate torte, flowerless if I recall correctly, and a gallon of Coke and rum."

"I hate me." I really did.

"Honey, you have a lot of company on this island, starting right up here." I searched my swollen brain for a witty retort to my wife's supportive words when a voice from upstairs lanced my aching consciousness.

"HOOT? It's dive time. Where you at?"

Drinking a shot of Culo Diablo tequila for breakfast was the only thing that could eclipse my desire to SCUBA dive that morning. I couldn't possibly answer with a loud enough response without my head exploding, and I peeled myself off the floor to stumble upstairs in my underwear. I had to tell him that I wasn't up to sunlight, let alone SCUBA diving.

'Hey Chuck, I...." His face was as bright and optimistic as was my soul polluted and dark.

"Hoot, put some shorts on, and let's go. Damn, your legs are skinny. I have everything loaded up and charged up the tanks. Jeb and Chiara are waiting in the Jeep. Grab Rosie and move it, puke boy, the weather isn't going to hold for long. A storm is coming in by afternoon. Oh, and you may want to rinse your hair. I'm afraid the fish might follow your head the way they do a hippo's ass underwater." I didn't want to give him the satisfaction of reaching up to touch it. Shit, I had to go diving. Staying home sick would provide him and Chevali with too much ammunition. I hated me more than I did that puppy-killing Percy Hayes.

The Caribbean Sea's boastful confidence in her blueness minimally offset the misery of riding in the back of Chuck's shockless Jeep. We bought a mobile breakfast and a couple of gallons of drinking water at the Mongoose Junction deli. I purchased a plastic gallon jug for myself. Before we arrived at the Fish Bay dive site, I had drunk it, partially rehydrating my oatmeal thick blood. Diving while in my condition was less than intelligent, yet my hangover made me more afraid of survival than of death.

"Ky, you look like shit. Are you sure you are up to this?" Chevali was attempting to be sympathetic.

"What are you babbling about?" I couldn't let him win the macho war that raged between us.

"You gotta be one hungover son of a bitch." He laughed his assumption at me. I was close to proving him right with a key lime pie shower but held it in. "Eh, I got a little headache, not bad."

I need to steer him into left field and away from my misery. "No shit man, doing well, got all the poison out of my system before going to bed. Slept like a baby. Hey, did I hear Baine correctly last night say that you two are going to have a push-up contest today?" This was abject bullshit, but I knew he'd take the bait. "Yeah, right, I could do more one-handed in a minute than he could do all fucking day with both hands." He turned to Chiara for backup, "You didn't hear Baine say that shit last night, did you?"

God bless her, "I think everybody heard him issue the challenge when we were leaving Fred's. He said that he set a record at the gym." Chevali looked at the sky, shaking his head. Chiara winked at me.

"We'll see." His confidence beamed as he flexed his right bicep and kissed it.

Hangover chiding put to bed. *Thank you, Chiara.*

My SCUBA tank was as heavy as if it were solid, causing me to sweat that which I had only recently borrowed from the water jug. Not trusting my poisoned brain and not being at peace with my SCUBA gear, I quietly asked Rosie for assistance. She attached my regulator onto my tank, rotated the regulator air to ON position, put my weight belt me on before entering the fresh morning water. It was like a seawater Imitrex for my whole-body migraine.

Vacation dives provide a relaxed time to observe happy fish in their environment and sway with sea fans in gentle currents to a silent underwater song. They are a tranquil distraction away from the hell of work. Rosie held my hand as we followed Chuck. He dove wearing old work gloves and carried a three-foot-long lobster stick with a wire noose at one end. Hugging the bottom at a depth of forty feet, I felt a slight tug on my hand and noticed that Rosie was also holding Chiara's hand. *Women innocently do that stuff all the time.*

Chuck powered ahead, his thick legs pumping rhythmic pulses to his yellow fins. He was forward-focused and not looking back. I did and noticed Chevali was missing. I had to see if he was safe and caught Chiara's attention. I rotated my palms up as if asking, "what, where?" She rolled her magnified eyes upward behind her mask and shook her head "*no.*" I pointed in multiple directions, and she indicated that he was back in the direction from which we had started. I motioned my hand downward to Rosie and then to the sand, "*stay.*" She understood and settled fins first onto the bottom, raising slowly billowing puffs of sand.

Chiara's petite hand clasped mine to lead me. My compass indicated we were on a heading of 25 degrees, North. We swam a hundred feet to find Chevali, totally oblivious to the fact that he was alone. I wondered if he had completed SCUBA training, as one of the cardinal rules was never to leave your dive buddy. I was holding his dive buddy's hand while he absorbedly searched under coral heads and around sand humps. I decided to teach him a lesson. With his attention focused downward and away from us, I swam up behind him and ran my index finger as far up the ass of his swim trunks as I possibly could.

Simultaneously, his muscular ass cheeks grabbed my finger, and his legs stiffened. He screamed with such force that his regulator shot out of his mouth and started free-flowing. This was not in my game plan. He whipped around, and I hurriedly stuffed my regulator in his mouth. He batted it away and found his own. Anger flashed in his narrowed eyes as I fought my own. In irritated Italian mimicry, I palm-slapped my forehead, and signaled for him to follow me, and took us on a heading of 190 degrees, South. Interestingly, Chiara held my hand again, not his. It was an innocent handhold, but I liked it.

We found Rosie and an animated Chuck waiting for us. He emphatically tapped his watch and his air gauge, indicating that we were wasting time and air. He curled his index finger toward Chevali and then stabbed the water next to himself, attaching a watery leash. Chevali got the message, and they swam away in unison. I assumed the center position between

Rosie and Chiara. Each one reached to hold one of my hands, sandwiching me between my two dive buddies.

Chuck was on a mission. He knew where the lobsters lived and earned the nickname of "Mr. Lobster" with the locals. He searched under coral heads, in caves, and skirted sandbars. This was no leisure dive. We were hunting. He would point to and then ignore two to three-pound lobsters, which would have been a prize catch for most divers. I wondered if we were hunting for something other than lobster.

He stopped at a massive jagged coral head with a large overhang casting a hard shadow in the sand, even at a depth of forty-five feet. The bright sand bottom made seeing underneath the coral head difficult. Chuck removed his tank, leaving his regulator in his mouth. He squeezed Chevali's hands to clasp his tank and indicated that Chevali would have to move it with him as he bellycrawled into the darkness of the coral overhang. He wiggled so deeply that Chevali also had to lay on the sand with his arms extended, pushing the SCUBA tank into the shadow. The only thing left showing of Chuck was his calves and fins, and after a few seconds, they began violently shaking.

Plumes of sand ejected from the dark space and covered Chevali. I immediately thought he was having a seizure and swam to them, hoping to somehow pull Chuck's bulk out from under the ledge. My mind raced through a thick acetaldehyde soup. *Keep the regulator in his mouth, let him vomit through it, don't rush to the surface, send Rosie for help while we resuscitate him. Shit, where would his Jeep keys be?*

A swift current carried the billows of sand off them and toward me. Chuck struggled to wiggle out but was still convulsing?

New torrents of sand clouds shot out into the water, re-covering Chevali. They moved together purposefully, yet his body continued to shudder and get yanked side to side. It was like watching an underwater exorcism scene. Some mystery force had the raw power to toss Chuck's mass around handily.

He emerged with a streaking orange flash that shot past Chevali, heading up toward the surface. It convulsed numerous times per second, making a squeaking sound with each thrust. The orange thing pulled Chuck by his lobster stick. Chevali, still holding Chuck's SCUBA tank, had to push off the bottom through the cloud of sand and swim hurriedly upward. Chuck, Chevali, and a gargantuan crustacean rocketed upward, strung out in a nearly vertical line, headed too fast for the surface.

The wildly flicking fantail was as wide as my hips. I couldn't believe that a lobster could pull two men through the water, yet they were ascending at an alarming rate. So I shot up toward them to help. I grabbed the handle of the lobster stick, and the monster's power reminded me of my one humiliating experience attempting to water ski. Our ascent slowed, and Chuck climbed his lobster stick, hand over hand, to grab the beast and its whipping three-foot-long antennae with leather gloved hands and hugged it. He fought to turn the lobster over, inspected for eggs under the carapace, and held a 'thumbs up.' He didn't let go of it until we were back at the Jeep when Rosie asked, "Did you know he was living under that particular coral head? You passed a half dozen nice-sized lobsters to get to him?"

"I saw him a month ago and hoped he would stick around until you guys got here. He's my biggest yet." Chuck radiated pride as he attempted to put the thing into a burlap bag.

"Oooh, no, baby. We're going home Deer Hunter style." Chevali said as he unwound a crusted tangle of nylon rope from the back of the Jeep. With one person at each corner of the horned gargoyle, we were able to tie the lobster, now named "Larry," across the Jeep's hood as a crustacean hood ornament.

Locals laughed and cheered, "OK, Mr. Lobster," as we navigated the narrow streets on the way to the Pussers bar for lunch. Chuck waved and smiled at his black and white friends like a rodeo queen making her entry lap. Tourists eyeballed the rolling aquarium and gave either smiles or sour scowls.

Chuck's personal Grape tree-shaded parking spot behind the bar was vacant...being on a sidewalk. Anybody else would've gotten towed, but a local cop, upon seeing Larry sprawled on the hood of Chuck's Jeep, waived us into his parking space. From under the brown canvas roof of the bar, a single "wow" spawned a crescendo of questions and laughter. Day drinkers and bartenders clamored to attain a view of Larry from over a short rail that separated the bar from Chuck's parking space. A few tourists took pictures. A well-fed woman wearing a floppy black hat and a pound of gold on her chubby fingers and thick neck chastised, "Oh my Goodness, never, never could something like this go on in the United States."

Chevali, the Henry Kissinger of crustacean relations, snapped, "Hey Doris, if you read anything besides fucking Fabio novels, you would know that we ARE in the United States." Petting Larry's thorny carapace, "and I'd bet you lunch that his skin is softer than yours." Her husband clutched her hand while glancing at Jeb sideways. He mumbled something, hurriedly threw money on the bar, drained his drink, and dragged his gape-jawed wife out of the bar.

Chuck recounted his epic lobster fight story while friends bought him Caribe beers. Soon, he was drunk, and I was worried about Larry getting too hot. I asked the bartender where I could buy some ice to cool Larry off. He lifted a five-gallon bucket of ice from under the bar, which I upended on Larry, who was still struggling to escape. I was able to relax and attacked my grouper sandwich, which soon made me dizzy with fatigue. I drifted into unconsciousness, sitting on my bar chair.

Chuck and I bound Larry's antennae with thick cotton string from the junk drawer of Tamarindo's kitchen to keep him from lacerating anybody who might open the refrigerator. Aside from a Cambazola cheese wedge and a milk jug, he took up the entire top shelf. A slurring Chuck gave confident guarantees that Larry would live in there without dying or rotting for at least a day. Tonight, he continued, was 'rib night' at Uncle Joe's Ribs, and we would address Larry tomorrow night. He weaved his way to the couch, plopped onto his back, rotated his stained ball cap over his eyes, and started snoring within a minute. His round, furry belly rhythmically peeked from under his T-shirt as it rose and fell. I took a hot shower to wash off sea salt and the remnants of the previous night's eruptions, laid on our soft bed whose sheets smelled of sunshine, spooned a naked Rosie and tumbled into a deep afternoon sleep.

-18-

BRAND NEW SECOND HAND

A woman's tonsil hemorrhaging scream and frantic slapping foot beats on the terrazzo floor above my head shattered my peaceful somnolence. Boddington's voice boomed, "What in the fuckin' hell..." as the woman's shrieks and foot slaps Dopplered off to the far edge of the deck.

"I think the Boddingtons may have found Larry. What do you think?" I talked to the jerking stern of Rosie's head. She didn't turn around, "Whoops, didn't see that one coming, shoulda put a note on the fridge or something, huh."

"Probably so, they're both from the Rockies. Doubt they ever saw a ten-pound lobster in a refrigerator before."

"That may explain the screams," she said.

"Bet you're right."

"Hey, speaking of screaming, I was a little distracted from my vacation duties last night when I came to bed," I said.

"You mean, came to floor." Her head tilted as she spoke.

"Yeah, whatever, but while in my unfortunate and unintended state of modest inebriation, I ignored my manly vacation dutles."

"I take it you are feeling better now?"

"Well, now that you mention it." I stroked her back.

"What did you have in mind?" I ran my hand across her ribcage to her right breast.

"Oh, that." Rosie rolled to her back.

I continued running my fingertips lightly along the contours of the border between tan and untanned breast skin.

"I don't know, honey. I still have some unsavory visions of you from last night that could ruin my mood."

I gently cupped her entire breast and chewed the side of her neck. She softly moaned.

"Let me see if I can tease those memories away from your imagination." I ran my tongue in little half turns from her neck to her breast, to her belly.

"It's not my imagination, asshole. It's a hardwired memory blazoned into my brain, but don't stop."

"Very well then, let me see if I can scrub those memories from your little brain with my tongue starting right down here...."

We joined the group on the deck after sunset. Heat radiated up from the deck's surface, which had been storing the sun's warmth all day. A mildly cool breeze wafted down the Island's central canyon to stir the air. Lightning flashes from a distant storm interrupted the moonless night's light vacuum. No thunder, only scintillating light scattering down, giving temporary faces to the voices in the dark. The sound of Chuck's Jeep signaled that the walk to town would soon begin.

Morning or evening, I loved the walk to town. It preceded another plunge into a lively segment of my temporarily peaceful life. Cruz Bay was never boring and promised new and unfamiliar smells, people, foods, and sometimes, unfortunately, alcohol in excess. After last night's adventure, I promised myself that I was going light on the rum. Chuck's curiously light footsteps for a man of his size played a familiar cadence as he approached the steps leading up to the deck. "Where is my Larry?" His silhouette moved from the shadows to the sliding glass doors that led from the deck to the kitchen. He was one of those big guys who moved as if he were dancing. Opening the refrigerator door and extracting Larry, he talked to the lobster, "Still alive and happy, eh buddy."

"Where's my drinking partner?" I was hoping it would be anybody but me. "Hoot, you on the deck or still downstairs sleeping? Come in and have a shot with me." His head weaved, searching the darkness beyond the glare of the glass door.

"I'm good, amigo, gonna drink light tonight, gotta save some brain cells for Bonefishing in the morning."

"Aw, come on ya pussy, it's rib night at Uncle Joe's, and they don't serve anything but beer." I was about to politely decline when I felt a slender, firm arm grab mine and pull me into its attached torso. A breast larger than Rosie's warmed my right upper arm as she walked me arm in arm toward the light of the kitchen. Jessica powerfully answered Chuck as we walked, "He's coming," then in a softer voice into my ear, "We're getting wasted tonight, Ky." The smell of alcohol already wafted heavily on her breath.

She stopped me at the sliding glass door and watched Baine. He was staring at the TV while wearing a baby blue polo shirt, buttoned up to the neck, Bermuda shorts, and loafers-no pennies, no socks. "He... I don't know? I can trust you, Ky. You're my doctor, I think you called in an antibiotic for me once, and you can't tell anybody anything I talk about, right?" She was pleading with me to hear her secrets.

"Sure, I guess," I answered and strained my brain to remember if I had even treated her for a hangnail.

"First, we drink." She whispered.

This is becoming stranger by the second.

"Chuckie, shots for everybody," Jessica said, giving Chevali a seductive smile. It was not unusual for Jessica to abandon her ultra-demure mainland appearance and temporarily escape the confines of her conservative life when on vacation. I had seen this measured transformation a few times in Hawaii and Tahiti. But her tone tonight was different. She wasn't showing cleavage but the majority of her breasts. The dress she wore had the texture of silver and orange flecked crepe paper that clung sexily to every curve of her body. I could always joke with Jessica, harder than most women, because we had the unspoken "no touch rule" of my wife's best friend. I was comfortable with it. She always privately said she liked it.

"Wow, great tits, oh and dress too." I started the games while Chuck and Jessica sipped their shots. "And I'm not seeing any panty lines, Miss Jessica." I chided.

"You're so astute, Dr. Elliott," she said as she lifted her dress to show her cellulite-free right ass cheek to us.

Baine was within eyeshot but paid no attention. She smiled with only half of her mouth and hung her head. "Hey, you doing a little rum with us?" She asked Chevali. He still wore a puzzled facial expression after the ass-cheek flash and didn't answer. For a few seconds, he stared at Jessica, shifted his gaze to the deck where Chiara talked to Boddington, then back to Jessica.

"Pour me a tall one Chuckie, we're celebrating the greatest lobster ever caught," Chevali said. The three of them gave poor Larry four toasts in the time I took to finish one shot. In celebratory drunkenness, Chevali pulled Larry out of the refrigerator, knocking the milk onto the floor, shooting it everywhere. He dramatically feigned a strained Larry-power lift over his head. Larry's dozens of legs haplessly bicycled in the air, searching for a grip to freedom. While laughing at the mess, Jessica bent forward toward him and softly, nonchalantly stroked her cleavage with the back of her hand. He raised an eyebrow, returned Larry to the refrigerator, and threw a few paper towels at the milk lake, leaving the remainder to the roaches.

"Time to go." Chuck said, "We gotta get to Uncle Joe's before the stupid tourists eat all the ribs." I raised my eyebrows at him.

"Oh, sorry, Hoot," and in a louder voice, "all the OTHER stupid tourists," and poured four deep roadies in plastic cups. The sound of a tropical downpour suddenly hammered the roof of Tamarindo. Jessica approached her TV absorbed Baine, "Time to go eat ribs, honey." Her voice was overly sweet and slurring. He didn't make eye contact with her but squinted at her shoes. "You look great, but why don't you put on the burgundy pumps."

"Screw your burgundy pumps. I'm going for comfort, not to entertain your.... Proclivity." Leaning closer, she said, "and to that end, Baineey boy, tonight I'm going commando." She stood erect, faced Baine, and her dress went up again. Baine jumped up and smoothed it back down. "Geez, sweetie, I only made a shoe fashion request." Then said to us, "Uh, by proclivity, she meant my bent for exclusive fashion."

"My ass, toe sucker." Jessica wobbled as he maintained a stiff smile and said, "She's full of it tonight, isn't she? Come on, sweetie, let's go eat ribs." He tried to lift the roadie out of her hand. She slapped his hand away. "Bent for fashion? And stay away from my drink. It's party time, your honor." Baine firmly steered her toward the sliding glass door.

"Toe sucker?" I asked Chevali.

"He's a damn divorce judge. Who knows what goes on in his chambers?"

Chuck, in a strangely paternal tone, said to Chevali and me, "Ya know, there are all kinds of things that bring men pleasure. You might not want to judge the judge too harshly. Like for example, you, Jeb, if it's not strange stuff, you have no interest. And you, Hoot, oh shit, you're married to my sister, I don't want to know." I laughed but also wondered what was motivating him to come to Baine's aid.

The night was young, and I had already taken my turn at the helm of the 'HMS Drunk Asshole' last night. Tonight, as my 'sit back and watch night' had already started. A collective drunken impatience drove the group to the deck. Chevali stepped out into the rain, cranked his face skyward, and drank from the storm.

The rain tapered down to a drizzle halfway to town. I was warm, wet, and noticed that I was walking with a newfound natural relaxation cadence. The pace of my breathing and walking had subtly changed. My gait slowed, and deep belly breathing replaced my shallow, staccato respiration. I was walking in vacation mode, even sober. With my wristwatch gone, my vacation time meandered between mealtime to rest time and adventure time. The unhurried pleasures of the Caribbean replaced bossy, hour-hand time. Down here, time was redefined as right now and experienced as whatever trivial pursuit in which I was engaged. *God, am I on St. John time ?* I questioned myself as each slow breath accompanied a couple of calm steps.

The balanced cadence of my expanding and contracting belly made me think about all the hours I'd spent in meditation, straining to relax into this Island's natural pace. My flip-flops weren't slapping the wet pavement as they did when I arrived. They slid in a laconic shuffle. I reached for Rosie's hand. Misty sweeps of tiny raindrops collected in my hair to run as rivulets into my eyes, blurring my already unfocused vision. St. John's physical and emotional comfort held me in their arms. The simple acts of breathing and walking in a steaming rain with my wife and friends became the essential things in my world. Above me, the low-lying clouds' rolling bottoms glowed, lit by the amber street lights. The mucky wet atmosphere that separated the stars from the cloud tops strobed with approaching lightning flashes. Perfect moments, like the sky's lightning approaching us, come when and where they want. I carelessly relinquished control to that moment.

Uncle Joe's Ribs' yellow and white tin-roofed, open-air restaurant stood between a busy street and a public parking lot. There, beer drinking locals leaned against their cars while Quelbe music rattled from car speakers. The St. John dialect, especially when lubricated with ethanol, sounded more like an intense argument than polite conversation. Unintelligible Tommy gun bursts of words splattered and mowed down any peace in their path. The return volleys and occasional reassuring laughs shot back with the sounds of acrimony. Bottles fell to the pavement and sometimes broke, while others clattered and rolled. Next to Uncle Joe's, a community billboard stood, plastered with pieces of paper advertising everything from puppies to baby sitters, yoga instructors, and rooms for rent.

Across the street, a Dominican Bar with no visible name flew a long Heineken banner as its only street-side decoration. The dull blue, hand-painted plywood exterior looked as if it had been a third-grade construction project. A lightless interior blasted the street with honking Dominican Bachata music. Drunken construction worker's unlaced boots dangerously drug leather jellyfish tentacles, inviting orthopedic disaster. They danced with beer bottles as their partners out into the street. Drivers nonchalantly drove around them or waited patiently for them to merengue back to the bar.

Uncle Joe's dining area consisted of a few plastic tables separated from the street by a short picket fence. The interior was open on three sides and contained refrigerators filled with ears of corn, little mystery tubs of side dishes, raw chicken and ribs on the lower racks, soft drinks on the upper racks. Uncle Joe cooked on a fastidious, handmade brick BBQ pit choked with meats smothered in a sweet, sticky BBQ sauce. The olfactory-seducing smoke rolled along the low tin roof to impregnate the still air, making the wait for food unbearable. Eating at Uncle Joe's was like being in a dry fishbowl. Walking tourists following their noses, eyed your food with cautious envy. Car drivers passing six feet from our table, sized us up, seemingly judging whether we were worthy of the island prize of Uncle Joe's ribs. They smiled once they saw Chuck and regularly stopped in the road, stalling the cars behind them in typical St. John fashion, "Chuckie, OK? Dis your family you said come visit?"

He'd respond, "OK. Yes..." I would smile through a beard of BBQ sauce dangling from my chin, waive a rib, and give the culturally appropriate "Good evening." After short, pleasant exchanges, they would slowly roll off, uncoiling the traffic behind them.

The no-name Dominican Bar across the street was the best dinner entertainment on island. Drunks danced and took wild swings at one another while swearing in a creole/Spanish hybrid. It was a one-punch fight with the loser's cap-clad head hitting the concrete if they connected. Hard appearing, overly made up, and painfully underdressed women entered the bar, disappeared into the hollow inky interior, and never reemerged. The exception to this disappearance rule was Latrina.

Latrina, a local West Indian crack addict, split her life into equal parts by living in jail, the psych ward in San Juan, and on the streets of St. John. Matted hair made her head seem distorted. She wore a long blue dress, festooned with all manner of island grime. Dental hygiene was noticeably not in her top fifty priorities, as teeth were a rare commodity in Latrina's head. Yet, she did have a signature bathing ritual to the horror of locals and tourists alike. Her favorite bathing spot was on the beach in front of the Pussers bar. Daily, to the dismay of the denizens of million-dollar yachts from all over the globe, Latrina would fling her blue dress in the sand, and without soap, roll in the water's edge. Sandy, the abandoned Rottweiler, would playfully bark and run around her. Once her emaciated body took on the appearance of a disemboweled soft dog toy covered in wet sand, she would rinse off in the oil-slick water, towel off with her dress, put it back on, and head to town.

Latrina was the only woman that night to leave the Dominican bar. She did so while screaming and boxing the air with clenched fists into the middle of the street. She turned to face the bar, raised her dress over her head, spread her legs, and yelled, "YOU WANT SOME A 'DIS?" After which, a Heineken missile launched from the bar hit its intended target, dropping her to the wet street. She laid, yelling up at the rain and lightning while cars cautiously drove around her. The sight of Latrina's cachectic jiggling legs, and empty burlap bags of an ass, stopped our voracious eating. Sauce-covered hands held motionless ribs in front of open, brown-stained mouths. Everybody's eyes darted to Latrina's supine form and back to their food until Jessica, slurring through her rum and spitting little pieces of meat, "Now that's an ass you could kiss," snorted and attacked her ribs.

"Chuckie, should we pull her out of the street so she doesn't get run over?" Rosie asked.

"SHIIIT, no, you touch her, and she will either hit or stab you, let her be."

From a side street shadow, a skeletal figure emerged with a plodding, camel-like gait. He bobbed with every splayed, barefooted step toward Latrina. He and Latrina evidently shared the same hairdresser and nutritionist. The right side of his head was afro-round, while the left half stood flat, making him look like a walking bookend. A squashed, partially smoked cigarette tucked partly hidden behind his left ear. He gesticulated with a white tin cup as he talked down to her in the street. A rusting brown sedan stopped at his side, barely missing Latrina. The driver wore a flowered plastic shower cap that dented the car's sagging ceiling liner spoke to the tall man, poured some Heineken into his cup, and drove off. I recognized his tin cup as a Pusser's cup, similar to the one still in my fanny pack from the previous day. The tall man offered a hand to help Latrina stand. She took ahold of his generosity, pulled herself to her feet, snatched the cup from his grasp, drank the contents, and staggered away while swearing at him. He stood, appearing confused and talking to himself in the rain, oblivious to traffic.

"Poor Tona," Chuck said.

"I'm assuming that's Tona?" I asked.

"Yep, he is a sweetheart local. Ya see him out on the streets every night, doing the DaTona five hundred."

"What the hell's the DaTona five hundred?"

"Oh, you'll see, he's harmless. He doesn't have all of his marbles and just wanders the streets all night."

"That bitch drank his beer," Chevali interjected, rising to his feet. He pulled a Heineken from Uncle Joe's refrigerator, threw a five-dollar bill on the counter, and walked out to Tona. He patted Tona's wet blue shirt, gave him the beer, and sauntered back.

Chevali reseated himself and reached to pick up a rib with the same hand that he'd patted Tona. Chiara squealed, "No, NOT thata hand." He leaned away from the table, poured beer on his hand, and wiped it on a stained and shredded paper napkin.

"That was kind of you, but why'd you do it?" Chuck asked.

Speaking through a mouth full of rib meat, Chevali said. "Two reasons. One, I hate it when bitches steal from men who are being kind to them. Two, we are all, every one of us, a simple stroke of bad luck away from being in his shoes, 'er, bare feet, oh fuck it, you get my point."

After dinner, Chuck wanted to check the community billboard outside the restaurant for used Jeep tires. We followed him and found a large color poster taking up the center of the board.

U.S. PARK SERVICE AND THE DEPARTMENT OF THE INTERIOR.

$10,000.00 REWARD LEADING TO THE ARREST AND CONVICTION OF THIS MAN SUSPECTED IN THE ASSAULT ON AN ENDANGERED SPECIES.

THIS PHOTOGRAPH TAKEN 9/13/1996 ON THE PRO-TECTED FLANNIGAN ISLAND

Beneath the writing was a grainy color picture of Baine with his wet suit pulled down to his knees, looking at the camera, squatting over a pile of rocks. On the bottom of the poster was an 800-phone number. Baine and Jessica stood motionless, staring at the poster with limp faces, his natural, hers from complete inebriation.

"Ha, nice grin there, your honor. I could use an extra ten grand to help pay for this trip. What's that phone number?" Chevali pretended to write the number on his palm.

"Shit Baine, we gotta get you off the island tonight. This is not good," Chuck spoke soberly. Boddington pulled a red bandanna from his back pocket. "Shit baby shit, boy you an outlaw. Here take this, put it over your face, Jessie James like. Nobody will ever recognize you with this disguise." Baine waived Boddington off and turned to stare wistfully at the lights of St. Thomas.

"OK, OK...I got a friend's Boston Whaler in the middle of Cruz Bay harbor I can use any time. We gotta get you off Saint John tonight, and on a flight. You have got to leave the islands before your picture makes it to the ports and airport." Chuck rubbed his forehead as he spoke.

"Well, how are you gonna get to it, swim?" I asked sarcastically.

Chuck stroked his clean clothes. "If I got to, I guess. Usually, I can hitch a ride on a dinghy, but probably not at this time of night". He snapped Baine out of his slack-jawed trance, "BAINE, MOVE, GO, NOW." Baine grabbed Jessica's hand, saying, "Come on, we gotta pack."

Jessica shook her hand out of his, "What's this WE shit?"

"What do you mean? Come on, let's go pack. We could go to jail, Jessica."

Her eyes focused a few feet behind Baine's head, "I'm not the one who shit in an endangered bird's nest. That was aaaall you. I'm in the middle of a fabulous vacation. Lots of adventures left to come." She eyed Chevali's face and then his crotch. "I'm staying put. Not leaving until next week, but you, Judge Bowel Boy, might want to haul your ass home and pack. BYE, and take the damn burgundy pumps too." She raised an unsteady hand and gave a Pope-like wave. Baine said nothing and trotted toward Tamarindo. Witnessing Jessica's odd drunken behavior made me wonder if there was some type of contaminate in our liquor supply that turned nice people into raging assholes, as it had me the night before. No... self-examination yielded the only true answer. Jessica was tonight, as I was last night, a plain drunken idiot. There can be pain in truth at times.

"I hope he can catch a morning flight before his picture is distributed to Customs. Anybody for a late-night swim in the bay, Hoot?"

"I'd love to, but I'm nursing a bruised esophagus. Probably shouldn't swim."

"Chevali?"

"Yeah right, Chuckie, think about it."

"Boddington?

"I'll stand on the shore, ya know, keep a watchin out fir them shark fins, give ya warning." He held his arms stretched out to his sides, alternately flapping them, "I'll shoot 'ya some semaphore." With each different arm position, he enunciated a letter, "B-I-G-F-U-C-K-I-N-G-S-H-A-R-K."

Chuck sounded exasperated, "Alright, alright, I got it."

"Oh, Ky," Rosie sided with Chuck's and turned back at me, "you go with him, keep him safe."

"Me? What the hell am I gonna do, be the trailing bait behind him? I'm a hungover shitty swimmer."

"I don't know," Rosie whined.

"Before we go swimming, let's check the Pussers bar. There are always sailors there with dinghies eating dinner or drinking." I said, not in the mood to swim in black water on a dark night.

I looked back at the poster as we walked off. Chevali had taken it down and was rolling it up.

We passed Tona as he made his rounds in the 'Da-Tona five hundred.' Locals and tourists frequently interrupted his vacant stare and mumbling self-talk, giving him cigarettes or pouring Heineken into his battered Pusser's white tin cup. Somehow that addled, mumbling, aimlessly wandering man inspired a level of misguided kindness in others. I wondered if anybody ever gave him food.

Boddington and I trailed behind the others. I bought us each a Heineken to drink as we walked. Tona approached us, and I stopped him, "Hey amigo, can I share my Heineken with you?" I asked as I reached behind me and unzipped my fanny pack. He answered with warm, sad eyes as he handed his filth-crusted cup to me. Even in the dim light, I could see its patina of brown-stained hand grease. Black crusty yuck clung under the cup's lip that would sicken a buzzard. I held it up to Boddington to inspect, and his smile inverted to follow the contours of his handlebar mustache. I rotated my torso, and while hidden from both of their eyes, exchanged Tona's cup for my new virgin Pusser's tin cup, and serreptitiously stuffed his cup into my fanny pack, and re-faced Tona in the dim yellow street light.

I poured my beer into the pristine cup, quickly held it up to Boddington, "Cheers," and took a couple of long gulps from it. Boddington gagged, "Good lord Ky, what the fuck are you doing? That cup is radioactive. Spit that shit out. What the hell is the matter with you?" His eyebrows slammed into his widening eyes, and he struck me in the back, "Spit it out, son...SPIT". I intentionally swallowed it with flare and smacked my lips.

"We are all God's children, my friend," I said while handing Tona the cup (with a Fifty-dollar bill wrapped around it as a silent thank you), belched, and walked on. Boddington was wordless for a more extended period than I had ever witnessed. He repeatedly grimaced at me, gurgled, and spat on the ground in a pseudocyesis of retching.

The nearly deserted, dimly lit Pussers bar played soft Brazilian jazz replacing the typically loud rock or reggae. One of the bartenders sat with his chin in his hand, trying not to fall asleep. A couple of pink, British accented mid-thirties women with tight sundresses stretched over ample bodies chatted, looking for last call takers. At the far end of the bar, an old grey, unhealthy appearing man sat nursing a shot. An African Grey parrot stood on the bar in front of him, holding a peanut in one foot, picking the shell away from the hidden meat. Next to the parrot laid a grey flannel bag, large enough for a pair of shoes. The old man wore a wrinkled, sun-damaged face and a florid rhinophyma mangled nose. He looked like an emaciated W.C. Fields without the Top Hat. His eyes spoke in sad volumes of a lonely life.

"I guess we're screwed," I said.

"No, we may be in luck." After squeezing past the British women who inspected him after he had passed, Chuck addressed the old man.

"Guys," Chuck spoke to us, "this is Ski."

Ski responded with unexpected, well-spoken English, "Nice to make your acquaintance," and presented a boney hand to shake. He appeared to be pleased yet unnerved by our mass attention and never held eye contact for long. The parrot worked, nonplused at her peanut. Chuck explained that an urgent situation required that he get to his friend's Boston Whaler moored halfway to Ski's boat on which he lived. Ski examined his shot, finished it, and quietly said, "It would be my pleasure."

I motioned for the bartender and paid for Ski's drinks. He thanked me with a nod and motioned tipping his nonexistent hat, then opened the grey flannel bag that lay on the bar next to the parrot by lifting the upper edge. The parrot dropped her peanut and walked deeply into it. Ski tied a grey, frazzled piece of string around the opening and lifted the bird, holding it close to his chest. All of us except for the Boddingtons followed him down to the water's edge. Boddington boisterously engaged the British women with the story of my drinking from Tona's cup, gesticulating wildly as they laughed.

Ski's ancient fiberglass dinghy ran no more than four feet in length. Her stern was in the water, and a single oar rocked slowly in an inch of water in her floor. She had previously been blue, but most of the color rubbed off, exposed the interlocking lace pattern of raw fiberglass. Ski wore shiny brown polyester pants cut off at mid-calf. He rolled them up to reveal lumpy, barnacled knees. Handing me the bird in the bag, he said, "Hold my Annie-bird soft but firm son, she's my world," his eyes followed her flannel bag like a young mother handing her baby to a friend for the first time. He pulled the dinghy into the water and invited Chuck to come aboard. He did, and it sank to the sandy bottom as water cascaded over the shallow gunwales. I couldn't help myself, "Time to back off the donuts, 'eh Chuckie."

He glowered at me, stepped out and upended the water from it, then pushed it farther from shore. First Chuck, then Ski precariously balanced their weights in the minuscule boat. The waterline was within inches of her oar locks. Ski looked up at me, "Please, son, hand me my girl." I carefully placed the bird in his trembling, tobacco-stained fingers. Chuck took short strokes with the oar until only their silhouettes undulated against the distant jumble of St. Thomas's street lights. Fearing that if they capsized, the bird would drop to the bottom of the bay, I stood on the shore waiting for either cries for help or the sound of a boat motor. A voice from the dark bay rolled along the water's surface, "Hey Hoot, tell Dumbshit to meet me where you are standing," just before a motor sputtered to life.

Tamarindo's lights were off, except for Baine's room. I asked if anybody wished to join me in a late-night dip to watch the bats.

Rosie said she wanted to go to bed and read. She kissed my forehead and told me not to be too late.

I slid my clothes off and eased into the coolness of the water. I heard Baine and Jessica arguing, a door slam, and saw Baine's outline scurry past the pool.

"Hey, Baine, come here, amigo," I spoke to the black silhouette obscuring the sparkling purple night sky. "I'm sorry things had to end like this for you, is there is anything I can do?"

"Thanks, Ky. I gotta fly back to the States before they catch me."

"Is Jess really staying here?" I asked.

"Yeah, she's kinda miffed. Wants to stay and work on her tan or something."

Right... work on Jeb.

I said, "Rosie and I will return her to you safely."

"I'm not sure that's what she wants."

"Of course, she does. You know women, sometimes they get drunk and say stupid shit that they don't mean. You guys will be fine. Chuck is waiting for you at the shoreline below the Pussers bar. Fly safe."

"Thanks, Ky."

"You bet, now go fast before the Sheriff shows up with his posse."

I had the pool to myself to enjoy the bat dive bombings. The night clouds played silently by intermittently hiding the moon. A passing warm rain hissed softly on the pool surface. The bats, backlit by the lights on the valley below, skittered as they drank from the pool. I was chin-deep and enjoying my solitude when I heard bare feet behind me padding toward the pool.

The shadowy figure eased into the pool and made its way toward me. Rosie was joining me, I thought, *how sweet*. Her hand silently reached out to touch me in braille fashion to determine my position in the pool. I leaned over and kissed her mouth. She smelled different, not bad, but different, and heavily of alcohol. I jumped back, splashing water up onto the pool deck, "Oh Shit, Jess. I'm so sorry. I didn't know."

"I know, I know, it's fine, please just talk to me. I'm confused and scared," Jessica said.

"Why didn't you go with Baine?"

"I can't take him anymore, Ky."

The bats were hitting a drinking frenzy, "Tell me...."

"Oh, this is so embarrassing. Please don't judge me." She paused, clutched my arm, causing her breasts to wobble on me. "Baine won't make love to me unless he plays with my feet, kissing them, sucking my toes, even dressing them up in puppet clothes. Since we've been down here, he's made me do footie Pirate puppet shows. He dresses my feet up in puppet clothes, for God's sake. Blackbeard versus Anne Bonnie. He makes me give him foot-jobs. He'd rather play with my feet than me. I'm sick of his weirdness. Tonight, I simply need a friend."

I reached down and held her hand in a brotherly fashion. *I just want to watch my bats*. She was drunk and hurt. I slowly spoke to her, "I love the hell out of you, so does Rosie." Her head dropped forward, and she talked to the water. "I'm a hopeless snob, and no real man would ever want me. I'm stuck with the Baines of the world. I'm pitiful."

"You're not pitiful, Jess. You're an emotion-driven human like the rest of us. And Baine, he's...he's a divorce judge. If I didn't have Rosie, I'd have chased you years ago."

"Really?" She asked excitedly.

"Absolutely, you're a 9.8 Jess. It's only my life's circumstances that have me acting like a gentleman. It's not sad. It's just life. But you and me baby, we're lucky to have each other. Look at us now, what two adults could be naked in a pool and be content with holding hands, sharing secrets and bats? Not many. I feel privileged to be your confidante."

"I guess you're right. Our secret." She put her head on my shoulder and quietly sobbed. I ran my arms around my crying, pitiful friend and watched my bats.

When I got to our room, Rosie was rhythmically snoring. I took a short shower and climbed hot, wet, and naked into bed. At deep competing levels, I felt guilty and proud of myself. I felt guilty for even fleetingly considering taking an opportunity with Jessica and proud for not listening to the little devil on my shoulder/under the water.

-19-

GONNA GET YOU

M y portly alarm clock sounded well before the sun had risen over Bordeaux Mountain. "Hoot, Hoot, where you at? We're waiting for you." Chuck was yelling from the deck above our rooms.

Rosie rolled to face me, "Hello, I was concerned that you might take to sleeping on the floor."

"Naw, I have quicker access to the things I need up here," I spoke to her chest.

"Pig."

"No, I mean my water glass." I patted my bedside table. "Gotta stay hydrated in this tropical heat."

"Hoot, move your ass up here before the Bonefish leave the island."

"Chuck's calling you," Rosie said, rolling her eyes up toward Chuck's voice.

"No, the Bonefish are calling me. He is only their emissary. What are you guys doing today?" I asked.

"Jimmy arranged for his friend to take all the girls sailing to Jost. Remember the poster on the light pole by sigmoid curve, the pictures of the sweet dog on the sailboat?"

"Uh, sure. What is Jost again?" I asked.

"Hoot, damn it, get up here, or we're leaving without you." Chuck was yelling as he paced heavily above our heads.

"It's a laid-back little island only a few miles away in the BVI. We always go to Foxy's or the Soggy Dollar bars when we come down here," she said.

"Have fun. See you tonight."

"Don't catch all the Bonefish. I love you."

"Love you too." I hurriedly bent over to kiss her and stopped at her mouth. I really did love her and was happy that I had handled last night the way I did. I kissed her longer than the normal quickie 'goodbye kiss.'

"Wow," she said, raising her eyebrows.

"I do love you, Rosie. Be safe and use sunscreen. Oh, and take care of poor Jessica. I'll bet she is gonna be a little hungover today.

"I will. Plus, now that Baine's gone, she can take that load off her feet and relax." Rosie said with no clue as to her words' meaning.

"Yeah, I'm sure she will have happy feet for the rest of the trip." I picked up my new Orvis rod for me and my old spare rod for Chuck.

Chuck was the only person upstairs in the main house. It took both of us rousting Boddington and Chevali to load them into the Herve Villechaize mobile for the drive to the trailhead leading to Reef Bay. Boddington and I rode in the back. Each turn showed juxtaposing scenes. The general pulled-back vistas were of hilly green islands scattered on a blue sea. A lineup of cumulous clouds extended in a chain from the Southeast to overhead and off toward St. Thomas. They were all uniform in size, shape, and height as if they were riding on an unseen cloud assembly line, marching Northwest toward the real world, a place I didn't want ever to think about again. I wanted Bonefish, Pusser's Rum, and warm nights of bats and laughter.

The closer-up roadside scene was that of an island in recovery with snapped trees, former homes in piles on the roadside awaiting disposal, and broad smears of human stuff in bushes and trees. Wrecked boats rimmed pristine, history-rich bays. "What a damn mess," Boddington yelled over the flapping truck cover. We were observing the same things. "How often do them hurricanes tear the shit out of this place, anyway."

"Hell if I know. Chuck says they can hit any year, right about this time," I said.

"What the hell would make people want to live down here with that kinda threat?"

I pointed to the top of the hills, "What's on the top of that hill?" I asked.

"Shit, I don't know, trees, monkeys, why?"

"Trees yes, monkeys no. But what DON'T you see that you will probably see on the mountains when you return home?" I asked.

"Damn it, Ky, would you quit answering my questions with questions. What the hell are you driving at?"

"No snow. No ice. No arctic blasts to send your nuts quivering under your diaphragm until May. Sure, there may be an occasional hurricane, but almost every day down here, nature is your friend. In a month, you'll be feeding horses in the snow while Chuck will be diving for lobsters in his underwear."

"Wouldn't be enough for me. Besides, where would ya ride your loud-ass Harley?" Boddington asked.

"Point taken. But that view could maybe make it worthwhile, right?" I pointed to the East, where the chain of the British Virgin Islands sprawled into a hazy distance. There were rolling, dark clouds behind them. I always took note of tropical cloud character since living in New Orleans. These were bad actors. I tapped on the roof of the pickup. "Chuckie," I thrust my nose up toward the rapidly building clouds behind the islands where the girls and his roommate were going today, "did you check the forecast? I hope that isn't Jost over there."

Chuck yelled from inside the cab. "Yeah, there is a little system building to the East, but not supposed to arrive here 'till later tonight. We're all good Hoot." My ears wanted to believe him, but my eyes told me not to.

"What the hell? We're on vacation. A little warm rain can't hurt us, eh Boddington?" I said.

He imitated casting a fishing rod. "Aint nothing getting between me and fishin today, buddy."

At the Reef Bay trailhead, the dark foliage tunnel disappeared behind the steeply descending muddy trail. The spider web hell was invisible in the faint early morning light. It was time to get even with Chevali for his toilet trick.

I put a finger to my lips while grinning at Chuck and said, "Jeb, why don't you go first and set the hiking pace. I know you're a little tired, and I don't want you to hurt yourself. It's a little muddy, so you might want to cinch your B-ball slippers down tight."

"These aren't slippers, asshole. They are the newest Air Jordan's. Kinda cool, huh?"

"Eh', I guess if you're gonna be dancing to hip hop," I said.

"I hope you didn't pay a lot for them because they're gonna get ruined," Chuck added.

"I bought them for this trip. I like high tops when I hike."

"This is more of a slog than a hike, and you may want to hold your fishing rod in front of you." Chuck cautioned.

I interrupted him firmly and quickly, "Don't sweat the rod position, just keep your eyes on the treacherous, muddy trail. Try not to look any more than a few feet in front of your feet. Always keep your head down, eyes on the trail. It's dark and slippery as hell. Don't want ya falling and bruising that pretty soft ass of yours," I said. Chuck grinned while mouthing the word "asshole" to me.

Chevali encountered the first thick web within a hundred feet. He talked about his sexual proclivities and watched the uneven ground as instructed when he recoiled as if kicked in the chest. He swore, stumbled backward, and fell in the mud on his back. "What the... Chuckie, what the hell?" Chevali spoke up and over his shoulder.

"I told you to hold your fishing rod up in front of you. By the way, he's on your chest." Chuck's right hand imitated a spider crawling on his own chest to his neck.

"Oh shit, shit, shit." He sputtered and fanned the leggy monster off him as it climbed toward his face. "Somebody else go first, how about you, son of a bitch," he said to me. I felt minimally vindicated as the steaming and muddy hillsides echoed Chevali's swearing.

"Yes, I will. Just remember it's crucial that you hold your rod up in front of your face," I said to Chevali.

"Ky, you're meaner than that bitch I took to Kauai last year. Boddington, you remember her, right?" Chevali said.

"I don't know if'n she was a bitch. I'm thinkin' she was just a little defiant concerning your less than flexible way of being, Chevali," Boddington said.

"Hey, flexibility was her only good asset," Chevali said as he pretended to hold her left hip with one hand and bend her over with his other hand, "nope, she was a bitch."

Boddington stopped walking and turned to Chevali. "Ya know, son, women can be like horses sometimes."

"Ha! Don't I know it. Did you see some of those heifers at the beach in spandex?" Chevali said.

"You are mixing metaphors, Jeb. Heifers is cattle," Boddington said.

"Who cares? They all walk on cloven hooves." Chevali dismissed Boddington's correction. Boddington slapped his own forehead.

"As I was sayin'. There's a big difference between a spirited horse and a bad-headed one. Same with women. Sometimes it's a thin line. A spirited horse has got him an opinion. And ya want an opinionated horse that gives ya that rare intersection of a little danger and excitement, wildness, and loyalty. A good woman with an opinion possesses them same qualities. It don't necessarily make her a bitch." Boddington said.

"Hey, if I want her opinion, I'll give it to her," Chevali said laughing.

Boddington turned to me, whispered the words, "Damn flatlanders," and continued talking to Jeb. "Well, Jeb, if you need a horse that ain't got no opinion, no spirit, then you ain't much of a cowboy, and if you need a woman who ain't got no opinion, then you ain't much of a man."

Chevali stared at Boddington for a few seconds, spit tobacco juice into the mud, and continued walking.

The ocean spread wide and blue beyond Reef Bay beach. St.
John's ragged South shore rounded its way into obscurity. The
sea and wind were calm as I began the pre-fishing ritual of
setting up my rod. It always seemed to take forever, and I imagined bored fish leaving the reef. I asked Boddington if he knew
what kind of flies to use for Bonefish and noticed his equipment. He had a baitcasting rod?

"What the hell is that?" I asked him.

He spoke to me as if I was stupid, "My fishin pole Ky, good
lord."

"I told you we were fly fishing, didn't I?

"Yep, but I ain't doin that sissy-ass fly whipping shit. I want
fish for dinner."

"Boddington, nobody eats Bonefish. We do catch and
release."

"Screw that man. If I'm fishin', I'm eating the bastards. I
want meat on the table, not some damn hippie fish hugging
experience." I looked to Chevali for help. He seemed perplexed
by his equipment. His reel was backward, and he was trying to
figure out how to wrangle the fly line out to the rod.

"Jeb, you ever fly fished before?" Chuck asked.

"Sure, lots of times in Alaska and the Bahamas, but I always had the guides to the bullshit work. That's what I paid
them for." Chuck already had his rig together and reached for
Chevali's. "OK, step one, put the reel facing forward." I turned
my attention back to Boddington as he dredged a blob of pink

goop from a small jar with his index finger. The wind carried a rotten fishy odor from it to my nose.

"What is that shit?" I asked.

"Powerbait, it'll get 'em every time." He responded with confidence. "Now, let's go catch us some bony fish to throw on the grill next to Larry," he said as he mushed goop onto a treble hook attached to a wire leader.

"A wire leader?"

"I did my reading. They say them bony fish have hard mouths, don't want them snappin' the ol twenty-pound test fluorocarbon. This shits' five bucks a roll at Walmart." I didn't want to squash his exuberance, so I just smiled.

We stepped quietly into the warm, calm water that colorlessly covered the shallow reef. The temperature and abundance of life pulled me into it, like going home. Within the liquid glass, tiny crabs, sea slugs, and fish cruised the sandy bottom for food. A stingray appeared from under a cloud of sand by my foot and flapped hurriedly away. "Whoa shit, glad I didn't step on that bastard," I said.

"Yeah, Hoot ya gotta do the stingray shuffle, walking in the water down here."

"The stingray shuffle?"

"Just shuffle your feet on the sand rather than stepping. That way, you scare the stingrays off rather than step on 'em and get stung." He shuffled his feet in short choppy, overly emphasized scoots along the sand.

"I understand. Walk like Chevali after he's soiled himself," I said.

"After what you did to yourself in the street the other night, Ky, you don't have much room to talk." I wondered if Chevali knew something I had forgotten in my drunken state. I stopped talking.

Boddington and Chevali spread out in unspoken predator pack mentality to find suitable positions to start casting. Chuck stayed back with me in the calf-deep warmth, watching a fish nuzzling a sea urchin upside down for breakfast. "Hoot, your friends are a blast. Thank you for bringing them down here. I needed the laughs."

"Thanks for helping Jeb. He likes being in nature but wasn't raised in it and doesn't know what to do other than enjoy it. On the other hand, Boddington is at home any place where there aren't walls or people."

"Oh really, I think they might prove you wrong." Boddington had already caught the bottom and was swearing, grinding his little baitcasting reel and tracing his fishing line to an underwater snag. Chevali had rolled out an impressive amount of fly line and with small wrist flicks, expertly commanded the entire length. He methodically drew the fly line and shot it forward at shadows in the water. I couldn't make out if they were Bonefish, but I was receiving an education on saltwater fly-casting technique by a man who couldn't put a reel on his rod.

"Shark, fucking shark, whoa baby, get outa here, you son of a bitch. Shark." Boddington's rod, tethered by his line to the rocky reef, arched forward as he cranked the reel. He high stepped in place, kicking at the water. "Shit, shit, screw off you bastard, this is mine." I reached into my fanny pack for my KA-BAR knife that an old friend had given me. Chuck threw his rod to the sand, and we ran into the water toward Boddington.

"Drop your damn rod, Boddington. The shark is after the Powerbait, not you." I yelled while splashing loudly, ruining any chance of catching Bonefish that day. Chuck passed me, pounding the water like a horse running through the surf.

"Screw that. I paid thirty bucks for this mother. He ain't

getting it." Boddington's rod took a fast, sharp downward bend as he stepped back and assumed a fish fighting position. The crank handle of his casting reel began rotating forward with a blazing speed of rotation. The shark had taken Boddington's Powerbait, dislodged it from the reef, and was now sprinting away from Boddington. The tone of his voice lightened, "Ha, I got me one boys, it's a fight to the death. I'll be puttin' ol' Jaws here on a stringer, directly." He was smiling, laughing to himself, and screaming epithets at the bolting fish.

I stopped my water churning run to watch him and drip seawater. Boddington's rod curved in an arc toward us, and a three-foot speeding blur shot past us then headed toward Chevali, who had stopped casting. His yellow fly line floated in limp rings in the water as he watched the Boddington show.

"Watch out Jeb, ifn' he hits you, he's liable to break a bone."

He didn't move and watched it pass him and head out to sea.

Boddington yelled, "Goddamn you, you ain't stealing my shit. Boys, I'm runnin' outa' line, what do I do?"

"Run Forest run," Chevali yelled, and Boddington did, lifting his knees almost to his chest, attempting to catch up with the torpedo at the end of his line. He moved Orangutan-like, running with his arms above his head. "Get back here. I'm gonna eat your toothy ass."

I asked Chuck if he ate shark.

"Not yet, but tonight may be a first."

Boddington disappeared underwater. He had run into one of the holes in the reef and fell wholly submerged. First to emerge was his fishing pole, then his fist holding it, then his balding and sunburned forehead. His torso shot upward out of the water, seemingly pulled out by his pole, and he was up running, coughing, and swearing again. The fight led him on a complete lap around the little reef while we retreated and watched from the shore. The frantic battle was slowing when Boddington yelled at us from chest-deep water.

"How the hell do I land this wild ass bastard?" The reef's water that had been crystalline before we stepped into it earlier was now disappointingly turbid. The only way to know the location of his shark was by watching his jittering fishing line.

Chuck shouted back to Boddington. "You want to start by getting out of deep water. All the commotion has drawn the attention of a few of his friends. Pull him closer to shore. You might want to do it now, Boddington." Two yellow fins, each sticking at least a foot out of the water, were closing in on Boddington. "Hey amigo, you may want to make it hasty. You got company." I used the SCUBA diving hand signal for 'shark' with an open hand, fingers pointing up, fin-like on the top of my head. He had no idea what I was trying to signal him and took his left hand off his rod, put his thumb to his nose, and wiggled his fingers, giving me the 'kiss my ass' sign. With the humor draining from the situation, I grabbed a fist-sized rock from the shore and threw it at one of the fins, nearly hitting Boddington. My aim was poor.

"What the hell, Ky, you trying to kill me?" Boddington said.

"Hoot, you throw like a girl." Chuck chastised me as he and Chevali began lobbing rocks at the fins. Boddington grinned back at us as they chunked their rocks with amazing accuracy. I felt stupid and irritated with my father for never teaching me how to throw.

"Thanks, boys. Ky, you keep the fuck away from the rocks." Boddington yelled. The torrent of thrown rocks kept the fins away from Boddington until he was on the wet sand, facing the point where his fishing line disappeared into the water. "Now what, I ain't got no net."

"Keep the line taught Boddington, I mean really taught," Chuck said and waded into murky the water. Boddington's pole shook, but he kept it pointing forward. Now opposite him in thigh-deep water, Chuck thrust his arms and face into the water and emerged with the shark's tail in his hands. "Walk backward, Boddington, keep the line tight between us, so he doesn't whip around and bite me." They worked in tandem with the shark strung out between them like a team roped steer.

Once on the dry sand, Chuck dropped his end, ran into the bushes, and emerged with a short, thick branch and beat the shark on the head until it was bleeding from its mouth and gill slits. He held it on the sand with the stick while it made futile attempts to bite the stick. I unsheathed my KA-BAR and drove it into the shark's skull with enough force to run the blade into the sand under its jaws. The fight was over.

I looked back at Reef Bay. It was murky brown and unfishable. Yellow fins patrolled the water in front of us a couple of times and disappeared. The day's bonefishing had ended, and my fly hadn't touched the water.

We hid from the sun in the cool sand under a Maho tree, and I pulled my baseball cap over my face and invited sleep. I was happy not to be alone. I imagined being out there with nobody around, fishing. Emotions of a confident solitude mingled with my unshakable fear of being alone in life. I was fine being by myself in nature. I preferred it most of the time. But dying alone, like both of my parents, frightened the hell out of me. I never worried about dying from cougars or bears or bike wrecks. My greatest death fear was to exit life alone in an ICU bed. Medically attended deaths are horrendous. With tubes in every orifice, you struggle to hold onto a life that's making every effort to escape. Your rotting body oozes yuck onto a plastic mattress designed to shed infected body fluids, so the next dying guy could soil himself where you died the day before. I prayed for my death in nature...only not right then.

From under my ballcap brim, I spoke to Chevali, "Fishing for Bonefish is like trying to force a lucid dream. Ya can't muscle it into happening. It's an expensive self-induced humility."

"Ky, Bonefishing is the sporting equivalent of paying to jack off. You spend an inordinate amount of money and effort building a skill that nets you nothing other than that worthless skill. Shit, even golf offers a remote chance of turning pro." He spoke as I drifted off.

I awakened to a battleship grey sky that hung like a hot and heavy carpet a few feet above our heads. The air wielded a pressure that spoke of trouble to come. "I'm thinking the little storm we saw building earlier is creeping in," I said.

"Hoot, you worry more than my mother. We have all day before it hits, and it's only a small system. It'll pass tonight while you snore in a drunken wet dream."

-20-

WHO THE CAP FIT

Rosie was leafing through the clothing racks at Foxy's bar when she heard the first rumble. "Jimmy, does Chuck wear muscle shirts?" She held up a shirt with a watercolor scene of a local man wearing a straw hat over his face, asleep under a palm tree. "No, he thinks he's too tubby to wear anything like that. I think he's perfect just the way he is. He is so self-conscious for a boy."

"He could always use a new baseball cap, right?" She asked.

"Oh my Goodness, yes. I keep telling him to ditch those grease pots he wears, but he insists on keeping them. He would love a Foxy's hat. That way, I can give an old one to the pit bull down the road to play with rather than eating the neighbor children." He cocked his head and smiled sweetly.

Rain pattered lightly on the tin roof of the little boutique, "Sounds like Virgin Island liquid sunshine." Jimmy was.... cheery and seemed to be content passing the time shopping with the girls. With each flowered drink he pounded, his hips loosened, and his head fell further back with giggling laughter. He had an armload of clothing and alternated turns with Rosie and Ramona to use the dressing room. At one point, he asked,

"Oh shit pies ladies, do these shorts make my ass look like a blimp in cotton?"

"All I can see is muscle rippling beneath the material, sweetie," Ramona answered. He giggled.

Rosie asked Ramona, "Does Boddington ever care what his ass looks like?"

"He doesn't give a damn. Weird, I mean Jimmy, huh?"

An unexpected lightning bolt struck the water in Great Harbor Bay off the island of Jost Van Dyke, shaking the cramped shop. Tim, the sailboat captain who they had chartered for the day, sat nonplused, sipping a rum at the bar. It was his daily life to load excited, sober St. John tourists onto his 28-foot sailboat, 'Bounder' in the morning, regale them with his sea stories on the way to Jost, and watch them drink and swim all day. He would reload them as drunks in the late afternoon to sleep on the deck of 'Bounder' for the ride home. Storms often blew in and out this time of year, and besides, he had consulted the weather channel a few days earlier, "No tropical development expected in the next 72 hours." He knew that the stray squall would carry the lightning off to St. Thomas within the hour.

"Is this anything to worry about?" Ramona asked Rosie in a concerned tone when the sprinkle turned into a substantial rain.

"Naw, it should pass in no time, then we'll go to Soggy Dollar for a Roti and a few Painkillers." Rosie held up a thong bikini with a likeness of a lascivious smiling Fox on the wisp of material in the front, "I'd look ridiculous in this, huh?"

"If you get one, I will too. We can shock the boys. What's a Roti and a painkiller?" Ramona asked.

"First things first, let me try it on, make sure it doesn't make my butt look like the moon squeezed in half by a rope." Rosie said as she searched the bikini rack, then asked Ramona, "Are you a size six, eight, what?"

"Thanks for the compliment, but I'm hitting double digits these days." Ramona turned to a bored appearing Chiara who was mindlessly leafing through men's shirts. "How about you, Chiara, want to join us in a Foxy's thong?"

"*Si*, I'd love to. Do they have any twos?"

"As in size two?" Rosie asked as she grimaced at Ramona.

"Si, that or a zero. I've been eating like a pig down here, so skip the size zero idea. It's hard to find clothes in my size. Let me check the Kid's section."

Softly, out of the side of her mouth, Ramona said to Rosie, "Oh poor me, the only place I can buy bikinis is at Pedophiles-R-Us. Bitch," causing them both to chuckle.

Rosie said, "She's funny as hell and has more brains than all the women Jeb has dated in the last three years put together. I've grown to love her."

Ramona replied, "Me too. Still, though, I'd like to spend just one night in her body, sleeping with Chevali. God, he is so, ummmm."

"Eh', I guess so in a jaded sorta way." Rosie's voice trailed off.

"Jade, marble, opal, I don't care, as long as it's Chevali's and hard," Ramona said, softly stroking her neck. But it would creep me out, being with a psychiatrist. I'd always feel like he was psychoanalyzing me."

"Ramona, as long as it has a pussy, he doesn't care if there is anything upstairs, let alone analyze it," Rosie said.

"Still, I'd love to give him something to analyze, spank, roll-over. Catch my drift?" Ramona said while spanking a pair of shorts on the rack next to her.

"Loud and clear."

Tim watched 'Bounder' in Great Harbor while the lightning and wind intensified. She was straining at her bow line attached to a small anchor in the sand fifteen feet beneath. He ordered another rum and sat back while his floating home and business bounced on wind-whipped waves, and a dark grey sheet of rain obscured his boat's outlines. Behind her, St. John and her neighbor islands hid the rain-choked atmosphere. When the lightning arrived, it invaded in waves from the ridge to the East of Foxy's to crash around them and then move out toward Bounder.

An hour of not visualizing Bounder had Tim tapping his fingers rapidly on the bar. The storm showed no signs of retreat, and he switched from rum to orange juice. Rain cascaded off Foxy's gutterless roof as a solid wall of water, further separating Tim from Bounder. Puddles in the wet sand conjoined, overflowing their banks and forming shallow rivers snaking toward the shoreline. While squinting out at the storm, Tim asked the bartender if he could use the bar's radio to contact other sailors in the area to ask about the storm. "This is lookin' like more than a passing squall."

The bartender handed him a two-way radio, saying, "Marilyn, she started deh same as dis, eh."

"Yes, she did," Tim said before making radio calls to fellow captains.

-21-

THREE LITTLE BIRDS

The hike up from Reef Bay grew more difficult by the minute. Rain and lightning snuck up on us by hiding behind Centerline Road and then suddenly rolling down the heavily wooded canyon. The tree canopy rocked in the gusting winds. High branches, broken and suspended the previous year, crashed down around us with a disquieting regularity. Damn, Chuckie, y'all didn't tell us we needed ta bring crash helmets for the hike," Boddington said as he eyed the swaying forest ceiling.

Chevali answered, "I'm not worried about my head. My new fucking Jordans are muddy as hell. These cost me an hour's work. Now they are ruined to shit."

"We could be squished or washed back down into the bay, and you are crying about your priss Nike boots. Jeb, I hope you can climb better than you fish," I said.

"Blow me, asshole. I've caught more Bonefish than you've had women or maybe even men for that matter. And besides, they are Jordans, not regular Nikes."

"You assholes, stop bickering like a couple of old women and concentrate on watching where you are walking. It's dark in here, and there are lots of trees and bushes you don't want to get tangled up in." Chuck sounded irritated. "Most of the stuff that grows here is either sharp or poisonous to the touch."

The mud of Reef Bay trail had transformed into a slick black soup. In the steeper sections, we slid back two feet downhill for every three feet climbed. The canyon bottom that had been silent on the hike down, gurgled with the sounds of tumbling water. It was dark enough to be early evening. "Damn, I hope Jimmy and the girls can get back safely through this. I'm a little worried about him them." Chuck sputtered on his words through a driving rain.

The uphill swim in the mud took an extra hour. My shorts and shirt were annoyingly heavy with rain and mud when we arrived at the truck. We each stripped down to our underwear, letting the hot rain wash sweat and mud off us. It did nothing to cool us. "Can you believe, hiking in the rain and still sweating your nuts off?" Chevali said to Boddington as he leaned against the truck bumper and drank from a gallon jug of water.

"Shit," Boddington replied, "if we were in Colorado walking in the rain, I'd be so cold my nipples would have already cut holes in my shirt. Now gimme some of that water, Jeb" and held a hand toward him.

"I'm hot enough to go naked for the ride home," Chevali said, "these damn wet shorts are chaffing my nut sack. What do you say, Boddington, let's skinny dip in this rain all the way home in the back of the truck, show our asses to the whole island?" I wasn't sure that Chevali was kidding. I knew him well enough to know his narcissistic, exhibitionistic personality traits.

"Hell no. I don't skinny dip. Seems like every time I do that, I develop some awful damn magical power." Boddington said, pretending to cinch his belt.

"You have a magical skinny-dipping power?" Chevali asked.

"Damn right. If'n I skinny dip, every man in the vicinity turns into a queer and every woman into a lesbian. It's weird. Everybody gets laid in some unnatural way, except for me."

"Well, Boddington, seeing your little dickie isn't gonna turn me queer," Chevali said.

"Well, maybe it could turn you into a lesbian," Boddington said.

"Already done."

Chuck interjected in a higher voice than usual as if his throat were tight, "Boddington, ask Jeb, he's the shrink, unnatural versus natural sex is a big grey zone." I wondered where he was heading with that one, but Chevali answered, "Right-O Chuckie. Normal, natural, unnatural, it gets all twisted up into a happy ball of sweating, hip-thrusting moaners. The shit that our post-Victorian society and religions have forced upon us is often in direct contradiction to where our Freudian id wants to steer us. It, your id, doesn't give a shit about society's guilt trips. It just knows what it wants."

Boddington leaned over to me and asked in a hushed tone, "Is id another, ya know, medical term for pecker?"

I answered, "It's your brain's pecker of sorts. It's the little voice inside the big head that makes us stupid and listen to our little head."

He was quiet and stared at me with rain water dripping off lowered eyebrows.

We stopped at the Dolphin Market to buy Pusser's rum and salad makings for the impending Larry the lobster's demise party. Boddington insisted on a can of beans in case the lobster wasn't to his liking. I picked up Sandy, the rottweiler, on our way home.

It was late afternoon when we got back to Tamarindo, and the flashing storm sat in Pillsbury Sound, obscuring St. Thomas from view. While the guys showered, I took the time to wash Tona's tin cup with soap, bleach, pool cleaning muriatic acid, and scrubbed it a half dozen times under boiling water. Once sterile, I inspected it. The dented cup with its chipped and faded enamel was mine now. I took a pinch of oatmeal, wetted it, and crammed it under the curled tin lip to dry for later.

The girls hadn't returned from Jost, and I was getting worried. My phone showed three missed calls and one message. Alley knew only to call me for emergencies. My adrenals sprang to life, loading my veins with a chemical cocktail that, like rum, could be my friend or enemy.

I listened to my phone message: "Ky, this is Baine. I'm stuck in the airport in Saint Thomas. I, uh, think I left my passport back at Tamarindo. Can you please ask Jessica to catch the next ferry and bring it to me? I have a flight out at ten thirteen tonight but can't get on it. Thank you. Oh, this is Baine, Jessica's Baine. Thank you."

The short-lived tropical twilight was barely perceptible when the voices of women awoke me. Rosie walked into the bedroom. Her flat and tangled hair hung on her tired face. Her wet clothes slowly swung as she moved.

"Hi honey, have a pleasant day sailing?" I asked as she dropped her bags with a thump on the tile floor. She fell face-first onto the bed and talked in a decrescendo monotone voice into the mattress. "Oh my God, what a cluster of a day we spent the entire day dodging lightning bolts swimming in the rain and lightning by Foxy's the weather sucked and we never even made it to Soggy Dollar when the weather finally started to clear we had to make a run for it back here and I think Jimmy is gay I want a shower and eat something besides alcohol can you help me pull these wet clothes off so I can shower do you know.... what.... we are.... dinner.... because I'm..." Her voice trailed off, and she stopped talking and started to snore face down. I removed her wet clothing while she slept.

I took my phone to Jessica to let her hear Baine's message. She was sitting on her bed wearing only a towel. The door to her room was open, and Chevali and Chiara looked in as Jessica burst into tears.

"That stupid ass, I can't escape him, not even on vacation. Ky, look at my feet. Are they sexier than these?" She held her breasts as Chiara and Chevali came into her room. Now I have to ride the ferry alone, at night, and go to St. Thomas to rescue his bird-killing ass."

"No, Jess, we won't let you go alone," I said, regretting my words, knowing I was about to do the right thing. *Shit.* I was going to have to go with her and miss the Larryfest. "Don't worry. I'll go with you."

"I can't let you." Jessica struggled through her tears.

"No, you go with her," Chiara commanded Chevali. "Ky is down here with his family for the first time in years. You go." I watched Jessica's eyes widen with Chiara's words.

"Huh? I don't give a shit about Baine," he said.

"Chiara scowled, "It's not about Baine. You wouldn't let Jessica go to St. Thomas alone, would you? Be a gentleman for once. We'll save some food for you both."

His eyes shot from me to Chiara to Jessica, "Uh, I guess not, damn. OK, OK, I'll go." His facial expression and words were flat. Jessica's expression changed to bright, and she immediately turned it back to sad before Chiara caught sight of her.

Chuck drove them to catch the 7 PM ferry. I watched their boat disappear into the rain and lightning from the deck of Tamarindo, and the lights of the ferry office shut off once they were out of sight. *Strange.*

When Chuck returned, he said, "Shit, they closed the ferries down for the night due to the storm. Jessica and Chevali are on the last one running tonight." I whispered in Rosie's ear, "Jeb's in for more than he bargained for. This ought to be interesting." She slapped my shoulder.

"More food and rum for me, ha," Boddington said before asking me if I wanted a shot of rum.

I held my Tona-cup out to him. "Hold on," I said and turned it over and, using my pocket knife, scraped the chunk of dried oatmeal out from under the cup's curled lip, flung it in my mouth and crunched it between my front teeth. "Hey, look, an appetizer from my friend Tona."

Boddington's face pinched, and his lips flattened. Instead of resting the rum bottleneck on the tin cup to steady it as he poured, he held it a few inches above my cup. "Shit Ky, you're gonna make me puke, watchin' you drinkin' and eatin' from that emesis basin. There is somethin seriously wrong with you, son."

I sipped from it, "Buddy, we are, right now, in the Universe's center of One Love... Love City. Tona is the gentle, wordless ambassador of this loving peace that holds all of us in her arms. Share his cup of love with me, brother." I held up to his quivering lips.

"Do not touch me with that fuckin' petri dish, or we are

gonna have a big problem, man," Boddington said while arching backward.

"No problem, my brother, but if you change your mind, it's yours to share," I said.

"Ain't gonna happen. Man, you need some damn Prozac or something. That's just wrong."

Larry's preparation was more difficult than expected. By the time the massive stewpot was steaming, and the fresh bottle of Pusser's was nearly empty. Boddington was manning the steaks outside on the grill and singing his version of filthy pirate songs to himself. Rosie and Chiara were making a salad while Ramona stirred Boddington's beans on the stove. I reached into the refrigerator and lifted poor Larry's horned carapace. He was cold when I placed him facing the pot of his impending torture. As he warmed, his dozens of little legs tried to propel him backward, away from the boiling pot.

"Damn it, Chuck, I can't do this," I complained.

"Do what, Hoot?"

"I hate, hate, hate it when live lobsters are chucked into boiling water, and they scream and churn death laps until they die. I don't want to do this." My words caught everybody's attention, and I felt the group come into sympathy with me.

"What the hell can we do. Ya can't drown him first?" He chided.

"Can't we pith him?" I asked.

"Pith?" Chuck puzzled.

"Ya know, brain him somehow. Kill him before the boiling water thing, so he doesn't have to suffer."

He smiled. "OK, but how?"

"Drive a spike into his brain?"

"OK, never done it before, but let's give it a try." I held Larry down with both hands on the kitchen counter while Chuck tried to push a large kitchen knife through his head. The blade bent and skidded off Larry's head.

"Hold on, my dive knife is thick as hell and wouldn't bend, let me get it." I wasn't about to give up and let Larry suffer. When I returned, Chuck held Larry down on the Formica counter as I put my entire weight on my dive knife, nothing, not even a dent. Larry's shell was too thick.

"Shit, we need a battering ram." I searched the Great Room bookshelf for my weapon. In the dim light and through rum blurred eyes, I pulled out the thickest book and took it to the kitchen.

"Hold little Larry down and hold the knife handle. I'll do the pounding." I said to Chuck.

He positioned the knifepoint between Larry's moving eyes, "I'm pretty sure his brain is here. Just don't drive the knife into my hand." I looked up from the lobster and knife as everybody wordlessly watched. Boddington stood still with the steaming steaks on a long metal platter, the size and shape of a ten-pound tarpon.

I took aim and hit the knife butt with measured force, driving it a few millimeters into his head. Not even close to deep enough, but the knifepoint made at least a small divot in his head, so I felt comfortable giving it a more formidable hammering. I did multiple times. The book was the perfect battering tool with enough mass to get the job done in a half dozen hard whacks. Larry's antennae went limp as the knife sunk deeply into his head. Larry was dead and hopefully hadn't suffered from much more than a transient headache before succumbing. I laid the book on the countertop and placed him into the rolling water: not a whimper or hint of a tail flick. Larry did not suffer in his cooking.

"Oh, shit Ky, I think you're going to go to hell," Ramona said as Larry began to boil.

Boddington chimed in, "Shit baby, that's a given, why I've seen him in action a few times, and there is a no place for his withered soul rubbin' elbows with angels. There was one time, where the hell was it, uh, just outside of Amarillo...."

"I'm serious." She stomped her foot down to stop his rumination and pointed to my battering ram on the counter, next to a bottle of salad dressing.

'HOLY BIBLE' in gold lettering was on the spine.

"Whoa shit buddy, if there was any doubt before," Boddington said and made the sign of the cross in my direction.

"There wasn't, trust me. Let's eat." My silent solace was that I had done the right thing but with the wrong tool. They say that the Gods have a sense of humor. I tested that theory again. The only things more extensive than the amount of food that night were the explosions of laughter and crashes of thunder as we partied, ate, and listened to reggae under the dry safety of the veranda roof.

Larry's severed head was almost the size of Rosie's, small by human standards, gigantic by lobsters'. His lifeless eyes stared at me as I washed dishes. I took him outside in the dark, away from the view of the others to the far side of the deck, thanked him, and threw him downhill to feed the bugs of the night, returning him to nature in a more dignified manner than rotting in a dump.

I stood in the dark, watching the storm retreat to the

Northwest as a warm wet breeze nuzzled me in my soft rum cocoon. Once again, as with every night for the last week (with one glaring exception), I didn't want the night to end. Back in the real world, I used sleep as a soft cudgel to scrape the stress of the day off me. Here, as much as I needed to catch up on sleep, it wasn't my friend. The unconscious hours robbed me of my St. John time.

"I'm going to take my rum into the pool and watch the bats. If anybody wants to join me, that's fine. If not, have a pleasant night." I said to Rosie and Chiara as they dried the last of the night's dishes.

The pool water pulled the heat of the day's hike out of my naked body. I leaned against the pool wall, neck deep, and waited for the bats to start their strafing runs. "You OK with a little company?" it was Rosie's voice from the dark.

"Absolutely."

I heard her slip into the water, "Damn, it feels wonderful to be naked in the water."

Chiara and I answered her in unison, "Yes, it does."

"Chiara, is that you too?" I asked. She was with Rosie.

"Si, I want to see the bats. Show them to me." She sidled up next to my right side.

"There's one. See it?"

"No, show me."

"Did you see it, Rosie?" She answered from the far side of Chiara. "Yech, those little bastards creep me out."

In total innocence, I put my hand on the right side of Chiara's head, grazing Rosie's shoulder with my hand. I pulled her to me and steered her head very gently to put her gaze in line with my pointing left index finger. I felt her left arm slide down to my waist to steady herself against me, but her hand continued lower and lay to rest on what became my immediate state of arousal. "Oh there, I think that's one," Chiara said.

This can't be happening... and with Rosie in the pool?

I had to think clearly. *There is no way for this to end well.* I tried to slide away from her slowly, but as I did, her left arm hugged my waist, stopping my retreat. Her right hand found my right hand, pulled it down, and placed it on her other hand at the upper junction between her thighs. I could feel her left hand under mine, rhythmically petting herself. She pushed my fingers through hers to join in her massaging. *No pubic hair?* She felt like a warm sliced peach. I could feel her internal heat contrasting with the lukewarm pool water.

Wait, she can't have three hands. I quickly counted them again. Her LEFT hand was around my waist... her RIGHT hand held my right hand, pushing my fingers through her LEFT-hand fingers that she was touching herself with. I didn't move or say anything. She continued to guide my hand, to slowly stroke and massage her in little circles. Chiara moaned and released my hand from hers, and it disappeared.

On the far side of Chiara, Rosie suddenly sucked a staccato breath and began breathing heavily. A hand slowly stroked me, and I stayed silent. A different hand softly picked my right hand out of Chiara's warm crotch and redirected it across Chiara to Rosie, cupping it firmly over her breast. I stayed silent. Chiara's first hand let loose of me and followed my arm to Rosie's breast. She then used her fingers over mine to pinch and roll Rosie's nipple harder than I would have ever done. I expected Rosie's loud, forceful protest, but Rosie yelped and said, "Again."

The bats had apparently picked up on the energy of the humans in their watering hole. They were attacking the water in swarms, reminding me of old WWII movies showing Japanese Zeros dropping in waves into American warships.

With my erection thumping in the water, I was sure to prove Archimedes correct and start the pool to overflowing. Chiara released my hand and turned her head toward Rosie. The sounds of kissing filled the otherwise silent night until Chiara turned her head to me and pulled my chin, guiding my mouth to meet hers. We kissed hard and wet. I felt bodies shuffle a bit, and Rosie's face joined ours. Our threes mouths openly, passionately kissed. Six trembling hands wandered and caressed. I expected a bat to try to join us. I stayed silent for as long as I could.

"Rosie, can we talk for a second." I broke the rising intensity of the moment.

"She pulled her mouth off of ours, "Sure."

"Are you Ok with this? I mean, this is way out of character for both of us. We've never, you know... We ARE happily married, right?" I asked.

"I'm very happily," she kissed Chiara, "married." They giggled. "Ky, I know this is out of character, but for God's sake, isn't that why you go on vacation to live outside of your normal life?"

"OK, but what about...."

She stopped mouthing Chiara's face. I could barely make her eyes out in the dark.

"Ky, this is it, your one and only shot at menage a trois in this life with me. After tonight we will never, in anger or levity ever, ever mention tonight ever again. This doesn't make it open season for either of us. It will never happen again. I love you and will be faithful to you for the rest of my life. If you want to stop, if you want me to stop, fine, done. No matter what happens, we will never repeat or discuss this again, or I will leave you. Are you in or out... are we in or out? You call it. Now." A mystery hand started stroking me again.

"In." It was like someone else answered for me, telling the story of my confused, turgid desires in one word.

"Hold on," I said. "Chiara, I can't do this to Jeb. He's my buddy. I won't. You guys go ahead." I hated myself intensely at that moment.

"Ky, don't sweat it." Chiara spoke, "I know that I am only his vacation chick. Do you think this is the beginning of a long romance between Jeb and me, sul serio? Next month he'll be banging some new airhead. He won't care. Does he love me? Hell no. Does he like me? Hell yes, a lot, I think. But that's all he can give me. Do I love him? No, but I could. But I know better. I don't know why, but I always find myself with guys like him. It's just, when I see you and Rosie, I see a love that I want, and if I can't have it long term, maybe, just maybe, I can squeeze myself into the middle of it for one night. Tonight."

"I'd be honored," I said. "We would be honored to have you with us tonight, Chiara. I hope Jeb won't feel betrayed. I mean, he's been off island for a few short hours, and here we..." She smiled and squeezed me with one of her three hands.

"Seriously, don't worry about him seeing this as a betrayal. He doesn't appreciate women the same way you do. That's what makes you a happily married man, and him a hound dog. Righta now, I'd bet he is boinking Jessica as we speak. She and I spoke after a few drinks at Foxy's. I know she has been after him forever. Sick, I know. Why do you think I told him to go with her? It's a favor to her. As they were leaving tonight, I told him to screw her brains out if he got the chance. The Universe listened and shut down the ferry service. Amazing how things work out." She smiled widely and tilted her head sweetly.

"If we go ahead, I still have to tell him," I said. I was serious.

"That's the right thing to do. But really, I doubt that this is the first time you and he have ever shared a woman, right?" OK, she had a point with that one.

Chiara grabbed my and Rosie's hands and waded backward toward the pool steps. After we got out, Rosie bent down and picked Chiara up in her arms and carried her toward our bedroom, occasionally kissing her. I followed in amazement from behind. Once in our room and on our bed, Rosie and I brought Chiara into the middle of our relationship for that night only.

-22-

REDEMPTION SONG

I awoke to the sound of the little brown bird whose body dips with every discordant note as it sang in the tree outside our window. Chiara was asleep, lying across both Rosie and me with her head on my low abdomen.

No, No, No, stay down. I communicated nonverbally to my pecker.

Remembering what Rosie had said in the pool, I tried to will myself limp, to no avail. I gradually but firmly pushed on Chiara's ear. Rosie's voice startled me, "Breakfast, anyone?"

Chiara crawled up to lay between Rosie and me. The room was quiet, too quiet. I was in a situation that I had never been in before. My world felt like a kid's finger painting where all the colors swirl together but aren't yet thoroughly mixed, not incorporated into a new color. I was heavy with guilt, happiness, confusion, and uncertainty about Rosie. I was worried for us and our future.

"Ho Fame, I'm hungry as hell." *Thank God for Chiara.*

"I would eat anything you put in front of me right now," I said. They each turned toward me and smiled.

"Ya know, it's not yet morning in Colorado. It IS still technically last night," Chiara said.

"Hoot, Hoot, where the hell you at?" Chuck didn't wait for

an invitation to come in and spoke as he entered our room. His freezing in place would have made any roadside deer proud.

"Good morning, Rosie, Hoot, and.... Chiara?"

I smiled and blinked, "It's not what you think. Chiara just came over for a cup of sugar."

"Hoot, you, I get it. Chiara, I don't know enough about you, but Rosie, my big sister whom I have looked up to for my entire life. Poor mom will be so disappointed." He was toying with us.

"One word, Chuckie," Rosie held up a fist in jest. He sat on the corner of the bed with an open-mouthed smile.

"I'd have never suspected you guys as swingers. I thought mom raised you right. Jeb's part of this little thing too, I imagine?"

The three of us answered an emphatic "NO" in unison.

"Huh, while the cat's away?" He still hadn't closed his mouth.

"Trust me, Chuck, right now, the cat is getting some new pussy." I was proud of myself. Rosie frowned at me.

"Chuckie, this is a new experience for both of us, we aren't swingers. We simply love Chiara." She made the situation crystal clear with that one.

"But big sister, it's so immoral." Chuck was pushing it, and Rosie stopped her retreat.

"Well, since the cats seem to be flying out of the bag this morning." More cat analogies, I was wondering if there was an undercurrent of a theme playing out here. "I have a question for you, my innocent little brother."

"Yes, my moral compass of a big sister, what's that?" The morning's strange levity was in a tailspin.

"I ask, in all nonjudgmental fairness," Rosie said.

"Yes." Fin said.

"Chuckie, is Jimmy gay?"

Anger flashed across his face, and he stood from the bed. "What, why, it's not for me to answer. Why don't you ask him? No, don't. Why would you accuse...? Gay?"

"I'm not making any accusations. It's only a question."

"Why?"

"Well, yesterday at Foxy's, he got a little drunk." Rosie's voice trailed off.

"That stupid asshole told you that he was gay? I'm gonna kill him. I gotta go." He started walking toward the door.

"No, he didn't, not in actual words," Rosie said.

Chuck stopped. "What the hell are you saying, big swinger? I mean big sister."

"Calm down. I'm not making any judgments here."

"What did he say?" His voice loudened.

"It wasn't what he said. It was how he acted. The more he drank, the more, well." Rosie paused.

"The more he drank, the more daffodil effeminate he got, right?"

"Well, yes. But I don't care. I love you."

He put his hand to his forehead, staring at the floor, and paced. "Yeah, what about you Hoot, how about having a faggot for a brother-in-law. Ya gonna make more jokes with Jeb and Boddington?"

"Hey, man, it's not for me to judge," I said.

"You're damn right it's not. Look around, notice anything unusual in your marital bed?"

"Whoa, amigo, did you hear me? Even without what you see here, I have no room to judge you."

"No, you don't, and how about you, my always do the right thing, big sister. You gonna look down your nose at me too?"

Rosie was red-faced. "Stop it, Chuck, you're being an asshole."

"Am I? You're as homophobic as Dad, Hoot, and the rest of them." Chuck was pointing his finger in multiple directions.

Rosie's posture straightened, and she spoke through gritted teeth, "Well, let me be succinct, little brother. Right now, I have another woman on my breath and..."

I added, "Yep, me too."

"The hell with you, Hoot. You, all of you hate me, so fuck you and your friends", he stared out the window at the bay full of sailboats. "Always making faggot jokes."

"Hold on, amigo, you don't get to tell me who or what I hate. I'm gonna explain something." I stood up and held a pillow in front of my crotch. "I love you, as you, not as something I think you should be. If I only loved perfect people, I'd have only Spike. So, dismount from your poor me, gay-high horse, and act like the man that you are, gay or not. And as far as you and I are concerned, show me respect, or shit is going to go down fast."

His eyes were welling up. "But you hate gays. You guys always make fun of them, us."

"That's not hating, it's simple, common stupid prejudice. You have it, everybody does regarding something or someone. It's wrong, but it's a fact. All I can do is work on mine, do what I can to lessen the influences of a crazy upbringing."

"Bullshit, you guys are **so** cruel. Jeb's a shrink, and you're a regular doctor, you guys should know better, be better than that." Chuck said wiping a tear.

"He is human and faulted just like you and me. Imagine what it's like being a doctor, worst of all, a shrink. Every day people confess their deepest, weirdest thoughts. It's your job to listen and not judge, but to help them come to terms with their screwed-up feelings in a world of self-righteous hypocrites. And keep all of it a secret. If you talk about your crazy patients, your perverted patients, even without using names, and the word gets out, you lose your practice, your license and get sued to hell and back.

"Oh, now you want me to feel sorry for you assholes?" Chuck asked in a mocking tone.

"No, but what do you think happens to all the stress that builds inside of doctors? Word by word, day by day, treatment complications and demanding patients who you have to treat like they're damn saints or they sue you? That pressure builds inside of you until you go on vacation someplace where nobody knows you, and ya asshole out, big time. You act out, drink, screw, swear, fish, and fight until you to go home and put the medicine-fire under your ass again. The worst of the worst is when you hear your OWN thoughts expressed by the batshit crazy patients. What the hell do you do with that? It's just more fuel in the fire, my fire, Jeb's fire. You don't have the right to judge him or me anymore than we do you."

"Screw this, I gotta go to work. I don't want you to go today. I need to think."

"I get it."

Chuck stormed out, leaving the bedroom door open.

"Porka miseria," Chiara said as footsteps moved in multiple directions on the deck above us.

"Hey, Chuckie." It was Chevali.

"Fuck you, faggot." Chuck answered.

"Oh shit." Chiara kissed us both on the mouth and ran naked for their room.

"What the hell do we do now," I asked Rosie.

"I need a brainless day at the beach. How about you?" She said.

"If you don't mind, I think I want to be alone today, not necessarily away from you, but I don't want to have to engage anybody. Does that make sense? Would it be OK if I took the pickup to Reef Bay and fished by myself?" I asked.

"Go ahead, baby. We can fend for ourselves."

"Thanks." Questions ran screaming through my head, but fortunately, not out of my mouth.

Rosie stopped me as I headed for the door, "Hey, I love you and only you. Last night never happened. No discussion, ever. I had a talk with Chiara while you slept last night. It was fun, it was exciting, it was.... once. You OK with that?" She asked.

"I am." I looked deeply into her eyes. I liked what I saw as we kissed.

"I don't understand how, but your mouth tastes wonderfully of pussy. What toothpaste are you using these days?" I asked.

"Go, chase your stupid ghost fish."

"Bonefish, Bonefish. I love you."

"Love you too."

The trail to Reef Bay hadn't dried a bit. Fallen branches from yesterday's winds littered the ground. I thought about how lucky we had been, not getting beaned by any of them.

Reef Bay flats was unfishable, obscured by brown turbid water from runoff. I sat in the wet sand and took in the overcast sky and jumbled waves. A grey day had followed a colorful night. I drank warm water out of an old Army surplus aluminum canteen my father had given me as a kid while my thoughts drifted to her firm athleticism. I followed visions of the night mingled with anxiety over Rosie's uncharacteristic enjoyment of another woman. Then there was the conversation with Chuck.

The smells of wet sand and salt air mingled to realign my thoughts with the present moment. It was going to be a day for exploration, and I made my plan. First, investigate the old sugar mill and then hike to the spring that Chuck said was the site of Caribbean Indian petroglyphs.

I realized that other pressing physical needs to be addressed, away, far away from the beach, and I entered the thick brush and searched for an appropriate tree. The rhythmic crashing of waves echoed along the shore as they chased the contrails of my thoughts through my clouded head. I slowly pushed my way inland through thick bushes. In the trees above me, flotsam hung like drying underwear. Chunks of plastic and boat parts clung twenty feet over my head, decorating the partly denuded branches like sickly decorated Christmas trees in a ruined boat hell. Thick roots arched in all directions from stubby mangroves. Plastic motor oil bottles and torn boat seat cushions colored the swamp in sadness.

Further inland stood a taller tree that could shelter me from the emerging sun. I scoured the ground to avoid repeating Blaine's bird nest mistake. Pieces of torn clothing made the wet ground look like a bloodless crime scene. A little white land crab stood on a piece of dark fabric with his claws raised toward me, defending it. It wasn't the clothing that had him in a defense posture.

A rotting disembodied human finger, mostly bone and joint gristle, was pointing my way. Another white crab feasted by pulling tiny chunks of tissue from the bones. Lengths of tangled, white rope dangled from tree branches well out of my reach, like cotton ice sickles. Flies and mosquitoes buzzed around my face and arms that dripped a soup of sweat and OFF. Even without touching me, their maddening numbers made my eyes itch. A suicide bomber aimed for an exposed ear canal and sent shivers down my spine as I squashed it with a fingertip, hoping not to drive its remains into my ear canal. The breezeless heat made me want to take clothing off, but visions of exsanguination by mosquito bites kept me miserably clothed. I followed the crab trails from the lifeless finger deeper inland. Thousands of crab footprints told a grizzly story of more remains to come and introduced me to the host of the crab banquet. I was happy to have had years of medical training to steel me from the wave of nausea that I denied myself.

A torn and twisted Zodiac lay wrapped in rope and light green vines. Human body parts lay scattered in a circle around the grey deflated raft. A human torso slumped partially beneath the raft, no skull in sight. The smell of decomposition wafted my way. As I approached, the ground moved with dozens of skittering crabs, their feast interrupted. A tightly wound rope around the waist of the bony corpse held him tight to the raft's grey skin. Dappled sunlight showed a glint of metal at the end of a twisted arm behind his back. Crabs had eaten most of his skin and muscle. His warped and deflated ass cheeks faced skyward, and he lay stuck in a permanent rear armbar. I moved closer, and crabs challenged me with open pinchers. Some of them were the massive land crabs that the locals ate. Their bodies were the size of softballs. This crustacean was off my menu, permanently.

The twisted arm remained attached to a hand with well-picked over fingers. A substantial golden ring hung on the bones of one of them. I figured that the contorted and humbly ass-up owner had no use for it. I covered my trembling hand with toilet tissue, initially intended for other purposes, to pluck what remained of a ring finger from the hand. I got more than I bargained for when it separated at the wrist, and I gave it a hard shake, sending maggots flying from the still moist palmar fascia. Crabs pounced on them, picking them up and shoveling them into their moving mouths. The ring was thick and heavy in my hand, a jeweler's rendition of a big cat head, green gemstone eyes, an open mouth of diamond teeth, and a protruding tongue of tiny rubies. It looked expensive. I couldn't tell if it was real or costume jewelry, but its heft spoke of the former.

I wadded it up in the toilet paper and jammed it hastily into my pocket. My curiosity rose to outweigh my common sense, reminiscent of the night before and spoke in two competing voices. One told me to leave the morbid scene to the police, and the other in true Caribbean pirate fashion, said to explore the potential riches of this dead sailor's misfortune. Paranoia pounded my head with my rapid heartbeat. I listened for voices and helicopters but heard only waves in the distance as the sun broke through the clouds. The temperature rose a dozen degrees. I rationalized that this wasn't necessarily a crime scene and that the cops could wait. An old rotting body recovery was not an emergency. I knew this well from being an impromptu coroner in Eastern Colorado when I was a medical Resident, moonlighting in farming community ERs.

It took a lot of pulling and sweating to overturn the filthy, flaccid Zodiac. In doing so, I exposed hundreds more crabs and roaches to their dreaded sunlight. I found three large plastic suitcases tied with thick rigging lines to the guest of honor of this fomite party. The suitcases were dark brown, hard-sided Samsonite. Yellow nylon straps embossed with a snarling cat face, bearing a resemblance to the ring in my pocket, encircled each bag. It was getting exciting, and even a stench rivaling the Manilla dump couldn't hold me back.

I cut one of the suitcases free and dragged it to the clearing under the tree that called to me in the first place. The suitcase had a small combination lock that prevented my gaining access to the contents, so I plunged my KA-BAR through the tough plastic siding and tried sawing to no avail. I picked up a rock of 'blue bitch,' a local granite, and used it to hammer the spine of my knife. The tightly packed contents were unyielding to my blade. I slowly hammer-cut a window the size of my head in the suitcase. Inside, layers of tightly wrapped plastic yielded quickly to my blade, exposing the contents to the morning sun.

I sat in the crab highway mud and couldn't think. Savage flies attacked my exposed facial skin and lips while dehydrated, pudding thick blood hammered my carotids. My mind exploded into a starburst from past to present and to a thousand different futures--the words 'what the hell do I do now?' churned in my brain. I had to make sense of this away from the stench and rioting crabs.

I struggled my way back to the beach and sat alone, sweating with my bulging yellow backpack between my legs, and watched pelicans glide effortlessly a few inches above the water, hunting. I envisioned myself with an eye patch and a parrot on my shoulder as questions tumbled around in my head like wet pants in a clothes dryer. The ghosts of slaves, pirates, and my feasted upon friend in the swamp all hid, whistling to me from behind the twisted mangroves of my imagination. I needed to leave and talk with Rosie.

I made my obligatory stop at the cybercafe in town, gathered the bad news, solved the problems, and swallowed stomach acid, which roiled into my throat with each email from home. My only consolation was the cafe's rolling reggae. My tan toes, free from the confines of shoes, tapped out a beat to UB 40 as I read my hate mail. Somehow, the overly simple rhythm that had been boring and monotonous in Colorado's cold air was soothing and appropriately familiar down here. It fit, loose and comfortable like my Brazilian sandals. I headed for home, Tamarindo.

The nauseating stench of decomposing and maggoty death boiled in the air for the second time that day. The hot uphill breeze carried an olfactory inferno of fishy redolence to the deck of Tamarindo. We were awash in an aura of lobster death. Larry's two-pound head, which I had flung in drunken haste over the deck the night before, was taking its odiferous revenge. Tropical heat and moisture had efficiently decomposed Larry's head into a state of scalding decay.

Jessica and Chevali laid on recliners on the deck, having returned from their night on St. Thomas. "Hey guys, good to have you back. Did you put Baine on his plane?" I asked.

"Yes, he made his getaway, but do you know what that horrible smell is? It stinks like rotting seafood." Jessica asked as if I had something to do with it.

"Have you done any laundry since we've been down here?" I answered, vaguely remembering seeing Larry's head flying from my hand in the blur of last night's kaleidoscope of memories. I heard Chevali laugh. A half-full bottle of Caribe beer sat sweating in the shade of his lounge chair. He was face down, shirtless, wearing the same blue and yellow striped shorts he had on when he and Jessica left for St. Thomas the previous night. His hair was greasy and matted.

"I'm serious Ky, this is awful." Jessica insisted.

"Why the hell am I the stink police? Tell mister melanoma over there to figure it out."

"Get your ass up and go stink hunting," I spoke to Chevali, who rolled away from me while flipping me the bird. His back was a red roadmap of new fingernail rake marks. Jessica's face reddening. I picked up her hand and tapped her nails, "Barbarous weapons, these in the throes of passion."

"Stop it. He fell drunk last night in St Thomas."

"Oh, and who did he fall into?" I said while patting her ass. Chevali laughed.

"Damn it, don't toy with me, Ky. Please find the source of that awful stink." She pounded her hand on her thigh.

I patted her ass again," I think I just did." I spoke to Chevali's hamburgered back, "Hey lover boy. You might want to put a shirt on before Chiara gets back." He laid motionless.

"Uh Jeb, you have a few small scratches on your back.... er.... from last night," Jessica said. Chevali rolled over to face us. "Chiara and I talked this morning. I explained my, uh, fall. She said there was a lot of falling going on last night all over the islands," and rolled onto his back.

"Is there a problem we need to discuss?" I asked. Chiara had beat me to the punch. I didn't want to chance to lose him as my friend.

"Let me grab a beer and join you," I said.

"I think you already did."

Jessica caught the meaning of our coded conversation, "You and Chiara?"

"Please don't tell Rosie. It was a one-time deal, never going to happen again. How about you kids? Where do you guys go from here?" By that time, Chevali was standing at my side, beer in hand.

I'd been in situations with adversaries holding bottles and always watched the bottle, having seen the damage inflicted by them. His knuckles were pink-holding it loosely. He pulled his sunglasses down his nose, so we were eye to eye. "One step, or fall at a time, I guess," he said. I held his gaze and asked, "You OK with this Chiara thing? Please tell me if you aren't."

He turned to face the islands that stretched out beyond us and made a sweeping motion over them with his beer bottle. "Ky, every other person out there has a pussy. Do you think I'm going to get possessive about one of them? If anybody was going to do Chiara, I'm glad it was you. She was great, huh?" He asked. Jessica was red-faced and loudly cleared her throat. He pushed his sunglasses back up onto the bridge of his nose and grinned at her. She turned and silently walked into the house.

"Jeb, I never kiss and tell." I almost took a high road, but it felt so rough and foreign. "But I will tell you that once when she came, she called your name." He beamed for a second, then scowled. "Once? Uh, how many times...ya know, did she...?"

The good fisherman goes to where he thinks the fish should be. The great fisherman knows fish and places himself where they are.

"Uh, I don't know. I stopped counting after we helped her

hit about half a dozen." "You're full of shit, Ky. How long did this little party go on?" He paused, "Wait, we?"

It hit me that she hadn't told him about Rosie. I had to cover for Chiara. "Yep, I tapped my crotch, "Little Mister Happy. Mr. Manos," I waved my fingers at him, "and Senior La Boca," I wiggled my tongue at him. And truth be told, my flyrod too."

The good fisherman hunts for fish, and if he sees them, casts to them. The great fisherman understands fish and casts to where he knows the fish will be.

"Fly rod?" He asked.

"Well, I had to make up for your skills somehow."

"Had to make up for.... what the hell does that mean?" His left eyebrow raised above his sunglasses.

"She screamed that I was bigger, I guess a lot bigger than you, but that you were better in some small ways. So, I had to put my fly rod to work."

The good fisherman sets the hook lightly so as not to injure the fish. The great fisherman holds his rod still to let the fish hook itself.

"Of course, I'm better than you, Ky." He smiled as he spoke.

"She said, 'in some SMALL ways." I don't know what that meant. But I had to bring in reinforcements, hence, the flyrod."

"Huh? And by the way, Ky, you aren't bigger than me. I've seen you in the gym showers before."

"That was when the little guy was sleeping. But when he comes to attention, which you will never witness, he's apparently a sight larger than that burnt match between your legs. Her words, not mine."

The good fisherman fights the fish valiantly. The great fisherman lets the fish fight its own weight.

"Bullshit, and what's the thing with the flyrod?" He asked.

"You haven't seen her ass cheeks today?"

"No, why?" His eyebrow went up again.

"Dude, it was all done at her insistence," I said.

"What?"

"Let's just say that by the time dawn came around, her little round ass looked like the red and white checkered tablecloth at Uncle Joe's ribs. If you know what I mean."

"She's not into that shit. She won't even let me handcuff her," he said.

The good fisherman plays the fish to the point of its exhaustion. The great fisherman plays the fish to only the brink of its fatigue.

"She obviously never schooled you in the art of shibari. She's a pro at it," I said.

"What the hell is shibari?"

"You're the shrink. You're supposed to know all about kink."

"Ky, I know kink, just not art. I'm a psychiatrist, not an art history major."

The good fisherman lands the fish with a net. The great fisherman guides the fish into his waiting hand.

"It's not important. In any event, she moaned your name once. Take it as a compliment."

He gestured to my overstuffed yellow backpack, "Shit Ky, you always overpack. Where'd you go today?" Chevali relented and changed the subject. I won.

The good fisherman eats his fish with gratitude. The great fisherman releases his fish to be caught another day.

When I returned to our room, it was like an oven. It had baked all day with the windows shut, the bathroom door closed, and the fan off. I could hear the A/C in Chevali's room grinding away, and for the first time, I was envious of his perpetually frigid room. I opened the sliding glass door, turned on the ceiling fan, and searched the spider-filled closet and musty drawers for a safe place to hide my backpack. There was no safe place, so I parked it in the corner of the room, hiding it in plain sight, and stripped to take a shower. For good measure, I threw my underwear on the backpack.

I opened the bathroom door and jalousie windows that Rosie had left closed for some stupid reason. Duct tape crossed the toilet lid and seat, holding them shut, and the toilet wouldn't flush. Chevali was playing more bathroom games. The flushing mechanism clanked in the empty reservoir. No water. I momentarily panicked, thinking that we had run out of cistern water until I noticed the water intake valve to the toilet was duct-taped in the off position. I bent over to peel the tape off the valve, and something cool dripped onto the back of my neck. I rotated my head up to see wet condoms draped over the artsy driftwood fish mobile that cheerfully rotated above me. I closed my mouth and shielded my eyes. The practical joke war was taking on a new urgency.

I was in the shower when Rosie and Sandy returned. Sandy stepped into the shower for a pet and then curled up on a bathmat. Rosie said that she and Chuck had a discussion earlier, that he was calmer but wanted to talk with me alone. She chatted excitedly about their day snorkeling the reef at Trunk Bay. Boddington had almost stepped on a stingray that fluttered from under his foot without stinging him. She showered with me, and then we laid under the fan for a nap.

We awoke to the sound of the group on the deck for the sunset, predinner drinks. It was the last night before the Boddingtons and Chiara were supposed to head home. The Pendleton Round-Up rodeo was going on, and Boddington would perform chiropractic manipulation on the horse and bull athletes. He was in high demand in the summer months. Stock Contractors needed their stars to be in prime bucking shape as they moved closer to the National Finals rodeo. Chiara too, needed to return to work and was on the same flight as the Boddingtons. Chevali planned on staying with us for an extra couple of days.

We joined the others upstairs to find that the Larry-stench was magnifying rapidly. Jessica wanted to call the property manager. Chevali suggested a plumber.

"Ky, I heard that ol' Jeb did you another bathroom joke. The boy was bragging about his artwork." Boddington patted my back. "Wow, duct tape and the rubbers? He said he's been saving 'em up for days. Man, I hope you got a plan to return the love."

"Not yet, but it'll come to me, or maybe it did, I'm not sure." He looked confused. "My mind has been a little scattered the last few days, but the hell with that, let's watch the sunset and start the big night off right with a little rum," I said.

"Never thought you'd ask. But for shit's sake, don't use that fuckin' tin cup. The sight of you drinkin from it gags me."

Two tin cup shots later, Boddington and I watched the pastel blue sky streaked with blazing pink altostratus clouds reflecting the retreating sun's fire. I'd never seen those colors in nature and honestly thought that artists like Redon and Van Gogh had invented them. By the time we had finished our third rum, the evening's muting sky and clouds were nearly the same shade of gray.

I glanced off the deck into the empty lot downhill from the deck. There it was, almost the size of a football, Larry's severed head turned even redder by the sun. Shit, surely someone was going to see him. I needed to retrieve him and throw him into a trashcan NOW. "Hey everybody, let's walk to town for dinner, beat the rush. Tonight is Chiara and the Boddington's last night, so we should take them wherever they want to eat. What do you think, Ramona, where you want to go?"

She thought for a minute, "I want to go to that place past Mongoose junction on the right, Morton's Mambo."

"Sounds great, let's pour some roadies and head out," I said and went inside to act as a bartender. Jessica was at the counter, holding the Pusser's bottle, watching Chevali and Chiara. "You OK, baby?" I asked.

"Yeah, this is painfully strange, as you can imagine," she said.

Out on the deck, Chevali had his arms around Chiara, "You have no idea, my girl." I lifted the bottle from her hand and poured us each a generous shot. She upended hers and held her glass out for another, "Here's to strange." We toasted them, "To strange, indeed."

I herded everybody out of the front gate and said, "You guys go ahead. My stomach is a little weird. I'll catch up with you in a couple of minutes." Rosie asked if I was OK, and I gave her a thumbs-down sign and patted my belly. "It's fine. I'll find you on the road."

Once the group inertia was carrying them downhill, I ran to the kitchen, grabbed the BBQ tongs, and ran down the steps to the vacant lot below the deck. In the fading light, I found Larry's sunburned head in the dirt. Adamant flies spun a thick tornado above him. It was hard to imagine the impressive magnitude of stench coming from anything other than Chevali. Both were rewriting the gas laws of Chemistry. On the way to the trashcan, an idea struck me, and I felt my grimace widen into a grin. I would be repurposing Larry.

I located the external air conditioner protruding from a half-boarded-up window at the back of the house that went into Chevali's room. It hung, hidden from view by the overhanging deck. I clunked Larry's head down on the buzzing, hot metal box to cook and fester while uttering a quiet "Sorry, Chiara." The airflow pulled the stench straight into the A/C.

I hurried downhill with Sandy to join the group and asked myself, "Why"? It was nearly dark, and I wanted to enjoy a little alone time with her. The vacation was mostly over, and it had been a touch eventful. I slowed to a walk with my hand on Sandy's head as she walked beside me. Her deep, slow breathing was like a metronome that made me walk slower, breathe deeper, and relish the moment. I had a new pile of pirate money and walked contentedly in tropical warmth to have dinner with my quirky friends. I was on an island a million miles away from reality. Possibilities for a new life rattled out of my brain like an old-time ticker tape machine. Once again, I was belly breathing without trying. Sandy and I took a short detour to her little cave, where we sat in the sand to look across the bay. People were coming ashore from the ferry, and tourists ate upstairs at Pusser's restaurant. Below them, locals and tourists were drinking and laughing in the warm evening at the Pussers bar. St. John's rhythms had infected me.

It wasn't paradise. The advertisement sales promise of a paradise was just a tool used to comfort my fellow dysthymics into wanting to buy a piece of it as a tee shirt or a villa. As I had experienced over the last week, I knew that the true paradise was not a material place but an internal landscape of dreams that could only materialize for a few scarce moments at a time.

Admittedly, some venues do open the door for their attainment more than others. Despite our ordinary lives brutally batting away vacations' brief pleasurable moments, their fleeting fulfillment becomes the engine that drives us through years of work and searching for them again. Each year, after fifty weeks toiling at thankless jobs, we force-feed ourselves ten days of vacation in "paradise." We accept this dysfunctional behavior because reality selfishly devours our dreams and beats the hope of attaining a real paradise out of most of us early in life.

I was temporarily feeling above that reality. Sandy snored with her head on my lap while I watched hundreds of people attempt to enjoy their versions of paradise. I lifted her head and scooted out from under her, told her to stay, and walked along the shoreline toward Morton's.

From outside the two-story restaurant, it was evident that I was in the right place. Boddington's voice spread out over the street and across to the bay's water with the restaurant's lights. I climbed the stairs and joined them, well into their cups. "Damn Ky, we thought you'd fell in. I was wonderin' how much we was gonna have to dip out," Boddington said.

The entire restaurant sneered at me as if I had yelled something crude. All I could do was smile like an imbecile and sit next to Rosie. Thankfully, she had ordered me a shot. I ran about half of the fiery coolness down my throat before I realized that something was different. I almost spit it out before it dawned on me that this wasn't rum, but tequila and good stuff. I smiled at Rosie. "Tequila?"

"Yep, Patron. I saw it behind the bar and ordered it for you."

"There is a God." Thus, I began the stumble into a Patron evening. I had missed them.

"To answer your question, Boddington, as to how much to

dip out. I'd say just enough to fill your soup bowl there. What is that in there, bowel bisque?" I raised my shot glass to him.

He frowned at his bowl, then at me. "Jeez, Ky, that ain't funny."

Two chairs sat unoccupied next to Jessica. "Who are those for?" I knew the answer as soon as I asked. "Chuck and Jimmy are supposed to be here any minute," Jessica answered from her seat next to Chiara. They chatted and laughed like best friends. I understood that I would never understand women, hell for that matter, men, particularly me. I ordered another round for the group and eagerly awaited my second Patron shot of the week. "Rosie, how are you doing? It's been a few crazy days, and we've hardly had a chance to talk?"

She gazed at me with a softness in her eyes that pulled me deep into her, "Ky, I could have never designed a better trip. I'm more in love with you now than I was when we first came down here. You were on the edge, buddy. It's been wonderful witnessing you transform back into you. The man whom I fell in love with is sitting next to me. Honestly, I'm a little worried about going back."

"First of all, the trip isn't over, and we have a couple of days left. I'm glad we planned it that way. Rosie, I do love you. I was a little worried after last night...."

She put a finger to my lips, "Never did it, or will it ever happen, nor be mentioned, ever. What wasn't, can't do us harm. Most fantasies should live in a place untouched by anything but our imagination, and if they are experienced outside of that protective cocoon, their purity is soiled and lost forever. Let's protect our cocoon." She kissed me with rum on her lips.

"How'd I ever get so lucky as to find and enter your cocoon?" I kissed her back. At that moment, the room was quiet and empty. We were alone on a deserted island, far away from anybody or anything. The only thing that existed outside of us was the taste of rum on her lips.

"Hoot, get a room." A hand swatted the back of my head.

"Do you mind? I was telling your sister how much saner she is than any of her goofy-ass family members."

Chuck sat next to Jessica. She grabbed his face with both hands and kissed him forcefully on the cheek. Boddington got up and slapped his back, "Boy, you're looking good, and you'll be better looking when I have another drink." Chevali threw an ice cube at his chest. "Hey, Chuckie, thanks for the hospitality. The Larry dive will go down as one of my favorite memories." Chuck smiled at me. He was the center of loving attention by the people whom he thought hated him.

Jimmy's eyes jabbed around the table and avoided mine when I got up and moved toward him. He stared up at me with the big eyes of fear. I shook his hand and whispered in his ear, "Welcome to the family, and welcome to the jungle baby." I caught Chuck's eye while still holding Jimmy's hand in mid-handshake and said to him, "We good?"

He nodded yes. I stood up straight and loudly said, "Well, what's it going to be tonight, girls, Pusser's or Patron? Cuz, the bar is full, and the night is young."

Chuck appeared shocked until Boddington added, "Them ain't girls, them is ladies, unlike Dr. Chevali there, he's just a shameless hussy."

"Boddington, except for your lovely wife, you wouldn't know a lady if she sat on your Texas lap dancing thighs," Chevali responded.

"The hell you say, Jeb, a lady like you got a mouth like a bass and knows how to use it," Boddington said.

Chuck waded in, "I agree, Jeb has a pretty mouth, But Boddington, if you had as many peckers on the outside of you as has been in your mouth, you'd look like a porcupine."

The people at the table next to us laughed out loud. And while the homophobic banter ricocheted between the three of them, I looked at Jimmy and mouthed, '*YOU OK?*' He smiled, appearing a bit calmer, mouthed the words "Thank you," and shook his head *yes*. Chuck, it seemed, was accepting being accepted.

On the walk back to Tamarindo, Chuck and I hung back from the group to smoke a cigar between us and talk. "Jimmy seemed a little nervous tonight," I said.

"Yeah, you gotta understand. You and your friends are an imposing bunch of macho assholes. It's not like you guys are easily approachable on matters of, well, alternative lifestyles."

"I know, but tonight you joined in with a few respectable verbal punches of your own."

"Sometimes, it's best to hide in the open, using the camouflage that your adversaries give you," he said.

"Each of those guys has their demons, skeletons, and faults that they hide just like you. Jimmy, not so much. If you guys want to keep your relationship hidden, you need to keep him away from the sauce."

"Yes, we talked. He apologized and said that he doesn't have the opportunity to play with girls very often and got too relaxed," Chuck said.

"Do you really see my friends as adversaries, see me as an adversary?"

"Hoot, I play for the other team. No matter how much you say you want to accept me, we are still not the same. You'll always look down on me. I don't like it but have to accept it."

"That's your Catholic guilt bullshit talking. Listen, I have a tattoo in my armpit that reads FTW."

"FTW? "What does that stand for?"

"It's a common biker tattoo. It means fuck the world."

"That's rude, typical you," he said.

"I'll take that as a compliment. Let me show you a picture I keep in my wallet." It was a shot from behind seven men in their respective motorcycle club vests, facing away from the camera, all with their arms around one another, embracing the guy next to him. Each had a different club's patch on their vests. "That's me in the middle, the short one."

"Nice picture, but I don't understand?"

"First, the tattoo. While at first blush, it seems rude, it isn't. It's a simple tattoo that's meant to educate civilians."

"What, that you are a violent asshole who beats little old ladies?" I shook off his sarcasm.

"No, actually the exact opposite. It straightforwardly means that I will live my life by my rules, my way. I have no desire to infringe upon your world. Live and let live. But I'm also not going to conform to your world necessarily. If you respect me, my world, my club, we will get along just fine. I'll do what I can to respect you. Hell, I'll buy you a beer. But if you mess with me, or criticize me openly, then asshole, we're gonna dance."

"Huh?" Chuck frowned.

"The picture is of seven individual motorcycle club members at a party in Cheyenne a couple of years ago. We all play for different teams, serious teams. This shows a moment of mutual respect amongst warriors in a time of fragile peace.

At some point in time, just about every one of those clubs has been at war with each other. Men have died in those wars. It's stupid, men are stupid, I know all too well, but it is what it is."

"So, what's your point, Hoot. Are we at war? You want to kill me?"

"No, dumbshit, just the opposite. Sane men, strong men, have the option to rise above their differences and, like in the picture, embrace one another as a sign of mutual respect for each other's team, club, or in your case, sexual preferences. Ya can't be at war with everybody who's not on your team. Life is too short and gets much shorter if you take that attitude. So, FTW, amigo, you be you and to hell with anybody who doesn't respect you."

"Lots to think about, Hoot," he said, looking out to the dark sea.

"Don't think it doesn't suit you, Chuckie."

He laughed and pushed me into a chain-link fence we were walking past and playfully called me an asshole.

When we paralleled Sandy's cave on the beach, I called her. She appeared out of the dark and jammed her nose into my hand as I walked. She stayed by my side as we walked uphill toward Tamarindo.

"Man, that dog is going to miss you. I doubt that she has ever been treated this well by anybody." Chuck said.

"Damn, leaving her, this place, even leaving you, is going to be tough."

"Rosie said that before you came down here, that you called St. John all kinds of shitty names. She was afraid you were going to be an asshole down here," Chuck said.

"Yep, I know. I'm under a lot of stress back home, more than I ever bargained for. I can't tolerate being a doctor anymore. I just don't want to do it."

"Yeah, I get it. In my life, all I have to worry about is sharks and homophobic assholes."

"Don't worry. There may be a light at the end of that tunnel. And who knows, some of it may shine on you too." I couldn't tell him any more just yet.

"What's that mean?" Chuck asked.

"I promise, I'll explain later."

"Whatever."

The three of us were behind the others arriving at Tamarindo, enough time for the rum to flow again. Jimmy was sitting next to Boddington, with his hand hanging on Boddington's shoulder, who was stiff and wide-eyed. Jimmy was drunk again.

"I've never understood how you macho guys can let their toenails get so long and gross," Jimmy said.

"Who gives a shit about toenails, man? Ya just stuff 'em in your boots and go to work."

"No, like I mean, what about your partner who gets raked by them in bed?"

Chuck's head swiveled toward Jimmy, and he quickly moved to get him away from Boddington. Chuck prattled as he guided Jimmy toward the sliding glass door, "Jimmy, are you are such a jokester. He is always complaining about HIS GIRLFRIEND, who wants him to keep his nails short. Typical of a guy, he lets them grow to ground squirrel length and claws HER legs up when they have sex. He picked up Jimmy's limp hand and waved it toward us. "Say goodnight to everybody."

Under the moon shadow of the eaves, he pushed Jimmy up against the house, and in a hushed voice, said, "Stay, asshole, don't move." Chuck rejoined the group and said his goodbyes. Hugs and arm slugs, kisses, and multiple 'absolutely next years' were exchanged. I went outside to stand with Jimmy making small talk, keeping him occupied and out of the mix. Chuck returned, "Thank you." He ushered Jimmy toward the gate and stopped, "Hey, Hoot, I got a question?"

"What's that?"

"Why the FTW tattoo in your armpit and not on your arms or chest like normal people?" Chuck asked.

"Because, present company excepted, if I have to show it to some asshole, I want them to have to look at my stinking, sweaty armpit to read it."

"I don't get it?" He asked.

"You don't have to. Now take princess pedicure home before he convinces Boddington to paint his toenails."

Chevali and Boddington said they wanted to sit outside, smoke cigars, and plan the next trip. I told them I'd consider joining them but had to put Rosie and Sandy to bed. Once in our room, I saw my yellow backpack and realized that I hadn't had a chance to tell Rosie about my find. I unwrapped the toilet paper-clad ring. While she busied herself in the bedroom, I washed it in the bathroom sink with soap and Clorox from the cleaning closet. I slid it onto my index finger. It was sloppy loose.

"Hey baby, while you were shopping, I did a little shopping of my own today. Want to see what I got?"

"Sure, let me put on the bikini I got at this cute little shop in Mongoose." She stepped into the room wearing a floral bikini top untied and hanging loosely over her breasts. In her hand was the bikini bottom. "Tie me up in the back." She gawked at my gold-draped finger, "What the hell did you buy? You don't wear jewelry, especially hideous crap like that?" I slid it off my finger. "Feel the weight," and dropped it into her hand.

"This can't be real." She scrutinized it. "My God, Ky, rubies, emeralds, diamonds, and the thing weighs a pound, have you lost your friggin' mind. This can't be. What is this?" She bit it, making a tiny indentation in the deep, lustrous gold. I didn't like seeing it in her mouth.

"Ky, this is stupid, even for you. This is real. The stones sparkle". She read an inscription inside the band out loud that I hadn't seen, "Los Hermanos leopardos... talk to me, Ky. This is the weirdest thing you've ever done. It's worth a year or two of mortgage payments. We can't afford this."

I gently held her hand. "It was a pirate's gift, and yes, we can.... NOW." I opened my yellow backpack and pulled out a brick of layered plastic wrap. I pulled back the cut edge and revealed the face of Benjamin Franklin. "A kilo of hundreds, and a shitload more just like this one. Do you like my ring now?"

Rosie picked up the brick and sat on the bed, carefully tugging out one-hundred-dollar bills.

"Ky, what in the hell?" I put my index finger to her quivering lips, "Shhhh," and laid out about twenty thousand dollars' worth of one-hundred-dollar bills on the bed and slowly pushed her down on them. We invented a new position that night, which I later referred to as "The Benjamin." Afterward, we sat on the money-bed and listened to the others on the deck above our heads as I explained the circumstances of my discovery.

"Ky, you took the world's luckiest bowel movement ever. Does anybody else know?" She asked.

"Hell no. First, I gotta figure out a lot of things before telling anybody but you, IF I ever tell anybody. You know the old biker saying about civilians keeping secrets, right?"

"Three can keep a secret if two are dead?" She replied in a questioning tone.

"Exactly, I don't want us to be the two who die because we

opened our mouths," I said while imitating slitting my throat with my thumb.

"Chuck might know what to do?"

"We're not exactly on great terms with him right now. Besides, if he let it slip to Jimmy, the next thing you know, our jugulars would be sliced open, or we're in prison. This is big. It could be big and good, or big and bad. I don't want to piss away this chance at freedom. Let's hold on telling anybody until we have this thing figured out."

"Sure, but how do we get this home? What about Customs? The police?" Rosie rambled as her eyes darted across the bed of love-sodden hundred-dollar bills.

"I don't have all the answers yet, it's all too fresh, and I haven't slept much. I gotta clear my head." I laid face down and fell asleep with one hand holding Rosie's, the other on Sandy's rising and falling ribcage.

-23-

Positive Vibration

I awoke with my heart pounding. Visions of the previous day's discovery and every possible unpleasant potential scenario for the money's disposition played in my head simultaneously. My brown bird, Sandy's sonorous snores and ferryboat motors firing up, comforted me. I was still in St. John and on vacation. I was alone in bed and got up to follow the sounds of the group grumbling upstairs. The source of their discontent was odiferously evident. Larry's revenge was in full swing.

"Good Lord, Ky, I woke up feeling sorry to leave, but with this, I'm gonna be happy as hell to go back," Boddington said while standing next to their bags and looking out over the bay. The morning sky was as bright as the air was sour. "Amigo, you two have made this week fantastic. You gotta make plans to come down here with us again, soon," I said.

"You know, I will. You got any idea what the hell is causing this stink? Bubba, this is unbearable," he asked.

I smiled widely and pretended to zip my mouth shut.

"You wily son old of a bitch, you know what it is, don't you?"

"Wanna see? You gotta keep it between us until you're on the ferry," I said.

"Can you make it quick?" Boddington asked.

"Twenty steps."

I led him below the house, around a blind corner, and gestured to Chevali's air conditioner cooking Larry's red head. He whispered as if we were hunting elk, "Remind me never to piss you off, man. You are a deranged bastard, and I'm kinda proud of ya." Boddington patted me on the back. "Them toilet tricks is coming back to haunt Chevali in a big way. But what about poor Chiara?"

"Casualty of war, my friend. Besides, it was only one night. It couldn't have been that bad. Let's go wake them up, or at least ruin their last shot at sex."

Their bedroom door wide open. The A/C was on full blast, washing their sleeping bodies with the air of rotting death. I thought it interesting that a stench had greeted us to Tamarindo, and one would also bid us farewell. Chiara hunkered under the sheets. Chevali was naked, face down, and covered in mosquitoes draining him of life.

"Hey, shithead," I called to Chevali.

His initial response was to swear and swat at the hordes of feasting mosquitoes on his bleeding, welted back, thighs, and ass.

"Get your lumpy ass up. Wow, is that smell is coming from your room? What the hell have you kids been doing down here, eating corpses?" I asked.

From under the sheets, Chiara said, "With this *odre di inferno*, there was no eating going on around here." Chevali laughed face down into his pillow.

Boddington whispered again, "Ky, you are the cruelest sombitch, I know."

"It's a gift. Let's eat breakfast. How long until you leave?" I asked.

"We have an hour or so, but I ain't sure I could eat here."

"Aghhh, you've gone soft on me. You've eaten at a lot of stinky 'Choke and Pukes' going down the road. This probably smells better than most of them," I said.

"Maybe so, pardner, maybe so."

I called into the airborne cesspool of their room, "Hey Chiara, get up, sweetheart, you got an hour before ya gotta leave." I was surprised that she was still in bed. "Shit, shit, shit, Jeb, I thought you were gonna set the alarm." She shot to her feet, facing us. She was wonderfully naked. Her face turned red, and one arm covered her chest while a hand shot to protect her shaven regions. "Boddington, shit, out."

"Uh, sorry, ma'am." he turned his head to me. "Wow, she's a cute little filly, lucky Jeb," he said.

"Yes, he is." I smiled.

Breakfast was quiet -- a heavy end-of-vacation air hung over Tamarindo with an unpleasantry rivaling Larry's fetid contribution. I was already missing the Boddingtons' and Chiara's additions to the fun that had defined the last week. The sound of Chuck's Jeep was, until that morning, a prelude to adventure, but that morning it was the sound of curtains slowly closing on the second act of a three-act play.

"Hoot." Chuck, by the tone of his voice, was back in more than one way. He loaded their luggage into his Jeep before coming to the kitchen. Ramona, Boddington, and Chiara alternately hugged the remaining four of us. Boddington slapped me on the back with the force of a horse kick. Ramona kissed my cheek and thanked me for performing their marriage. Chiara hugged Rosie first and then turned to me. I wasn't sure what to expect, and I noticed both Rosie and Chevali watching with more than casual interest. She rose to her toes, and I gave her a quick, brotherly hug and a benign smile. This was not the time for a show of familiarity. Her embrace was physically warm but emotionless. "We'll all have to get together at our place after our pictures get developed and share them," I said to the group. Multiple short but enthusiastic responses followed, and they were gone.

We sat around the large teak table under Tamarindo's veranda, drinking thick but necessary coffee. The pleasantly sticky wind was picking up and heating rapidly. I thought about the cold, dry air that the three of them would be landing in later today and pushed hard to remove that vision from my mind. I never wanted to see another Coloradowinter snow, the inside of my office or a medical patient ever again.

"Rosie, can't we just send home for Spike and the parrot and have someone sell all of our shit, stay here and be hippies?" I asked.

"Sounds wonderful."

"Me too. I don't want to go home either." Jessica added.

"Yeah, fuck going home. I'd bet there's enough psychopathology in the tourists alone that I could have a little practice down here." Chevali added.

An uneasy silence held us as the brown bird sang his amelodic songs. Sandy panted and got up a couple of times to drink water. I spent my quiet time crafting a dozen potential schemes for my newfound money (and a tiny amount of the cocaine I'd held back from one of the suitcases) until Chuck's whining Jeep brought me back. He returned with a pink jar in his hand, "Hoot, Boddington wanted me to give you this, said you should chuck your yuppie fly pole and start catching fish for dinner." He dropped a bottle of Power Bait in my hand. He raised his nose like a dog scenting a deer, "Wow, that smell is worsening. Let's check around the house. This is horrible."

I didn't want to take a chance of ruining my practical joke on Chevali. "We can do that later. I don't want to spend vacation time being responsible. Let's do something fun, we only have a couple of days left, and I don't want to waste time stink-hunting," I said.

"Whatever, you have to live in this. What do you want to do instead? Anything you want to see, place to go?" Chuck asked. At some point, I had to go back to Reef Bay and rescue more pirate money, but I wanted something different today.

I spoke to Rosie and Jessica, "What do you girls think, what sounds fun? And no damn shopping."

"We didn't get a chance to enjoy Jost because of the storm. I would love to go back for the day." Jessica said.

"I'd go to Jost any day," Rosie added.

"What's it got that St. John doesn't?" I asked.

Chuck said, "It's got a totally different vibe, more laid back. There are some cool things to see."

"More laid back than this?" Chevali questioned. "Time would have to move in reverse."

"That's the point. Let's do it. I'll call Tim and see if he's booked for the day." Chuck didn't wait for a consensus and went inside to make the call. I had no desire to go. I just wanted to relax for a day in the shade, on a beach, and read.

"Are you guys sure it's worth the hassle?" I asked.

Rosie said, "Relax, Ky, let go of your need to control everything and go with the flow for once. You're into going to Jost, right Jeb?" She pointed to him.

"Uh, I think I'm with Ky on this one."

Before I could thank Chevali, Chuck reappeared. His bouncing stride belied his rounded bulk, "Hurry up and pack your snorkel gear and your passports. We're meeting Tim at the commercial dock in ten minutes."

"Shit." I looked to Chevali for backup. He stood and said, "I guess it's a sailing day."

"Do you have time to go home for your passport?" Rosie asked Chuck.

"No problem, I don't need to." He answered.

"What do you mean, won't you'll need one like the rest of us?"

"Sure, but I leave it in the glove box of my Jeep."

"I guard my passport like a Grizzly with her cub. Your glove box does it even lock, right?" I asked Chuck.

"No, why?"

Tim motored us from the dock to Bounder in a miniature Zodiac. He looked like the poster child for underutilized sunscreen. His complexion was copy paper white, and precancerous lesions defined the skin of his face and arms. He was soft-spoken, and his spray of white hair had the consistency of a wire brush defying gravity. He generously invited us aboard his floating home. At the top of the swinging wooden stairs leading up to her deck from the water, hand-carved wooden dolphins served as hand knobs and welcomed us to Bounder. He politely showed us around the boat's cramped interior.

Bungie cords held well-worn novels and ship's lore books on dark wooden shelves. A weary, diminutive two-burner gas stove spoke of his solitary life at sea. The boat, while crammed full, still felt somehow empty. I lingered below decks as the others went topside. Tim's little world dragged me emotionally to that gray continuum stretching from alone to lonesome and on to lonely. I wondered where he spent most of his time along that desolate line. I knew I'd have to be on the far side of loneliness to open my home to strangers as he did daily. I felt sympathy for him and wanted to treat him kindly.

Topside, Rosie, and Jessica laid in the shade of the mainsail while Chevali sprawled in the sun. Curled next to him was a dog that had the same hair color and texture as Tim's. Her nose was sunburned and appeared as if it had been so every day of her life. I wondered if doggie sunscreen existed. *Where does she relieve herself?* Before finding a place to lay down, I searched for stains and spoke to Chevali.

"Who's the new bitch." I gloated silently in my double entendre.

"She's a lady, asshole. Her name is Bilgepump." He responded without making eye contact, "Tim's first mate."

"Bilgepump, seriously? Probably his ex-wife's dog. He must hate her."

"Quite the opposite, he said that she saves his sanity daily. I don't need to educate you about the value of a dog in a man's life. Hell, I'd been wondering if you were going to leave Rosie here and take Sandy home."

"Ha, the thought crossed my mind. Sandy wouldn't argue as much. Probably be a lot cheaper to feed."

"I heard that," Rosie snapped from under a frilly scarf that lay over her face.

"Sorry, honey, just kidding." I said as I shook my head 'no' to Chevali.

"I can see through the scarf, Ky. You're in trouble, and we haven't even left American waters yet." Rosie said sharply.

"I know that's a see-through. I can see your face perfectly."
I lied.

"Oh really, which eye is open?"

Shit, she's got me. "Left," I said in all confidence.

Rosie made a honking, buzzer noise that made Bilgepump raise her head.

"Who's left, yours or mine?" I asked. "You know doctors read x-rays with the patient's left on our right. It gets confusing sometimes... I love you."

"NO, you won't." She shook her index finger at me.

"Go to sleep now, dear."

Confident that I had confused her with the x-ray thing, I laid next to Bilgepump and held her tail. She moaned and put her head on Chevali's belly and her back leg across my chest. We were sharing a lady.

I enjoyed how Bounder moved through the water as opposed to motorboats that crashed into waves and beat the water. Bounder's sails pulled her up to meet each wave crest, catch an accelerating breath of wind, and glide down the far side slope. That little kick of acceleration at the top of each wave rocked my limp body while the sail rigging clanked at the same tempo as the wave accelerations. It was physically serene. Nature was gifting us forward propulsion for free.

I awakened to a slowing of wave pulses and rigging rattling before Tim started the boat's motor. It purred with confidence. Over the edge of the deck, it appeared as if I could put my hand down and touch the coral heads, which plodded along beside the boat. A few hundred yards ahead, Jost Van Dyke arose from flat, transparent emerald waters. We motored toward a small, vacant dock. Beyond it, a solitary yellow house stood in the middle of a sundried mudflat. To the left, grazing goats and a twisted dirt road led to a couple of houses clinging to a steep brown hillside. It had the same lonesome feel of the East side of St. John.

To the right of the deeper bay stretched a still and silent shallow saltwater flat, readily ten times bigger than Reef Bay's. It ambled a few hundred yards to a smaller, totally deserted island. Car-sized mangrove islands dotted the flat's placid water. Powerful, wind-blown waves broke on the far, East side of the flats. Nobody was fishing in what seemed like the perfect place for Bonefish. I didn't see any spectacular beach bars as Rosie and Jessica had described. It was a peaceful, hot, and desolate place. *A man wouldn't want to live here unless you already had a wife and dog.*

"Hey, Chuck, where are all the bars?" Chevali spoke my mind.

"On the other side of the island, Good God, Jeb, it's not even ten o'clock," Chuck answered, "I asked Tim to bring us here first. I want to show you guys something cool."

Before we could finish tying off to the dock, Bilgepump jumped down onto it, ran for the shore, and promptly relieved herself in draft horse fashion. Question answered. Beneath the pier, hundreds of fingerlings swam as if magically confined to the shadows. The clear water revealed a couple of car tires and an outboard boat motor on the bottom, each covered with a fuzz of light green sea grunge. Adventurous fish swam from the shadows to play around these and dart back to the safety of shade and pier posts. Chevali fired a mouthful of tobacco spit into the otherwise pristine water. A couple of small blue fish swam up to it to investigate and thankfully refused the take.

Walking onshore, a firm mixture of sand and brittle white mud reflected the sun's heat up to my legs like a mirror. Tim led us to the unoccupied yellow house with plastic tables and chairs under a bare tin roof. He pulled a paperback from his back pocket and started reading. Chuck motioned for us to follow him back out into the sun. "Where in the hell are you taking us? It's hotter than shit." Chevali said and flung Copenhagen from his lower lip into the sun-bleached, hard-baked ground.

"Relax Jeb, you whine like a little girl. I promise it will be worth the walk," Chuck said.

He led us along the shoreline of the shallow flats in the direction of the waves that intensely punished the island's Eastern, Atlantic edge. We turned left beyond a mangrove swamp that smelled like Larry's head and traversed a goat path uphill where rocks and cactus demanded thoughtful attention so as not to bloody or impale my toes. To our right, a hill slanted upward and the sound of pounding waves. Occasional puffs of sea mist wafted over the short hill to minimally cool us. We walked until Chuck proudly swept his hand in the direction of what looked like a thirty-foot wide toilet bowl of smooth-worn rocks and broken coral. Steep black cliffs and thick jungle surrounded it on three sides. The water in it was calm and appeared to be draining. *But to where?*

A jumble of human body-sized rocks formed an imperfect dam to separate the Eastern edge of the toilet bowl from a ten-foot-wide, hundred-yard-long solid rock channel that led out to the heaving Atlantic. The bay where Bounder moored was calm and languid, but the unbridled eastern Atlantic bucked rough and chaotic. A stiff crosswind tore sheets of water off the tops of chugging white caps. The toilet bowl water was peaceful and only a few feet deep, a perfect calm wading pool in which to cool off.

"NOW, get in, hurry," Chuck commanded rather than suggested. We joined him, barefoot and picking out way into the toilet bowl. He adamantly urged us to join him squatting waist-deep in the little pool. A churning wave sped toward us through the rock slot that led from the Atlantic to the edge of the rock dam. It slammed into the rock barricade, and water flew up over our heads. The toilet bowl filled quickly, not from the rainbow over-spray, but *UP* from the bottom, filtering through the rocks of the toilet bowl floor.

A loud fizzing noise overshadowed the breaking wave sounds as millions of bubbles tickled their way up my chest and shot two feet into the air, popping and spraying onto my face. I rocked limply in what felt like a twenty-thousand-gallon glass of freshly poured champagne. Rosie's face blurred. Her eyes and mouth smiled, wide open, blinking, and laughing. The pool partially drained, and a second wave bashed the rock dam as the process repeated itself. Bubbles, exploding above the pool's surface by the millions, obscured my vision. In a few seconds, they were gone. The receding water tried to pull me toward the dam, and I had to struggle to keep from being swept into it. Between waves, everybody talked loudly through their laughter.

When the wave set ended, gentle water puddled in the toilet bowl once again. I vibrated with the tickle of the scrubbing fizz until the tropical sun drove the sensation away. Seabirds clutched to the sides of the rock walls above us and seemed to enjoy watching us while they preened themselves. A conspicuous silence descended. Previously lurching whitecaps on my inner ocean of emotional afflictions quieted behind my conscious mind's rock dam. Peace welled upward beneath palm-sized Sergeant Major fish swimming in circles at my feet. I wondered how they survived the watery torrents of their tumultuous little world. My ears choose to cling to the silence and let the group's talk fade away. I sat back in the water while sand pebbles washed into my shorts and scrubbed my ass cheeks with the water's gentle rocking.

Once more, another foreign and enticing rhythm of the Caribbean had embraced me. The body rocking butt scrub followed the cadence of reggae in my head. Marley's sound waves seemed to drive the water's waves in moving me. I was in love with this place, my friends, my family, my moment. I realized again that I could not manufacture perfect moments, no matter how hard I tried. They're infrequently, unexpectedly sprinkled on us by forces much greater than ourselves, creating pristine memories that only death can steal from us, I thought.

My memory skittered back to what should have been such a moment. I was standing on an auditorium stage, receiving my medical school diploma, and looking down on the crowd of student's families. In that second, four years of intensive pre-med education, followed by four years of the abject tortures of medical school, all came to fruition. I had worked harder for that moment than most people ever worked through the entirety of their lives. I had endured fear, humiliation, and uncertainty and incurred immense financial and sleep debt to feel that sheepskin in my hand. When it touched my palm, it mercilessly threw me back to being a skinny kid in a drab apartment, swimming in secondhand tobacco smoke, and listening to a miserable song for the thousandth time. My mother cried, quietly mouthing the song's words while performing fellatio on the two most important men in her life, Jim Beam in his bottle and the Marlboro man. But on my graduation day, Peggy Lee sang the words of "Is That All There Is" only to me. A generous wave slammed the rock barricade, showering us with warm salt water, and washed the incongruous song-word jumble out of my brain. Peggy thankfully drowned beneath the screams and laughter while thousands of sharply bursting seawater champagne bubbles flushing my tear-blurred eyes.

-24-

FREEDOM TIME

Once back on Bounder, Tim motored out of the calm bay and into a stiff wind off the Atlantic. It was near noon, and wave spray cooled my skin. The mainsail jolted taut as it caught the wind, and we slid downwind to the South side of Jost until Chevali collected the luffing sail as we entered White Bay. The ocean's surface water behind the island's wind shadow wobbled like Jell-O. The fish below us carried out their little life dramas amongst giant coral heads of red, blue, orange, and white. Their shapes and colors undulated, trading places with each other. Chuck cast Bounder's anchor into the sandy bottom between the coral worlds, a hundred feet from shore.

On a deserted, blazing white beach sat a small blue and white open-air bar surrounded by palm trees. Tim extinguished the motor, and a muted tranquility pulsed with the sound of my heartbeat in my head. To the West, pelicans gathered above the tranquil bay, circling and then folding their wings, diving headfirst into the bay. Even from a hundred yards, their head-splattering smacks into the water broke the silence. It didn't look like a fun way to make a living.

"Let's go." Chuck assumed command.

Tim and Chuck flung their shirts off while Rosie and Jessica stripped down to their bikinis and jumped overboard.

Bilgepump nervously paced the white-topped deck and barked down at them.

"Hoot, what are you waiting for? Oh, and bring your flip-flops. We're going for a little walk."

"I'll catch up with you guys in a minute," I shouted to the back of their bobbing heads and went below decks to find a suitable hiding place for my passport. I filled a dented metal bowl with water from a rhythmically ejaculating kitchen mini faucet, placed it on the deck for Bilgepump, and leaped into the luscious cool water.

Hot sand gave way to my digging toes as I huffed uphill toward the little bar. A well-worn, upside down, blue, and white dinghy chained to a palm tree laid in the sand in front of the bar. "**SOGGY DOLLAR BAR**" was hand scrawled across her bow. The open-faced bar was the size of a large closet. Police and fire department uniform patches from all over the world lined its white ceiling rafters. Clothespins over a wire held hundreds of dollars' worth of American money in various stages of wetness behind the bar.

"Ah, Soggy Dollar, I get it," I said. Chuck frowned at me like I was stupid while placing a decorated white plastic cup in my hand. It was wet and cold. Floating Islands of fine sawdust clung to the drink's ice cubes in what looked like skim milk. "What's this?"

"Painkiller, the specialty of the house." Chuck grinned as he spoke, then drank.

"No, I mean the floating shit," I asked.

He pulled his drink from his mouth, and little chunks of sawdust clung to his mustache tips and filled the gaps between his front teeth. He was oblivious. "Hoot, it's Nutmeg, look." He pointed to the bartender rasping a brown nut across a cheese grater over a drink.

"Nutmeg? Nutmeg is a powder that comes in a little jar. My aunt used in making pumpkin pies," I said. He glared at me, "Just drink it." I figured I'd oblige him and pretend to like it.

Coconut, fruit, rum, and nutmeg alerted my sense of smell well before the liquid rolled onto my tongue. I loved this Painkiller thing before I tasted it. I felt as helpless as a crack addict after her first time at the glass pipe with my initial sip. I wanted to order another round for everybody before the bartender ran out of ingredients. My thirst doubled with every swallow.

"Well?" Chuck asked.

"Holy shit, I never liked sweet drinks before, but this and Bushwhackers could make me want to have a beach bar down here just so I could have these every day," I talked with nutmeg grounds crunching between my molars.

Then...IT HIT ME.

I'd been sucker-punched twice in my life. Once at a biker wedding in Prescott, Arizona, and the other at a cowboy bar parking lot in Reno. I think that alcohol may have played a part in those experiences. I never got the chance to repay the bastards who put me to sleep those nights. But this, this was a different type of sucker punch. Instead of putting the lights out, this sucker punch turned them on.

In my mind's eye, a vivid movie played in reverse order of events. First, I saw a bright vision of me standing in the sand behind my own beach bar, serving smiling, bikini-clad women. Second, I saw myself closing my medical office door for the last time and hanging a black wreath on it. Then there was a scene of me pulling pirate cash out of a briefcase and paying cash for my new bar. I next watched me ship boxes of pirate money from St. John to Colorado. Lastly, I was having sex with Chiara and Rosie again? *Oh well, you aren't responsible for your thoughts, only your actions. At least that's what my shrink, Jeb Chevali says.*

I rode the euphoria of my epiphany for a few seconds and summarily shot it down as an implausible fantasy. For the next hour, no matter how many subjects I covered in conversations, a distinctive physical sensation of the emotion of my little bar fantasy persisted. My fleeting beach bar vision produced a unique vibration someplace between my heart and stomach.

"Hoot, we're taking a walk," Chuck asked me to unpour myself from a perfectly fitting hammock strung between two coconut trees. I gave him my best sigh of contented laziness. It didn't work, and he shook my resting place in an unpleasant rhythm. I wasn't going to win this battle. "Where to?" I asked.

"I want to show you something that you've never seen before. Let's go now before anybody else wants to come," Chuck said. I rolled out of my perfect hammock and onto wobbling, Painkiller relaxed legs.

We walked to the far East end of the beach, "Here's where you'll need your flip flops." With feet as tender as a newborn puppy's, I didn't ask why. We ascended black stone steps cemented into the hillside, then hiked in the sun on a dry path along a steep hill face that traversed a cactus-loaded landscape. To my right, waves softly broke below us on the rocky cliff. Between the U.S. Virgin Islands and us, taut, half turban-shaped sails pulled sailboats over blue waters out at sea. I wanted to be on every one of the dozen islands in sight and on Jost all at once. My beach bar sensation surged between my heart and stomach, and I stuffed it into the sack of impossible dreams that bulged in my brain. I forced my gaze downward so as not to kick a cactus or fall off the cliff.

"Where the hell are you taking me?" I asked as another deserted white sand bay came into view. Two sailboats lay at anchor. A woman's voice bounced off the flat water up to us from at least two hundred yards away, asking someone what they wanted for lunch.

"Right down there." He indicated a spot midway in the arc of the little bay. Footprints in the sand led to the water's edge from a break in the bushes and trees. Except for the footprints, the beach and jungle behind it were devoid of signs of humanity. I wanted to ask more questions but dutifully followed him.

Uphill from the footprints on the beach, deep in the trees, stood a small blue building the size and design of a thousand square foot New Mexico rancher home. A white and lumpy, life-size statue of a man built from seashells guarded the entrance. He wore a pointed hat and had stubby thalidomide-like arms. He was even anatomically correct with a cone shell as his pecker. A small, hand-painted sign above the door read **"IVANS STRESS FREE BAR."** Beneath the words, someone had painted a red and yellow sun. Glued bleached seashells lined the door jams. Framed pictures of an old black guy playing guitar and singing were the only wall decorations. Most were water-stained, faded, and hung crooked, an easy target for thieves. "That's the bar's owner, Ivan," Chuck said. The place was cool and vacant.

The spartan furniture was in the ubiquitous Caribbean plastic table and chair motif. The untended bar was handmade from unpainted plywood and the size of a raised bathtub. Behind it, an open door led out into the bush. A rusted metal ice cooler covered with peeling beer logo stickers dripped a small pool of meltwater into waterlogged sand. Behind the bar, a cracked chalkboard displayed the cost of drinks: two dollars for alcohol, three dollars for soft drinks. There was no cash register atop the uneven bar, but only a mayonnaise jar. Attached to it by rusted wire was a handwritten rough-edged cardboard sign. "DRINK $$," written in pencil. The barback was full of bottles of rum, vodka, whiskey, cans of warm soda, and plastic cups in neat rows. In the sand next to the metal cooler, a Styrofoam ice cooler had written across it, "ICE." Spiderwebs and dangling dead bugs covered the dark inside corners underneath the bar.

"Are you serious?" I asked, "nobody here. Ya just pour your drink and leave money?"

"Yep, this is Ivan's honor bar. Pretty cool, huh." Chuck smiled as he spoke.

"I've never heard of an honor bar. Any other place else in the world besides here, this place would be stolen empty in twenty minutes." I said.

"Yep." He put some money in the jar, "Pour up, Hoot, I gotcha covered." I'd already had enough alcohol at the Soggy Dollar and poured myself a Coke over ice. He pulled a Caribe beer from the old cooler by skittering its rusted top to the side.

"I love this, man. This is the coolest bar I have ever been in." I said as my mind ran to the hundreds of cowboy, biker, and stupidly fancy bars in which I had wasted thousands of dollars. The sand floor smelled damp. Paint was missing in the hard-to-reach spots near the ceiling corners, and bird songs echoed off the barren walls through glassless windows. Before we left, I reached into my pocket, found a twenty dollar bill, and put it in the money jar. Chuck motioned to me with his beer, "I already paid for us." I held my coke can up to a curled, water-stained picture of Ivan singing and said, "I know, but this place is entirely too important for the balance of the universe ever to let it go under."

We drank as I swayed in a tire swing under a huge tree between Ivan's and the beach. Chuck sat in a webbed nylon chair that was missing half of the straps. "Amigo, are we alright?" I asked.

"I'm good. If we weren't, I'd have never brought you here. This place is too perfect for assholes."

"Is that why Jeb didn't come with us?" I asked.

"Yep. I know that you guys sound a lot alike, but I think you have a different mindset than he does."

"Thanks, but despite all of his bluster, he is really is a good guy."

His vision focused far out to sea as he paused for a few seconds, taking a long pull from his beer, "Hoot, I live in a strange world where people can love me but hate what I am. I can't give my trust to many people, especially down here. The locals hate gays, they call us Antiman, and if the word got out, I'd lose everything I had ever worked for, lose the life I love. So I need to know who my enemies are."

"Yeah, amigo, I get it," I said

"You aren't gay. You couldn't possibly get it," Chuck slowly shook his head, still looking at the bay.

I laughed a little, "Chuck, you're right. I couldn't understand the gay thing, but as far as enemies go, I'd challenge you to put a motorcycle club patch on your back and walk into a strange biker bar alone. If you see guys wearing patches from unknown clubs, you don't go to the bathroom alone and keep your back up against something solid. You don't know if they are going to play nice or try to prove something at your expense," I said.

"Well, at least yours is a choice. I am who I am. I don't have a choice. And why in the hell do you do that stupid club shit anyway? It seems like a lot of hassle and danger for no good reason. Couldn't you just CHOOSE to ride your motorcycle with no patch and not have to deal with those other assholes."

"Pardon my being crude, Chuck, but putting another guy's dick in your face IS a choice."

He turned to face me, leaned forward, and spoke in an emphatic tone. "It's not just about sex, Hoot. It's where I choose to give and find love that feels right to me. You parade around like some Billy Badass with your little club bros to make yourself feel tough."

I took a deep breath to stay calm. "Chuck, I've chosen club life, that's true, and I don't want to sound too macho or whatever, but I do so because I am tough, not because I pretend to be. I hate describing myself like that, but it is in the company of like-minded men that I feel most comfortable, just like you. When I'm around most candyass doctors, all they can talk about is golf, their expensive houses, or their overindulged children's Montessori educations. I'm as uncomfortable around those cardigan-wearing pseudointellectuals as I would be in a snake pit. I speak Harley, not Mercedes. At the end of the day, both you and I choose who we hang around with, for the same reason."

Chuck cocked his head, "How in the hell could that be?"

"Because I love the way a hard man's ass looks in black leather chaps," I said and winked at him.

"What the hell? Huh, what, Hoot, you're not Ga...?" he dropped his beer into his lap.

"Jeez, man, I'm kidding. But seriously, it is about love and maybe fulfilling unmet needs due to a shitty upbringing.

Perhaps it's about addressing fears head-on or fulfilling a sense of belonging to something bigger than me. But in the end, no pun for you, love."

"Love, biker love. You gotta be kidding me?" He smirked.

"There is no more sincere love, except for a dog's. In all no-bullshit honesty, how many people can you say that you would happily kill to defend them or their families, and they would do the same for you? In a split second, no hesitation, kill or die for?"

"My family and maybe two or three others, why?" He asked.

"I have hundreds across the country and thousands across the world. "When I meet a man with our patch on his back, I know what he had to do to earn it and what he will do to keep it."

"I don't buy it, Hoot, I just don't buy it."

"I'm not asking you to. Let's walk back to Soggy Dollar. I'm hungry as hell."

After each day of challenging adventures, I loved returning to my pleasant, temporary home, Tamarindo. "Holy shit, this is unbearable." Jessica was more expressive than usual. "Ky, you HAVE GOT to figure out what is causing this smell. It's making me sick." She was assigning me the stink duty again.

"If I had any idea where to start, I'd do so. We just gotta hope that it goes away." I heard Chevali coughing and whining from his room below the deck. "Fuck, this is unbearable. I think it's worse inside my room than out."

"Oh now, now Buddy," I called down to him, "are the Gods of stink picking on you? Just remember we're all miserable up here, too." I bounced in silent laughter, smiling at Rosie.

"No, I'm serious, Ky. It's worse in my room, shit you gotta come down and smell this," he plead.

"With an offer like that, how can I refuse."

I found him in his doorway, fanning himself with his bedroom door. As usual, he had left his A/C on all day. Putrid Larry-head steam was billowing out of it.

"Ky, this is unbearable. Smell my room, fucking smell it." He had a panicked tone to his voice.

Putting my head into his room, I pretended to inhale, then stepped back into the hallway and took deep audible breaths through my nose. "No, no, I think it's worse out here. Maybe the sluggish air movement in the hall somehow concentrates it. Good thing you got that A/C running to stir the air, though."

"Do you think it's really helping?" He asked.

"After smelling this out here, I can tell you that I'm going to turn ours on. I think A/Cs have a filter in them that might help. Besides, the cool stink is better than the hot stink. So, leave it on. It might be the only thing separating you from death." I said, envisioning his used condoms swinging from my bathroom mobile, dripping onto my neck.

"You're probably right, thanks."

"My pleasure, buddy."

I left him standing with his door open, taking an air shower in front of his air conditioner.

-25-

Redder Than Red

Later we gathered on the deck for sunset. Fortunately, an off-shore breeze minimally decreased the Larry stench. I began to question my actions as I enjoyed the semi-clean air.

"Who's up for a roadie-rum?" I asked the group as they stood in silence, watching gravid pink clouds fading to grey as the sun ducked behind the edge of the ocean. Jessica and Rosie declined, saying they wanted an early dinner. Chevali said, "I'm going to hold off for now. That smell has ruined my taste for anything", he smiled at Jessica's ass as she bent over the deck's handrail. "Almost anything."

"Hey guys, come here, you gotta see this." Both Jessica and Rosie leaned forward over the rail, looking downhill. I asked, "Whatcha got?"

"Cats. A herd of cats, it's like they are launching an attack." Rosie's head weaved as she watched cats filtering through the bushes, moving in mass uphill. They had apparently smelled Larry and were on the hunt. "Here, cats and land crabs filled the empty niche left by the absence of buzzards, I said. I recognized the black and white cat from my night of vomiting. *Bastard*.

"Let's go down and follow them, see if they can lead us to the source of the stench," Chevali said excitedly.

I had to think fast, not wanting the cats to spoil my practical joke. "Hey guys, it's turning dark. The last thing I want to do is stumble around in bad light and hurt myself before dinner. If there is anything to find, the kitties will show us in the morning." Somehow telling the truth and being deceitful at the same time was serving my needs. *I'm going to have to remember this ploy for the future.*

Rosie pulled me aside, "I want to eat and go to bed early. Tomorrow is our last day. I want to have a good night's sleep to be ready for anything tomorrow. So I'm asking you nicely to please get rid of Larry tonight once we get home."

"We'll talk." I knew this was only a temporary weakening on her part.

I walked with animated purpose toward the front gate, away from the menacing feline pack, and jiggled the gate handle, "Let's go eat."

Is Chuck joining us tonight?" I asked as we walked downhill.

Rosie answered, "he said he'd meet us at a bar after dinner. It's in the same building as the Pussers bar."

This was my second to last night of walking to town. I was already missing what I was doing now and feeling stupid for feeling like that. Everybody was quieter than usual, and I wondered if they felt my same premature sense of loss.

"Hey Rosie, how are you doing?" I asked.

She answered, "you said earlier that you could live down here. Were you serious?"

"I was serious at the time, but even if we could make a go of it financially, the logistics of moving down here would be a nightmare. And, I'm not sure you could be as philosophical as Chuck about the lack of amenities here. The only reason to move would be to find peace, not trade one set of problems for another." I tried to ignore my newfound and recurring beach bar-spark sensation fluttering in my low chest.

"Or Mister Negative, you could think of it as choosing peace and ignoring the loss of stuff that you REALLY don't need." She talked on as I worked on re-stuffing the beach bar dream into the 'unobtainable dream sack' in my brain.

"Shit, now you're talking psychobabble like Jeb," I said.

"Did someone call my name?" He asked from behind us.

"Yeah, we were just talking about bad breath." He exhaled into his hand and sniffed a couple of times. *Narcissists are such easy targets.* He spoke to Jessica, walking at his side, "Here, smell my breath," and forcefully exhaled at her as if fogging a mirror.

She laughed and pushed him away, "Get away from me, you weirdo. I know where that mouth has been."

"Maybe that's what all the cats were coming for, Jeb. Have you brushed this week?" I asked.

"Screw you. I brush twice daily."

"I'm not talking about your hair, pretty boy," I said and grinned at a scowling Rosie.

"Will you two please stop it," Rosie said, "I want to have a light, pleasurable evening and not listen to the two of you bicker like two old women." I held up my hand to entice a high-five from Chevali, which he readily obliged.

We were nearly to town, and the sound of The Pussers bar pulled my eyes to it and the restaurant above it. "There's Pussers. The food is supposed to be decent. Let's try it," I said.

We sat at a table overlooking a dark sea. Slowly rocking sailboats moored in the bay reflected the town's lights on the water between them and us. Little lights wandered in lazy circles or frantic jumbled figures at the tops of their masts, depending upon whether a ferry disturbed their rocking slumber. Strings of small bare white bulbs lit our table from above, strung like Christmas tree lights on red-painted metal rafters, open to the night sky. The railing between us and the air above the Pussers bar was also red and glossy. Laughter and conversation wafted up from the bar to meet the scents coming out from Pusser's kitchen.

"Drinks before dinner?" A tan, young waitress in a white and blue apron broke my mind's wandering. I unzipped my fanny pack and pulled out Tona's battered white tin cup and held it up toward her and asked, "What are the chances of filling this with a double Painkiller?"

"I don't know. Nobody has ever asked." She wore the pained facial expression of a woman denying a request for a dance. Her eyes begged me to retreat off the dance floor and find my place in the lonely shadows of the rejected drinkers. Instead, I placed Tona's tin cup in her soft hand and closed her fingers on it with both of my hands. "Well, I guess this will be a maiden voyage for both of you," I smiled and batted my eyelashes, thinking that she might like older men. She blinked back, "SCREW YOU." I hoped she wasn't going to spit in it.

"Always charming the young ones, aren't you, Ky," Chevali said and spit a mouthful of tobacco juice over the rail. A woman squealed from below at the bar, "EEEW, I think a bird or something just shit on me. Oh--my--God, it's so gross."

"Yep, amigo, I learned all my charm from you," I said, realizing that about anybody else would have been embarrassed, but not Chevali. He calmly reached across Jessica to the table next to us and grabbed a used Coke can, and drained it on the floor by her feet. "Spittoon," he said and put the can between his legs. The waitress reappeared with their drinks and my chipped cup, filled to the brim with Painkiller. We each ordered Roti and ate with the swirling peace of a calming wet and warm sea breeze.

After dinner, we headed to the bar to meet Chuck. It's dark, hand-carved wooden sign, 'The Ancient Navigator,' hung in a concrete hallway. Large, open arched windows emitted the typical dull, fluorescent glow of a dive bar. The base of the windows was a couple of feet above the walkway. Thick wooden shutters that could close and protect the bar from an angry sea hung like ears on either side of the windows. I stepped over a window ledge to enter the bar. A dartboard hung from a pockmarked wall that had a Manuel Ortega-like complexion, resulting from hundreds of drunk-thrown darts.

Metallica raged from an old jukebox in the far corner of the dimly lit room decorated with pirate-themed paintings. A moose head-sized ship's Maidenhead dripping with panties and bras projected forcefully beside the long, mostly empty bar. Behind the bar hung well-worn whips, riding crops, a black leather cat-o nine tails, and a pair of incongruous handcuffs. The bar-top was charred plywood hid under generations of yellowed urethane, cigarette burns, beer logo stickers, and stains forever entombed in layers of hardened goop.

Chuck sat at the bar, engrossed in conversation with a man sporting slicked back, black hair. Waves of grey wove their ways through the sides above his ears as if glued to his head. His dark face supported a spray of deep wrinkles at the corners of his eyes, while his shiny forehead alternately flattened and wrinkled as he talked.

I smiled benignly at the man and put my finger to my lips as I snuck up on Chuck. His eyes deflected to catch mine and went back to Chuck. With a straw from a glass at the bar, I softly brushed Chuck's right ear. He swatted at the imaginary bug and kept talking. I waited and ran it down the back of his neck. His hand smashed his neck.

To my left, a well tattooed, thick but not obese female bartender with long, raven hair watched me silently as I gingerly ran the straw across Chuck's ear and withdrew it quickly. "Damn it." His open hand struck his ear with a whop. I smiled at the bartender. The poker-faced black man with whom Chuck was conversing asked the bartender for two more drinks. I waited, and as he turned on his stool to face the bar, I ran the straw into his ear canal and left it.

"Oh, Jesus." He stood and fanned his ear, shaking his head. The bartender threw an ice cube at him, and his friend apologized to him for his complicity.

He threw the straw at me. "Damn you Hoot."

I asked the buxom bartender, "Would you find poor Chuck a can of OFF?" She just smiled a wicked smile that seemed somehow familiar and put a bottle of Pusser's rum in front of him and his friend. Then, she opened a can of Coke and refilled their glasses with ice.

Her chest would have been the envy of civilians, sailors, and women alike. Her voluminous, round breasts were tattooed with a four-masted ship and its skeletal pirate flag, riding the waves of their magnificence. A fashionably tattered, lowcut shirt exposed all but the bottom of her ship's hull.

"Shit man, you order the whole bottle?" I asked Chuck.

"No, Hoot, this is how they do it here."

The black man splashed a few molecules of Coke on his ice and filled his glass with rum.

"Rum is cheaper than Coke here, so they let you pour your own drink," Chuck said.

Chuck poured his drink, and the bartender put the Coke can behind the bar, leaving the rum bottle. "Hoot, I want you to meet an old friend, Aldous. He's Jimmy's uncle." I shook hands with the man. His long shiny fingers were smooth and warm, yet his palm was calloused and rough. He smiled through absent maxillary incisors.

Chuck said that they had made quite a bit of money over the last year salvaging wrecked sailboats. He explained that some owners wanted their boats brought up whole, others were interested in rescuing specific items.

"What kind of stuff do they want you to bring up?" I asked.

"Mostly hidden safes, locked suitcases, briefcases."

"You're not worried that you could be recovering illegal stuff?"

"We never ask, and we never look. The idea is to make money, not get killed." Aldous continued, "Tell him about Pizza Face." Next, they searched the room to see if anybody was within earshot.

"We have a big-time drug dealer poking around from Columbia, a violent, bad mother raper, asked us to be on the lookout for his boat. Aldous's daughter is with the V.I. Police department, and works with the DEA a lot. They have been trying to catch this guy for years, but he's too slippery. He asked us to watch the South side of the island for his missing yacht."

"Huh, the South side, I'm always about 90 degrees off down here, isn't where Reef Bay is?" I asked, not wanting to hear the answer.

"Yep," replied Aldous, "he believes that Marilyn sank his brother's boat."

"You gonna help him?" I asked Chuck.

"No. Rumor has it that people around him develop the bad

habit of wearing," he put his hand up to his throat and pretended to slit it with his thumb, "Columbian neckties." I moved down here to never wear a necktie again."

"I like that idea too," I said as Chevali and Rosie walked up to us.

"The girls want to go home early. Oh, Hi Chuck." Chevali said.

I watched Chuck's expression. "Hey, Jeb, meet my friend Aldous." They shook hands and launched into small talk.

"Hey babe, what's up?" I asked Rosie.

"Jessica and I are tired. So we're gonna go home and read. I'll pick up Sandy on the way home."

"Are you sure?" I asked.

She bent forward and kissed me, "Have fun, I'll be fine. But please get rid of Larry before you come to bed. Do it for me if you love me."

That last statement, "Do it for me, if you love me," always irritated me. It was her way of saying that if you don't do it for me, you don't love me -- a double bind.

"We'll talk about Larry when I return home." She thumped me on the forehead and left.

I smiled and held up two fingers to the bartender.

"What's your desire?" She bent forward, and her arms came together, squeezing her breasts and deforming her ship tattoo into a black and white taco. She held her position while her eyes rotated upward, catching me looking. Thankfully, Chevali was also watching the pirate ship destruction derby and saved me from embarrassment.

"Two Caribes," I said.

"Will that be all?" She asked.

"No, actually, "he said.

Her face reddened when she made eye contact with him. *A blush?* "What would that be?"

"Your ship is missing something," Chevali said.

"I love my ship." She seemed put off by his statement. "I like totally researched The Queen Ann's Revenge before I got it. So what's the matter with it?" She pushed her arms closer again and dropped her head, inspecting the deformed ship.

"Yep, it's missing something, alright." Chevali insisted.

"Nuh-uh. Do you know pirate ship history or something?" She asked.

"Enough to know what that tattoo needs."

"Well, what?" She asked.

"Sea men, mine to be exact. Oh, and my Caribe, please." I expected her to yell at him, but she calmly released the ship from her arm vice, letting it settle back to a natural position of glory. When she returned with his beer, she took a step backward and slid it in her cleavage between the fore and aft of her ship. Then, cradling it securely without using her hands, "Come and get it if you're brave enough."

Chevali smirked and reached for his beer which was dripping condensation between her masts. She leaned seductively back, making him stretch over the bar while she ran a hand back toward the wall of torture instruments. She plucked something off a wall as he bent fully over the bar. She leaned forward, letting him rotate his beer from between her breasts, and delivered a hard slap on his back with the cat-o-nine tails. The wallop echoed across the room. He yelped and recoiled, spilling beer over himself and her wobbling ship as she laughed. I noticed the veins standing up from her muscular striking arm.

"You bitch, that hurt." Despite his words, he had a playful expression on his face, as did she.

"Respect me, or I hurt you." She shook the torture device at him.

"I respect your strength, but you're gonna have to earn my respect if you want it." He tipped his beer to her and nodded his head.

"Why would I give a shit about you or your respect?" She asked.

"As I said, your tattoo needs my decoration, but my sea men don't climb aboard any old ship, and I need another beer. Your ship is floating in my old one." Chin up, she ignored him and walked to the customers at the end of the bar.

"You best be careful, son, that young woman has a reputation for being bloody strong and making men pay to play," Aldous warned.

"Is she a whore? I can usually spot those from a mile away. It's a professional hobby of sorts." Chevali said.

"Oh no, quite to the contrary," He spoke with perfect, elegant grammar and a slight British accent. "Despite her appearance, I don't know of a single man to board that ship, so to speak. But I do know of a few who ended up, rather shall I say, taken up for the hawks."

"Taken up for?" Chevali questioned.

Chuck interpreted Aldous, "She likes to beat the shit out of men. I'd go for it if I were you. She doesn't look that tough to me." Chevali watched her move behind the bar, studying her like a coyote watching a suburban poodle. "I'm up for a challenge." He flexed his bicep and kissed it, a favored if not overused move of his.

"I'd have my running trainers on if I were you, son," Aldous warned and continued talking about sailboat recovery. I worried that my dead pirate friend was the Columbian drug dealer's missing brother. I needed to hike back to Reef Bay, take whatever I could in the morning, and not grow a Columbian necktie.

When the bartender returned with his beer, I asked Chevali, "You coming home with me or staying to let this chick humiliate you?" The bartender raised an eyebrow at me, and I recognized her. She was the bartender from Woody's.

"I'm staying. I got a bunch of sea men and hawks that need to be set free," he said.

"I think you misunderstood the expression about the hawks," I said through a grimace.

"Who cares? I have a four-masted challenge to attend to."

"Well, amigo, I don't know which you'll need more, a rubber or a crash helmet. Good luck," and climbed out of the bar's arched window. Looking back, I saw Chevali behind the bar, pulling a riding crop off the wall and slapping his palm, while tattoo girl was locking the massive wooden front doors. *I wouldn't want to be either of their asses tonight.*

Yowling cats were competing with Larry's presence for my annoyance when I got back to Tamarindo. I felt guilty for a fleeting second. Downstairs, Rosie was in bed engrossed in a cowboy novel, and the mood was as sour as the air. "Hey baby, I need to borrow Sandy for a minute. Gotta chase off a few of those damn cats who are trying to steal Larry." I said and kissed her on the top of the head.

Without her eyes leaving the page, she said, "Larry MUST go, his welcome has worn out. He's making all of us miserable."

"I know it's a little inconvenient, but we only have one more day left."

Rosie slammed her book down, "That's exactly my point. I don't want to spend my last day here, miserable because you want to play some boyish practical joke."

"But it grows funnier with each passing maggot." I was sure I could humor her out of her sour mood.

"Let me put it to you this way, I not going to have sex when it smells like this. Do you get MY drift?" Her eyebrows raised with 'drift,' a sure sign of her seriousness. This was almost an ultimatum, the ultimate challenge in marital relations. "Aw, come on, you've had sex in stinkier places than this, right?" I was still flying with the humor approach.

Rosie growled and kicked her heels into the bed, "Damn it, Ky, this isn't funny anymore. I want our last day here to be romantic, not stinky. I worked all year to help pay for this damn vacation. The last few days have been overwhelmed by your screwed-up sense of humor, making all of us sick either you get rid of Larry or I will, and if I have to do it, I guarantee that our house is going to be a lot colder than the snow when we go back." Tortuous little arteries in her sclera bulged like skinny sunburned fingers holding her eyeballs. She wasn't catching my humor. So, I acquiesced in the name of relational respect, plus I really wanted to get laid. "Ok fine, you win. Larry will go away in the morning."

"No, NOW." She was being unreasonable, but I decided to indulge her. "Fine, come on, Sandy, protect your buddy from those nasty cats." She groaned, stretched, and came to my side.

"At least there is some love in this room for me," I said as I petted Sandy.

"Remove Larry from this property, or that's the only love you will know for a long time."

I went upstairs for supplies. Jessica was sitting on the

couch, holding a glass of red wine and listening to classical music. A single candle lit the room, and her short see-through negligee covered some of her cleavages. She stared through me. "He didn't come home with you." Her tone wasn't accusatory but had a wandering quality, lost. My first instinct was to cover for Chevali, tell her he was still drinking with Chuck. "No, he didn't." I didn't need to lie.

In the candlelight, Jessica was sadly beautiful in her vulnerability. She had always been a close, platonic friend, and I wanted to hold her to make her feel better and would have if I couldn't see both of her cleavages. "You Ok?"

"I'm fine. Just feeling like a fool. Why Ky why?" Jessica spoke through tears.

"Why what? Why is Jeb such an idiot? Why would he leave someone as attractive as you here alone?"

"No, why, I guess, I mean more like, why do I chase men off? I try to make myself attractive. I have a superb education and make more money than most of the losers I date. Yet, they always go away. Why?"

"Jess, listen to me, please. Men are pigs. Men are stinkin' pigs. Plain and simple, all of us, every friggin' one of us, pigs. It is as much a part of us as women being flatulent." That made her laugh and blow snot and tears on her chest. She reached up and pulled me down to her and wiped with my shirt. "Ky, shut up, you aren't a pig. You're just a man."

"Baby, there's nothing wrong with you, you are beautiful, but you said it best when you described the men you date as losers. Come on, Baine, Jeb, what the hell?" I kissed her on the head. "Hold that thought. Sandy and I have to go stink hunting." I said as I yanked a rusted magnetic flashlight off the refrigerator.

Sandy and I stepped outside, "Let's find some kitties, girl." I grabbed her basketball-sized head, aimed it at a cat about ten feet away, and said, "Get it, get it." She loped three strides forward to the cat, who appeared to recognize her, rolled onto its back, and playfully swatted Sandy's face. Next, she licked the cat's belly until It purred. "Fine, I'll do the job alone."

The ground below Chevali's A/C unit was thick with cats. They circled like sharks and made futile uphill jumps to reach Larry. When I got close, they acted as if it were feeding time and rubbed their flea-covered, mangy bodies against my legs. I found solace in Larry's crimson head, still draining his juice into the A/C unit intake. Even if I disposed of him, his lobster-love would live on for the next day. I skidded Larry off the A/C and into a plastic PUBLIX shopping bag with a stick.

As I walked downhill toward sigmoid curve with Larry's putrid head in the shopping bag, I held it out to my side to avoid any unwanted drips hitting my legs. Cats followed at my heels, mewing and fighting each other for the yuck splatters. Mosquitoes found a couple of spots where my OFF had sweated off and feasted mercilessly. There was nothing pleasant about that evening's walk.

I threw Larry into one of the street-side trash bins at Gallows point, giving Sigmoid curve more ammunition to earn its name. Downhill, Chevali was walking toward me, whistling to himself. I waited for him in the streetlight shadow of a large tree. When he was a few feet away, totally oblivious to my presence and bending over to pet a cat, I lowered my voice into a deep barltone.

"Hey asshole, leave the tabby alone, she's mine." He stumbled forward, trying not to step on the cat, whirled around, landed in a crouched position facing me, and backed up to a telephone pole. Dim yellow street lights cast long, poorly defined shadows down his face, "Ky, what the hell are you doing down here?"

"Just out for a walk with my friends," I said, gesturing to the cats who were leaping into the trash bin.

"You're fucking weird." His lower lip was swelling.

"Crap Jeb, were you jumped? Let's go find the son of a bitch." I held my rusty flashlight up like a club.

"Not he. She." He grinned. I could see blood in his teeth. "She got a little rough and didn't want to give it up until I kinda pinned her down. Man, that is one strong bitch."

"You're making it sound like you raped her."

"Hell no, at the turning point in the process, it was just the opposite. I was about to give up, and she, well, beat the shit out of me until I did her. It was strange but fun. I think there might be some Daddy issues in that closet."

"Ya' think papa Jeb? And it sounds like you just added another skeleton to that sad closet," I said.

"Maybe so, but I think we both kinda liked it."

"Well, doctor, I guess that makes you as screwed up as she," I said.

"I doubt that," he said, pulling his shirt up, "She doesn't have these on her tits." In the pale light, I could see bite marks and hickeys on his chest. The bite marks were complete upper and lower rows of teeth, red and surrounded by purple bruising. Some were slightly bleeding. His nipples were swollen.

"Damn, Jeb you look like you fell into a shark tank," I said.

"Maybe, but you should see her ass." Cats were raucously fighting and screaming in the trash bin.

"Jeb, you're more of a mess than I ever knew."

"I know, I know. And I wouldn't admit this to anybody but

you, but I think I love her. She is the prettiest, roughest, and most exciting piece of ass I've ever had. Seriously Ky, all bruises aside. That is one complex woman. I can't quite put my finger on it. She's a psychiatric conundrum. I'm intrigued."

"No, you're beaten to shit. Did she hit you in the head? Besides, you know better to fall in love with psychopathology," I said.

We walked uphill to Tamarindo and away from the Larry orgy. "Yeah, I know, I gotta regain my footing. I think I'm a little high on adrenaline right now. But, maybe you're right." He looked far uphill as he spoke.

"By the way, Jess is hurt. She was hoping for more from you. I'm talking emotionally, not sexually," I said.

"Ky, I never said anything to her that would obscure my shallowness. She's a sweet girl and will make some elitist, rich asshole a great wife. She knew damn well before we went to St. Thomas, who she was going with."

"I know, man, just be nice to her, please. Jessica, like you with your female Mohammad Ali, doesn't always have control of where her heart goes, no matter what her head tells her."

"Leave the shrink-talk to me," he said.

Tamarindo was dark, and the only sound was of Coqui frogs. The music in town had died down, but Larry's stench continued despite his absence. I hoped it would dissipate by morning so Rosie could come to her senses.

Before I fell asleep on the cool sheets, I set Rosie's travel alarm for five AM and my last chance to retrieve the pirate money. I was facing a total of three hours of sleep. I lay face down, with one hand on Sandy's rib cage and one stuffed between Rosie's motionless ass and the mattress.

-26-

RAINBOW COUNTRY

T houghts of ischemic injury entered my head when my right
hand refused to listen to my conscious commands. I had not
moved all night and had developed wife-ass-induced carpal
tunnel syndrome. Then, after multiple shakes, it started the
pins and needles recovery process. Once it was functional, I
stuffed all our handbags, backpacks, and nylon rope into my
yellow backpack and tied the ankle ends of my long fishing
pants in knots.

Sandy and I drove in the dark to the parking mudpuddle
above Reef Bay. By flashlight, I used my fishing rod/spider
sword to get us down to the dead drug dealer safely before the
sun breached the hill to the East.

I jammed pirate money into bags, daypacks, and my fishing pants that I'd fashioned into a doggie backpack. I stuffed
money into my shirt pockets and down my pants and tucked
money into the incongruous white sox I was wearing with
my Reef Walkers. Each bag and pack were solid and heavy.
I moved the eleven remaining unopened plastic-wrapped
money kilos to higher ground above the swamp. In true pirate
fashion, buried them under the only Monkey No Climb tree on
the hillside. My unconscious mind had a plan and insisted that
I take a couple of handfuls of cocaine in my plastic sandwich

bag. I hated having the toxic shit even touch my skin. I left the rest for the already jittery crabs.

I trundled up Reef Bay trail with two jam-packed daypacks and a large floral bag jammed with pirate money bricks exposed at the top. I packed my pants and shirt full to the point of nearly ripping, and I hugged two unopened kilo bricks of money under my right arm. I was so money-bound that my strides were half of their usual length. The money was an excellent insulator, not letting a single BTU escape my skin's surface, causing me to stop frequently and catch my breath. The sun was beaming down in silvery shafts through the jungle treetops and warming the morning air as I finally leaned against the truck and vomited from exhaustion. Sandy dropped like an overburdened mule in the mud to cool off but still smiled as she panted.

Rosie left a note for me at Tamarindo. They were going for French Toast and then to Trunk Bay. I had to hurry and coerced Sandy into the shower with me. I washed the mud off us and wracked my brain for ways to ship the money home. I skidded naked into the bedroom in time to shelter Rosie's shopping bags from dog water as Sandy shook. And there it was, a large Donald Schnell Art Studio box containing an expensive ceramic hanging lamp embossed with miniature sea horses, chunks of stained glass, and seashells mushed into the sides of the lamp before its firing. The box was sturdy, and old newspapers padded the lamp. I dried us off and went shopping.

I purchased ceramic fixtures, lamps, and outdoor light covers and requested that Sinclair's polite local sales kid provide me with multiple oversized boxes. Each box was custom decorated with the Donald Schnell Ceramics of St. John logo. I asked, "I don't want to sound condescending, but is it alright if I pack them myself at our villa and bring them back for you to ship?"

"Sure, but I pack des every day and never a complaint bout dem pieces being broken deh mail."

"I believe you, but you don't know my wife. If anything arrives broken when we are back home, I'll have to drive all the way back here to exchange it." He guppy-mouthed for a few seconds and appeared to think better of commenting on my stupidity. I'd just spent thousands of dollars with him, and I expected he wasn't about to jeopardize the sale. "Whatever you say, let me get deh cartos and packin' material."

Back at Tamarindo, I unfolded sheets of newspapers, covered each in layers of one-hundred-dollar bills, and rolled them into what looked like gigantic marijuana joints. I folded and stuffed them inside the lamps, wrapped them around the lamps, and jammed them into the corners of the boxes. Each box held tens of thousands of dollars, all hidden inside rolled tubes of the inconspicuous newspaper. When I delivered the boxes back to Sinclair, he commented on their weight and was concerned that my packing job would be too expensive to ship. So I gave him a crisp pirate hundred for the extra trouble and my credit card number for the shipping costs and drove to join the others for an afternoon at the beach.

Tamarindo's pale orange skin welcomed us back from our last afternoon at Trunk Bay. Sandy barked us home and ran in happy dog circles until I petted her. Her trusting eyes made me wonder what was going to become of her after we left. I hadn't let myself think of that much until now. My black girl-friend was going to return to her little cave under the street. Who was going to feed her? My throat tightened in pre-tear discomfort.

"Rosie, we have to talk," I spoke to her back as she rinsed our SCUBA gear.

"It always worries me when you start a conversation that way." She put the hose down.

"What are we going to do with Sandy when we leave?" I said.

"Oh hell, Ky, I was afraid of this," Rosie said.

"What do you mean? She loves you too. We can't just turn her loose again. She could starve or hit by a car or beaten by locals. We can't let that happen. We have a responsibility now." She looked down at Sandy, then at me with that blank stare of impatient love.

"What do you propose?" I asked.

This is a good sign. Since I had no plan yet, I gave the most intelligent answer I could muster. "Uh, I don't know. Give me a little while to think about it." This answer induced a deep sigh and hands resting on her hips, thumbs pointing forward.

"*Not a good sign.*"

"Ky, we're leaving on the eight AM ferry. Shouldn't you have thought about this earlier?"

"I'm taking that as a yes?" I spoke through a grin.

"Take it as... you are a dumbass who is incapable of planning anything." She was softening. I could sense it.

"Maybe Chuck could ship her to us? Ya know, put the dog in a cage and drive her to the airport." The visual image was less than plausible. "Maybe she could live with him until we fly down here again and put all the pieces together then?" I said.

"Have you talked to Chuck about this? You seem happy to volunteer his services for something that's going to be a huge pain in the ass."

"Uh, not yet," I said. *That was a poor answer.*

She continued to hose her SCUBA fins and wet suit. "Damn it, Ky," she said. *At least it wasn't a 'no.'*

The sun began its nightly tumble into the sea off St. Thomas's left shoulder. I didn't want to miss this one, and I didn't want to see this one, the last sunset before returning to reality. *Shit.* I helped Rosie hang the SCUBA gear on the railing to dry and went inside to pour our sunset rums.

I returned to find Rosie sitting on the deck with Sandy's head in her lap, petting her and softly crying. "Damn it, Ky..." Sandy would be finding a way to Colorado. I sat next to them with my thigh against Sandy's firm body, handed Rosie her rum, and held my glass up to the sadly setting sun, "To another kid in our future." We drank in silence.

Jessica played the classical music station from Puerto Rico in the main house, and Dvorak wafted strongly out of the screen door into the evening. The moment felt of family, of home, and a sense of uneasy peace. The only appealing thoughts of returning to Colorado were of the club and my animals. They all hung like a velvet yoke around my neck. Without them, I could have easily torn up my return ticket.

"I shipped the money to Colorado today."

"You did?" She asked, with her head cocked. "How are we going to deal with it when we go back?"

"I have a perfect plan, don't worry." I lied to make us both feel better.

We showered and dressed for dinner. I wore my typical tee shirt, flip flops, and short pants, and Rosie wore a bright orange flowered sundress. She always made me appear poorly dressed but also made me look better by being with me. "I guess we gotta go to the stupid, most expensive restaurant on the island tonight for Jessica," I said, feeling irritated but still happy to do it for Jessica.

"She said that she just wanted to eat in town and get back to pack, Rosie said."

"Wow, that's a first," I said.

"Yeah, she doesn't want to spend a lot of time around Jeb."

"I haven't seen him since this morning. Let me see if he's here."

Downstairs, Chevali was absent. Larry's fading stink was his room's only occupant. Upstairs, I found Jessica sitting next to a note. "He left this for you." She said, handing it to me.

"*Hey asshole, I'm on my own tonight. If I don't make the flight, I'll catch up to you back home!*" A faint bloody fingerprint covered the exclamation point. I knew his destination.

"I guess it's just we three and Chuck tonight," I said to Jessica.

"Ky, do you want to go home?" Jessica talked to her rum.

"Hell no. How about you?"

"Neither do I."

"I know, baby. At least you do have Baine to go home to." I usually try to measure my words before saying them. This was an unintended exception. I felt stupid the minute they dribbled out. She slowly lifted her head and met my eyes. "Really? You think I'm lucky. I'll go home to have my feet cherished and my heart ignored." She downed her rum. "Pour me another, Ky.

Gotta finish the bottle tonight, or it gets wasted." The bottle was nearly full.

"Sorry, baby, I didn't mean to...."

"To what, tell the truth. I'm going back to my successful tennis at the country club, smartly packaged life. I have nothing to return to that makes me genuinely happy. Sure, I have my BMW, Pings, and the most exclusive shoe collection in town, but I have no life. Nobody who cares, at least nobody who isn't a sicko. I guess that makes me one too."

"No, no, look at it this way. How many bored housewives would kill for a regular foot massage?" My humor always worked on her. She was stone-faced.

Her eyes left mine, "When Jeb made love to me, he consumed me, ravished me, all of me, EXCEPT for my feet. He made me feel like I was the best that he had ever had. Ky, a woman just needs to be taken sometimes, taken hard, taken away, taken deeply into her own vulnerability and femininity. He did that for me multiple times. He used me for MY own pleasure. Does that make any sense?"

"Sure, I take myself for my own pleasure all the time," I said.

"Damnit, I'm serious. I need NOW, what I didn't even know I needed before him. And to top it off, he has a small penis. He's a little guy just like you, yet he makes big love."

A little guy like me? While I usually enjoyed discussing myself, I didn't feel the need for the conversation to go down that rabbit hole.

It made me wonder if Rosie talked about me to her friends? I imagined her saying after a few glasses of wine, "*If he could make only love to me with his ego instead of his little pecker,*

I'd be a satisfied woman." I shook my head to get Rosie out of my thoughts.

"Hoot, where the hell you at?" With my being engrossed in a sexual discussion, I hadn't heard Chuck drive up.

"In the house with Jess, and a bottle of Pusser's that needs killing. Haul your gelatinous ass in here and drink." Jessica's lower eyelids were holding back dammed tears.

"Hang tough, baby. There is more big love in store for you, I promise." She pulled my shirt and wiped her nose with it. Obviously, the rum was hitting her brain. Chuck entered the room as she was finishing. "Jessica, you need a napkin or something?"

"No, I have Ky's shirt." She was feckless.

"Just an intimate moment between friends," I said.

"Huh, you seem to have a lot of those these days, Hoot. Where's Rosie?" Chuck asked.

"Right here." Rosie was standing in the doorway, listening to the conversation. Jessica snorted back a nose-full and swallowed, "Hey Rose." Rosie made eye contact with me, grimaced a slight smile, and answered. "Hey, Jessica." That was an awkward, innocent moment, and I needed to change the subject, "Jessica, are you sure you don't want to go to Chateaubriand, or whatever it's called for dinner?"

"Chateau Burgundy, honestly, I don't care. I'm not hungry. Anywhere is fine."

I saw this as a reprieve, "I'd vote for Uncle Joe's ribs." Surprisingly, everybody agreed. *Saved.*

Short bursts of conversation about fun memories from the previous ten days interrupted our subdued meal. Jessica barely ate or spoke. Chuck, Rosie and Jimmy plotted their next trip to Colorado for Christmas. The Dominican bar across the street was silent. The only aspects of the evening that were consistent with previous nights were the mosquitoes and the wet heat. I ate somber ribs while squishing mosquitoes on a slouching Jessica. Before we left, Rosie said to me, "I want to steer Jessica away from the Ancient Navigator on the walk home. The last thing she needs to see is Jeb and the bartender together."

"Agreed," I answered. Chuck quietly suggested that we should check on Chevali to make sure he was still alive. We headed to the bar while Rosie steered Jessica home.

The bar smelled of full ashtrays, mildew, and spilled beer. The bare fluorescent lighting gave it the charm of a Mexican jail. From the arched doorway, we watched Chevali talking across the bar to his latest conquest. Her shoulders and muscular thighs made her attractive in an athletic way, and her maritime tattoos fit her as part of the bar's decorations.

"There's the spider and the fly. Oh, what a tasty morsel he is. Look at him. He has no idea." Chuck said, and Jimmy giggled. They knew something that they weren't revealing.

"What are you guys talking about?" I asked.

"Oh nothing, it's just that they are such an interesting couple." Jimmy giggled, and Chuck waved him off.

I studied the pair. Chevali was gesticulating, telling a story. She laughed with her head back and covered her chest with a large hand. When she laughed, her Adam's apple was a bit too large. Suddenly I understood their joke. Chuck, Jimmy, and the bartender were all members of the same tribe.

"She's a dude, a friggin' dude, right?" I said.

Chuck's eyes widened on me. "Shit Hoot, not so damn loud, keep it quiet. This island is an unforgiving place for people like her...us."

"I'm right?" Of course, I didn't expect to be right. But, for Chevali's sake, I didn't want to be right and had to play it cool.

"Sort of," Jimmy said.

"Huh? I'm confused."

"She was born a female, but with the wrong plumbing. A few years ago, with the help of a financial benefactor, the bar's owner, her ex, flew to your state for sexual reassignment surgery." Jimmy said.

"Jeb is in love with a tranny?" My surprise outsprinted my sensitivity.

Chuck grumped in a harsh tone," Why, do you disapprove?"

"It's not my place to approve or disapprove. Ya know, to each his or her own. But it is a touch ironic, eh?"

"Yep, but are you going to warn him that he's dating a Trans?" Chuck asked.

Good question. I felt like I should warn him, but from what, I wasn't sure. He was a big boy capable of making his own choices. He had used his charm on who knows how many women for his enjoyment. I suspect not always to their betterment. Maybe this was the Gods using him as a cat toy for their entertainment for once.

"I love him enough to let him explore the world on his own. Stranger shit has happened a time or two in the history of mankind. No, this isn't my call. Besides, happiness is fleeting and rare. Who knows? Now, how about a drink? I need it." I said.

Chuck slapped me on the back, "let's leave the lovebirds alone and kill the bottle of Pusser's at Tamarindo instead."

"You two go ahead, I'm tired and need some sleep. It's

been an interesting time meeting you, Dr. Elliott. I hope to see you soon." Jimmy said.

"The pleasure has been mine. "Take care of old stinky here for me until we return." He patted my back uneasily.

When we arrived back home, Rosie was talking to Sandy in our room, and a light shone beneath Jessica's door. We took the Pusser's and a can of OFF to the deck under the stars, leaned back in sunchairs, and sipped rum. Music and laughter from town moved up to us in waves. Coquis sang by the hundreds from all directions. "Man, what a trip this has been." I said to the sky, and Chuck replied, "I could never have imagined it would turn out as it did. I expected a few dives, some drinks, and time to shoot the shit with you and Rosie."

"You've been an excellent tour guide, host, divemaster, and most importantly, the brother-in-law I have missed for years. I apologize if I've been insensitive to your situation, it took me by surprise, and you can see that, right?" I asked.

"Sure, Hoot, I hope you can see how I'd have expected you to judge me. I mean, you guys are the living definition of homophobic, macho assholes. I'm sorry if I overreacted. I can be kinda oversensitive. I wasn't prepared for this come out, ya know?"

"Yep, I get it. But most importantly, man you need to know that I meant it when I said that I love you like a brother. There are NO qualifiers in that. With me, it's all or nothing. It's not that I don't care if you are gay because that would be an implied judgment. I love you, brother. That's it," I said.

"Love you too, man. But what are you going to do with Jeb? Somebody is going to get hurt. You don't think he'd hit her if he finds out, do you?"

I felt a smile come to my mouth, "If he did, she would kill

him. I'm not worried about her safety as much as I am his. She beat the shit out of him the other night, and I think the sick bastard enjoyed it. He went back for more tonight. Right?" I said.

"Yeah, not many men have. She has a bit of a history here." "I'm thinking that she has a lot of history wherever she has been." I held my glass for Chuck to clank. "To the homophobic macho asshole and his trannie with great tits, amazing tattoos, and a hell of a right cross."

When I got to our bedroom, Rosie's bags were neatly sitting at the doorway. She had a Louis Lamour novel on her chest. Sandy was asleep in the corner, on my dirty clothes. I was too tired to pack.

"Hey baby, how ya doing?" I asked.

"Better than poor Jessica. She's pretty low. I think she was thinking of Jeb as her magic ticket away from Baine."

"Rosie," I said, "she's been after him for years and knows all his issues. If she fell for him, it wasn't because he wasn't anything but being his genuine asshole self. He has never tried to put the best foot forward with her, or anybody for that matter. He'd spit chewing tobacco juice in front of the Queen."

"I know, but she gave him her heart, not just her body."

"Come on, Rosie, they were alone for a night, not months. She fell in love with her ideal vision of him, not the real him," I said.

"Ky, you'll never understand women."

"Maybe you are right." I wanted the subject to go away.

"You are as big of an asshole as he is. Come here, kiss

me anyway." Our mouths met, and I sensed toothpaste on her tongue. I worried about what my mouth tasted like and started to pull back out of courtesy. She put her hand firmly behind my neck, halted my retreat, and kissed me harder. "But you are my asshole." She reached up and pulled my hand to her breast. "Now, make love to me one last time before we have to leave paradise."

"Rosie, this island isn't paradise. We take paradise with us, wherever you and I go together." I slid my hand off her breast and placed it over her heart. "There it is, beating under my hand, my paradise."

-27-

SATISFY MY SOUL

I never liked alarms, but that morning I hated Rosie's travel alarm more than death. At the ferry dock, she hugged Chuck goodbye. My farewell was not just to him but to St. John and, above all, to Sandy. I don't cry much, and never in public, but when I kissed the top of her anvil head, I saw a tear fall and disappear into her black forest of hair.

"Chuck." He was blurry. "Please take care of Sandy until we can figure out how to get her to Colorado." I reached out to shake his hand, and when our hands met, I transferred a dozen pirate, one-hundred-dollar bills to his palm. His eyes narrowed, and he glanced down into his palm. "Huh?" He said.

"For dog food, a bed, and some toys, a Vet check, wormer, ya know."

"You don't have to do this. Rosie already asked me to watch over her 'till you guys figure it out," he said.

"Will you?"

"Of course, Hoot, she's family now." He said while stroking her head. "Besides, I need someone to guard my Jeep."

"Where's Jeb? They're boarding the ferry. We gotta go, or we're going to miss our flight." Rosie searched the dock with her eyes.

"He's a big boy and will figure it out for himself," I said.

Jessica held up her middle finger to the island, "I hope he's face down in a dumpster."

Chuck whispered to me, "Hell hath no fury...."

"Yup, and just for clarification's sake," I asked him, "does that apply to gay dudes too?"

Speaking through a smile, "It's worse, dumbass. I'm gonna miss you, Hoot. Come back soon and get your girl."

I thought about a stack of well-packed, handmade lamps in Donald Snell boxes on a plane somewhere between here and Colorado. "I suspect our return may be a bit sooner than either of us have planned. We'll talk. Oh, by the way, how would you feel about being a part-owner of a Caribbean beach bar?" I asked.

"With who, you?" Chuck asked as Rosie nudged me up the gangplank to the ferry.

I said, "Only if we flip a coin to see who cleans the shitters."

Rosie pushed me through the door, and I didn't get to hear his answer.

The decrepit diesel engines started with a slap of what sounded like loosely fitting and soon to dislodge engine parts. The captain ground her into gear, and she lurched forward, dumping people into their seats.

In the secure U.S. Customs area of the San Juan airport, we stood in line with passports in hand. Across the expansive grey and featureless room, a U.S. Customs agent walked a Beagle on a leash. To his right, a DEA agent, both men in menacing black uniforms and boots. Glocks rested on their hips. They murmured to each other while visually scanning hundreds of us in a non-moving line. The DEA agent made eye contact and walked toward me in a straight line. I felt a little river of sweat run in front of my right ear. I bumped Rosie and, with my hand opposite the approaching agent, put my keys and wallet into her hand.

"Baby, no time for questions and answers. I may not be seeing you for a while. I'm a complete idiot. I love you." Before she could answer, the DEA agent walked directly to me and said, "Sir, we would like your cooperation."

I was sunk. *"How the hell could he know what I had in my pocket?"*

It could only be an ounce or two of the pirate cocaine, so surely my sentence wasn't going to be too long. My entire career, home, practice, and future were all gone because of an idiotic plan for revenge.

How could I be so stupid? Did they have some special x-ray or something? Was there residue on my checked baggage?

My club brothers occasionally discussed prison. I did not want to end up as a shower bitch. The room grew hotter.

Play it cool, Elliott.

"Sure, how can I help you?" I smiled and asked.

He didn't spin me around and cuff me but reached into his shirt pocket and pulled out a folded square of aluminum foil the size of a few stacked 3x5 cards. "We are doing training with our drug dog. He pointed to the Beagle fifty feet away, facing away from us. If you would, place this in your pocket, act normal, and let the dog find you in line. Will you help us sir?"

What the hell? Is this some game to doubly entrap me? Why go through all this bullshit and not just cuff me now?

I envisioned huge unwanted swarthy hands soaping my

back in a prison shower. I searched for a place to run. *SHIT, trapped.*

"No problem, officer." I took the packet and put it in my back pocket. Rosie's eyes bugged out like mine in my future shower scenario that played in my mind. She said nothing. The room was getting hotter. "This place could really use a few ceiling fans," I said as we moved to the yellow line in front of the U.S. Customs officers in their elevated glass box. The Beagle sauntered up and sat by my right foot, waving his accusatory little white paw at me. Done, screwed, sunk... shower bitch-me.

"Hello, officer," I said.

"Don't address me, don't look at the dog, and for Christ's sake, don't touch her." I kept my eyes straight ahead and said, "No problem officer, I just don't trust those hairy, baying little bastards." I figured I might as well make the jury laugh with my recorded conversation.

"Give it to me now." He demanded. I started to reach into my front pocket for the pirate cocaine but figured I'd play the game, enjoying my freedom for another few seconds, and handed him the foil packet from my back pocket. He snatched it without a 'thank you' or 'you are under arrest,' grunted and tossed a tennis ball to the snitch Beagle, and they walked away. *Ugh, Feds.* I was experiencing my third one-in-a-million of this trip. Finally, the room cooled off to lead-melting temperature.

In the Dallas airport, we had a two-hour layover. So I excused myself from Rosie and Jessica, saying, "I'm gonna walk around for an hour or so, don't want to develop a blood clot." Once out of sight, I headed for a row of public telephone booths to make a phone call.

"Right Team insurance claims center, Ft. Collins. How may I direct your call?" A hollow voice said.

Knowing that they record every call, I affected my best New York Puerto Rican accent, "Hola, this is Ignacio Mcgillacutty, Internal investigations at the Dallas Western regional office. What the hell is going on with jor phones up there? I've been trying to reach, what's her damn name, that woman who is that Huele Bicho Percy Hays' supervisor for an hour and keep getting cut off. Goddamn it, put me through to her now."

"Y-Yes, sir, I'm sorry for the inconvenience. I have no idea what the problem is." The hollow voice stammered.

"I don't need you to know how to repair carajo phone systems. All I need you to do is your insignificant job and direct my damn call to Hays' supervisor. By the way, what is your name? I'm writing this chit down."

There was a click, and Liberace music played over the receiver. A voicemail recording came on, "Hello, this is Jean Tourniquet, I'll be out of the office until Tuesday. Please leave a message."

Continuing in my accent, "Percy, this is Louis. I have another shipment of... monkeys (I have no idea why I used that term), and puto, these are GOOOOD monkeys. Better than usual. Very potent, snowflake-pure monkeys. I'm gonna send a little snort to your office address again. If you and your business partners like it, call the 800 number with the amount you want, and I will contact you about delivery. Vaya." And hung up.

I purchased a hard-bound book at the airport trinket store, "Christian Morals and the Modern Wife," stamps, and tape. Then, in a men's bathroom stall, I ripped the center portions out of the inner pages, making a hollow the size of an egg, and placed the baggie of pirate cocaine in it. I wrapped the book in a brown paper bag, and addressed it to Percy Hayes at his Right Team address, and dropped it in the little post office box by the McDonalds. *Here ya go, you puppy-killing son of a bitch.*

"I thought we were going to have to come looking for you. You're as bad as Jeb." Rosie was irritable when I returned.

"Relax baby. I just had to do a little work. All good now. I'll tell you later." I smiled as I answered her.

"What are you up to? You have been weird and mysterious all day. You still owe me an explanation about that stunt in the San Juan airport. Are you losing it? Is the stress of returning home getting to you? I'm worried." Rosie tapped her finger on her lips.

"Just putting a little plan into action. I promise, tonight I will make it all clear. After a short pause, I asked, "Is there any such thing as Bartender School?"

"You're scaring me." She said with her head tilted.

-28-

KINKY REGGAE

hevali threw open my back-office door. It had been weeks since I'd seen him. "Hey asshole, did you see the TV news today? Amazing shit." I shook his hand. Mine was sore with healing paper cuts from unpacking boxes of Donald Schnell lamps over the last week.

"No," I said, "I quit watching the news three years ago, too damn depressing. Why, what's up?"

"They busted Percy Hayes, that asshole adjustor from Right Team. He was running a drug ring out of their office. The News showed him in his purple jumpsuit, being led away in handcuffs by guys in sunglasses and cheap suits. It was fucking great. There was even a German Shepherd cop dog barking its ass off at him."

"Huh, another one bites the dust. If only the Shepherd knew how many puppies that asshole had sent to their deaths, it would have eaten him. Let me buy you lunch. We need to talk," I said.

We walked on a slippery wet carpet of brown and yellow Fall leaves covering the sidewalk. A featureless grey sky hung above our heads. My hands were cold, even in my ski gloves. I hated Fall, not because of Fall itself, but because it led into Winter.

"How's life back here in the real world?" I asked.

"Ah, you know, an office full of whackos expecting me to spew forth some life-altering wisdom that will make up for their fucked-up childhoods. So how are the crybabies in your office?" he asked.

"Tearful. Man, I was hoping a vacation was going to make coming back to this shit easier. But, instead, it somehow made it harder," I said.

"You're dumber than I thought, Ky. Did your mother breast or bottle feed you?"

"Eat me, psychobabble boy. I'm serious. I don't want to be here, doing what I do, and have to face another damn winter."

"Well, maybe you need to be grateful instead of bitching about it. You have a lot to be happy about. You need to start by examining all the good shit in your life," he said.

"You're right, and I do every night before I go to sleep. But I keep hearing my mother's voice telling me I'm not worth it."

"Voices in your head? You need Haldol. Take a deep breath. That's life, baby. It's not supposed to be perfect. What the hell do you want to do, live in paradise, drink rum and chase fucking ghost fish with your little pink flies all day?"

I stopped walking. The cold, dry wind irritatingly parted my hair on the wrong side, "Why the hell not? Why not go for broke, Dr. Chevali? This is it man, the one life we are given. It ain't a dress rehearsal, you know? If we don't grab the golden ring, then someone else will take it, right? What did Maxwell Maltz write, 'if you don't follow your dreams, you're destined to follow the guy who followed his,' or something like that," I said.

"Ky, that was 1950s pop psychology. We know better now."

"Oh really, we know better now? Look at the world. Do you see us as a species being happier now than we were then? I'd bet it's just the opposite. We live in a morally and toxin-polluted environment, a hypercompetitive, gluttonous consumer-driven economy where we measure our value as humans by our car's value, you Porsche driving elitist prick. You sincerely think we are better off?" I asked.

"No, but true happiness is attained by setting realistic goals. Otherwise, you fail and reinforce that sense of worthlessness that your sadistic first-grade math teacher instilled in you. Reality sucks. It's a hard life, and comparing your real life to the superficial veneer of other people's lives in an alleged paradise will only make you crazy," he said.

"I didn't think it was appropriate for shrinks to use the word crazy?" I jabbed my finger into the side of his head.

"In your fucking case, there is no other adjective. Anyway, they have all the same problems and worries and fears that we do. The only difference between living in paradise and Ft. Collins is a function of daily temperature. So, count your blessings and buy me a big greasy burger."

"Done. But my reason for asking the question wasn't to receive free psychoanalysis but to ask you a simple question. Don't label it as crazy. Just Rorschach it and give me your first guttural response. Cut the right-brain filter and answer from whatever serves as a heart in your chest. After that, tell me about Tattoo girl and what happened after we left," I said.

"OK fine, what's the question?" He took in a deep breath and forcefully exhaled, making a long puff of condensed breath that hung frozen in the air between us.

"Would you like to be a partner in a beach bar in the Caribbean with me and a couple of other people like Chuck and maybe Boddington? Live part-time here and part-time there. Ski in winter, play on the beach in the summer?" I expected a snort and lecture on my psychopathology.

"Yes, no fucking hesitation, yes, and I have the perfect bartender," he said.

"Excellent, done. I'll work out the details and get back to you in a few weeks."

"I'm in. Now feed me."

"Right. But, tell me about Tattoo girl. You kids going to be pen pals?" I asked.

"Better than that, she should be here in a couple of weeks to see if we can make a go of it."

"A go of it? What the hell are you saying? A go of it, as in going steady, hold hands, raise a family of spoiled children and watch her ass grow like a thunder cloud?" I asked.

His lips tightened, and he looked at me directly. "Well, sorta, I guess, everything but the kids."

I played dumb, "I get it, man. I never wanted the little nipple wreckers either. Every time I see a young couple pushing a baby carriage full of squalling sausage, I thank God I never inseminated anybody," I said.

"Ky, has anybody ever told you that you are a cynical asshole?"

"Every time I talk to myself in the mirror, why?"

"If you were a patient, I'd fire you so as not to waste my time," he said.

"I love you too, Dr. Bastian of sanity, and speaking of hamburgered nipples, we were talking about you and Tattoo girl, I believe. She's coming here? You can't be serious. What are you thinking? She is batshit crazy. This is called a recipe for disaster, and not just for your dentition."

"Ky, you're talking to a shrink. Let me explain something to you. As far as the world of psychiatry is concerned, everybody is crazy. It's just a question of whether they are crazy and boring or crazy and interesting. She is crazy and interesting."

"So was Hitler, from a clinical standpoint, but that doesn't mean I'd want him as a roommate," I said.

"True, but Hitler didn't have her tits, and there is something else I need to run past you, kinda serious. I trust your opinion." He looked away.

"What's that?" I asked.

"You and I have shared a lot of things, travel experiences, bottles of tequila, small women, and big secrets, right?" His brow furrowed.

"Jeez, this sounds serious. What is it, amigo? Are you invoking Boy's secret mode?" I asked.

"Yes, I guess I am. But, all bullshit aside, you and I can be ourselves around each other, 100%, and never judge, right?" He asked.

"If I stood on an elevated moral platform from which to judge you, I would, happily. But I don't," I said.

His gaze rotated up toward the Rockies. "Ky, you know that I'm not gay, right. I never took one in the ass, never will. This gate just doesn't swing that way. I'm a man, a real man. I love women, I love tits, I love pussy, I...."

"She's a tranny Jeb." I stopped his rationalizing and pain.

His head snapped to face me, "How'd you know? What the fuck? You think I'm a pervert, don't you?"

I took the painful high road and decided not to toy with him. He was a loyal friend, and no matter what faults he had, I saw no reason to make him more uncomfortable with his new, confusing reality.

"Adam's apple, hands, and biceps," I said.

"Huh?"

"Jeb, her biceps, and Adam's apple are larger than most linebackers. Great tits and ass, but unless she is part Clydesdale, no woman is muscled like that."

"I'm in love with a... sort of a dude. BUT, just for the record, she is FULL tranny, no pecker, ya know." He paused. "Am I a faggot? What the fuck do I do?" He asked.

"Why are you asking me? You're the shrink."

"I know, but that's my job. I can be objective about other people's fucked up lives, just not my own."

"No, you're not gay."

"You're sure?" He was pleading.

"Really. You're fine, but just as an aside, can you help me pick out some new curtains for the office? I'd value your opinion if you know what I mean."

"Goddamn it, Ky, I'm serious, what do I do with this, with me, with her?"

"You want my sincere answer?" I asked.

"Yeah, shithead, or I'd have never asked, and please quit fucking with me. I'm scared. Scared of me." Chevali said.

"Love her," I said.

"Huh?"

"Love her."

"You serious?"

"Jeb, ten minutes ago, you were giving me your sage advice about accepting an imperfect life. Now I'm giving you the same advice. It's OK to love an imperfect human, mostly because you're one too."

"What if anybody finds out, I will be the laughing stock...."

"FTW, baby. If they, whoever the hell THEY are, can't accept you for who and what you are, then they don't matter. If they try to force their opinions on you, break their heads open. Simple." I opened my shirt to show him my FTW tattoo.

"Close your shirt asshole, before someone thinks you are exposing yourself to me. And besides, what's that gaudy shit hanging around your neck?" He referred to my new gold Leopard pendant, which I had a jeweler craft from the dead pirate drug dealer's ring.

"I found this down on St. John. It's a real gold leopard face, real diamonds, rubies. Cool as hell, huh," I asked.

"Sure, if you're a pimp. But aside from your appalling lack of taste in jewelry, do you think I'm wrong for falling in love with her?"

"Buddy, this is a short life. You know damn well that we don't always have control over where our hearts will go. You are responsible for your actions, not your thoughts. Don't you spout that kind of platitude bullshit to your closet queen patients every day?"

"Yes, but that's them, and this is me. And fuck you, I'm not a closet queen," he said.

"Jeb, we are all just bouncing clowns riding the big happy circus wagon in the Fellini movie called life. Enjoy the ride. I love the hell out of you, and so long as she won't beat my ass, I look forward to partying with... What's her name anyway?

"Daisy." He said, straight-faced.

"No, don't screw with me, Daisy? Come on."

"I'm serious. Her name is Daisy."

"Only you, Jeb."

-29-

Time Will Tell

" H ey Bullhead, when you come back, we need more Pusser's and a couple of cases of beer before the rush tonight. I made a list." Jason, my club brother, called to me over the music of Peter Tosh while I loaded my fly rod and Sandy into my Jeep. Tropical breeze driven shadows of palm trees were drawing circles on the thatched roof sign above his head, "The Last Drop Bar and Grille." I walked to him as he talked to a dark man with a lunar landscape, acne-scarred face sitting at the bar.

"Yep, been here about two months, got another month left in my rotation before heading back to the mainland," Jason spoke while wiping a drink-sweat pond in front of the man's drink.

Pointing and smiling at me, Jason said to the man, "Meet one of the other bar partners, Bullhead." He introduced me to the serious-looking man, "Brother, this guy just named every kind of bird in sight. He's a bird expert, has a degree in birdology from Columbia, the country." He asked the man, "What's your name again?"

"Che Garcia," as he shook my hand, I noticed him inspecting the gold leopard pendant around my neck. His rutted, hairy face turned into a throbbing crimson. "Beautiful necklace, sir. May I ask as to where you were fortunate enough to obtain such a fine work of art?" He enunciated his words with a crisp Castilian accent while covering the same leopard face, but as a ring on his left hand. My mind raced in a dozen directions.

"About six months ago, I was at a pawn shop in Old San Juan Puerto Rico, searching for antique plates when I saw it and just had to have it. They said it was from an estate sale on the island of Vieques, I think."

THE END

About the Author

R.A. Parker lives and works in Hawaii. When not indoors working or writing, he spends every waking moment outdoors riding his horse, his mountain bike or on his paddleboard.

Ky Elliott is a burned-out physician persuaded by his wife and closest friends to take a much needed vacation to a location that he has no desire to visit. On the island of St. John in the U.S. Virgin Islands, Ky and his friends discover more than warm weather, soft seas, and cold drinks. Their trip turns into a series of humorous adventures into uncharted waters above and below the ocean's surface and bedsheets. In the name of fun, the most significant challenges they face are from iguanas, lobsters, and their egos. All the dogs portrayed in this novel, apart from one Beagle, are as the higher beings.

THIS NOVEL IS POLITICALLY INCORRECT. None of the characters or their actions are politically sanitized, not to offend the reader. This novel portrays various races, cultures, sexes, and sexual orientations as being imperfect, true to human nature. Many of them act with what some could consider inappropriate manners. None of the characters represent any specific person, dead or alive, but are conglomerations of people who arrived in the author's head as he wrote this novel. They are not intended to represent/misrepresent any race, culture, sex, or sexual orientation… except for the male characters, who portray the idiotic side of humanity called "men."

The protagonist in this novel is a FICTIONAL CHARACTER. His actions and thoughts do not reflect those of the author…other than him being a stupid male. The story is an amalgamation of imagined events, not a memoir. It contains a lot of swearing and alcohol drinking because some adults swear and drink. It depicts potentionally objectionable sexual situations because humans by their nature are "naughty." Some scenes contain violence, OK I think you get the point. The labels of "bad" and "good" as applied to human behaviors are value judgments and subject to interpretation. On the surface, this novel is a mindless story about imperfect friends vacationing in a fun tropical setting. Minimally below the surface, it is a critical essay on the puerile behaviors of people who, despite their best efforts, learn about their fragility and discover humility while on an island vacation.

"Men are pigs." Ky Elliott.

Made in the USA
Las Vegas, NV
14 October 2021

32330573R00224